Final Target

Books by Steven Gore

Final Target

Final Target

Steven Gore

Poisoned Pen Press

Poisoned Pen Press

First Edition 2010

10 9 8 7 6 5 4 3 2 1

Library of Congress Catalog Card Number: 2009942188

ISBN: 9781590587492 Hardcover

The people and events described or depicted in this novel are fictitious and any resemblance to actual incidents or individuals is unintended and coincidental.

Poisoned Pen Press
6962 E. First Ave., Ste. 103
Scottsdale, AZ 85251
www.poisonedpenpress.com
info@poisonedpenpress.com

Printed in the United States of America

For Liz,
the love of my life and gentle critic
who taught me the craft of storytelling,
one question mark at a time

Prologue

Eighteen Months Earlier

More surprising than spinning out of control, than smashing through the railing, than tumbling trunk-over-hood down the hillside; more surprising even than the sheet metal buckling around her, was that she was dying in English. The woman tried to die in Russian, then in Ukrainian, but the words had forsaken her. Even her given name had fled into the swirling dust at the bottom of the ravine. She remembered only what others called her: Katie.

Katie grieved the loss of the inner voice of her childhood, as she knew would her parents, then comforted herself with the knowledge that they'd never find out. The police officers standing with an interpreter at their apartment door would say she died instantly, sparing them the horror that their only child suffered any final thoughts at all.

In truth, she felt no horror. Nor panic. Nor dread. There was just the rush of wind in the eucalyptus, as if an overture to the passing of her life before her eyes. But her mind drifted not into the past, but to another place in her present: her SatTek coworkers gathering a mile away, under coastal redwoods surrounded by acres of spring grass. She wondered whether they would miss her, backtrack along the twisting road when she didn't answer her cell phone, or notice the broken railing as they drove home sunburned and bleary-eyed, then scramble down the hillside to find her body. She wished she could freshen her makeup and comb her hair, just in case.

Katie inspected the red soil blanketing the gray vinyl interior, then looked through her burst side window at dust dancing and gliding in a beam of morning sunlight. She heard the rustling of tiny feet in dry leaves. Perhaps a rabbit, a gray squirrel, or a finch returning to its work, pecking at wildflower seeds scattered by the three thousand pounds of steel and glass that had thrashed the hillside.

A warm gust churned the air. She smelled her mother's kitchen in the bay leaves sweating in the overhanging branches and in the sage and fennel crushed by her car. She then saw herself at the dining table a month earlier, hunched over her laptop, heart pounding, typing a San Francisco address, and then later, hands shaking as she slid a letter into the corner mailbox.

Dear Mr. Special Agent in Charge:

The president of Surveillance and Targeting Technologies of San Jose, California, is engaged in a massive—

Which of them knew? Which of those she saw in her mind's eye just a mile away, starting charcoal, setting up volleyball nets, pinning down the corners of tablecloths with ketchup and mustard bottles. Those men tossing footballs and glancing over at the women in little outfits they'd never worn to the office. The women trying not to giggle at white nerd-legs stuck into brown socks and clearance-rack Nikes or stare too long at the Cancún-bronzed chests of the men from the loading dock.

Which of them knew? A chill vibrated through her body. *Which of them knew that she knew?*

The lenses of her eyes changed focus from the thistles and nettles beyond the fractured windshield to the pale green Tupperware lying upside-down on the dashboard, her potato salad still sealed inside. Wasted. Even back home in Lugansk among the collapsed coal mines, even in the worst of times, no one wiped off blood to eat the food of the dead. It would be—*What did Father Roman say?* It would be like eating the bread of the Eucharist without the sacrament.

Katie closed her eyes, her shallow breath once again infused with bay and sage and fennel—then a wrenching vertigo, as if she'd been tossed from a sailboat twisting in a hurricane. *My name…I need…to know…my name.*

She wanted to smile when it finally reached out to her from the whirlwind…*Ekaterina.* But there wasn't time.

Chapter One

"Come on buddy, don't die on me. Don't you dare die on me."

The rain-slickered EMT pressed hard on the side-by-side bullet holes in the fifty-year-old jogger's sternum while a paramedic slipped an oxygen mask over the man's nose and mouth. The runner was splayed out on a predawn sidewalk fronting ten-million-dollar mansions in San Francisco's Pacific Heights.

"Come on, man. Hang in there. You're gonna make it. You're gonna make it. You just gotta help me."

"One, two, three, lift," and the victim was moved from the wet concrete to the collapsible gurney. "One, two, three, lift," and the gurney was raised and rolled toward the fire department ambulance.

"Any ID?" a beat-weary patrol officer asked as the gurney slid into the back.

"Nothing. Just this hanging around his neck." The EMT tossed over a silver chain and house key. "Sorry, I couldn't get his name."

The cop rotated the key between his fingers and inspected it under the streetlight as if puzzled by how a jagged sliver of metal could imprison him on duty long after his shift. He shook his head slowly, then looked up. "Am I supposed to try this thing in every fucking door in San Francisco?"

"Just do your job," the EMT mumbled as he ran toward the cab. "Just do your job."

◇◇◇

Private investigator Graham Gage lowered the barbell onto its crutches, then grabbed his ringing cell phone from the carpeted floor of his basement gym.

"Graham, it's Spike."

"Can't be." The wall clock read 5:37. "The only Spike I know is still lying in bed dreaming about bass fishing." Gage expected a clever response. He didn't get one.

Spike's voice held steady. "It's about Jack Burch."

Gage felt his heart twist in his chest. He pushed himself up from the weight bench, then braced the phone against his shoulder and ripped off his lifting gloves. Spike was the lieutenant in charge of SFPD Homicide.

"How bad is it?" Gage asked, heading toward the stairs to the main floor.

"I don't know. It just came in."

"Where's he now?"

"Hold on…3E44…What's your 1020?"

Gage took the steps two at a time. He caught a jumble of voices and static as the officer answered.

"They're just pulling into SF Medical," Spike said.

A crack of thunder drew Gage's eyes toward a wall of windows in the living room of his Oakland post-and-beam house. He had expected to see the lights of San Francisco across the bay, but a late-October alloy of fog and storm clouds sweeping in from the Pacific had enveloped the city. Even the oak branches that framed his view were webbed in gray, their resident birds mute, invisible, cowering against a squall advancing up the hillside.

"What happened?" Gage asked as he climbed toward his third floor bedroom.

"The uniforms on the scene are telling me it was road rage. Witnesses said he'd just started jogging from his house when a guy blew the stop sign at Webster and Pacific. Jack yelled something and the asshole did a U-turn, fired a couple of shots, then took off. A neighbor recognized Jack as they put him into the ambulance."

Gage knew his friend's morning route, knew the intersection. Animated stick figures reenacted the shooting in his mind as if in a virtual re-creation. He fought off the image of an early morning downpour washing Jack Burch's blood into a leaf-clogged gutter.

"Anybody ID the shooter?" Gage asked.

"Nobody we've talked to yet, but chances are slim. The commute hadn't started and there weren't many runners and dog walkers out because of the weather."

"And the car?"

"Generic every which way, and nobody caught the plate."

Spike's radio crackled in the background. Gage heard him double-click the handset to confirm receipt of the message.

"What's that?" Gage asked.

"They asked me for his next of kin."

Gage froze at the top of the stairs, then caught his breath, steeling himself for the answer before he asked the question. "Did he..."

"No. Sorry, man. It's not that. They just wanted contact info."

Gage exhaled. "Put me down until his wife gets there."

"Where is she?"

"With Faith up at the cabin. I'll call her on the way."

In his bedroom, Gage slipped on a pair of Levi's, then reached for a gray hooded sweatshirt, and slid it over his body like armor.

Chapter Two

The city began to emerge as Gage drove down the pine- and oak-treed canyon toward the Bay Bridge. The clouds had lifted enough to expose a pattern of lights hinting at the shapes of buildings spread around the San Francisco financial district. His mind's eye perceived what he still couldn't quite make out: the top three floors of a steel and glass Montgomery Street office tower, home to Jack Burch's international law firm. His thoughts then drifted up toward Pacific Heights, still masked in gray, now and forever stained in his sight. He then imagined a faceless driver in an anonymous car disappearing into the mazelike city spreading out before him.

Gage glanced at his dashboard clock as he crested the cantilever section of the bridge, beginning the decline toward the waterfront: 5:59. He punched on the radio, already tuned to the local CBS News affiliate. He didn't know how long it would be until some nurse or clerk or paramedic leaked Burch's shooting to the press—but he knew how long it would remain there: weeks, maybe months. It wasn't imaginable that the man who charted the courses by which half of the Fortune Global 500 navigated the world's turbulent markets had been randomly shot down in the street. The cable news channels would demand a Greater Meaning, perhaps even a Conspiracy. Day after day. Night after night.

The 6 A.M. national feed began with the collapse of Silicon Valley's Surveillance and Targeting Technologies and the outbursts of betrayal from its devastated shareholders. Networks had hovered over the SatTek story for days like news helicopters at a crime scene, the downdraft creating a turbulence of uninformed speculation that seemed to feed less on new facts than on itself. The disintegration of a key manufacturer of components for anti-terror and missile guidance systems had left the cottage industry of analysts at a loss for explanations, though not for words, and a new surge had been triggered by the arrival of U.S. Marshals to secure the chaotic SatTek facility.

Through a breach in the veil of drizzling fog, Gage caught a glimpse of Mount Sutro rising two thousand feet above sea level. The radio and television tower stood poised like a monstrous, three-pronged gigging spear, clouds masking its barbs. Anger surged when he realized that the news channels would soon abandon SatTek to obsess over Burch's shooting, and through that obsession lay waste to Burch and his wife's intimate lives. He took in a breath, then gripped the steering wheel as his body warmed from within. He exhaled when he recognized the source: how much easier it was to rage at the media than at a faceless and anonymous—what? Thug? Lunatic? Assassin?

Gage jabbed the off button, then stared at the pavement ahead and at the lane lines bracketing him: a familiar path now leading him into the unknown. He drove the rest of the way listening only to his racing thoughts against the background of the gusting wind, the raindrops tapping his windshield, and the rhythmic sweep of his wipers.

◇◇◇

Gage spotted Lieutenant Humberto "Spike" Pacheco at the end of a wide hallway, leaning against the wall outside the packed emergency waiting room. Thick arms crossed above his belly flared out the front panels of his navy sports jacket. It revealed a middle-aged paunch that belied the childhood nickname he carried with him when he had joined Gage at SFPD thirty years earlier.

"Any word from the doctors?" Gage asked softly, a step away.

Spike shook his head as he looked up. His dark face and bloodhound eyes revealed nothing. He wasn't about to give passersby fodder for speculation, later to be whispered to tabloid reporters as fact: *Then this private eye came up. Tall. Solid-looking. About fifty. Not a snap-your-neck-tough-guy type, but you could tell he works out. First I thought he was like a college professor or something. Now I'm thinking that he looked a helluva lot more like a cop than the short, fat detective—that guy couldn't run nobody down. Somebody told me the PI said he was going to...*

"What about the shooter?"

"Not a damn thing." Spike's tone was low, grim.

Murmuring flowed from the waiting room. Gage glanced inside at the families of the night's wounded huddled together in plastic chairs under brutal fluorescent lights. The air was heavy, almost sweating, reeking of unwashed bodies ripped from sleep by sickness or violence.

Gage and Spike turned as one as Dr. Ajita Kishore approached. She acknowledged Spike with a quick nod. They didn't need an introduction. The trauma surgeon had sought him out a hundred times before on that same square of speckled tan linoleum, more often than not to report that a shooting or stabbing or beating had become a homicide.

Kishore looked up at Gage, her deep-set South Asian eyes expressing a compassionate familiarity, even an affection, that he hadn't expected.

"You must be Graham," she said. Her accent was Indianized British. Formal, but not distant.

Gage nodded, his jaw set tight for the worst, his eyes riveted on her.

She held his gaze. "Mr. Burch raised his hand and mumbled, 'Graham, tell Graham' just before we put him under. Something in his voice told me you'd be here when I finished. He must trust you very much."

"How is he?" Gage asked.

"Alive." Kishore pressed her fingertips against the green surgical scrubs covering her breastbone. "It's not just damage from the slugs, the CAT scan shows his brain absorbed a tremendous shock when he fell. Unfortunately, he's now slipped into a coma."

Gage smothered the urge to ask the questions to which he knew Kishore couldn't have answers: How long would it last, and how would it end.

Kishore looked at him apologetically. "We put him on a ventilator. We couldn't count on his brain functioning well enough to maintain his breathing."

A timer started counting down in Gage's mind. The science hadn't changed that much in the quarter century since he'd left SFPD Homicide. Given his age and the severity of his injuries, three weeks was all Burch had to fight his way out of the coma and avert a descent into a lethal vegetative state—if he survived the next few hours.

Kishore cast an expectant look toward the emergency entrance. "Has his wife been called?"

Gage nodded, finishing her sentence in his head: *In case he doesn't make it.*

"She'll be here by ten o'clock. She and my wife—"

A glimmer of a question caught him short. He fought his way back from an uncertain future to the image of Burch raising his hand—and to his own past as a young detective: riding in ambulances, then following gurneys to operating room thresholds, pursuing facts binding a victim to a shooter, or a dying declaration linking a wounded killer to his crime.

"Do you know what he was trying to say?" he asked Kishore.

The doctor shook her head. "I'm sorry. That's all there was."

They stood silently for a moment, then Kishore furrowed her brows as if she'd taken a wrong turn in a familiar city. "I assumed you'd be Australian, too." She inspected Gage's graying brown hair. "Maybe his older brother."

Gage's mind leaped back a half a life. Looking down from a dusty one-lane bridge, spotting a ruddy fisherman waist-deep in the Smith River, wading boots losing traction on the descending tail of a submerged sandbar with boulder-strewn rapids gapping and foaming below. Then Gage racing downstream, sliding down the hillside, crawling out on a fallen log above the rapids…reaching…reaching…reaching toward the young man flailing in the torrent, the crush of water filling his waders—

Gage blinked, then refocused on Kishore, his answer unspoken: *Brothers are bestowed by chance and nature; friends you love by choice.*

Kishore squeezed Gage's upper arm, then turned toward Spike. "Can I talk to you for a minute, Lieutenant?"

Gage watched them walk down the hallway, hoping to read more of Burch's future in her manner and gestures. Kishore stopped fifty feet away and rotated her hand in front of her chest, then dug into her pocket and handed Spike a small plastic bag bearing a white label. Gage knew what it contained: two mangled slugs caked with Burch's blood, now seeming less like evidence and more like sacred artifacts. Spike cradled them in his hand and looked back down the hallway at Gage. He nodded in silent comprehension, then slipped them into his breast pocket.

Gage turned away and reached for his cell phone to call Faith. She answered on the first ring. He heard her all-terrain tires rumbling on the pavement. She and Courtney Burch were just south of Mount Lassen in Northern California, entering the desolate expanse of the Central Valley. Gage told her the truth, counting on her to mold it into softer words to pass on.

He found himself staring at the screen after he disconnected, imagining Burch's playful face, hearing his accented voice during the calls and messages that marked the turning points in their lives. "Graham, it's Jack, guess what, best man? Courtney said yes…I just got the bar results. If that bloody champagne hasn't become vinegar…We're on our way to the hospital. I can't believe it, in a few hours I'll be a father. Me. A father…It's about my mother. I'm flying home to Sydney…We just got Courtney's MRI. It's spread to her lymph nodes…call as soon as you can."

Gage looked up and spotted Spike striding toward him, followed by two uniformed officers. Spike directed the pair toward the ICU, then said to Gage, "Let's go outside."

◇◇◇

As they walked from the emergency entrance into the parking lot, Gage found that the rain had stopped. The cloud-filtered light falling on the blacktop seemed vague and directionless; even the shallow puddles rippling in the breeze reflected nothing but gray.

Spike stopped next to his police-issued Mercury Marquis, then looked up at Gage.

"I've ordered round-the-clock security."

"You really think the shooter's coming after him?"

"I don't know. It's something Kishore said." Spike formed his small hands into a tight circle like a bull's-eye. "It was like Jack was wearing a target and the shooter scored two tens. Side-by-sides into his breastbone." Spike widened his hands, as if framing Burch's heart and lungs. "If he scored two fives, Jack would be dead. That's damn accurate shooting for a maniac who's pissed off and on the move."

Spike opened his car door, withdrew a black leather folder, then flipped it open. "Even though the witnesses are describing road rage, I have to ask, has Jack complained to you about anybody threatening him?"

Gage shook his head.

"You know what he was working on?"

"The usual. He was in Geneva for a few days, then in Moscow."

Gage had answered mechanically, then felt a wrenching expansion of the world as Russia, which had faded into an icy stillness since his return two weeks earlier, now came monstrously alive: a hydra head of criminal and political threats feeding off the corpse of the former Soviet Union—and willing to destroy those, like Jack Burch, who had interfered with their feast.

Spike peered up at Gage. "Weren't you just in Moscow?"

Gage nodded slowly as a slide show of Slavic mug shots flashed through his mind.

"Did it have anything to do with Jack?"

Gage trusted Spike as a man, but if a gangster had reached across the Atlantic to assassinate Burch, no local cop could help Gage punch back.

"Not directly."

"What about indirect—" Gage's opaque eyes and tone of irrevocability strangled the word in Spike's throat. He reddened. "Don't stonewall me on this thing, Graham."

"It's not my decision. As long as there's a chance he'll survive, it's up to him what gets revealed about what he did over there. I'm not taking that away from him."

"And if he doesn't?"

Gage fixed his eyes on Spike. "Then I'll decide."

"Come on, man," Spike's voice turned pleading. "For all we know the guy who did this is boarding a flight back to Moscow right now."

"Then it's already too late."

They stood silently at the impasse until Gage found a middle ground that he knew would leave Spike stranded.

"I'll tell you what's been in the European press and you can take it as far as you want."

Spike nodded.

Gage paused, trying both to tear his mind from the image of the bullet holes in Burch's chest and to find a way to make a complicated story short, simple, and vague enough that Spike couldn't extract any leads from it.

"This was the issue," Gage finally said. "After the fall of the Soviet Union, crime bosses and politicians in Russia and Ukraine began using the natural gas trade as their private piggy bank. Billions of dollars were extorted by the *maffiya* to fund arms- and sex-trafficking schemes. Billions more were siphoned off by Russian and Ukrainian presidents to finance their political campaigns.

"The gas is Russian, but the pipeline that carries it to Western Europe is Ukrainian. And last year Ukraine tried to force Russia to give them a bigger cut of the profits by shutting off the flow. The EU went ballistic. Forty percent of what they consume comes through Ukraine. They threatened to build a line of their own through Turkey from gas fields in Central Asia."

"But that would just put them at the mercy of a different set of crooks."

"Exactly. That's why the EU chose the known over the unknown and brought Jack in to restructure the market. He realized that the key was to eliminate all of the intermediaries used to skim money and replace them with a single transparent authority, a kind of joint venture run out of a third country that would have its books open to the world."

They ceased speaking as an elderly doctor parked his car in the next space.

Spike waited until he had walked toward the hospital and out of earshot, then said, "I can understand why the Russian and Ukrainian governments might cave in; for them it's a foreign policy issue. But not the gangsters. I just don't see them backing off."

"Let's just say that they came to understand that all of Western Europe would be inspecting this thing with a microscope, and decided to show restraint."

Spike raised his eyebrows in a knowing look that assumed what he was trying to discover: that Gage had been Burch's emissary. "They decided on their own, or were persuaded?"

Gage cast Spike a reproachful look. "I don't know. Maybe one led to the other."

From the moment Burch asked Gage to join him in Moscow, he had understood that a public disclosure that they'd approached the underworld would cast doubt on the legitimacy of the plan, for everyone watching would assume that there had been a secret quid pro quo.

Spike shrugged. "If you say so." He jerked his thumb toward the Richmond District north of Golden Gate Park, now a Little Russia. "But persuasion isn't exactly the weapon of choice around here these days."

A month earlier he'd complained to Gage that the mayor had summoned him to City Hall, less concerned about the slug-ridden corpses of what the newspapers were calling "Russian businessmen" than about stray bullets and November elections. Spike had called Gage as he drove away from that dressing-down, infuriated not only by the pressure, but by his own helplessness in solving murders ordered by gangsters overseas whose identities and motives he had no way of ascertaining.

"Are you sure they didn't change their minds?" Spike asked. "Hitting Jack would send a message that it's going to be business as usual."

Gage wasn't at all sure, but the answer wasn't one Spike could help him get, so he fixed his eyes on his friend and answered, "Yes."

Spike held his gaze for a moment, then conceded by drawing a line across his pad.

"What else was Jack up to?"

"IPOs. Bank mergers. Nothing anybody goes to war over."

Gage glanced down the long hospital driveway toward the street. Commuter traffic inched by. Overfilled trolleys crawled along the wet pavement. Another ambulance rolled up to the emergency entrance followed by a patrol car, lights flashing, arriving with the last of the night's victims.

Spike followed Gage's eyes, then pointed at the windows lining the ICU and sighed. "I always figured it would be you or me lying in there."

"Until two years ago, I had no doubt it would be Jack." Gage made a steep gliding motion with his arm. "The way he used to rocket down the ski slopes like some oblivious teenager. But that all changed when his wife was diagnosed with breast cancer. First he flared up the way he always would, ready to take on the forces of nature. But two weeks in, he realized it was all about chemistry and physiology, not force of will. Courtney's or his. It crushed him, really crushed him."

"Tough for a guy like that to feel helpless."

"It was more than that. He felt..."

In grasping for words, Gage saw what habit and familiarity had obscured when he'd spotted Burch three weeks earlier climbing out of a limousine in front of the tsarist-era Baltschug Hotel in Moscow. His cheeks hung on his thinned face, his square shoulders had rounded, his gray tailored suit was ill-fitting and misshapen. Where they once faced each other eye-to-eye at six-two, Gage remembered looking slightly down as they waited to check in.

A lump in Gage's throat caught him by surprise when he found the word. He swallowed hard. "Fragile," Gage finally said, struggling to keep his voice even. "I think he felt fragile for the first time in his life."

Spike folded his arms across his chest, as if trying to resist seeing Burch, and maybe himself, through the eyes of Gage, a man who'd never felt the least bit invincible, even as a young cop kicking doors and always the first one in.

"Jack was terrified that he might leave Courtney a widow," Gage said, "sick and alone. So he kept himself out of harm's way and tried to control everything around them." His eyes caught the glitter of fine drops now settling on Spike's roof. "He would've stopped the rain when she stepped out of the house if there was a way to do it. They just adored each other."

"Why was he willing to leave her and go to Russia?"

"He wasn't," Gage said. "She insisted because she missed the joy he took in his work. He recovered some of the old Jack in Moscow, and life seemed secure enough to start running the hills again when he got back." Gage glanced in the direction of Pacific Heights, then shook his head slowly. "I wish he hadn't, or at least—"

"Don't even think it. You can't be everywhere." Spike flipped his notebook closed. "I know it looks grim, but it's not over yet. There's still a chance he'll make it."

Gage looked up at the ICU, then down at Spike. "How many shootings did we work together?"

"Hundreds, I guess. Would've been thousands by now if you hadn't gone private." Spike's eyes widened as he finished the sentence, knowing Gage had trapped him.

"And how many victims survived slugs in the chest?"

"Well…I mean…there must—" Spike threw up his hands. "Your heart's aching over what life did to Jack even before he got shot, but your mind keeps churning like a goddamn mainframe, calculating the odds of whether he'll survive." Spike's face reddened in frustration, almost in anger. "And nobody's gonna see the rage you feel until the end of this thing, and maybe not even then. Sometimes you scare the hell out of me."

Spike pulled out his car keys and gripped them in his hand.

"Ever since we were kids you thought differently than me; saw the world differently. Different from anybody I ever met. For a while I fooled myself into thinking we were following the same path when SFPD recruited us, but we weren't.

"I'll help you however I can, Graham. But for the first time in our lives I think you're holding things back from me." Spike's lips went tight for a moment, then he took in a long breath and exhaled. "It makes me afraid that the road less traveled is going to take you off a cliff."

Chapter Three

Stuart Matson, president of SatTek Incorporated, faced Assistant U.S. Attorney William Peterson across a conference table on the eleventh floor of the San Francisco Federal Building. Peterson was flanked by an FBI agent on one side and an IRS agent on the other.

On Matson's right sat his attorney, Daniel Hackett. His other flank was exposed.

Thunder reverberated through the steel-framed building and into the book-lined room as Peterson pushed aside his unfinished morning coffee. He aligned two government-issued Paper Mates along the top edge of his legal pad, and said, "Mr. Matson—"

"Just call me Scoob," Matson said, attempting the ingratiating smile that had begun to fail him a week earlier when he found himself in the crosshairs of a securities fraud investigation.

"Mr. Matson, this is what we call a Queen for a Day. It's your one and only chance to convince me to allow you to cooperate with the government."

Matson curled his hands inward toward his chest and adopted the practiced indignation of a professional salesman. "I thought *you* were asking for *me* to cooperate."

Peterson shifted his eyes to Hackett. "Your client doesn't seem to grasp that we'd just as soon take this case to trial." He turned to the FBI agent at his side. "What's the loss?"

"Almost three hundred million dollars." The agent's voice was flat. He fixed his gaze on Matson, his face as expressionless as a spreadsheet. "And counting."

"So we're talking what? Twenty years? Thirty?" Peterson looked back at Hackett. "What do you think, Counselor? I'm sure you've done the math."

Matson thought back to the day the SEC suspended trading in SatTek stock. Sitting in Hackett's office. The lawyer's black-haired, hawkish little head bent over the thousand-page Federal Sentencing Manual, working his mental calculator, then summing the total in a nightmarish bottom line: Unless Matson won at trial or delivered others to Peterson's chopping block, he'd spend the next three decades sleeping in a concrete box, eighteen inches from a lidless steel toilet.

Peterson glared at Matson. "I don't have time to waste on this." He then pushed himself to his feet and reached down to gather his files.

As the six-one and two-hundred-thirty-pound former NFL linebacker loomed over him, Matson saw himself as he knew Peterson did: the twenty extra pounds bunched around his small frame, his soft hands with their manicured fingernails, and his face that fell just short of handsome; a chin just a shade too small, eyes just a shade too narrow, and a nose just a shade too large.

Matson blinked away the image and embraced another, one he'd earned through four decades of struggle, of standing outside his body, of molding it and training it: the steady gaze, the ingratiating smile, the trustworthy handshake, even the perfect golf swing.

"Wait." Hackett shot his palm up toward Peterson. "Wait. Scoob wants to continue." He swung fully toward Matson. "Right, Scoob? You do want to continue?"

Matson clenched his jaw, face reddening, furious that his freedom might hinge simply on whether the prosecutor turned toward the door. He answered, staring at Hackett, not at Peterson. "Sure. I wanna continue."

Peterson jabbed his forefinger down at Matson. "And that means no more game playing about why we're here."

Matson knew that was exactly what he'd done, made a couple of preemptive moves, trying to avoid becoming Peterson's pawn, but he looked up and said, "I'm not playing a game. I just want to know where I stand."

"Does that mean you're ready to listen?" Peterson asked.

"Yeah. I'm ready to listen."

Peterson sat down, laid out his files, and then fixed his eyes on Matson.

"You know, I know, and your attorney knows that you've been lying for years. To the SEC, to shareholders, to your employees, and to your family. The first thing you need to prove to me is that you're ready to step up, be a man…"

Matson imagined the prosecutor mentally pulling back his fist, then pausing before the punch.

"And just tell the truth."

The jab landed, and the expression of satisfaction Matson saw on Peterson's face meant that he'd seen it hit.

Matson straightened in his chair and folded his arms across his chest. He reminded himself that this wasn't a done deal; he could still walk out, hire a half-dozen Hacketts to fortify the defense table and force Peterson to prove an intricate securities scheme to jurors whose credit card balances testified to their inability to understand even compound interest.

And Matson realized something else: It wasn't just him sitting there wanting something, Peterson wanted something, too.

"I won't ask you everything," Peterson continued, "only enough to decide whether to allow you to go forward with your cooperation. And what…exactly…does that mean?"

Matson smiled to himself; it wasn't a question, but a setup. He felt a comforting familiarity in the cadence, the beats between the words. He'd done it a thousand times himself, motivating sales teams pushing everything from silicon switches to SatTek stock: *And what…exactly…does an activity quota, or a unit target, or a sales goal mean to you?*

Peterson snapped him back to the present. "It means you better prove you can give us people we couldn't indict without your testimony. If we've got them anyway, we don't need you.

We'll make a deal with somebody else. And trust me, the ladies are already lining up."

Matson cringed as a half smile flashed on Peterson's face. He felt shaken and weakened rather than repulsed by the prosecutor's scorn.

Voices in the hallway penetrated the conference room; muffled words followed by laughter. Matson imagined it was a joke another prosecutor would later share with Peterson. And in that moment, Matson grasped that life would go on unchanged for Peterson regardless of what happened to him. And with that realization, the balance shifted: He knew he wanted it more than Peterson did.

"If we accept your proffer, we'll work out a plea agreement with Mr. Hackett. That's why we call this a Queen for a Day, like the old TV show." Another half smile appeared on Peterson's face. "The one who tells the best story wins the crown and goes home with all the goodies."

Matson blew past the sarcasm and reached for the prize, overcome for a moment by the urge to just give in, say whatever the prosecutor wanted, and escape the mess his life had become—

But Peterson yanked it away. "Of course, there's no way it'll guarantee you won't go to the joint."

Matson gritted his teeth against the suffocating nightmare of toilet fumes wafting toward his face.

"It comes down to this," Peterson said. "The more people you give us, the less time you'll do."

Matson pasted a smirk on his face. "And who makes *that* little decision?"

"Me," Peterson said. "I do."

Matson rolled his eyes. "I figured."

"You have a problem with that?"

"Technically, the court decides on the sentence," Hackett said, looking back and forth between the two.

"Technically." Peterson said the word with a dismissiveness that told Matson that there wasn't a judge in the entire Northern

District who'd rise up on his hind legs to challenge Peterson—at least not over SatTek.

"Technically," Matson repeated, shaking his head slowly and picking at a fingernail.

"Your attorney and I have agreed that you'll proffer information regarding the involvement of others in the stock fraud itself and in the use of offshore companies to accomplish it. Is that also your understanding?"

Matson nodded, now panicked by the admissions Peterson would extract from him and wanting to push away from the table and bolt toward the door—but he could feel neither his arms nor his legs.

"You also need to understand that the government appreciates that you have a Fifth Amendment privilege against self-incrimination. And it's no secret to anyone in this room that by implicating your coconspirators you'll be incriminating yourself."

Matson found himself continuing to nod, as much to Peterson's words as to his even tone; there was no pulling back of a rhetorical fist, no rising toward a setup; there was just a relentless pushing forward.

"But in exchange for you waiving that privilege, nothing you say to me will be used against you unless...are you listening?" Matson nodded a final time, then lowered his head. "Unless we reject your proffer, you proceed to trial, and your testimony conflicts with what you say in this room."

Matson's head jerked up, eyes betraying the bewilderment of a rodent snared in a steel trap. "Are you saying I won't be able to testify in my own defense?"

Peterson leaned forward and crossed his forearms on the table. He glanced at Hackett, then bored down on Matson.

"If you had a defense, Scoob, you wouldn't be sitting here."

◇◇◇

Peterson took Hackett aside just outside the conference room after they broke for lunch. He remained silent until the agents had directed Matson out through the lobby door at the end of the long hallway.

"I'm concerned about security at SatTek," Peterson said, "but we can't keep U.S. Marshals down there forever. I need your assurance that pissed-off employees won't try to get even with Matson through sabotage or try to cushion their fall into unemployment through theft. For all I care, they can steal every stapler and coffeemaker in the place, but if I discover that any military-grade hardware has slipped away, I'll make sure the judge hammers Matson regardless of whether he cooperates in the fraud investigation."

Hackett tilted his head toward the inside of the room. "After what just happened in there, the last thing Matson wants is to have both you and the judge ganging up on him. Trust me, if anything gets smuggled out, it'll be over his dead body."

Chapter Four

We heard it on the news, boss."

Gage looked up from where he sat in the sparsely occupied ICU waiting room. In his hand was a notepad on which he had outlined the reassignment of his own cases to his staff. Although time stood still for him, it surged forward for his corporate clients around the globe, and the enemies that threatened them wouldn't be calling a truce because of a shooting on a San Francisco street.

Hector McBride, an ex-DEA agent, and Derrell Williams, an ex-FBI agent, pulled up chairs close to him.

"How's he doing?" Williams asked, peering up at Gage through wire rims that glinted in the overhead fluorescent lights.

"Not good," Gage said.

McBride hunched his huge frame forward, then tilted his head toward the door. "We saw some of Burch's people heading toward the elevator."

"I sent them away. They were so distraught, I was afraid they'd scare Jack's wife. There's nothing they can do here anyway."

Gage handed Williams the list. "The only urgent one is my antitrust case. If we don't move fast, the client is out of business. Take care of it yourself." He then looked at McBride. "Get out to the Richmond District. See if your old informants have heard anything."

"You think it's Russians, and not road rage like the news said?" McBride asked.

"I don't know yet, but it's all we've got to go on."

The three of them rose. McBride scanned the other people in the room, then leaned in toward Gage and lowered his voice.

"We're right behind you, boss, and we're gonna get this asshole. There's no fucking place he can hide."

◇◇◇

Faith caught Gage's eye as she climbed down from her SUV in the hospital parking lot. He walked around and opened the passenger door and immediately understood. Courtney Burch's clear, sweet eyes told him that the tidal wave of the attempted murder of her husband hadn't yet hit her.

The women were still dressed alike in plaid shirts and jeans for a clear fall day along Hat Creek, now darkened by gunshots. In Gage's mind, they had always been opposites bound together like the north-south poles of a magnet. Faith: tall, slim, auburn hair; hazel eyes that peered out at the world as if it was composed of puzzling fragments, each to be held up for inspection. Courtney: diminutive, olive-skinned, black-haired, soft features; a woman for whom life was to be taken whole.

Gage hugged them both, then reached his arms around their shoulders and guided them through the hospital entrance and up to the second floor ICU to await permission to see Burch.

"Have the police found out anything more about who did this?" Courtney asked, after they sat down together in a corner of the reception area.

Gage shook his head. "Not yet, but they'll pass on everything they learn. Spike is keeping the case himself."

Courtney's face drained of color. She looked up at Gage. "But Spike is in homicide."

"They handle assaults, too," Gage said quickly, hoping she wouldn't ask why.

Courtney caught the motion of a patrol officer checking in with hospital security, then heading through the double doors into the ICU. The meaning registered on her face. "Is he safe here?" Panic rose in her voice as her eyes darted around the room, then froze toward the hallway as if masked men were about to storm the hospital. "Graham, is he safe?"

Gage reached around her shoulders and squeezed her tightly. "I'll make sure he's safe."

Courtney looked up at Gage as if searching for a handhold in a tsunami. Her shoulders slumped as she burst into tears and buried her face in her hands.

The seawall had finally crumbled.

◇◇◇

"I called Spike while I was in the cafeteria," Gage said, handing cups of tea to Faith and Courtney a half hour later. "There'll be a Take Back the Streets rally tomorrow where Jack was shot. Spike and I'll be there trying to turn up more witnesses. All they've got so far for an ID of the shooter is that he's slim and was wearing a Giants baseball cap."

He sat down next to Courtney. Both he and Spike needed a question answered, one that made the shooting less anonymous and more terrifying.

"Was there anyone Jack was afraid of?" he asked.

"Is that why there's an officer protecting him?" Her eyes locked on his. "You mean this wasn't random, that it wasn't road rage?"

"No. That's not what I'm saying." Gage held her gaze and offered her reassurance he didn't feel. "It's only in case the shooter thinks Jack would recognize him. Nothing more." He tried again. "Was Jack troubled by anything at work?"

Courtney took a sip of tea, then gripped the paper cup in both hands, close to her chest. "More than troubled. Furious. The Russian finance minister tried to backdoor Jack after you two left Moscow."

Gage's eyes narrowed. "What was that about?"

"Nepotism and money." She turned toward Gage. "The minister tried to have his son appointed managing director of the natural gas joint venture, positioning himself to divert funds. But Jack called him the day before yesterday and backed him down."

"Any fallout?"

"Someone leaked the call to the *Financial Times*. Jack thought it made his part of the project look political."

"It *was* political."

"Not for Jack." She struggled to smile. "For him it was like playing with Tinkertoys."

Gage finished her thought: "And he didn't want bullies interfering." He didn't finish his own: Not wanting the bullies interfering was no guarantee that they wouldn't. He let it drop and looked elsewhere. "Was Jack worried about anything else?"

Dr. Kishore emerged from the ICU before she could answer. They rose as the doctor walked toward them. Gage introduced her to Faith and Courtney. Dr. Kishore took Courtney's hands in hers, but had nothing new to offer; just kind words and no promises, and permission to see her husband.

As the surgeon walked away, Gage led Faith and Courtney down the hallway toward Burch's door. He opened it and stepped in first, trying to absorb some of the shock that he knew would jolt Courtney. He stopped at the foot of the bed where Burch lay surrounded by a cockpit of monitors and attached to a half-dozen drips. The only sound was the whoosh-snap of the ventilator, its breathing tube taped to the corner of his mouth. Gauze encased the top of his head, his forearms were mottled with bruises, splotches of yellow and blue surrounding needle punctures. The dim light shadowed his pallid face and his closed, sunken eyes. Burch already looked like the aged man that Gage hoped he would survive to be.

Courtney walked past Gage, took her husband's hand, then leaned down and kissed his forehead. She sat in a chair next to the bed and gazed at him for a few moments before lowering her head to rest her cheek on the back of his hand. Her black hair, finally regrown after radiation and two courses of chemotherapy, flowed over their hands and onto the sheets.

Gage felt Faith's arm reach around his waist, then her head press against him. He slipped his arm around her shoulders as they watched Burch's slowly rising and falling chest. Moments later, Gage felt Faith tremble as she fought back her tears, and an ache tore at his heart as the stick figure to which his imagination had held fast, now transformed into blood and flesh.

◇◇◇

Gage and Courtney watched mist glittering in the yellow halogen parking lot lights triggered by cloud-darkened, afternoon skies. He had led her to a quiet spot just outside the hospital entrance to converse out of the hearing of the nurses and technicians tending to Burch. Faith remained at his bedside.

"I'm sorry to keep pressing you on this," Gage said, "but I need to know whether there was anything else bothering Jack besides the Russians?"

Courtney reached out her hand and watched the mist drift between her fingers, almost as if she hadn't heard his question. Finally she answered: "SatTek."

Gage felt his stomach tighten. "Why did—" He caught the motion of a television news truck pulling in from the street. He grabbed Courtney's arm. "Let's get back inside."

He led her to the cafeteria, then into the employees' dining room, where reporters wouldn't think to look. They took seats next to each other, facing away from the door. He pushed aside empty paper plates, soda cups, and crumpled napkins, then called Spike, who promised to block the media from bringing cameras beyond the hospital lobby.

Gage seized the broken thread of their conversation, now seeming more like a live wire. "Why SatTek?"

Courtney shook her mind free of the descending media storm and the tens of millions of eyes that would soon drill like termites into their lives. "I don't know. Jack wouldn't say."

"Then how do you—"

"He's been obsessed with the SatTek television coverage for the last week; alternately angry, then dejected, switching among the cable news channels, then searching the Internet, fixated on every rumor about the collapse."

Gage reached for the lesser evil. "Did he lose money when the stock fell?"

Courtney lowered her head. "It wasn't that."

"You mean SatTek was a client?"

She nodded without looking up.

"Since when?"

"Two years ago. A referral from a venture capital firm in New York."

There was a momentary silence, but neither of them said the obvious. SatTek had approached Burch just after Courtney was diagnosed. Gage and Burch had spent days together, sitting outside the Stanford Cancer Center as she first underwent surgery, then radiation, and finally chemotherapy. Burch had fled from the uncertainty of her future into talking about his work, the intricacies of each deal, seeking some alternate universe, safe and controllable.

"Why didn't he mention SatTek to me?" Gage asked.

Courtney finally looked at him. "He couldn't. You were still working on that TM-Micro trade secrets case. He read about your testimony in the *Wall Street Journal.* SatTek was about to make a huge purchase of TM-Micro products, big enough to push their stock up five or ten percent. He didn't want to create the appearance that he leaked insider information."

She paused for a moment and her eyes went vacant, then her brows furrowed.

"Is that it?" she asked, searching Gage's face. "Is SatTek the reason Jack was shot? Some lunatic shareholder?"

Gage shook his head. "Not likely. Stockholders come gunning when companies collapse, but not with weapons, only with class action lawyers. If it was otherwise, Enron headquarters would've become a war zone."

Courtney's face showed she wasn't convinced. Her gaze drifted down toward the brown Formica table, then held there as if searching for a constellation among the littered bread crumbs.

"It just can't be random," she finally said, looking up. "It just can't be. Isn't life supposed to mean something?"

◇◇◇

Gage sat alone in Burch's room, next to his bed, his hand resting on Burch's. Faith had gone with Courtney to call his family in Sydney and hers in Portland.

Random. The word repeated itself in Gage's mind, carrying with it a feeling from his early years in homicide. He'd drive up to Twin Peaks or Russian Hill and look out over the nighttime city after a murder, especially one without witnesses, without leads, without hope. A wave of uneasiness would shudder through him as if he were staring into a vast emptiness, as if he, too, was about to lose himself into the abyss in which the victim had disappeared. That unease would soon give way, replaced not by a feigned and swaggering squad room confidence that pretended away the unknown and unknowable, but by a resolve that was as palpable as the relentless breeze flowing in from the ocean.

He'd gaze down at the lights and the shadows and at the twisted grid of streets, listening to the rumble of traffic and the howl of tugboats on the bay, then he'd get back into his car and turn the ignition, and—

Gage heard the door swish open behind him. He looked over, then stood as Courtney approached the foot of the bed.

"Graham," she said, looking down at her husband. "I need you to find who did this. I need to know he'll never come back to hurt Jack."

"I'll protect him," Gage said, "but I can't promise that I'll find the man. Sometimes it isn't possible."

"Just knowing you're out there searching will give me a feeling of security, of stability." She hugged herself as if fighting off a chill. "I just feel so…so…"

"Adrift?"

"Yes, adrift." She peered up into his eyes. "How did you know?"

◇◇◇

As Gage walked past the waiting room an hour later, car keys gripped in his hand, he heard Spike's voice, distant and tinny. He glanced over at the television hanging from a bracket in the far corner: CNN. The ticker told the story: "International lawyer

Jack Burch shot down in San Francisco. Russian and Ukrainian presidents to issue a joint statement regarding the future of the natural gas agreement."

The small screen showed Spike along with Dr. Kishore and the chief of police standing in the hospital lobby behind a dozen microphones. A BBC reporter yelled out a question.

Gage didn't break his step. He already knew the answer.

"No," Spike said, staring into the camera, "we have no leads."

Chapter Five

Let's start with Edward Granger," Assistant U.S. Attorney William Peterson said, beginning Stuart Matson's afternoon session. "We'll do Jack Burch next."

Lyle Zink, the FBI agent seated to Peterson's left, slid an enlargement of a driver's license photograph toward Matson. It showed a white male, mid-sixties, brown eyes, long in the face, and self-possessed enough to smile at the Department of Motor Vehicles camera.

"Is that Granger?" Peterson asked Matson, who stared at the photo for a moment, then nodded.

Zink flipped it over and laid a pen on top.

"Sign the back," Peterson said.

Matson glanced at his attorney, who gave him a slightly off-center nod. Matson signed. Zink then added his own name, the case number, and the date.

Peterson fixed his eyes on Matson. "Tell me about how you first got hooked up with Granger."

Matson looked around the table and thought back to his first job after college. Burdened with student loans, he'd grabbed the first one that was offered, knowing that he wouldn't stay long. *I got thirty-plus years in the car business*, the sales manager at the GM dealership told him the day he started. *Trust me, kid, nobody likes buying from a victim. Be a man.* At that moment, Matson grasped that he knew more by instinct than his boss had learned in a generation. Five minutes later, he weaseled an old guy into the driver's seat of a new Cadillac he didn't want, then slipped into the passenger seat, hung his head, and lied about his wife dying of leukemia. It was the first of three cars he sold that day.

Showtime.

"Looking back," Matson said, "I guess you could say I was sort of a sitting duck."

Matson paused, then leaned forward and rested his forearms on the table.

"You've got to understand what kind of a guy Ed Granger is. When he was with Westbrae Ventures in New York, he was huge. Huge. Then all of a sudden he shows up in California and comes walking into our country club. A member named Herb Wilson had invited him. They'd been in the Harvard MBA program together years ago. Herb's wife tells my wife that the *Wall Street Journal* article about Granger retiring was just a puff piece. That he'd actually been forced out. Real hush, hush, and nobody at Westbrae was talking.

"I asked Herb to introduce me, and it was weird. Granger seemed to know who I was and even knew about a turnaround I'd done at Premier Switches."

Matson noticed a smirk on Peterson's face.

"Look, a turnaround is a turnaround whether you make a better product, or find a way to sue your competition into oblivion." He thumped a forefinger on the table. "I chose Plan B and it worked."

Hackett reached over and grabbed Matson's forearm. "Take it easy, Scoob. Premier isn't the issue."

Matson took in a breath, then nodded.

"I knew from the moment that Granger shook my hand that he was on the prowl, and decided right then that I was going to wine him and dine him and three-putt and double-bogey thirty-six straight holes if that's what it took to get his blessing. I'd spent twenty years waiting for a break, and I wasn't going to miss this one.

"When I met him at the country club two days later, I came ready to pitch the hell out of SatTek, but he was already a step ahead of me.

"Granger was sitting at the bar when I walked in. We started with a little small talk. Golf handicaps, that kind of thing, until my drink arrived. Then he eased into the subject, casual-like, and told me that he'd done a little research on SatTek's financials.

"I froze up. Panicked because he might've figured out that SatTek was just treading water. The Grangers of the world don't invest in swimming holes. They want to ride the raging river. They're chasing new technology, not the old, even if it's the best in its market.

"I gave him the pitch anyway because that was all I had. I ran through the whole product line: everything from how our acoustic detectors can pick up a terrorist sneaking across the desert ten miles away, to how our video amplifiers can drop an air-to-ground missile into a coffee cup. I really pounded it. It was the best presentation I ever made.

"After I'm done, Granger smiled at me and gave me a fatherly pat on the shoulder, and said, 'You don't need to sell me, I'm already sold.'

"I felt like an idiot. Granger is a guy with a reputation for knowing everything, and I just pointed at the sun and told him it was daylight.

"I got flustered. I think I even turned red. But he ignored it and said, 'Have you thought about bypassing the venture capital route altogether, and taking SatTek public?'

"For a second, I thought maybe he got dumped from Westbrae for senility. What the hell do you think guys like me daydream about? I'll tell you what. It's standing on the podium at the New York Stock Exchange, ringing the bell, and then watching your share price explode through the roof.

"But I had no reason to think that would ever happen with SatTek and I admitted it. I told him that there was too much pink on our balance sheet and that the SEC would just laugh at us.

"Granger stared down at his bourbon for a while, took a sip, and then looked back at me and said, 'I guess we'll just have to wipe the smiles off their faces.'

"Man, what a rush. At the time, it felt like he was putting his arm around me, including me in something. But looking back now, I realize it was just him setting the hook.

"Then he swiveled his stool toward me. I remember his exact words:

" 'What you've got to understand, Scoob, is that success in business has very little to do with whether you're in the red or in the black. It's about how aggressive you're willing to be.' He paused and stared me right in the eyes, then he said, 'You know what that means, right? Aggressive.'

"I really wasn't sure what he meant, but I nodded anyway and asked him what he had in mind. But he didn't tell me. Not right then, anyway. He just pointed at my chest and said, 'Whatever it is, Scoob, don't waste my time. You're either going to be in or you're going to be out.'

"The fact is, I was in even before I walked through the door."

Chapter Six

At seven on the morning following Burch's shooting, Gage displayed his identification to the security guard stationed behind the counter in the glass and steel lobby of the financial district tower housing Burch's top floor office. The balding man in the gray uniform waved it away and offered Gage a toothy grin.

"Don't you remember me?" the guard asked.

Gage inspected the man. There was something familiar about the Howdy Doody cheeks, but Gage couldn't connect the face with anything in his past. He shook his head.

"I'm Sonny Powers. I was a bailiff when you were with SFPD."

Gage smiled and stuck out his hand. "D Day."

The courtroom riot in 1982 known as D Day had ended the career of the then-twenty-six-year-old Powers with a crushed knee. Gage was testifying in the homicide trial of three members of the D Block Boys, when four gang members in the gallery jumped the barrier to overpower the bailiffs. The clerk remotely locked the door, and the escape attempt devolved into a pointless melee. Gage shoved the judge under the bench, then weighed into the mix. He last saw Powers writhing on the marble floor while the paramedics tried to stabilize his leg.

Powers struggled to his feet to shake Gage's hand, then held up the day's authorized visitors sheet. He pointed at Gage's name and the suite number. "You here about Jack Burch?"

"His secretary came in early to gather up some files for me before the press showed up. I didn't want to become part of the story."

"How's he doing?"

"Not good." Gage glanced back toward the storm-soaked street where a television truck pulled to a stop to feed a story to the early morning news. "Looks like I'm too late. I better get upstairs."

Gage started toward the elevators.

"Don't worry," Powers called after him, "they won't get by me. I've had enough of those assholes trying to sneak in and out of here."

Gage spun back. "What do you mean?"

"A janitor popped the back door to let one in a while ago. Said he was a producer from ABC News, that *20/20* show, and wanted to use the freight elevator to bring up equipment." Powers gestured toward the monitors on his desk. "I saw him come in." He adopted an authoritative tone. "I read the janitor the riot act and told her to go find the guy and bring him down here."

A rush of anger followed Gage's recollection of the only other thing he knew about Powers: He'd ended up as a court bailiff because he was incompetent as a street cop. Gage cringed at the thought of Burch's secretary, Anne-Marie, already at her desk organizing the SatTek and Moscow files: distraught, preoccupied, and vulnerable.

"How do you know he was with ABC?"

"The janitor said he showed an ID, just like all of them." Powers reddened, then limped toward the end of the counter, as if abandoning his post to look for the man. "You don't think he's the guy who shot—"

"What did he look like?"

"Dark windbreaker. Black hair."

Gage tossed Powers a business card. "Call my cell so I'll have your number." He then pointed at the entrance. "Lock the front door and block the back exit." He sprinted toward the elevators and into an express toward the forty-third floor. His phone rang as the doors closed. He verified that Powers' number showed on the screen, then punched the end button.

The elevator seemed to rise in slow motion. The annoying pinging seemed to be counting down rather than up. A final ping signaled the door opening in the empty lobby of Burch's firm, lit only by the storm-muted sunrise. He listened for a moment, then headed down the long carpeted hallway toward Burch's office in the opposite corner of the building.

As he crept along the wall, the snap of metal on metal broke the silence. It sounded to Gage like a file cabinet or a desk drawer. He edged toward the hallway corner and looked around it. Sharp fluorescent light emerging from a small storage room striped the gray carpet thirty feet away. Burch's office door was open fifteen feet farther down.

Another snap, then the slap of a file and the shuffling of papers. The noises seemed to come from the storage room. Gage imagined the layout. Banks of file cabinets on the right and left walls. Copier at the back. Table centered in the middle.

Gage heard a groan as he approached the threshold. He balanced on the balls of his feet, and then peeked into the room. Anne-Marie lay on her side in front of the copier, hands and feet bound, packing tape over her mouth. She flinched at the motion in the doorway—

A fist shot toward him from around the doorjamb. It rocked him with a punch to the stomach. The burglar surged forward, jamming his shoulder into Gage's chest, and ramming him into the opposite wall. Gage slumped to the floor as the man fled down the hallway.

Fighting for breath, he crawled toward Anne-Marie to untape her mouth, but she shook her head as if to say, *Go after him.*

Gage pushed himself to his feet and reached for his cell phone.

"He's coming down," Gage gasped to Powers as he staggered down the hallway.

A scream sliced through the still air as Gage took the turn into the reception area. The just-arrived janitor stood flush against the wall behind the desk as Gage ran by, her face red, her eyes still wide as she pointed toward the closing elevator.

Gage yelled for her to untie Anne-Marie, then pushed open the door to the stairs.

Leaping more than running, Gage grabbed the steel railings and swung himself around each turn. He imagined the burglar arriving at the first floor and running toward the entrance, bouncing off the locked doors, then searching for the stairway to the underground garage and the rear exit. Gage guessed that Powers would only have to fight the man a minute or two to give him time to catch up.

But the sound of the rear door slamming as he ran down the last flight into the garage told Gage that Powers hadn't been up to it. When he burst through the back door into the alley, he spotted a bulldog of a man shielding himself with Powers and dragging him toward the intersection a hundred feet away. Gage ran toward them, arriving at the cross street just after the burglar pushed Powers into the path of a garbage truck and then jumped into the back of an already moving van.

Gage ran forward and reached down for Powers as thirty-five thousand pounds of steel squealed and skidded sideways into the slick intersection. He yanked hard on the front of Powers' jacket, dived over him, and rolled with him into the next lane.

He didn't hear the truck shudder to a stop. He felt only the heat and smelled the burned rubber of the tire next to his head. And the only sounds were his pounding heart and exploding breath, and the sobbing of Powers lying next to him on the rain-soaked blacktop.

Chapter Seven

Assistant U.S. Attorney William Peterson opened an FBI evidence envelope and removed a packet of incorporation papers for companies in Vietnam and China.

"We ended yesterday afternoon with Granger suggesting you set up offshore," Peterson said, sliding the documents across the conference table to Matson. "Have you ever seen these?"

Matson flipped through the pages. "These are the companies Jack Burch set up."

"Then let's talk about Burch—and say whatever you would've said before he got shot. Road rage is SFPD's problem, not ours."

Matson's eyes widened. "You didn't let on—"

"Don't worry. We didn't tell them you're cooperating."

Matson nodded and opened his mouth to speak, then hesitated, unsure what to say or how to say it. "Can I talk to Mr. Hackett for a minute?"

"Sure." Peterson looked at his watch. "Take all the time you need. Agent Zink can show you to an empty office."

Matson looked at Zink, his face registering for the first time. *A chinless rodent.* Matson imagined himself slogging through a dark, cavernous sewer, swarmed by miniature Zinks, crawling up his pant legs, nipping at his balls.

"I think Scoob and I'll go downstairs," Hackett told Peterson. "We'll grab a cup of coffee. Talk down there."

Zink escorted them out of the U.S. Attorney's Office and into the hallway by the elevators. Matson started to speak, but

Hackett hushed him with a raised finger. They rode in silence down to the second floor restaurant and took a table in the far corner, away from other attorneys and their clients strategizing before court or commiserating afterward.

"Can't we just give them Granger and maybe the accountant?" Matson whispered, eyes darting around the dining room as if he was afraid he might be recognized.

"No. The deal is for Burch. He's the prize they want."

Matson flared and fixed his eyes on Hackett. "And I'm gonna look like a scumbag snitching off a road-rage victim." His voice rose. "You see what the press is saying about him?"

"Not so loud." Hackett reached over and grabbed Matson's arm. "Not so loud."

Matson leaned in and lowered his voice. "They're making him into a fucking saint. Charity-this and charity-that. His wife's heroic battle against cancer. Immigrant success story—like fucking Australians don't grow up speaking English."

"Keep your eye on the ball, Scoob. You're only worth something to the government if you can give them somebody they want. That's the reason they're willing to take the heat in the press for letting you walk. They think Burch was in on it and they've got a paper trail right to his desk. They think every lawyer who deals offshore is a crook or money launderer. So you're just telling them what they already believe."

Hackett pointed at Matson, his voice insistent. "And there's something else. Peterson is aiming at SatTek because it's a hard target that the public can comprehend, not like some squishy securitized loan scam. People can't make sense of that shit. But SatTek they can, and they need a face to go with it. So far, that face is yours, but Peterson wants it to be Burch's. Don't give him time to go weak-kneed and decide it'll look better to use Burch to roll on you. Because I'll tell you what'll happen: Burch'll go in and say, 'My wife was sick. I wasn't thinking straight. Mea culpa. Mea culpa.' Pretty soon everybody's thinking he's *your* victim instead of *you* being his. And trust me, nobody's going to be calling him a snitch. They're going to say he's a fucking hero for turning you in—so you better get him before he gets you. Understand?"

Matson felt like a school kid just sent to the corner. "Yeah, I understand."

"And, as your lawyer, I have to tell you one more thing. You need to tell the truth. One lie and this proffer evaporates. You won't be able to get it back. DOJ policy."

Another lawyer covering his ass, Matson thought. *He's supposed to be covering mine.*

Matson and Hackett rode the elevator in silence back to the eleventh floor. The receptionist guided them through the bullet- and bomb-proof glass security doors and down the long hallway to the conference room. They found that Peterson and the agents had removed their jackets and loosened their ties. There were bottles of water and sandwiches collected on a side table. It seemed to Matson that the only thing missing was a picnic bench and a red-checkered tablecloth.

"Ready, Scoob?" Peterson asked after they returned to their seats.

"Yeah, I just needed to make sure I was on the right track. I don't want to blow this."

"We were talking about Jack Burch."

Matson looked dead straight at Peterson. "Burch was in on it from the beginning. We couldn't have done anything without him. No way. We didn't know diddly about the offshore world. We were novices, he was the pro—as slick as they come and looking to make a killing. And I felt like a fucking rabbit in his crosshairs.

"I'll admit that I was nervous driving up from San Jose to meet Burch. Granger wanted me to do it alone even though it was new territory for me. I'd spent my life in manufacturing and sales. You make something solid, something real, and sell it. But the meeting with Burch was something I had trouble wrapping my mind around. It was only about air and paper.

"Sure, SatTek had hired lots of lawyers. Contracts. Real estate. Intellectual property. But Burch was in a different league from them. It hit me how different when I got off the elevator on the forty-third floor. The views from up there are more than amazing. They're unnerving. The whole financial district. The Golden Gate. Blue sky all the way to the horizon.

"I gave my name to the receptionist and took a seat on the couch. Plush. Soft leather—and I got sucked into the damn thing. My suit jacket got all bunched up. My briefcase was dangling over the edge. Before I had a chance to recover, Burch walked in. Tall. Intense. Almost senatorial—and I'm sitting there like the village idiot.

"First I got embarrassed, and then pissed, thinking that the couch was set up as booby-trap to put outsiders at a disadvantage.

"As we walked down the hallway toward his office, I told myself that I needed to get focused and get my head in the game. One amateurish screwup and Burch might drop-kick me out of there. Then a warning from Granger came back to me. 'Self-control is key,' he'd said. 'Be careful what you say and how you say it. The rules are different from what you're used to and the most important one is this: No one says exactly what he means if he wants to get what he came for.'

"I hadn't grasped what Granger meant at the time, but two minutes after I sat down in Burch's office, I understood exactly.

"Burch read over some notes on a legal pad, then looked up and said, 'Ed Granger hasn't told me the details of what you want to do, other than it somehow involves selling nonmilitary-grade sound and video detectors in Asia.'

"Even though it must've sounded like I was reading from a script, I answered him the way Granger told me to: 'The plan is to give ourselves an international presence in anticipation of going public.'

"I waited for Burch to nod like Granger said he would, then I looked him straight on and said: 'We're looking to create a flexible structure, one that you might even call aggressive.'

"Burch's eyebrows went up a little and he got a half smile on his face, and right then I knew that I'd hit just the way Granger had trained me. Crushed it three hundred yards down the fairway.

"Hell, when I look back on it now, I think Burch understood where Granger was headed with this thing long before I did."

Chapter Eight

At 9:30 A.M. Gage pulled into a parking space behind his red-brick converted warehouse office along the Embarcadero. The weather had gone sideways, rain pounding the driver's side window and sending rivulets streaming across the windshield. He decided to wait it out, for San Francisco storms squalled, rather than swept, their way across the city, cresting and troughing like surging waves.

Gage's head and ribs had merely felt stunned and bruised during his meeting with the senior partners of Burch's firm after the burglary, but were now stiff and throbbing. Since no bones had been broken, he was certain that by the end of the day nothing would be left but aches and twinges.

Everyone assembled in the windowless boardroom an hour earlier had understood that a press report exposing the breach of their files not only would provoke an onslaught of panicked calls from corporate clients around the world, but would make the firm the focal point of the media's speculations about the shooting. With the consent of both Burch's secretary and Sonny Powers, the firm had therefore agreed not to risk a leak by calling in the police, but rather to leave the investigation in Gage's hands. He knew that they trusted him not only as Burch's closest friend, but also as someone each of them had worked with since the founding of the firm.

Nevertheless, in the strained faces of the men and women sitting around the conference table, Gage had observed a silent acknowledgment that the clock was ticking down toward the moment when they would lose control of a story whose implications, both for Burch and for the firm, were as ominous as they were opaque.

◇◇◇

When the rain hesitated, Gage walked around to the passenger side of his truck and grabbed two boxes of files and an overstuffed folder he'd taken from Burch's office. He braced them against the wall and punched his security code into the back door pad. Once inside, he climbed the steps toward his office. The crisscrossing, floor-to-ceiling I-beams installed throughout the building by earthquake retrofitters made the stairwell feel bunkerlike in the muted fluorescent lighting.

Emerging on the third floor, Gage heard the voices of three of his investigators making calls to the midday East Coast, or perhaps to end-of-the-day London or Frankfurt, or to nighttime Moscow or Dubai or Kolkata. He knew a dozen more were settled in before their monitors on the two floors below, learning enough about Gage's own cases to fulfill the reassignments he'd made the previous day. Others on his staff of former FBI, DEA, and IRS agents were at work in those far-off cities, and in others, searching for facts and witnesses to explain why stock prices suddenly plunged or how trade secrets had been stolen or where embezzled money had been cached.

After hanging his rain jacket on a corner rack in his office, Gage walked to the nearest of the three casement windows facing the bay. Wind-driven raindrops swept across it sounding like cascading dominoes, then attacked the next, and the next. He watched fog swirl in, obscuring the front parking lot, and thought back to the day he had paid off the building: he and Burch sitting on the landing, drinking beer as the sunset gave the bay a reddish glow, their friendship somehow anchored in the brick and the concrete and the steel.

But standing there now, gazing into the grayness with Burch near death in the ICU, Gage realized that the illusion of permanence had been nothing but a self-deceiving denial of mortality.

As he turned toward his desk he noticed a stack of messages left for him by his receptionist the evening before. He separated out the ones from reporters, crumpled them up, and threw them into the trash. He selected one from the remainder, a Russian name with a Washington, D.C., area code, and slipped it into his shirt pocket.

"Alex?" Gage spoke into the intercom as he sat down. He didn't have to complete his request before Alex Z answered, "Be right there, boss."

On any other morning, Gage would've had to walk downstairs to Alex Z's office to get his attention, for the skinny twenty-six-year-old's ears would've been wrapped in headphones, his mind immersed in trails of data dancing across his monitor. It was Alex Z's job to think and to turn data into information that Gage could use, and if he needed blaring music to make that happen, Gage had always been willing to accommodate him.

But for Alex Z, as for everyone else at the firm, everything had changed since the shooting of Jack Burch. Gage had heard it in the voices of every employee who'd called him in the last two days. He knew that each, just like Alex Z, would be working with a divided mind: half concentrating on their cases, half listening for Gage's voice on the intercom.

The wild-haired, Popeye-tattooed Alex Z arrived a minute after Gage's call. He still looked like the disaffected computer science graduate student who'd sought out Faith, an anthropology professor at UC Berkeley. He had already surrendered his fellowship and was in search of work that would be more meaningful than simply making the world seem smaller and move faster. Faith had brought him home to Gage like a stray dog from the pound, and during the succeeding five years Alex Z became the one in the office on whom Gage most relied to help him bring order to the chaos of facts and events from which complex cases are formed.

Alex Z looked over at Gage's jacket as he walked toward the desk and shook his head at the street grime smearing the arms and elbows and the split seam at the right shoulder.

"Jeez, boss, you okay?" Alex Z asked as he dropped into a chair.

"It's nothing serious."

Alex Z glanced again at the jacket. "Has the press gotten ahold of what happened?"

"The firm agreed not to say anything about it, even to the police, until I look into it."

"But what if he was the shooter?"

Gage shook his head. "He wasn't. He was at least forty pounds heavier than witnesses described, and I don't want to take a chance of SFPD leaking Jack's connection to SatTek to the press."

Alex Z drew back. "No shit? SatTek? Man, the media is going to tear Mr. Burch apart. You see what they're doing to the company president? They're picking through his life like it's a garage sale at the *National Enquirer*, and nobody even heard of him until a week ago."

Gage thought of the press still camped out at the hospital and on the sidewalk in front of Burch's mansion, and of news cycles that needed feeding.

"That's why we better figure out what Jack's part was before the media paints a bull's-eye on him." Gage pointed at a chaotic foot-high stack of documents he'd piled on the conference table centered in his office. "Those are Jack's SatTek files. They were scattered all over a storage room and his office. The burglar ripped them apart looking for something. There's an index in there somewhere, see if you can figure out if anything is missing."

Alex Z rose. "How soon?"

"Jack's wife wants me with her at a meeting with his doctors early this afternoon. She's afraid she's not thinking clearly. See if you can have it ready by the time I get back."

"Just tell me what you need and when you need it, boss. I'll be available 24–7."

Alex Z's two lives converged in Gage's mind. His indispensability occasionally made Gage forget that Alex Z had a second life, what sometimes seemed a second identity, as the lead guitarist for a popular South of Market club scene band.

"You didn't cancel—"

"The moment I heard the news, and everybody in the group is on board with it."

Alex Z turned away to gather up the documents, then looked back, brows furrowed. "If the break-in is connected to SatTek, doesn't that mean the shooting is, too?"

The words reminded Gage of his throbbing shoulder, as if the connection between the two was visceral. But he knew that the web of relationships that formed Jack's world wasn't that simple.

"Until we know a lot more we're going to have to treat it as a coincidence," Gage said, "just like the natural gas deal. It's merely a blip on the screen over here, but it's front page news in Europe." He thought of the message slip in his pocket. "Over there, everyone is assuming that Jack was shot to prevent it from going through."

"So, for the Europeans, SatTek is like a tree falling in a forest."

Gage nodded. "But not for us." He again reached for the telephone. "Let's get to work finding out who's hiding in the trees."

Alex Z pointed at a sealed file box stamped with Burch's firm name sitting on Gage's credenza. "What about that?"

"It's something Jack and I worked on in Afghanistan. I figured I better keep it locked up over here. We did a few things that might be misunderstood in light of SatTek."

◇◇◇

Gage punched the radio button preset to NPR while driving back to his office from the meeting with Burch's doctors, whose vague answers and shrugs revealed nothing more than the limits of their science. He caught the closing segment of *Marketplace*, the afternoon business report, devoted solely to SatTek.

A Brookings Institution Fellow asked, "Where was the Securities and Exchange Commission during the last two years?"

A Harvard Law professor demanded, "Where was the Justice Department?"

It seemed to Gage that neither had answers that even satisfied themselves, much less their listeners.

The host concluded the program as Gage turned off Market Street onto the Embarcadero and drove along the pier-studded bay: "Where, exactly, do hundreds and hundreds and hundreds of millions of dollars go when a company collapses? When a stock descends? When monitors silently flicker in empty cubicles and customers' e-mails go unanswered? Where, exactly, is Nowhere?"

◇◇◇

"Looks like Matson and Granger hired Mr. Burch to set up SatTek's international operation," Alex Z said, sitting down next to Gage in the third floor conference room and flipping open a binder. "It was run out of a holding company in London. The managing director is a chartered accountant named Morely Alden Fitzhugh IV."

"Sounds like the name of a kid who got beat up a lot," Gage glanced over at Alex Z. "Old money?"

"Once. His family was the last of the line to join the middle class. Now everybody works for a living. His little enterprise is called Fitzhugh Associates."

"Which means there aren't any."

"You guessed it. A one-man show."

Gage gestured toward Alex Z's binder. "Does he have a Web site?"

"Nope." Alex Z turned a few pages. "But here's a screen shot of the one from the London holding company. It's as polished as they come. They sure wanted to make the thing look legit." He pointed at a photo. "That's him."

A bookish man in his early forties, with dark hair and rimless glasses, looked up from the page. Gage recognized what he was trying to project: didn't cheat at bridge, lunched on the same thing at the same restaurant at the same time every day, except Tuesdays. On Tuesdays, he got his hair cut. A well-chosen image for an accountant, Gage thought, perhaps too well chosen.

"How about the Asian companies?" Gage asked.

Alex Z opened a second binder. "No Web sites, but here's an old PR packet from Mr. Burch's file."

It showed the directors of the Chinese and Vietnamese companies to be cookie-cutter Asian managers. Both were engineers with prior experience in electronics, though not in the precise field of sound and video amplifiers. Each stared uncomfortably at the camera, hair not quite combed, cowlicks springing upward, heavy black-rimmed glasses resting on flattish noses and set off by well-fed pudgy cheeks.

Gage looked back and forth between the faces, then back and forth between the photos of the companies' headquarters.

"I better send someone over to take a look," Gage finally said.

His eyes came to rest on Hawei Electronics located in Southern China, and wondered if it was what the NPR commentator had been searching for: the outer edge of Nowhere.

Chapter Nine

You ain't paying me enough to become a floater in the South China Sea," Brian Early whined from Hong Kong as Gage sat down behind his desk the following morning.

Gage shook off the image of the pale and comatose Jack Burch that he'd carried away from his and Faith's 8 A.M. visit. He glanced at Burch's SatTek file and Alex Z's research binders that he'd worked through the night before, then looked at his watch. It was after midnight in China, which meant that Early had gotten the job done in less than twelve hours, or at least had tried.

"What are you talking about?" Gage asked.

"I went to that address in Guangzhou you gave me."

Early was the entirety of Pacific Rim International Investigations Limited. Ex–U.S. Customs agent stationed in Hong Kong for the last five years of his twenty-seven-year career. Married his Filipina maid and stayed. She really loved him. He loved himself, and talking.

"I haven't gotten that chilly a reception since we did that software piracy case in Beijing." Early laughed. "But at least this time the folks didn't have guns."

"I just told you to look, Brian, not touch."

"Well, it was like this—"

"Whenever you begin like that, I start to feel a little queasy. What did you do? And skip the detours."

Gage grabbed a legal pad from the top of the credenza behind him.

"Okay. You know that old Gertrude Stein line about Oakland? 'There's no there, there.' Well, there was almost no there, there."

Gage looked up at the ceiling and exhaled loudly enough for Early to hear. "Brian?"

"What?"

"You're already on a detour."

"Okay, okay. Gotcha. I hopped a train across the border to Guangzhou and took a taxi to the building. The office number you gave me was on the seventh floor. No elevator. I hiked up and peeked in. A picayune office. A couple of middle-aged women pushing papers. I just said the company name, Hawei, and got the big chill. Then one of them starts chanting, '*Bu zai zhe li, bu zai zhe li.*' Not here, not here."

"Was it once?"

"It was there all right. Two guys were waiting for me when I got back down to the street. Wanzi and Panzi or maybe it was Kung Fu and Dung Fu. Anyway, Wanzi gets in my face and says, 'Can I help you?' and I say, 'No thanks.' And he says, 'It's not here.' So I say, 'I just figured that out, pal.' And then Panzi puts his hand on my shoulder and says, 'So you won't be coming back?' and I say, 'Nope, no need to.' I kinda pawed the sidewalk for a few seconds with my knockoff Nikes, then skedaddled out of there."

"Come on, Brian, that hardly qualifies you for hazard pay."

"That's not the end of the story."

"You went back?"

"Couldn't help myself. Last night. Late. Real late. The building is in a district of the city that the Great Leap Forward leaped over and where nobody, at least on the legit side, ever made any real dough after China joined the capitalist road. The whole area is deserted at night except for a noodle place on the first floor and a karaoke bar down the block. Just the bouncer and a couple of hookers poking their heads out. So I go around the back. The noodle shop's door is propped open for ventilation. I figure I'll have a little look-see. Maybe I can work my way into the rest of the building. But once I get inside, the only door goes to the basement. What the hell? I go down there—smelled like rotted pig guts.

"Looks like everybody in the building uses it for storage. Bunch of caged-in compartments, heavy chicken wire. Dried noodles, office supplies, old files, that kind of stuff. One of 'em got a big, industrial-strength canvas tarp over everything inside. So I grab a broom and get down on my knees. I jam the handle under the edge of the tarp. Weighed a ton. No leverage. But I got the corner up, and guess what?"

Gage felt his body stiffen even before he said the word. "SatTek."

"Damn right. Must be seven, eight hundred devices. Millions of dollars' worth. Millions. Made in the good old USA. They were marked LNA. That stands for 'low noise amplifier.' I looked it up on the Net. I found something about China using nonmilitary-grade detectors like these in a new flood warning system. They pick up vibrations from older dams that may be starting to weaken."

"Could you tell when they were shipped over?"

"Nope. Could've been anytime up to when SatTek collapsed—maybe a last shipment Hawei hadn't paid for yet."

"That can't be right. These are made to spec. Hawei wouldn't have ordered the devices unless it already had a contract to resell them." Gage paused, wondering what SatTek had tossed into the Chinese black hole. "You get a sample?"

"Nope. But I was thinkin' I should try, when this greasy T-shirt comes in waving a cleaver at the end of his string-bean arm. He's yelling, '*Zie! Zie! Zie!*' You know, 'Thief. Thief. Thief.' I'm still on my knees, thinkin' he's gonna chop my head off. So I grab my stomach and I kinda slur out, '*Wo he zui le*' like I'm drunk and gonna puke. He points the cleaver at the door, then back at me like, *What're you doing in here?* I reach in my pocket and he raises the cleaver again. I pull out my hand, real slow, empty, no money, like I've been robbed. I say, '*Ji nu*,' you know, 'Hooker,' like she came down there to do me and robbed me instead. And the guy starts laughing and points me toward the door."

"Can you get back in?"

"No way. Right after I grabbed a taxi to scoot to the train station, I looked back and saw Wanzi screeching up in a Mercedes G55. It's like a Land Rover, but costs twice—"

"Brian?"

"Okay, okay. Sorry. Once greasy T-shirt told 'em what I looked like I'll bet they moved the boxes out of there, pronto. In fact, I'll bet Wanzi or Panzi is sittin' down there right now with an AK-47 waiting to blow my head off."

"What about flying over to Ho Chi Minh City to look at the other one?"

"It's your money, but I think whatever was there is gone, too."

"Just to cover the bases. You know any Vietnamese?"

"Sure *Con dĩ cuóp tôi* ."

"What's that mean?"

"It sorta means, 'The hooker robbed me.'"

Chapter Ten

It never crossed my mind that your two bookends would be brought together like this," Faith said, standing in their granite-countered kitchen.

Gage took in a long breath, then exhaled. "Neither did I."

Faith always referred to Spike and Burch as a slightly mismatched set. Immigrants from different worlds. Spike, as a five-year-old carried on his farmworker father's shoulders wading the Rio Grande. Burch, an Oxford-trained barrister flying in on British Airways, first to add a law degree at Berkeley, then to storm the U.S. legal profession.

Now one was investigating the attempted murder of the other.

A break in the rain had allowed Gage to uncover the barbecue on the redwood deck and cook salmon steaks while Faith made rice and fixed a salad. They carried their plates to the dining room, where windows framed San Francisco against the backdrop of offshore cumulus clouds and a variegated pink, yellow, and red sunset.

Gage propped his forearms on the table and rested his chin on his interlaced fingers as he stared out at the bay.

Faith reached over and rested her hand on his shoulder. "He may make it. The doctors are telling Courtney it's going to be a long haul."

"Come on. I was there. That wasn't a prognosis, it was just a way to muzzle her and keep her from demanding answers they don't have."

He filled Faith's wineglass, then outlined what he'd learned about Burch's role in SatTek.

"I love Jack as much as you," Faith said, "but I've got to ask. Why are you so sure he wasn't at least partly responsible? Maybe the lesson he learned from Courtney's illness was that the world's not a fair place, so there's no reason not to grab what you can."

Gage shook his head. "Not Jack. He never believed money was a substitute for immortality."

"Maybe, but he wouldn't be the first to express rage against the world as greed."

"I don't see it."

"Maybe you don't want to see it."

Gage pulled back and looked at Faith out of the corner of his eye. "Ouch."

"When it comes to Jack, you have a way of overlooking how impulsive he can be. It's been that way since we were in graduate school. You, the philosopher forgiving human folly, and him, the reckless daredevil."

"He's just a little adventurous."

Faith threw up her hands. "See?"

Gage smiled. "Touché."

"And there's something else." She reached over and took his hand. "Loyalty sometimes comes at a price that's too high to pay."

"You don't mean bailing out—"

"No. Just be careful. That burglar at Jack's office could just as well have shot his way out." She pointed at Gage's bruised shoulder. "You can pretend that doesn't hurt, but I wince every time you take your shirt off."

They sat quietly, watching the horizon drain of color. Fog wormed its way through the Golden Gate, led in by three oil tankers making for the Chevron Refinery along the north bay.

Faith spooned salad on each of their plates, then broke the silence. "Anyway, isn't it possible that somebody in the natural gas deal was behind Jack's shooting?"

"Others are asking the same question," Gage said. "I returned a call to Ambassador Pougachev yesterday morning.

State Security reported to him that I'd been seen with Jack in Moscow—"

"State Security?"

Gage waved off the implication. "Since the cold war ended, they have a lot of time on their hands."

"Graham…"

"Nothing to worry about. All Pougachev wanted to know is whether Jack brought me in to fix something that was broken. He was preparing for interviews with *Agence France-Presse* and *Der Spiegel.* They weren't satisfied with the Russian president's answers at the press conference about whether Jack's shooting would interfere with completing the joint venture. Winter is coming and houses need to be heated."

"Does he think there's a connection?"

"I don't know. Pougachev is less interested in the causes than the effects."

Gage cringed as the world narrowed to twin images of Burch lying helpless in the hospital and of a self-satisfied Pougachev sitting across from them in a Washington, D.C. restaurant a few months earlier, sucking on crab legs.

"Jack's being gunned down means nothing to him," Gage said.

"But after that dinner you two had with him, Jack said—"

"He's never been able to understand that for the Russian elite, people are nothing more than a means to an end. He actually believed those bureaucrats from the finance and energy ministries when they expressed sympathy for Courtney and all she went through. They were really just probing for weaknesses. It was painful to watch, but I couldn't take it away from him."

He pointed at Faith's plate, wanting to lighten the moment. Nothing he could say now could reverse what happened back then.

"You should have a little more salmon," he said. "I'd hate to think this poor fish gave his life in vain."

Faith ate a small piece, then pushed on. "Does Pougachev know that you met with organized crime bosses?"

"That's another bit of information he got from State Security."

"Did he ask if Jack brought you into this?"

"I told him Jack didn't bring me into anything."

"Did you tell him you volunteered?"

"He wasn't perceptive enough to ask." Gage smiled. "He doesn't have your skills in cross-examination." He watched Faith blush. "In any case, he knows he can't get heavy-handed. I know too much. He tried to pursue it gently with a 'We have our ways' in a German accent, but ended up sounding like a cartoon character, so he had to let it go."

"Jack'll get a kick out of..." Faith's voice trailed off. An image of Burch struggling for life entered both of their minds.

Gage quickly filled the silence. "We'll tell him."

Faith returned to her probing. "But how can you be sure those gangsters didn't change their minds and demand a cut? Shooting Jack might buy them some time."

"I'm not sure they'd want to raise the stakes that high. Interfering with the flow of natural gas into Western Europe right now would be seen as much as an act of terrorism as blowing up a power plant—and it would mean destroying the wall between domestic law enforcement and international intelligence they've always taken refuge behind."

Faith pushed her plate away. "I don't know, they're unpredictable people."

Although she was an anthropologist, she wasn't offering a description, but a warning.

"I'll be careful," Gage said, reaching over and squeezing her hand. "But I'm not going to figure out who shot Jack until I figure out why. And that means retracing Jack's steps and trying to spot whatever came out of the shadows to blindside him. If it was road rage, then the trail will end where he fell. If not..."

Gage ended the sentence with a slow shake of his head. They both knew there was no way to finish the thought, so they sat in silence, the weight of inevitability pressing down on them.

Faith picked up her wineglass again and stared into it before speaking. "In some ways I have a hard time fixing Jack in my mind anymore. He's changed so much. Like the Afghan Medical

Relief dinner last fall. Accepting an award for charity work was out of character for him. It was almost like grandstanding."

"I asked him about it on the flight back from Moscow. Turns out he saw something Courtney wrote for her cancer support group, a phrase about invisibility being oblivion. He wanted an excuse to put her on a podium; talk about her in front of all of their friends. In retrospect, it was a very dangerous thing to do."

"Dangerous?" Faith said, glancing over, her eyebrows raised. "The dinner was in the grand ballroom of the St. Francis Hotel, dear, not at some falafel stand in Baghdad."

"Not that kind of dangerous. He risked drawing attention to the offshore bank accounts and front companies we used to smuggle medical supplies through Pakistan, and those are exactly the kinds of deceptions the U.S. Attorney might accuse him of using in SatTek."

Gage flashed on an image of Burch and him sitting with a Pashtun *jirga* near the Afghanistan border three years earlier; Burch extending his hand holding a hundred thousand dollars of his own money, the first of a series of payoffs to tribal leaders so they'd let the material pass unmolested through their territories.

"To say nothing of currency smuggling and bribery."

"But that wasn't part of any fraud," Faith said, voice rising in their defense. "Just the opposite."

"But it was fraudulent. And we could've gotten twenty years in Lompoc."

Faith flinched. "I wish you wouldn't say things like that."

"Sorry. As Jack would say, no worries. No U.S. Attorney would dare go after us for what we did over there. Anyway, SatTek may be the case that proves the rule."

"Which one is that?"

Gage reached for Faith's plate, set it on top of his, then looked over and winked the same exaggerated wink with which Jack Burch always preceded his punch lines. "If they ever get us, it'll only be for something we didn't do."

Chapter Eleven

Mr. Hackett, there's a Mr. Peterson on line one."

Daniel Hackett hesitated before picking up the receiver. He lived for these calls, but despised them all the same. He knew he'd get what he wanted; it was just that the whole thing made him feel like a weakling and a fraud. Peterson had the power, so he could play it and Hackett however he wanted. And the only way to keep his dignity was to sign on, join the team, ally himself with the prosecutor against his own client.

"I think we can do a deal," Peterson said. "I've talked it over with the case agent. We're convinced Matson can give us Granger and Burch, and I know you won't let him keep talking for free."

Hackett adopted a firm tone; his first move in a fox-trot where Peterson had already taken the lead. "You got that right. I think I've let him say as much as I should without something on the table."

"But there's too much money involved to let him walk."

"I warned him that would be your position."

"It's not my position," Peterson said. "The Corporate Fraud Task Force wants everybody in this case doing jail time."

Hackett knew that Peterson really meant it wasn't the task force's position *alone.*

"So what's next?" Hackett asked.

"A plea agreement. It'll be sealed until I've indicted the others. And he'll have to plead to the sheet."

Peterson said the word "sheet" as if the indictment would be handed down like the Ten Commandments, not spit out of his own computer—but Hackett didn't challenge him. The dance wasn't over. "What will it be?"

"Conspiracy to commit securities fraud, conspiracy to file false reports with the SEC, and money laundering."

"Money laundering?" Hackett feigned surprise. "You've got to be kidding. The sentencing guidelines are ridiculous. He'd rather roll the dice."

Peterson paused as if deciding whether to drop the money laundering count. As if. They both knew before the conversation even began that Peterson wouldn't insist on it. The pretense of negotiation was merely a bone tossed for the sake of Hackett's dignity and to give him leverage with his client. Now he could tell Matson that he hung tough with Peterson, made him dump the heaviest charge.

"Okay," Peterson finally said. "No money laundering, but it'll have to be all the rest."

"What about time? Uncertainty is stressing the guy out. Let's agree on something now, at least a range."

"No can do. His sentence will depend on his performance. Heads on a platter. Can you sell him on the fraud and false reporting?"

"Probably. It's just that I don't think he's clued in his wife yet. And he better be wearing riot gear when he does. She thinks he actually earned it all."

"And I'll bet she's been spending like he did."

"Her personal shopper at Neiman Marcus has been named Employee of the Month like clockwork since the day she first laid down her credit card."

Peterson laughed. "When this is over, she'll be doing layaways at Kmart. No way she really believed your client earned that kind of money on his own."

Hackett leaned forward in his chair, as if Peterson was actually in the room to observe the significance of what he was about to say.

"Don't underestimate the guy. Matson may have started out as a kind of a Silicon Valley used car salesman. And I know he looked pathetic during his Queen for a Day—all these guys look that way spilling their guts. But once Granger got him started, it didn't take him long to learn to play the offshore game. He even got pretty good at it. That's why he'll be a damn good witness for you. He's a lot lighter on his feet than you think."

"Take it easy, Hackett, you don't need to sell me on the guy, except for one thing. Matson seemed to get a little squirrelly when we got to talking about Burch. Is he afraid Burch will try to cut a deal and roll back on him?" Peterson didn't wait for an answer. His voice hardened as he pushed on. "You can tell him I'm not making any deals with Burch. If he ever walks out of that hospital, he's gonna spend the rest of his life in federal prison—whether your guy delivers him up or somebody else does."

Hackett wanted it to be Matson, *needed* it to be Matson. He wasn't about to humiliate himself losing the case in trial. "When can you send over the plea agreement?"

"This afternoon. Most of it's boilerplate. I just need to plug in a statement of facts."

"And those would be?"

"Granger laid out the overall stock fraud strategy and Burch executed it using the dummy offshore companies."

"Sounds fair. I'll get Matson in here to sign it."

"And we want the money. All of it." Hackett visualized Peterson pounding his forefinger on his desk. "If we catch him lying about where it is, there's no deal and the money laundering comes back in."

Hackett had already given Matson that lecture.

"When do you want him in court?"

"Day after tomorrow. The sooner I can get him in front of the grand jury, the sooner I'll get the indictment. *United States of America v. Burch, et al.* All the Burches of the world do is help fraudsters like Matson and Granger, and they make an obscene amount of money doing it. When the rest of them watch Burch doing the perp walk past the TV cameras with his tail between his legs, being hauled off to the joint, they'll all be closing up shop. Every one of them."

"You mean if Burch survives long enough to get convicted."

"No. He just has to live long enough for me to get him indicted."

◇◇◇

Hackett set the phone back on its cradle, then looked through his window past San Francisco's western avenues toward the Pacific Ocean. He never quite understood the arrogance of jingoistic prosecutors like Peterson, amateurs who didn't have a clue about international business. How, exactly, could U.S. corporations operate in dozens of different tax jurisdictions, dozens of national sovereignties, accommodating dozens of competing masters around the world, without lawyers like Burch?

His gaze settled on the Transamerica Building. What about Transamerica International registered in Bermuda? Or Bank of America Securities in London, Santiago, Singapore, and Taipei? Did these arms of U.S. companies spring out of foreign soil through spontaneous generation?

Why were the tough-guy prosecutors like Peterson always so damn naïve? Hackett already knew the answer: It was because they lived in a simple, unambiguous world, structured by simple rules. They believed who they wanted and what they wanted and did so absolutely.

Hackett comforted himself with the thought that he saved Matson's ass because that's what he got paid to do, and had gotten paid almost half a million dollars to do it. Anyway, he didn't know the truth. He hadn't been there, in Burch's office. He didn't know what Burch said, what Matson said. It was all he said, she said. That was the law of conspiracy. Nothing more. Nothing less.

Did Burch cross the line once in a while? Maybe. Maybe not. Who knows? But Peterson taking the word of Matson? Did he really believe that stunted, pastel-packaged liar was reborn a saint when he slithered into the Church of the U.S. Attorney, the Chapel of Cooperation? It was worse than merely naïve; it was damn stupid.

Hackett leaned back in his chair, wondering what would be the cost to Burch of that naïveté, that stupidity—but not for long. Hours spent thinking about abstract matters weren't billable, and the clock was ticking. He reached for the intercom, then hesitated and dropped his hand to the desk.

Decades of criminal defense work painted a picture in his mind; it showed him how it would end. Even if it was just a failure of due diligence: Burch too preoccupied with his wife's illness to pay attention. Peterson would make not knowing look like not wanting to know; and make not wanting to know into greed. Using the hammer of his office and the anvil of a jury composed of peons looking for someone to blame for their own liabilities and others' enormous assets, Peterson would metamorphize Burch's negligence into willful conspiracy. That would be the price Burch would pay.

Burch is already judicial roadkill, Hackett thought. *Even his pal Graham Gage won't be able to yank him out of the way of this steamroller.*

Gage. *Shit.* He'd forgotten about Gage. Every insider in the legal community knew how close they were. And he was out there, somewhere—

But there's nothing Gage can do for Burch. Conspiracies are about words, and the words Peterson is listening to are Matson's.

Hackett breathed again and a blurry future snapped into focus: One way or another, guilty or innocent, Burch would have to take a plea. Despite Peterson's grandstanding about giving Burch life, he'd offer twenty years, maybe twenty-five, and Burch would take it. Only idiots go down in flames.

And while Burch might be a crook, he wasn't an idiot.

Chapter Twelve

Gage and Spike were working the Take Back the Streets rally in Pacific Heights. Neither had spoken the words, but both knew they needed a witness to do what Burch might not live to do: identify the shooter.

Four hundred joggers and cyclists blocked the sloping intersection of Webster and Pacific. Uniformed officers ceded the street at Spike's order and redirected traffic to the surrounding neighborhood. Television reporters with trailing camera crews worked the crowd, searching for anyone who knew Burch or Courtney, reaching for fragments of fact and grasping at rumors.

"Whoever shot him was looking for a fight," a taut, middle-aged man wearing a black ASICS running suit told Gage and Spike.

"How do you figure?" Gage asked.

"I jog here every day. A lot of us run in the street to avoid the dog walkers and the strollers. Some of these asshole drivers go out of their way to force us off the road. I heard some people saying that the shooter had flipped off the runner." The man scanned the throng, then pointed at a young couple in matching gray sweat suits standing next to a stroller. "There they are. I've got to get to the office. If you need anything else, you've got my number."

As Gage and Spike started toward them, a local television reporter blocked their path. She jammed a microphone in Spike's face, then looked at the camera.

"I'm with Lieutenant Spike Pacheco of the San Francisco Police Department...Lieutenant Pacheco"—she cocked her coiffured blond head toward the crowd behind her—"can you confirm the rumor that Jack Burch was shot because of a love triangle?"

Spike grabbed the top of the microphone and twisted it out of her hand, then glared at the cameraman. "Turn that fucking thing off." Then toward the reporter, his brown face reddening with rage. "It's not good enough for you that the guy's lying in a coma? You've got to try to destroy his reputation, too? For what, Jane? For what?"

He looked over at Gage, who shook his head. *Let it go. Don't let her create a story where there isn't one.*

Spike tossed the microphone to the cameraman, then jabbed his forefinger at her face. "You do this kind of shit one more time and nobody at SFPD is ever gonna talk to you. You might as well go back to doing the farm report in Boise."

Gage grabbed Spike's arm and led him away. "Take it easy. Get the press officer out here to run interference for you. I don't want your face showing up on television again, and mine ever. We can't let the guy see us coming until it's too late for him to get away."

Spike glared back over his shoulder. "Asshole. Who the fuck does she think she is?"

His fury faded as they walked along the edge of the crowd toward the young couple. He displayed his badge as they approached.

"Thanks for coming out, Lieutenant," the woman said. "We were hoping to speak with you."

Gage pointed back from where they came. "A guy told us he overheard you two say something about the shooter flipping off Jack."

"That's not what I said." The woman's voice hardened, as if being misquoted was a personal assault. "I said that I saw a driver's left hand, framed in his window. For all I know, he was scratching his nose. It was dark outside and his car was dark inside. The car was heading east, like us, but Jack was running the other direction. It was only a few minutes ago, when we overheard someone describing the car and its route, that it crossed our minds that the driver might've circled the block and went after him."

Gage looked at Spike, who nodded. That's what Burch was trying to communicate with his raised hand as he was wheeled into surgery. *Graham. Tell Graham.* For the first time Gage felt Burch's dread that those words and that gesture would be his last—and no one would ever understand.

"Male or female?" Gage asked.

"Male. I'm sure about that."

"Race?"

"White. Maybe Hispanic, but light-skinned."

Spike obtained their telephone number, then he and Gage headed back into the crowd.

"I'm still thinking the guy was a helluva good shot," Spike said. "Two trigger pulls and two hits. Side-by-side."

"At least we know he's left-handed." Gage stopped and turned toward Spike. He held up his left hand, forefinger extended and bent. "I think they saw the shooter's trigger finger."

◇◇◇

Spike grunted as he dropped into the driver's seat of his car an hour later, then glanced over at Gage. "We're just going through the motions. The guy who shot Jack is gone. Long gone. And the partial description we've got is all we're ever going to get. And I know you're thinking the same thing. I saw you checking out the streetlights, figuring how the shadows fell. There's no way Jack could've seen the shooter."

"We don't know that yet. He was moving. The shooter was moving."

"I know what you're trying to do, Graham, but neither one of us has ever been good at wishful thinking."

Gage watched Spike's pupils flit side to side, as if he was torn by an inner conflict that extended beyond the morning's frustrations. "What's going on?"

Spike took in a long breath and exhaled. "Since I took your spot in homicide, I've been doing the same thing every day—gunshots, autopsies, and *chingasas* on dope. Most of my life doing the same damn thing."

"But you're the best—"

"Bullshit. There's no best in police work, just degrees of failure. And I've had twenty-nine-point-nine-nine-nine years of it."

Spike fell silent for a moment, then he sighed and looked at Gage. "You got out when you'd seen all there was to see around here. Your world is London, Hong Kong, Moscow. Me, I spent the whole time trapped in a few square miles, a place that looks like a crushed potato. And it's like I've just been watching the same damn movie over and over and over, and the ending never gets any better."

Gage crossed his arms over his chest, then settled a little in his seat. "You know why I really left? More than anything?"

"I thought you wanted to go to grad school, read some philosophy books, ponder the deep thoughts."

"There were things I wanted to think through, and Cal was a good place to do it, but that wasn't the real reason. I just never fit in. Most people in the department were there to prove something, get over something, or hide from something behind the badge."

"What about me?"

"You were the exception. You were trying to save the world. Every day coming into the squad room, big smile on your face."

"And you?"

"I didn't have your optimism."

"Well, I didn't save much of it."

Gage glanced toward four uniformed cops standing together by a patrol car, sipping coffee, ignoring the milling crowd. "More than your share, and more than any cop I ever knew."

Spike's eyes went vacant, then he nodded. "Now I get it."

"Get what?"

"What you said just before you resigned. You said it was like we were all in different departments together." Spike smiled to himself, then rotated his thumb toward Gage. "You know what we used to call you behind your back?"

"I never had a nickname."

"You just didn't know it because nobody had the guts to say it to your face. We called you Buddha. Like when you got your detective's badge, the other guys beaming like the teacher gave them a gold star, you looking like somebody handed you a glass of water."

Gage shrugged.

"But that wasn't the truth." Spike looked out at the intersection where Burch was shot down. "No cop ever felt the tragedy in a homicide scene more than you. You just didn't show it. While the rest of us hid behind callousness and gallows humor—or even just the mechanics of how the thing happened—you'd immerse yourself in it, imagining what happened as if you'd been the guy lying inside the chalk marks."

Spike fell silent, then shook his head. "I don't know how you did it. If I'd tried to do it your way all these years, I'd have blown my brains out by now."

Chapter Thirteen

That wasn't so bad, was it, Scoob?" Zink asked as he walked Matson toward the elevator from the Magistrate's Court on the sixteenth floor of the Federal Building. U.S. Marshals guarded the door while Matson uttered the single word that ratified his transformation from citizen into convict. The only witnesses were Peterson, Zink, Hackett, the magistrate, the clerk, and the stenographer. As far as the rest of the world was concerned, the hearing never happened.

For Matson, it really was bad. So bad Matson felt himself splitting in two. Or maybe three or four. He remembered looking around the courtroom, his eyes flinching at the light, his stomach turning. At the same time, he felt a nauseating hollowness, as if his mind was a shriveled nut inside a shell bouncing down a hillside.

Walking away, rerunning the scene in his mind, it hit him. *It was just a goddamn play.* Everybody knew their parts, played them like they'd read the same lines a thousand times before. There was Peterson. Huge, dominating. Zink. A rodent waiting to gather up the scraps. The magistrate. Just a judge's helper. A guy who wasn't smart enough or didn't kiss enough political ass to get appointed district court judge. The magistrate would do what Peterson told him to do. And Matson would do what Hackett told him to do.

Hackett. *How much money did I pay that shyster?* Matson asked himself as Zink led him down the hallway. *Whose side was he really on? What did he tell me?*

"When the magistrate asks whether you were threatened into entering the plea, answer no, got it?"

"But they were gonna throw away the fucking key if I didn't."

"So what? If you say yes, there's no deal."

What's all this about the truth? It's all about lying at the right time, just like business. These people are hypocrites.

Matson noticed that he was now in the elevator, descending, just him and Zink. Hackett had abandoned him at the courtroom door.

Matson knew it was his voice that answered, "Guilty," but his mind, cowering in an internal crevice, hadn't pushed the word out. Hackett simply trained him to say, "Guilty, Your Honor," and he did.

How did I get into this mess? Matson asked himself as he and Zink got off the elevator on the thirteenth floor. *I shouldn't have listened to Hackett. He's a punk. Fucking snitch lawyer. I could've beat this case. What've they really got? Nothing. That's what Granger said.*

Zink stuck a security badge on Matson's suit jacket, then walked him through the armored entrance into the FBI office. A few steps inside, Matson saw a wooden door, a sign taped to it bearing the single word "SatTek."

"This is where we'll be working," Zink said, directing Matson inside.

Matson took a step across the threshold. Instantly all of his parts snapped together.

To his left was a poster board covered with photos. His. Burch's. Granger's. Fitzhugh's. *They know about Fitzhugh.* Next to that a world map. Red-headed pins impaling San Francisco, Guangzhou, Ho Chi Minh City, London, Guernsey. *They know about Guernsey.* To his right were flowcharts taped to the wall. Money. Accounts. Companies. Straight ahead were file boxes. SEC. SatTek. The China company. The Vietnam company. Cobalt Partners. *Damn, they know about Cobalt, too.*

Matson felt an itchiness, like there was a gun barrel pointed at that edgy little spot between his eyes. He finally understood Hackett's phrase, "a slam-dunk case."

He dropped into a blue cloth-covered chair, hands clammy, as if watching the dentist's drill approaching before the Novocain kicked in.

Zink sat down behind the desk, then withdrew a white legal pad from a drawer.

Matson studied Zink's face, sickened by his willful failure to suppress his self-satisfaction, his pride of ownership.

Matson couldn't say Granger hadn't warned him. "If you cooperate, they'll own you. You'll think you're gonna get over on 'em, but you won't. Nobody does."

And Matson had promised him, "I'm not makin' no deal. No way. Fuck 'em. I'm not sayin' shit."

But that was before Hackett told Matson how much time he could do and before he decided that there was no fucking way he was going to do it—not if he was going to have a life after SatTek.

Hackett had also told him something else, maybe the most important thing. As long as he kept setting up other targets, the prosecutor would stop aiming at him, and that would give him time to feather his nest for a soft landing. And Matson knew that unless he did a little more feathering, he'd crash real hard.

"Let's start with Fitzhugh," Zink said, his pen poised. "How much did he know?"

◇◇◇

"I flew to London and checked into the Park Lane Hilton by Hyde Park. At 6 P.M., I went down to the lobby bar to meet him. He looked up soon as I hit the door and caught my eye. I'm jet-lagged as hell, so I order some coffee before I sit down. I don't want to miss a word of what he has to say.

"Helluva name. Morely Alden Fitzhugh IV. But it fit with him being an accountant. Thin, pale face. Conservative black suit. The only thing that didn't match the profile were his Bono-type eyeglasses and a gold Patek Philippe chronograph. I later saw a watch just like it at Tiffany's. It cost about thirty grand.

"We talked a little bit, and once he felt comfortable with me, he went into his spiel.

" 'Mr. Granger told me that SatTek is on the verge of greatness, and that you're the right man at the right time.' Then he leaned over the table and lowered his voice. 'I know you trust Mr. Granger and Mr. Granger trusts me. And you know the offshore world is about trust. We're not gangsters and there aren't any courts with real substance that can deal with even minor disputes. So it's up to the parties to work together, fairly. Everything aboveboard.'

"That shook me up a little. There was no reason to bring up gangsters. We were just doing business. But I wasn't there to argue, so I let it go.

"Fitzhugh paused for a few moments, then he adopted a sort of effeminate pose and said, 'Mr. Granger has, as I understand it, assumed the role of, shall we say, adviser. What's it called at the Vatican? *Consigliere.*' Then he punches the air with his forefinger, like in punctuation. 'That's it, *consigliere.*'

"I'm not the pope, and I told him that.

" 'But every enterprise needs a principal. That's you. My function is solely as a fiduciary, someone to advise you on financial matters and to whom you may issue instructions in complete confidence that they will be faithfully executed.'

"There was only one problem with that: Granger told me that I was supposed to be following his orders; not him following mine."

◇◇◇

Matson watched Zink finish writing down the last sentence on his legal pad, then said he needed to use the bathroom.

Zink escorted him down the hallway and pointed to the men's room door. Matson entered and stepped into a stall, but just stood there. He didn't need to pee, he needed to think. Something else had happened in the Park Lane Hilton lounge that evening, and Zink had no right to pry into it.

◇◇◇

As the waitress approached with his coffee, he had noticed a woman sitting alone at the bar behind her, twenty-five feet across the room. The contrasts among her black chemise dress, pale skin, Asiatic eyes, and Slavic cheekbones had unnerved him. She seemed foreign in a more profound way than any woman he'd ever seen.

His eyes followed hers as they swept along the row of bottled whiskeys doubled by the bar mirror behind them. Their eyes met in reflection. He looked away, but was drawn back. And as he gazed into the dark pupils looking back, he felt a depth and solidity in himself that he hadn't experienced before, and realized that somehow, in a way he didn't yet understand, the world that Granger had invited him into was making him into a new man.

◇◇◇

"Did you meet anyone else in London?" Zink asked Matson as they walked from the bathroom into the FBI's kitchen to fetch coffee.

Matson hesitated for a moment, then answered, "No. Not really. Granger told me to keep a low profile. Just slip in and slip out. So that's what I did."

Matson leaned back against the counter, hands crimped over the edge.

"There's a whole world out there I didn't know even existed," Matson said. "All these people doing international business. It's hard to explain. Everybody's in their own heads."

Zink filled a cup and handed it to Matson.

"People meet. All they have in common is the deal, whatever the deal is. Always on the move, like they're never really anyplace. They just take the deal from one airport to another, one hotel to another."

Zink smiled to himself as he walked Matson back to the SatTek room. Matson wasn't an idiot. He had avoided answering the question. Zink knew he'd answer it eventually, once he realized that the government wouldn't let him keep any secrets.

Matson would be dotting i's and crossing t's until he developed carpal tunnel of the brain. He just didn't know it yet.

Zink knew how to work informants, and decided that it was too soon to push Matson. He made an excuse to go back to his own office to give Matson time to adjust to the idea that eventually he'd have to give it all up.

He left Matson sitting, arms folded, staring up at the ceiling.

◇◇◇

Matson had returned to the hotel after dining with Fitzhugh. He had glanced into the lounge on his way toward the elevator and spotted the woman still sitting at the bar. He stopped in the doorway. A man stood to the left of her, his hand gripping her elbow. She jerked her arm away and rotated her stool away from him.

Matson found himself walking toward them. He heard the man say in a slurred American accent, "Just one drink, honey. Come on, just one drink."

Before the woman could answer, Matson stepped up next to him and said, "Let it go."

The man turned toward him. Red-faced. Fists clenched. "Mind your own business."

Matson held up his hands. "Take it easy." He made a show of scanning the others drinking in the lounge. "Whose side do you think these folks will take?"

The scraping of chair legs on tile broke the silence. The man glanced back over his shoulder at two men who were now standing and glaring at him. He swayed as he turned back toward Matson, then shrugged and walked away.

She turned toward him. "Thank you." She spoke in what Matson took to be a Russian accent.

"He just had too much to drink," Matson said, then noticed that her hands were shaking. "Would you like me to sit with you?"

"Very much."

Matson climbed onto the bar stool next to her. "Can I get you something?"

"Please. Whatever you are having."

Matson looked down the bar and spotted tall glasses of Guinness before a young couple sitting at the end, and ordered two pints.

"I'm Alla," she said. "I saw you here earlier."

Matson blushed, then glanced away as if checking the bartender's progress on their order. "I'm Stuart, and I saw you, too."

"I was so relieved when you walked up." She smiled. "I thought you were about to tackle that man."

"Tell you the truth, I wasn't sure what I would do. We have an expression in the States. It's called playing it—"

"—by ear."

He drew back and looked over at her. "You know that one?"

"I love language, especially American expressions. Out in left field. The wrong side of the tracks. Between a rock and a hard place." She tapped her chin with her forefinger. "Let me see… how about, Hey bud, what line are you in?"

Matson didn't respond.

Alla grinned. "That was a real question."

"Oh." He blushed again. "I'm the president of a company in California. London is the base of our international operations."

The bartender set two pints on cardboard Guinness coasters.

Matson wasn't sure what to say next, so he escaped into watching the bubbles rise to form a soft, rich head.

Alla pointed at the glass. "Sometimes the bubbles go down."

Matson shook his head. "They can't. It's air."

"Things aren't always what they seem. Watch closely."

She leaned down toward the glass, eyes focused on the body of the beer. Matson's head followed as if magnetized. He found himself lost in the swirling of her perfume.

"Pick a bubble. A little one."

Matson focused on one caught on the glass. It broke free and swept downward.

"Son of a gun." He leaned back and looked at her. "How'd you know?"

"I studied engineering in college in Ukraine. In Dnepropetrovsk."

"In what?"

"Ne-pro-pe-trovsk. Just say Neper. I'm from a village nearby."

"You mean a village, village?"

"Yes." Alla laughed, her eyes twinkling in the candle flame. "A village, village. Thatched roofs, cow in the backyard, chickens trying to sneak into the house."

"And from there to a college where they let you study beer?"

"It was sort of political."

"Come on..." Matson said, unable to suppress his incredulity.

"It's true. Students had so much hope after the collapse of the Soviet Union, only to see gangster capitalism take its place. We all found ways to express the horror we felt. My way was fluid mechanics. The outside world only saw the large bubbles rising in the center. The elites. But that created a vortex that forced nearly all of the small bubbles downward. The middle class became impoverished and the lower class became destitute. And when their standard of living rose, it was paid for with the suppression of the freedom they had earned. My experiment was a metaphor."

Matson studied her face. "And what kind of bubble are you?"

"One that escaped."

He raised his glass. She clinked hers lightly against his, then each took a sip.

"Why here?" he asked.

"For Americans, London is merely a charming place to visit. For me, for all Central Europeans, it's...I don't know how to capture it in English...I guess you could say that London is our Ellis Island."

"If you don't mind my asking, how can a village girl afford to live here? This is an expensive town."

"I saved a little money and I live simply." She shrugged, and the light went out of her eyes. "Eventually I'll have to go back to Ukraine. I dread it. It's suffocating. It's what we call *peregruzhennost*. I don't think there is an English word...Maybe you would say...overburdening. That's it. Overburdening. Eventually it will break me."

Chapter Fourteen

Hey, Graham. There's a rumor going around that the attorney general is looking for a new poster boy for corporate crime." The voice, high-pitched against the low chatter of a busy pressroom, belonged to Kenny Leals, a *New York Times* reporter, and the only journalist who had Gage's cell phone number. "The Enrons and Global Crossings and Arthur Andersens just ain't cutting it anymore. The way I hear it, they've decided that it's time for lawyers to take a hit—and they're hard on the prowl for a guy to take the first swing at."

Gage sat forward in his desk chair, but kept his tone casual. "Have they put a name on it?"

"Not yet, but I was shooting the breeze about SatTek with an old-timer at the *Chronicle* and she said you and Jack Burch were pals, so I figured I'd give you a buzz. Rumor is that he's somehow connected to the company. But I can't confirm it."

Leal let the words linger, as if anticipating an easy confirmation, but Gage wasn't about to become a second source.

"What do you have so far?" Gage asked.

"For one thing, a memo that went out to the local U.S. Attorney's Offices a few months ago." Leals chuckled. "It reads like one of those sales incentive deals. You know, the guy who sells the most refrigerators wins a cruise on the Love Boat. And there's a lot of buzz in the Justice Department about the SatTek collapse."

"There are lots of fraud cases around—"

"But this one has resonance, maybe because it's a defense contractor. In any case, it's the kind that gets stronger and stronger as the clock ticks down. And trust me, you can hear the tick, tick, tick all around Washington." Leals hesitated, then said, "How about a call if Burch is the fridge that wins somebody the vacation? I promise the *Times* will give him a fair shake. I've never let you down before."

◇◇◇

"You've got to give me something," Gage demanded of the man on the other end of the line a minute later. "You run the division. You know what's going on."

"No can do." The voice was gravelly from too many cigars over too many years. "I can't even tell you the name of the Assistant U.S. Attorney who's handling it. They don't want any bits of the investigation dribbling out. They want an explosion heard around the world."

"How about a heads-up if Jack's a target?"

"And find mine on the block? No way, Graham. No fucking way. If there are any leaks in this case, the attorney general will start dusting off polygraph machines."

Gage glanced toward a refrigerator-sized safe anchored to the concrete floor in the far corner of his office and filled with documents that could end careers.

"Seems to me you've got a short memory," Gage said. "It wasn't that long ago that you were riding a log toward a political buzz saw—"

"I know. I still owe you, but this isn't the time. All the decisions in this case are coming from the top—they're bypassing the Criminal Division altogether. It's in the hands of this new Corporate Fraud Task Force. That means the attorney general and the FBI director. I've got no say about whether Burch gets indicted."

The man paused. Gage imagined him gazing out of his Justice Department office window toward Pennsylvania Avenue.

"It's a new world," the man finally said. "The public is sick of lawyers skating in these fraud cases, and the White House is listening. Somebody like Burch—I'm not saying Burch—but somebody like him is the perfect guy to hang a noose around. He's at the top, he's made a bundle, and he's an immigrant—the politically correct guy to take the fall for the crooked lawyers behind all of the other scams. He's the ideal target." The man chuckled. "Sort of a sacrificial kangaroo."

"You're leaving me no choice but to—"

"You helping Burch is like a surgeon operating on his own brother. Not a smart move. Good intentions in the wrong place gets people into trouble. It's already gonna be a huge indictment and I'd hate to see your name add to it, charged with obstruction. If I was you, I'd fold my hands in my lap, sit quietly, and wait for the show to start."

"Look, he's had a tough—"

"And I feel bad for him, and his wife. But this happened long before he was shot. If he was part of it, he was part of it. If he wasn't, he wasn't. You start tearing into this thing yourself, Graham, and you're the one who's going to get torn apart."

Chapter Fifteen

Was Fitzhugh a competent guy?" Zink asked Matson as he bent a pizza box and stuffed it into a trash can in the windowless, timeless debriefing room. Zink had learned over the years that pizza to a snitch was like a warm bottle to a baby.

"When I first met him," Matson said, "I thought he was just a pipsqueak. But I found out real fast that he sure knew his business. Like perfection in motion. A guy like that could make a fortune in the States. Not like Burch, but still a lot of money. Say you want to set up a corporation in California. You know what you have to go through? How much you got to spend on lawyers and accountants? Sure, you could buy one of those do-it-yourself kits. But you know you're gonna get sued. Everybody gets sued. You think the one-size-fits-all is gonna protect you?"

"No, it's not."

"Damn right. So you gotta start with a slick lawyer like Burch. A guy that creates the strategy. And he's gonna charge a bundle. You know what his hourly rate is? You got any idea? Eight hundred and seventy-five dollars an hour. You know what that is a minute?"

"No."

"I figured it out. Fourteen dollars and fifty-eight cents. One minute. But you're not paying for a couple of minutes. You're paying for hours and hours and hours. Burch's like a quarterback who calls his own plays and can throw the long bomb. The guy you pay to see. Fitzhugh? He's more like a small running back that eats up the field, two, three yards at a time. Bang, bang, bang."

Matson took a last bite of pizza, then leaned back in his chair. His eyes glazed over for a few moments, then he shook his head and blinked hard. "The whole thing was such an adrenaline rush, I sometimes wonder if I really got into it for the money in the first place.

"We flew on a turbo-prop to Guernsey in the Channel Islands. The whole thing was right out of a movie. Pinstriped suits and black briefcases; even the women. As we circled over the English Channel to land you could see the coast of France. Like a knife edge.

"The island's outlying areas were as open and green as fairways, but St. Peter Port was all granite buildings and narrow cobblestone streets. Little wind tunnels. Right in the middle and sitting high up like a fortress was the Old Government House Hotel where we stayed.

"After we checked in, Fitzhugh took me to a firm of solicitors and introduced me to a partner, Charles LaFleur. Looked like Fitzhugh's twin, but twenty years older.

"LaFleur had three binders lying on his desk. The incorporation papers for companies he'd already set up. Azul Limited in Panama, Blau Anstalt in Liechtenstein, and Cobalt Partners in Guernsey. They were just empty shells waiting to be filled.

"Each one was already staffed with fake directors. They call them nominees. For Cobalt Partners, they were bartenders on Sark, another one of the islands. The nominees don't make any decisions, they just sign papers that LaFleur puts in front of them. No questions asked. Open bank accounts. Transfer money. They don't know why they're signing or who the real owners are.

"It's all a game of just pretend. But if you don't play it, you can't operate out there.

"LaFleur said that for extra insulation—that's exactly what he called it, insulation—he wanted to put Fitzhugh down as the real owner.

"Right away my antennae went up and locked on. Fitzhugh had said that the offshore world was about trust, and I didn't know these guys from Adam.

"I realized right then that I needed to control at least part of it myself. I knew it was a risk to have my name on anything, but I told them I wanted Cobalt Partners for my own.

"Fitzhugh jerked back and looked at me like I just put a gun to my head. But we both knew he had no choice but to go along. After all, he's the one who said I was the pope.

"But from the moment we walked out of there, and as much as I refused to think about it, I knew I was eventually going to get scalded."

◇◇◇

Zink rose from behind the desk and walked to a file cabinet. He returned with a stack of bank account records. He laid them out in front of Matson.

"Whose idea was it to set up the Cobalt bank account at Barclays in London?"

"Mine. I like the city and I was thinking I might want to..." Matson's face reddened as his voice faded.

"Hook up with a woman there?"

Matson drew back. "How the devil did you know about her?"

"I asked you a yes or no question about whether you met anyone else in London"—Zink smiled—"and you answered with 'not really.'"

"She was a helluva lot more than just a hookup. She's the most amazing woman I ever met. I really wanted to get back there to see her again before Granger needed me in the States, but we got stuck overnight in Guernsey because LaFleur had to redo the Cobalt Partners paperwork and get the nominees to sign off.

"Fitzhugh took me to dinner at this little restaurant called The Best End, right on the bay at the northern edge of St. Peter Port.

"After two glasses of wine, I loosen up a little and I put it to Fitzhugh straight: 'What's your angle?'

"He just deflected the question back. 'I assume it's the same as yours.'

"I pushed a little harder and said, 'But you don't look like a guy who's doing what you're doing.'

"Then he sat up and took on a tone like he was on the witness stand. 'I do nothing other than establish and manage companies and bank accounts. I've done my due diligence. I have no reason to believe that the underlying SatTek transactions don't serve legitimate business purposes. And, more importantly, neither does anyone at the Southeastern Fraud Squad or Scotland Yard.'

"I sort of raised my eyebrows and asked, 'Aren't you supposed to wink now?'

"Then he smiled his first smile in the two days I'd been with him, and said. 'You just missed it.'

" 'Did I miss LaFleur's wink, too?'

"And he deadpanned back, 'Apparently.'

"That little back-and-forth changed our whole relationship. From then on, we were like partners.

"After dinner, he led me through the center of town past international banks like Barclays, HSBC, and UBS, and past law firms like LaFleur's that handle the offshore tax-dodging of companies like ExxonMobil and Halliburton.

"But he didn't do it to impress me or prove to me that I was in good company. It was more like he had turned into my tutor and wanted me to understand how things really worked out there, and why they worked that way.

"He stopped at the front steps when we got back to the Old Government House, and then turned toward me. I could tell that this was what he'd been leading up to. His voice got real intense.

" 'Not a hundred million dollars,' he said, 'but a hundred billion dollars have collected on an island the size of a ten pence. And it's all because people here know how not to ask one too many questions. What you call deniability in the States has been perfected into an art on Guernsey. While American students are taught the Bill of Rights and the Constitution—the fixed law—here they absorb the science of legal relativity. Illegal? Says who? By whose rules? By what right?'

"Then he smiled again. 'And everyone learns to wink before they can even say mama.' "

Chapter Sixteen

I thought your pal in Washington told you to fold your hands and sit patiently on the sidelines," Hector "Viz" McBride spoke into his two-way outside of Matson's forested Saratoga home just before daybreak.

Hector McBride was ready to jump on Matson's tail. McBride was a big man. The biggest man nobody ever saw. Around Gage's office he was simply referred to as Viz, short for the Invisible Man.

"He knew that wouldn't happen," Gage answered from where he was parked a half mile away.

Viz laughed. "Didn't we all."

Alex Z was sitting in the passenger seat next to Gage. He'd come along to talk about the case in a world where, as Viz always told him with a grin, "the rubber meets the road, kid." Alex Z never knew what he meant, but it always made him nervous.

Gage heard Viz's engine turn over.

"Time to go to work, boss. Scooby Doo's just pulling out. He's in a silver BMW, four-door, 760Li. Heading southeast toward Big Basin."

Viz reported in five minutes later. "He's not on his way to his office. Not even toward San Jose. He just turned north on the Saratoga-Sunnyvale Road, toward the 85."

"I'll swing around."

Matson indeed took the 85. He drove north until he hit the 280, then the 101 along the bay toward San Francisco.

"He must be going downtown," Viz said.

Gage and Viz traded places, then followed in silence until Matson approached the financial district.

"Looks like he's aiming toward Van Ness Avenue," Gage said.

Matson turned east from Van Ness just after passing the gold-domed City Hall, then swung around the Federal Building and parked in the lot across the street.

"Viz, I don't want him seeing me yet and I want you out here snapping pictures. I'm sending in Alex Z."

"What? Me?" Alex Z recoiled toward the passenger window. "You said I could just come along for the ride."

The man who spent his nights performing onstage before crowds of adoring women was panicking in the wings.

Gage grinned. "It'll be something you can tell your children about."

Alex Z shook his head. "Did I tell you I don't want kids?"

"Too late, hop to it."

"What do I say if—"

"Say you got busted in an ecstasy case."

"But I don't use ecstasy."

Alex Z's eyes tracked Gage's as he scanned his earrings, tattoos, and unkempt hair.

"But everyone will think you do."

Heart pounding, Alex Z climbed out of the car and followed Matson through the security checkpoint and into the elevator. Matson pressed 11, then glanced over at Alex Z.

"Thanks, I'm going there, too," Alex Z squeaked out.

Matson stepped out of the elevator on the eleventh floor. Alex Z followed him down the hall into the lobby of the Office of the United States Attorney.

Alex Z took a seat, then waved a clammy hand toward the receptionist behind the bulletproof glass, mouthing the words, "I'm waiting for my lawyer."

Matson walked up to the counter.

"I'm here to see Mr. Peterson."

Two minutes later, after the receptionist handed Matson a stick-on security badge and buzzed him in, Alex Z slipped back to the elevator.

"He went into the U.S. Attorney's Office," Alex Z told Gage when he got back into the car. "He asked for someone named Peterson."

"Damn."

Gage noticed Alex Z's hands shaking. "It wasn't the answer I was hoping for, but good job getting it."

He radioed Viz. "The little punk is setting up Jack in exchange for a get-out-of-jail-free card. Go down to SatTek. The workers still there are either unemployable elsewhere or real tight with Matson. Try to figure out who's who, but be careful. We're going to have to stay in the shadows until we can shine a little light on the inner workings of this scam."

Chapter Seventeen

Zink looked over his notes from the previous day, wondering how much Matson was holding back. He didn't glance up, but sensed Matson inspecting his thinning hair.

He knew more was churning in Matson's mind than was coming out of his mouth. Fifteen years in law enforcement taught him that's the way crooks were, even when they were telling the whole so-called truth.

Matson studied Zink's lowered head, wondering how Zink became an FBI agent. Hackett told him that Zink's career stalled out six years earlier, something to do with a sexual harassment complaint by one of the secretaries. He didn't even put in his name for promotions anymore. Now just a day laborer, counting the months and years until his retirement, which Matson could see was still a long way away.

Matson decided that thinking of Zink as a rodent was probably a little unfair. Zink didn't choose his scrawny features; they were a result of his parents unwisely choosing each other. He could only be held blameworthy for failing to mitigate his physical disadvantages. Plastic surgery might've helped, Matson thought, but he knew of no operation that could enlarge Zink's minuscule ears. Matson figured he'd ask his wife. She had personal experience bumping up against the limits of plastic surgery.

Actually, Matson thought, *Zink's not a bad guy. Just doing his job. I can work with him, but he's hard to read.*

Zink felt Matson trying to gauge how he was doing. He knew snitches always did that. Are they pleasing their masters or not? Are they saying too much or too little? They're always wondering where's the finish line. Of course, there wasn't one. It took most crooks a long time to figure that out, and Matson hadn't even started.

He stepped to a chalkboard, then charted out the companies Fitzhugh set up in Guernsey.

"Now tell me about the bank accounts," Zink said, turning around, and wondering how much of the truth he would get.

Matson got up and walked to the map on the wall. He pointed at a city next to a lake in Switzerland, just north of the Italian border.

"I didn't even know where Lugano was until the day before we flew in." He faced Zink. "Ever been to one of those Swiss banks?"

Zink shook his head.

"If it weren't for the brass plate mounted outside that said 'Banca Rober,' I'd never have known what it was. No teller window. No signs advertising mortgage rates. Just security like the CIA and a bunch of little offices."

Matson sat back down. "You know why Fitzhugh chose Lugano?" He laughed. "A woman. Isabella. This pipsqueak set up the Azul Limited and Blau Anstalt accounts there just so he could get laid."

"Just like you."

Matson blushed, then flared. "I'm not the one who chose to run this thing out of London. She just happened to be there."

"Sorry," Zink said. "I didn't mean for it to come out that way."

"Hell, not only did I not know why he chose London, I didn't even know how the scam was going to fit together. All Granger had said up to that point was that he wanted to put a structure in place. I didn't even realize that when I told Burch we needed a flexible structure, I was telling the truth. And at that point, it was all form and no substance."

"Did the banker know that?"

"Of course he did, but you couldn't tell by looking at him. He was about as expressive as a dead carp. He had the account opening forms filled out even before we walked into his office. Fitzhugh introduced me, then threw out the phrase, 'strategic partnerships,' and the guy slid the papers across the table for him to sign. Like some choreographed dance. I'm laughing as we're driving away because the banker didn't even ask what the companies did.

"I elbowed Fitzhugh and told him that I must've missed the wink again. He just grinned and said, 'No wonder, in Switzerland it's the nod.' Then he pointed toward a mountain across the lake, punched the gas, and said, 'Let's go see Isabella.'"

Zink's ringing cell phone interrupted the story. He gestured at Matson to stay put, then answered the call and stepped out into the hallway, closing the door behind him.

◇◇◇

Just like you.

Matson felt a surge of anger as Zink's accusation came back to him.

Alla wasn't about getting laid, he thought, *but punks like Zink wouldn't understand that.*

He had met thousands of Zinks at sales conventions all over the country. He had once been one of them himself, and even had still been one when he arrived in Lugano. But that changed a half hour after leaving Banca Rober.

Fitzhugh had wound through town, then along the northern edge of Lake Lugano and up the switchbacks etched into the side of Monte Bre. Just below the summit, he pulled to a stop in front of a tan stucco house. Matson paused to look down at the city lights, then followed Fitzhugh inside and into the kitchen where Isabella was waiting. Tall, slim, shoulder-length black hair, spaghetti-strapped red dress covered by a knee-length white apron. She turned as their footsteps sounded on the marble floor.

Stunning. Heart-wrenchingly stunning.

As he stood there looking at her, Matson remembered a line of German poetry that a girl he dated in college liked to quote. It had stuck with him over the years even though its meaning had always been obscure: "Beauty is the beginning of terror."

Right then he understood why he had ended up with a Madge, instead of an Isabella or an Alla.

Matson accepted a glass of wine from her and then followed Fitzhugh into the dining room, the table set with English bone china and the candles already lit.

Throughout dinner Matson watched the playfulness, the intimacy, and an acceptance of each other that made what he'd been taught were the institutional bedrocks of society, like marriage, like his own twenty-year marriage, seem hollow. And the hours would've been entirely joyful, even blissful, were he not haunted by the suspicion that he'd wasted his entire life.

Zink reddened as if Peterson was making a comparison, not merely a statement. Peterson ignored it.

"Doesn't this guy have any weaknesses?" Zink asked.

"You mean besides being loyal to a crooked lawyer?"

"Yeah, besides that."

Peterson hesitated. There'd always been something that bothered him about Gage, but he'd never before had the need to articulate it. He struggled until he found the words. "He doesn't go to Giants games."

Zink squinted up at Peterson. "I don't get it."

"Gage misses out on some of the best things in life. It's like they're invisible to him."

The blank look on Zink's face told Peterson that he didn't understand.

"Put it this way. Gage's got two close friends: Burch and a homicide cop over at SFPD he grew up with in Arizona. Neither one would invite him to a ball game. Not that they're not close, they are; like brothers. Not that they wouldn't want him to come, they would. But they know Gage couldn't do high fives when there's a home run or do the wave with everybody else. I guess you could say he's kind of trapped inside himself."

"Some of the best times I've had were at games with my buddies, hooting it up."

"Me too. Toward the end of my career with the Raiders I sometimes wished I was up in the stands instead of down on the field. Playing hurt is lonely. You can't immerse yourself in the game and give in to the blind instinct that great plays are made from. In fact, I can't imagine Gage playing football or baseball or basketball. I'm kind of surprised he was ever a cop—it's the ultimate team sport."

Peterson folded his arms across his chest and stared down at the linoleum floor, trying to puzzle out why.

"And I think I know the reason," he finally said, pointing toward the courtroom floors above and looking back at Zink. "It's something Judge Conrad said. She worked for Gage while she was in law school after she quit the FBI. She told me that he's always aware of what he's thinking. It's like he never lets his mind wander unobserved the way people do when they're cheering or fishing or just watching a sunset."

"Is that a strength or a weakness?"

Peterson took in a slow breath and exhaled, almost as a sigh. "I don't know, but it must be a burden sometimes."

"What do you want me to do about him?"

Peterson didn't respond, momentarily confused by a feeling of envy. He shook it off and answered, "Nothing. He won't find out anything. Burch can't talk, and Matson and Granger are the only ones who know everything that happened. And only one of them is talking—and just to us." Peterson glanced at the SatTek sign on the door, then back at Zink. "Don't have Matson come to the Federal Building anymore. Gage may put a tail on him. I don't want him to figure out that Matson is cooperating."

Zink grinned. "Until he reads the indictment?"

"Yeah. Until he reads the indictment."

Chapter Nineteen

Zink telephoned Matson, directing him to an FBI safe house in Palo Alto and telling him only that they needed to have a heart-to-heart. He cringed during the entire drive down. He dreaded having this conversation with Matson, this touchy-feely crap. He almost gagged when he spotted Matson and his lovelorn little face waiting on the doorstep.

◇◇◇

"Her name is Alla Tarasova. I didn't even learn her last name until after we'd slept together when I got back from Lugano.

"She was pretty much on her own. Divorced. Her mother is dead. Never close to her father. He moved out of Ukraine when she was a kid and set up a business in Budapest. She hasn't talked to him in years. Hates him so much that she resents the way Russians and Ukrainians have to take their middle name from their father's first name. Hers is Petrovna. Alla Petrovna. It was like a burden to her, so she refuses to use it, even when she introduces herself to Russians and Ukrainians.

"We lay there in bed the next morning, looking out over London.

"Sure, it had crossed my mind that her aim was to use me to get a green card, so I decided to test her a little and asked her what she wanted out of life.

"She's really into language, so she told me this word, *uyutnost*. It means 'coziness.' Then she said, 'If there is love and intimacy, even the poor can have *uyutnost*.'

"After she said that, I knew she wasn't after money.

"It almost made me cry.

"Then she told me intimacy was something she never got from her ex-husband, and that Ukrainian men are horrified by it. She explained it by giving me another word, *trast*, and said that for women it means 'passion,' but for men it means 'terror.'

"It's ironic when you think about it. The first words people usually learn in another language are 'hello,' 'good-bye,' and 'thank you.' And there I was learning 'coziness' and 'passion.'

"I asked her straight out whether that's why she slept with me, just because I wasn't him and I wasn't Ukrainian.

"And here's where she could've looked up at me with baby-girl eyes and told me what I wanted to hear, but she didn't.

" 'Who knows why,' she says. 'Because it happened, today happened. Isn't that enough reason?'

"Sure as hell was."

◇◇◇

"Pathetic," Zink said, as he dropped into a chair in Peterson's office at the end of the day. "Fucking pathetic. Can't I get back to some real investigation?"

"What do you have in mind?"

"Fitzhugh."

"What's Matson say?"

"That he's as dirty as they come. Knew everything. Been running these kinds of scams for years."

Peterson thought for a moment. "I wish I knew what was going to happen with Burch, so I could decide who to make deals with."

"What are you hearing?"

"There seems to have been some improvement. He's moved his hands—but not like he's actually responding to anything." Peterson jerked his arm. "That kind of thing."

Peterson tapped his forefinger on the edge of his desk. "It'll look bad if the press thinks we're singling out a road-rage victim—especially a guy like Burch. They've been making him into some kind of hero. The U.S. Attorney won't like it. He likes press coverage, needs it for his campaign for governor, but not that kind."

Peterson gazed out of his window toward the tree-covered Presidio and the Pacific Ocean beyond. "Let's make the case look real international." He looked back toward Zink. "How many countries so far?"

"Switzerland, United Kingdom, Panama, Liechtenstein, China, Vietnam."

"That's the way we'll play it. Let's indict Burch as soon as he's conscious—"

"You mean if."

"Yeah, if...along with Fitzhugh, Granger, the stockbrokers, and maybe some bankers in London and Switzerland. They all knew the whole thing was bogus." Peterson grinned. "We'll call 'em fugitives. International fugitives. The boss loves feeding that shit to the press. And Burch won't look so much like a victim, even if they have to roll him into court in a wheelchair."

Peterson glanced at his wall calendar. "You better break off what you're doing with Matson and scoot over to London before Fitzhugh goes underground. He's got to be hearing drumbeats by now."

"I'll call the guy in the Serious Fraud Office who got us the Barclays Bank records."

"Tell him we'll send a Mutual Legal Assistance Request as soon as we get Washington's approval. In the meantime, maybe he can start checking out Fitzhugh—but carefully."

Zink rose to leave.

"We don't want this guy spooked," Peterson said. "So make sure they don't haul him in until we're ready."

Chapter Twenty

Whoever dumped Fitzhugh's body into the Thames on the day Chief Inspector Devlin and Agent Zink were to knock on his door wasn't a fisherman, a meteorologist, or a sailor. Instead of drifting out to the North Sea, Fitzhugh's remains rode a tidal surge upstream, driven by winds blowing in from the east. Fishermen dropping lines off Victoria Embankment, where he was found wedged between a skiff and a piling, considered and debated the matter for weeks. The consensus, ultimately, was that Fitzhugh must've been dropped into the river at St. Katharine's Docks, perhaps even dragged down Alderman's Stairs. In any case, certainly no nearer than the Tower Bridge. After all, the paper said Fitzhugh hadn't been dead all that long when the young solicitor walking in the darkness along the river toward his office in Blackfriars vomited at the sight of Fitzhugh's headless and limbless torso floating by.

◇◇◇

Chief Inspector Eamonn Devlin was disappointed. While some officers viewed the murder of a criminal as just deserts, Devlin figured it was no more or less than a timely escape from justice. He often fantasized about becoming the Lord High Executioner, thinking it a shame that the position no longer existed.

Devlin wasn't personally certain Fitzhugh was a crook, but when the FBI rings up and asks you to perform discreet inquiries, and when an agent arrives bearing a most solicitous letter from Washington, it wasn't much of a leap.

By the time he'd noticed the homicide entry on the morning bulletin, Fitzhugh's two arms and one leg had been recovered. By noon, when Zink arrived at Devlin's office, Fitzhugh's head, which had been bobbing along and unnerving tourists near the Houses of Parliament, had been netted by a passing tour boat captain.

Just before 2 P.M., Devlin received word that Fitzhugh had been provisionally identified based on a missing person's report filed by his wife when he hadn't returned home the previous evening.

Devlin walked Zink down the hallway in the City of Westminster's Agar Street Station to meet with Inspector Rees of homicide, who'd been assigned the Fitzhugh case, unofficially categorized as a Humpty-Dumpty.

"What's your interest in Fitzhugh?" Rees asked, as they stood in his small office.

"Securities fraud," Zink said. "We were going to indict him in a few weeks."

Rees grinned. "Instead, he'll be reassembled."

Devlin frowned.

"Sorry, Chief Inspector. Sometimes we...I..."

"I don't think our guest appreciates your attempt at levity."

"Yes, Chief Inspector."

"It's okay," Zink said. "I'm used to it. I started out as a street cop."

"What was the cause of death?" Devlin asked.

"A slim sharp object entered his thoracic cavity from the rear and came to an abrupt stop in his right ventricle."

"Any similars?"

"By victim? Chartered accountants. None. By method? A few."

"Suspects?"

"In Fitzhugh? None. In dismemberments? Russians or Chechens." Rees looked toward Zink. "Of the fifty-four nationalities in the City of Westminster, few others have the stomach for this kind of work. But anything is possible."

"Motive?" Zink asked.

"Until you arrived, we had no thoughts beyond the likelihood that it was a contract killing or, of course, a domestic manslaughter followed by a desperate attempt to dispose of the body."

"Have you searched his home and office?" Devlin asked.

Rees shook his head. "That's next on the agenda."

"Why don't you take Agent Zink with you? I'm certain he'll be interested in examining Fitzhugh's files."

"Yes, Chief Inspector."

"And I'd like you to copy me on your reports."

"Yes, Chief Inspector."

◊◊◊

As Zink was boarding his Heathrow flight back to San Francisco, he telephoned Matson, ordering him to appear at the Palo Alto safe house at 3 P.M., fifty-five minutes after his scheduled landing.

Twelve hours later, Matson's sunken-eyed, ashen face stared at Zink on the other side of the coffee table.

"Who have you been talking to?" Zink demanded.

"No one. No one knows."

"Burch gets hit just before we're about to lean on him. Now it's Fitzhugh."

"I haven't said anything to anyone. Not even my wife."

"Bullshit. What about Granger? When did you last talk to Granger?"

"A week ago. But we didn't talk about the case except he said he wasn't gonna make a deal. I was gonna tell you about it when you got back from London."

"And when were you going to tell me about your connection to TAMS Limited? I found the papers in Fitzhugh's house."

Matson blanched. "I was gonna…"

Zink sprang across the table and grabbed Matson by the shirtfront, yanking him from the sofa.

"You were gonna what? I could go to Peterson right now and get your ass indicted by sundown. Is that what you want? Hide one more thing from me and that's what you're going to get. You got it, you little shit?…I said, you got it?"

"Yeah, I got it," Matson squeaked out. "I got it."

Zink pushed Matson back down, but remained standing, glaring at him. Matson flinched when Zink reached into his briefcase for a legal pad, still astonished that a man that small could be so strong, and so quick.

Zink yanked a pen from his shirt pocket, then sat down.

"Tell me every fucking thing about TAMS fucking Limited."

"It's nothing." Matson wiped the sweat from his forehead. "Just a company Fitzhugh set up. Burch was supposed to do it, but he was busy or something. TAMS owns a flat in London. Alla lives there. I wasn't hiding it. We haven't even gotten to the stockbrokers yet. They came long before TAMS. You got to have money before you can buy anything. Even though Granger had gotten the SEC to let us issue the shares, we still had to find somebody to sell them for us. That's how we hooked up with Northstead Securities."

Matson took in a breath and exhaled, then leaned forward on the couch.

"The guy we dealt with was named Yuri Kovalenko. You should've seen this monster. Granger and I walked into his office in San Diego and sitting behind the desk was a guy with a huge, shaved head and hands like a meatpacker.

"Kovalenko had a spreadsheet all ready. It showed that SatTek was supposed to issue Northstead some shares at two dollars each, and that they would keep whatever they could sell it for above that. The stock goes up to five, they get three; goes up to six, they get four. It pissed me off. They could be making twice as much as SatTek.

"I wanted to get up and walk out right then, but it hit me real hard what kind of guy I'm talking to, and I'm not sure who to be more frightened of, the SEC Enforcement Division or him. But I figure I need to say something, so I tell him that the SEC will only let us pay a commission. A few percent. Kovalenko looks at me like I'm a fool and points this sausagelike finger at me, but Granger cuts in and says how much of a risk Northstead is taking in the deal and blah, blah, blah."

Matson emitted a nervous laugh. "The only one who was at risk right then was me."

Zink smirked. "Don't tell me you're claiming you got coerced into doing this by Kovalenko?"

"No, I'm not saying that. I was still thinking that if we did things just right, and brought in enough money, even at two bucks a share, we could grow SatTek into a big company. Five million shares meant ten million dollars for SatTek. That and a little leverage and we could buy up some of our competition."

Matson rose to his feet and started pacing.

"Kovalenko took us into a big trading floor, about forty guys working the phones, and then across the hall to meet an old man they called the Maestro. A droopy-jowled guy with the worst rosacea I've ever seen. I never learned his real name. His job was to push the stock. Plant stories in the press. Spam out stock tips.

"Granger was pissed at me when we left because I had challenged Kovalenko and I was pissed at him because he was always treating me like a child, and I was sick of it. But we needed to get cash coming in, so the next morning I did what he told me. I called the stock transfer agent and had him issue five million shares to Northstead and then two million each to Cobalt Partners, Azul Limited, and Blau Anstalt."

Matson paused, and his eyes went vacant for a moment.

"Right after I hung up the phone, I got a real sick feeling in my stomach." He looked down at Zink. "You ever go to a magic show in Vegas?"

Zink shook his head.

"The magician asks somebody to come up on the stage, then he does a little razzle-dazzle, and suddenly he's holding the guy's wallet and everybody in the audience is laughing at him. I decided right then that I wasn't going to let that happen to me. I called the guy back and had an extra two million shares issued to Cobalt Partners. Then I told the lawyer in Guernsey to have the nominee directors sell them as soon as the stock hit five dollars a share and send the profit to my Barclays account in London."

"And that's the first money that went into TAMS?"

Matson nodded.

"Did you tell Granger and Fitzhugh about the additional shares?"

"Fuck no."

Chapter Twenty-one

When Gage arrived at his office after a futile morning meeting with Courtney and Burch's doctors at SF Medical, he found that Alex Z had converted it into a war room. Conference tables. Easels. An additional computer workstation. Redbrick walls now bare, waiting for poster boards bearing flowcharts and chronologies.

"SatTek was self-underwriting," Alex Z reported as he sat down across the desk from Gage. "They sold a lot of the stock themselves. The rest through a brokerage firm called Northstead Securities."

Gage sat poised behind his desk, chin propped on his folded hands.

"It's owned by Albert William Ward, a broker hanging on to his license by a thread." Alex Z pointed toward the floors below. "I asked all of our ex-FBI people to use their contacts at the SEC. It turns out that he's been on their radar for a long time." He slid a Securities and Exchange Commission Litigation Release across the desk. "The Enforcement Division slapped his wrist a few years ago. He laid low for a while, then came back as Northstead."

Gage picked it up and read it over. "Is he still in Colorado?"

"No. San Diego. Off Highway 5 close to downtown, right near the Hyatt Regency." Alex Z grinned. "I mean real, real close by."

Gage drew back, brows furrowed. "What does the Hyatt Regency have to do with Northstead?"

"I made you a reservation for tonight. Late check-in."

Gage shook his head and smiled. "I think we've been working together too long."

"Your flight is at 7 P.M. out of SFO."

"I'll be on it."

"Pretty soon after SatTek went public, they used some stock to buy an engineering software firm in Ireland. No cash changed hands. A shares-for-equity deal. Three million shares worth about fifteen million dollars."

"And the shareholders put up with that?"

"Some didn't like it but it went through anyway. They thought SatTek was straying from its business plan with no justification."

"Still, that's quite a chunk."

"SatTek did everything in chunks. There were eleven big shareholders. The biggest were Blau Anstalt, Azul Limited, and Cobalt Partners."

"Blue companies."

Alex Z's face washed with puzzlement as if he'd gone color-blind. "Blue companies?"

"*Blau* is 'blue' in German. *Azul* is 'blue' in Spanish. Cobalt is blue as the deep blue sea."

"You think they're linked some way?"

Gage nodded. "It's not likely to be a coincidence. Any blue ones on the domestic side?"

"Nope, but there's a large shareholder in Nevada. The registered agent is named Chuck Verona."

"Send someone out there to find out who he is and what else he's into." Gage pointed at an easel bearing a fresh pad of poster board. There was already too much to keep track of in his head. "Then chart all of this out."

"I'll do it tonight."

"You don't have to spend—"

Alex Z shook his head. "I know I'm just a computer guy but something smells real bad about what happened to Mr. Burch. So I'll be living here until you figure it out."

◇◇◇

Gage reached for the phone to make a call as Alex Z headed back downstairs to his office.

"Tiptoe?"

"Yeah?"

"This is Graham Gage."

Gage heard Tiptoe chewing. He was always chewing. Gum. Tobacco. Beef jerky. He said it kept the rest of his body steady, especially his hands. His life—spent performing black-bag jobs for the good guys—sometimes depended on it.

"What's cookin'?"

Gage heard his lips smack.

"I've got a little situation. You doing anything tonight?"

"Depends on what's on the Playboy Channel and how much you wanna spend."

"A thousand."

"I think my cable just went out."

"How long would it take you to get to San Diego?"

"That also depends…"

Tiptoe's jaws fell silent.

"Fifteen hundred."

"Two hours."

"The place is called Northstead Securities."

◇◇◇

Alex Z had a rental van reserved for Gage when he arrived at the San Diego International Airport. American. Gray. Anonymous. Tinted windows.

Gage made a quick run down Pacific Highway, glanced at the bay and the Naval Air Station on North Island, then cut a few blocks inland. Northstead Securities was located on the ground floor of a U-shaped glass and metal office building north of downtown. Parking places filled and surrounded the U.

At 8:45 P.M. Gage slipped into a parking space shadowed by a Torrey pine. The lights inside Northstead were still on; a few brokers remained. Gage didn't need to bug the place to know what was going on. Every boiler room he'd ever investigated was the same. Twenty, thirty, forty cubicles. Guys, all guys. Not members of a team or a group or a staff, but a crew that moved like a toxic cloud. When it was time for Northstead to evaporate, they'd condense somewhere else and adopt a new British-sounding name with the resonance of marble columns and old money: Oxford Capital or Oxford Securities or Oxford Investments, Stratford Asset Management or Stratford Equities or Stratford Partners.

Through the floor-to-ceiling windows, Gage surveyed the brokers working the phones, pumping and dumping penny stocks, an archaic nickname for those selling for less than five bucks, and often, Gage knew, not worth a cent. As he watched their bobbing heads and gesticulating hands, he imagined the pitches Northstead used to push SatTek, ones appealing to the war on terror, the military's need for SatTek's proprietary technology to fight it, and its stock being a way to make a patriotic killing in the stock market.

Gage saw two of them jump to their feet, high-fiving their half-height cubicles. A sucker bit.

Moments after the last of the brokers turned off the lights two hours later, a potbellied little man in a hooded sweatshirt and jeans appeared out of the darkness. He opened Gage's passenger door and climbed in. He cradled a black canvas bag on his lap.

"Can you get us in?" Gage asked Tiptoe.

"I've already been inside. They had a little electrical problem earlier. It fucked up their security system."

"And you fixed it?"

Tiptoe grinned. "I caused it."

Gage pointed at the lights glowing in a third floor window. "Do we need to worry about them?"

"No. They're just kids running a start-up. As long as they don't spot us going in, we'll be okay."

◇◇◇

An hour later, Tiptoe jimmied the lock and stepped through the double glass doors. He pulled out a tiny flashlight, turned toward the wall, and punched in the code to disable the alarm. Gage scanned the parking lot, then followed him inside.

They stood silently, letting their eyes adjust to the semidarkness. Only the screen saver on the receptionist's monitor and an exit sign at the end of a short hallway provided light.

Gage spotted a restroom sign and an arrow pointing down the hallway, then whispered to Tiptoe, "The file storage room is probably down there."

Tiptoe slipped away while Gage skirted the reception station and the glass partition behind it, then headed along the carpeted floor toward the half-height cubicles of the boiler room. The empty desks seemed like epicenters of thousands of tragedies: retirement savings lost, college funds wasted, and houses in foreclosure.

Gage's foot slipped on a piece of paper. He flicked on his flashlight. A handout for the brokers. The title: "Human Motivation." And below that, the scales of justice with one side labeled "Greed," the other "Fear."

He moved on, then stopped halfway down the aisle and pointed his flashlight at a desk. A lead book. A thick blue binder. "Do Not Remove. Property of Smith Barney." He flipped it open. Names. Telephone numbers. Pages and pages and pages of leads. Smuggled out and sold to Northstead for cash that had been stolen from previous victims. Tacked above on the cubicle wall were scripts for pushing new stocks. One was for a company promising renewable energy using a process the brokers weren't allowed to disclose and, Gage suspected, didn't exist.

Headlights swept the window, backlighting the closed blinds. Gage snapped off his flashlight and ducked down. Headlights once again. This time bearing down. Then off.

Gage reached for his cell phone. Tiptoe's number was set for redial. "A car pulled up." He crawled to the window and peeked out. The driver's door opened. A man stepped out. His starched white shirt glowed in the parking lot's halogen lights. Black hair. No more than thirty-five. Six foot two. Broad-shouldered.

Must be one of the brokers, Gage thought.

Then the passenger door opened. A woman. Blond. A walking centerfold, but hair a mess. She reached into her purse. The parking lights of the car next to his flashed.

The broker steadied himself on the hood of his Lexus as he made his way toward her. He opened her driver's door, then reached his arms around her. His hands groping under her skirt, reaching between her legs. She giggled and pushed him away. She slid into the car and he staggered to the sidewalk, rocking side-to-side, and watched her drive away.

The broker turned toward the office entrance, keys in hand.

"Tiptoe," Gage whispered into his cell phone. "He's coming in."

Gage ducked back into a cubicle just a second before the office exploded with light.

"It's me." The slurred voice was speaking into a phone. Words coming out as "Itch me." "Sorry. I had to work late...Dinner meeting with a client...yeah...it was Kovalenko's idea. Fucking slave driver."

Kovalenko. Kovalenko. Kovalenko.

The name rocketed around in Gage's head. Burch's face came to him first. A bull's-eye encircling it. Only then did an image appear: Semion Kovalenko, an East Coast gangster.

Wait. That can't be right. Isn't Semion Kovalenko dead? Who's he talking about?

"Yeah," the broker said, "at the office to get some papers... gotta take a pee, then I'll be home."

"He's coming your way," Gage whispered into his phone.

But he wasn't.

Gage heard the thud of the man staggering against the corner of the first cubicle. "Son of a bitch." Then a laugh and "I'm fucking wasted." The voice was moving closer.

Gage glanced around the carpeted cubicle. The desk and chair and filing cabinet occupied half the space—and Gage filled most of the rest.

The metal joints of the cubicle walls creaked when the broker pulled on it to maintain his balance as he worked his way down the aisle.

Gage knew he couldn't fight him. Their combined four hundred pounds crashing into walls, buckling partitions, and shattering windows would leave an irreparable battlefield—and send Kovalenko—or whoever he really was—on a hunt for the invader.

The carpeted wall bulged out as the man grabbed on to it just a yard away.

When the broker stopped again to steady himself, Gage snatched a pen off the desk and tossed it in a high arc toward the glass partition behind the receptionist's station. Gage sprang to his feet as the man turned toward the sound of metal clicking against glass, then stepped up behind him. He locked his hand over the man's eyes and clamped the crook of his elbow across the man's neck. The man tried to pry away Gage's hands and punch at Gage's head, adrenaline rushing to overwhelm the alcohol that had deadened his brain—but not enough. The broker finally went limp. Gage lowered him to the carpet.

Tiptoe's head peeked from the far hallway and he pointed at the light switch by the door. Gage shook his head, then met him halfway, next to the glass partition.

"The guy's car is in front," Gage said. "Anyone driving by will think he's working late."

Tiptoe glanced down the aisle toward the body. His eyes widened. "You didn't…"

"He'll be okay. Hopefully, tomorrow morning he'll just think he passed out." Gage picked up the pen, then looked back toward the hallway. "What did you find?"

Tiptoe shrugged. "Not much. The cabinet drawer in the storage room with the SatTek label is empty, except for one file. I photographed everything inside. And there were a few folders mixed in with some others in a drawer called Cambridge Investments. The only name I saw was for a guy named Verona, from Nevada. His name was also on some papers for something called Golden West Properties. It owns cars with this address on the registration."

Gage pointed at the storage room. "Keep searching." He then headed down the aisle toward what appeared to be the manager's office. An image of Burch's face in the bull's-eye once again appeared in his mind. Then his stomach tensed. *Kovalenko.*

He called Alex Z. "Do a news archive search for me. Semion Kovalenko. He was involved in a Russian organized crimes stock scam in New York."

He stepped into the boss' office, but didn't turn on the light. He scanned the desk with his flashlight. Stacks of correspondence.

"Alex? It's not Semion, but Yuri."

Gage inspected the sparse room as he listened to Alex Z's keystrokes in the background. No pictures on the walls. No filing cabinets. No diplomas or broker's licenses. A high-back leather chair and two smaller ones that looked like they'd been salvaged from a skid-row dentist's office. No computer on the Office Depot desk. Just a twenty-line phone and an adding machine. Gage opened each of the drawers in turn. Nothing about SatTek.

Finally, Alex Z spoke. "I found it. A *Business Week* article. Three years ago. Yuri is Semion's brother and was the muscle for the operation. Says here the broker-dealers were terrified of him. Semion was murdered just before he got indicted and Yuri did almost twenty months for refusing to testify."

"In the fraud trial?"

"No, in the trial against the guys who gunned down his brother…looks like he got shot, too."

"An old-school gangster. Any kind of testifying is snitching." The almost bare office now struck Gage as a stage set. A way for Yuri Kovalenko to tell whoever sat across the desk that he had nothing to lose—so don't cross him. "He must've terrified Matson, too."

"Hold on. It looks like there's a link to another story…Jeez…the bodies of the killers were found dismembered in Central Park two days after he was released from jail."

Chapter Twenty-two

Oceanside's Pleasant Acres wasn't near the ocean, wasn't pleasant, and had no acreage beyond the legally required ten-foot strip between it and Good as Gold Pawnshop on one side and Nguyen's Nail Salon on the other. And it didn't strike Gage as the sort of place a stockbroker would expect to spend his declining years.

"Albert will be so pleased to have another visitor," the receptionist said to Gage. "And you are?"

She was a fleshy middle-aged black woman wearing a yellow shift. Reading glasses hung from a "What Would Jesus Do?" lanyard. Her off-kilter name tag, riding high on huge and structurally supported breasts, said "Dolores B." She seemed thrilled to have outside company.

"I'm Mr. Ward's nephew. This is my first chance to get to this part of the country in years. How long has he been here?"

"He came right about my birthday. So about twenty-three months."

"Then happy birthday."

Dolores beamed. "Thank you kindly. I hope he remembers you. Even if he doesn't he'll be so pleased to have a visitor."

She turned a sign-in book toward him. Gage wrote in the name Gary Ward.

"He's out in the patio," she continued. "Just go down that hallway." She pointed to her left. "There's a sliding glass door near the end. He's dressed. We get them dressed every day, you see."

Gage walked down the corridor, counting six rooms and a nurses' station, unattended. Two patients per room. The wall next to room four bore a handwritten label: "A. Ward." The roommate was dressed, and asleep. The room smelled of urine, cigarettes, and instant coffee. Gage slipped inside, then quickly searched Ward's closet. The elderly man stirred in his bed, rolling first toward the wall, then back. Gage froze until the man started snoring again, then checked the chest of drawers. There wasn't a scrap of paper, even a wallet, to show that Ward had any life at all before his abandonment at Pleasant Acres.

Gage found Ward sitting alone in the patio but for a shriveled woman propped in a wheelchair at the far end. He was staring up at metal chimes, rusted and silent. A glass of orange juice rested on a low wrought-iron table, untouched. Standing, he would have been five foot ten. Good complexion. Still had most of his silver hair. Looked his age, seventy-two.

"Mr. Ward?"

Ward squinted up at Gage. "Am I supposed to know you?"

"No." Gage adopted a sympathetic but respectful smile, as if he'd come to learn from an elder. "But I'd like to ask you about the great work you did with Northstead Securities."

Ward looked down and repeated the name to himself, then back up at Gage, his face scrunched up in puzzlement.

"What's that?"

"Aren't you Albert Ward, the stockbroker?"

"Me?" Ward's face reddened in frustration and in anger, as if he could no longer bear to walk down memory's path only to find himself at an abyss. "If I'm a stockbroker, I would know it. Wouldn't I?"

"Yes," Gage said, reaching out and squeezing the bewildered man's shoulder, "you would know it."

Gage walked back to the reception area where Dolores was seated behind the reception desk.

"Dolores," he said, "I don't think it's a good day. He didn't even remember my father."

"Unfortunately"—Dolores sighed—"most days are like that now."

Gage watched her fondle the cross on the chain around her neck, as if seeking strength to bear nature's ruthless unpredictability that revealed itself daily in the ossifying mind of Albert Ward. He felt a tenderness for her, a righteous woman trapped by her own history in a job with no future, tending for people with no past.

Gage glanced down at the sign-in book. "You mentioned other visitors?"

"Mr. Kovalenko comes once a month, of course, just for the paperwork and to pay the fees. And..." Dolores stood up, then leaned over and glanced down the hallway. "I'm not sure I'm supposed to tell you."

"If it's something important, someone in the family should know." Gage took her hand and looked into her eyes. "If you can't rely on family and our Lord Jesus, who can you rely on?"

"You're right, of course." She glanced around again. "You see, an FBI agent came to visit Albert. Zink, his name was Zink. I remember because our old pastor at Love Temple Church of God in Christ was named Zink. It was such a tragedy when he died. We almost renamed the church after him. A saintly man. Except he was black and this Zink is white. But that was on another of Albert's bad days."

"Did Agent Zink say what he wanted?"

"No. He just talked to Albert for a few minutes just like you, then he got a box from Albert's room and left."

"Do you know what was in the box?"

"Just papers. There was a time when Albert liked to look through them. I'm not sure now he even remembers it."

"Has Mr. Kovalenko visited since then?"

She shook her head.

"Dolores, I think the family would appreciate you not telling Mr. Kovalenko about Agent Zink until we can look into the matter."

"Of course. If I was Albert, I'd want that, too. And…" She looked around again. "I don't like that Mr. Kovalenko. You know how some people have a feature that's just scary. You know, like eyes, especially eyes. But with Mr. Kovalenko it's not his eyes. You can't see nothing in his eyes. But he's got these big meaty hands, ugly and sweaty. Like…like …"

"Like he could crush your neck with just one of them?"

"Yes. Dear Lord. Yes."

Chapter Twenty-three

Is this how they pumped it up?" Gage asked Alex Z on the following morning. They stood in front of a set of four-foot-by-five-foot charts Alex Z had hung on the walls of Gage's office that displayed dates, events, and share prices.

Gage scanned the first two entries. The stock had been issued on June 5 at two dollars a share, then jumped fifty cents a day later when Investor's Blue Sheet made a strong buy recommendation.

"I take it Investor's Blue Sheet is just an arm of Northstead Securities," Gage said.

"It's run by a defrocked stockbroker. He calls himself the Maestro."

"Made to order?"

"All *made up* to order."

On June 8, the stock jumped another fifty cents based on a rumor that the Chinese government was placing a thirty-seven-million-dollar order for sound amplifiers to be used as part of an early warning flood control system.

"Who started the rumor?" Gage asked.

"My guess? Maestro the Scumbag." Alex Z almost spit out the words. He glared at the chart, shaking his head. "This whole thing really pisses me off. When I think of the naïve people who fell for this scam. . ."

Alex Z lowered his head and exhaled, then waved his hand toward the share prices, as if each represented a tragedy in someone's life. "Actually, it's worse than that. For the first time ever, I imagined myself old and vulnerable. I felt queasy, almost seasick." He pointed at a graph to his right and made a chopping motion with his hand that tracked the plummeting of the stock at the end of the scam. "Imagine what the older shareholders went through watching their futures collapse."

Gage reached his arm around Alex Z's shoulders. "Maybe we can help them get some of their money back, and give them a chance to start over."

"I don't know, boss. I haven't been able to figure how the scam worked. And if we don't know how they did it, we won't be able to figure out where the profits went."

"Let's work on the how first, and the where later." Gage dropped into a chair and looked up at the chart. "Did the Chinese ever buy anything?"

"SatTek put out a press release saying that they were still in negotiations and that was the end of it, but the share price didn't drop back down."

Alex Z pointed at the next entry. June 10. The stock had jumped to nearly four dollars a share based on a report that AB Labs was considering a buyout of SatTek.

"And that didn't happen, either," Gage said.

"AB Labs' denial was taken as an attempt to keep the stock price down until they made their move. Meanwhile Matson, Granger, and an engineer started doing road shows. Granger to lend financial credibility, Matson to do the sales pitch and the engineer to explain the technology…And one more guy. Retired from the CIA. He talked about counterterrorism and military applications—"

"To combine the fear of growing old with the fear of dying young in a terrorist attack."

"And it worked. The stock kept ratcheting up. You can even see little jumps every time Homeland Security raised the threat level."

Gage scanned down to the next item. June 14–18. SatTek had been one of the most actively traded stocks on NASDAQ, and the price jumped to almost five dollars a share.

"One of the most actively traded on NASDAQ?" Gage asked. "You've got to be kidding."

"Four brokers were responsible for most of the volume. It looks like Northstead just traded the stock among them, millions of shares, back and forth, and around and around. All the activity put the little investors into a frenzy, wanting to get in on it. A couple of days later the stock hit five dollars and thirty-five cents—and then the dump. All of the offshore companies, the blue companies, Cobalt, Blau, and Azul, started selling and the little people started buying heavy. Northstead's boiler room couldn't sell the stock fast enough."

"Which stock?" Gage asked. "From the blue companies?" He didn't wait for Alex Z to answer. "Couldn't be. SatTek would've fronted a separate chunk to Kovalenko."

Alex Z nodded. "And Northstead didn't even pay SatTek for it until after they sold it off. They didn't take any risk at all."

Gage studied Alex Z's chart. "What happened after the stock sold out?"

"SatTek filed its quarterly report with the SEC. Looked perfect. The company was booming like a son of a gun. Tons of money coming in, like from the Asian companies Mr. Burch set up. They paid in full and placed another ten million dollars in orders, each."

Gage's body stiffened. He stopped breathing. He could almost hear the cell door slam in Jack Burch's face. He now grasped Peterson's theory: Without Burch there couldn't have been a SatTek fraud. He created the Chinese and Vietnamese companies, and they were the key to the entire scam.

Alex Z searched Gage's face. "What is it, boss?"

Gage looked up. "Where'd the Asian companies Jack set up get the money to pay for the products?"

Alex Z shrugged again. "From sales, I guess."

"Think. We know they didn't do that. We found the devices SatTek sent to China piled in a basement, covered with a tarp. Same thing in Vietnam."

Alex Z stared at the charts, as if the pattern would somehow emerge on its own. "But I don't…"

Gage pushed himself to his feet. "The money to pay for the products came from the blue companies."

Alex Z shook his head, almost a double-take. "What?"

"The money…to pay…for the products…came from the blue companies."

Gage picked up a black marker and began charting.

"Look."

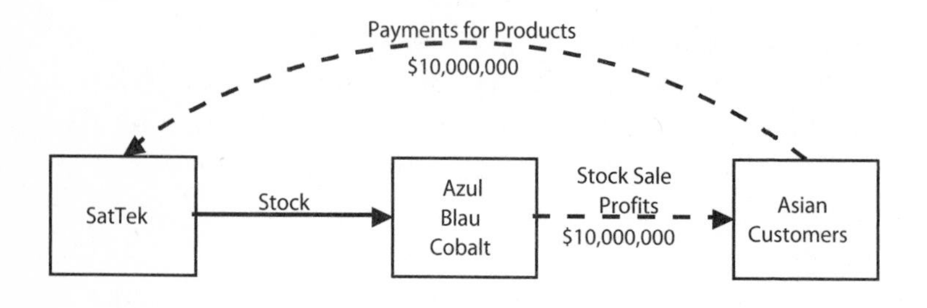

Alex Z traced the lines with his forefinger. "But…" He locked his hands on top of his head and closed his eyes for a few seconds, then looked back at Gage. "You mean SatTek pretended to sell millions of dollars of products to the Asian customers to convince the SEC to let them issue stock…"

Gage held up a finger. "Step one."

"Then used the blue companies to sell the stock…"

Gage held up a second finger. "Step two."

"Then the blue companies wired the money to the Asian customers so they could pretend to pay SatTek for the products they had pretended to purchase?"

"Exactly." Gage rotated his hand. "Step three was a pirouette. SatTek paid for its own products with the money it made from selling its own stock."

Alex Z looked back at the flowchart, eyes wide, almost awestruck. "It's the perfect crime."

Gage sat down, then grabbed a pen and a legal pad from the conference table. There was a box missing from the chart.

"How many shares went offshore right after they went public?"

"At least eight million."

Gage thought out loud as he wrote. "If the blue companies sold the stock for an average of five dollars a share..." He performed a quick multiplication on his pad. "That's forty million dollars."

"Right."

"Even after the blue companies paid SatTek sixteen million dollars for the stock and sent ten million to China and Vietnam, they still had fourteen million left."

Alex Z whistled. "That's a whole lot of money."

"And that was exactly the goal of the whole scheme—Matson and Granger have got to be behind all of the blue companies."

Gage stood up and added to his flowchart.

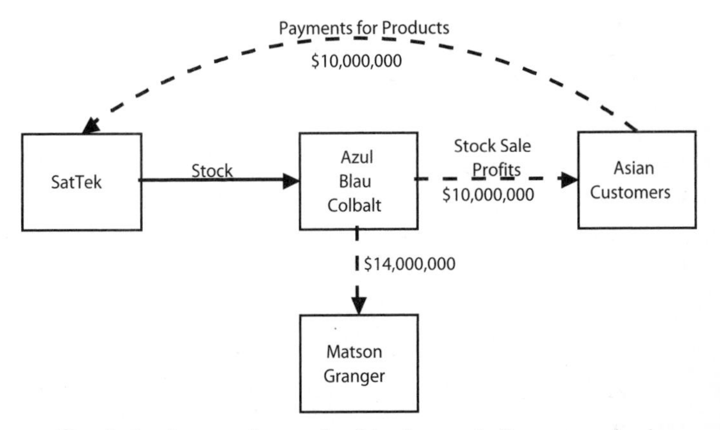

"And that's not the end of it, boss. A few months later, the SEC authorized SatTek to issue another twenty-five million shares, then another thirty after that."

Gage looked back at the flowchart, his stomach in a knot. What if he was wrong and Faith was right? What if Burch's rage really had turned into greed?

One thing he knew for certain was that when Peterson presented his own flowchart to the jury, the bottom box would read: Matson, Granger, and Burch.

Chapter Twenty-four

The train is leaving the station," William Peterson told defense attorney Sid Lavender. Peterson propped his legs on his desk, leaned his oversized ergonomic chair back to its limit, and locked his hands behind his head. "Sid, your client better get on board."

"Come on, Billy-boy, I've been taking these cases to trial for twenty-seven years. No way you'll convict Ed Granger, relying on Matson and Zink. Zink couldn't investigate a plumbing leak. Why do you think he never got promoted?"

Lavender loved the game and loved to go to trial. He'd rather go to trial than have sex, eat prime rib, hit a hole in one, or win the lottery. In fact, trial *was* his lottery except the odds always were that he'd win. White hair, chubby face, playful smile, everybody's favorite uncle. Juries adored him and prosecutors could never bring themselves to hate him.

Lavender unbuttoned his suit jacket, took a sip from his Starbucks latte, then grinned at Peterson.

"How do you spell impeachment? M-a-t-s-o-n," Lavender said. "Granger's got lots of stuff on Matson. Lots and lots. You'd be better off taking the case civil."

Peterson slipped his feet off the desk.

"You've got to be kidding, Sid. Let Granger kick all the dirt he wants at Matson, they'll both be covered in dust."

"Who's kidding who?"

"Whom."

"Okay. Whom. You've got to prove that Granger knew what Matson was up to. It's he said, he said. You got Granger's signature on anything? He own any of those companies? You got his name on a single overseas wire transfer? Can you even trace any of the shares to him? No, no, and no. How many was that? No. He was just an elder statesman offering a little advice to a guy he thought made a good product. All he got were consulting fees. Not even a quarter mil. Trust me, he feels betrayed… No, heartbroken…" Lavender sighed and placed his hand on his chest. "That's it, heartbroken and betrayed."

Peterson waved him off. "Save it for your closing argument."

"You don't really have anything. At least anything solid. I know it and you know it."

"Sid, Sid, Sid. I'm not giving you a peek at my case unless your guy wants to do a Queen for Day about what he knows."

Lavender set his cup down on Peterson's desk, then leaned forward, reaching out his hands, palms up.

"Hypothetically speaking—get that? Hy-po-thetically. Who's left for him to give? You got Matson. Granger never even sat down with Burch." Lavender drew back. "What? He's supposed to roll down on a bookkeeper at SatTek? What'll that earn him? Two days off a ten-year sentence? Four days off twenty?"

"I think you better have a heart-to-heart with your client," Peterson said, tapping his middle finger on a file folder bearing Granger's name. "This isn't the first time he's come up on the radar. As soon as he stops lying to himself, you'll be knocking on my door. If he doesn't come in, it's *dasvedanya*, baby. I hear Lompoc in the fall is just lovely."

"That's the last word?"

"Yes."

"Which one?" Sid grinned. "Lovely or *dasvedanya*?"

"You're enjoying this too much, Sid." Peterson slid aside the file "Anyone else on the agenda for today?"

"Nope." Sid rose to leave. "But put on your trial suit. Granger won't come crawling in. I think he'll roll the dice in front of a jury."

"It'll be fun," Peterson said. "We always have fun in trial. Just don't use that peel-the-onion metaphor again to describe my case—it's getting old and smelly."

Sid spread his arms like a farmer showing off his crop. "But for jurors it conveys the aroma of spring planting. And don't forget, it takes a little manure to grow something really tasty."

Peterson smiled and shook his head, "Sid, Sid, Sid."

◇◇◇

Zink was sitting in Peterson's office when he returned from escorting Lavender to the exit.

"Is Granger coming in?" Zink asked.

"Nope." Peterson dropped into his chair. "At least not right away."

"I've traced a few million dollars of Matson's and Granger's money to Liechtenstein. It all went through Blau Anstalt. The authorities froze the accounts but Granger's nominee directors are fighting our bank record demands in court. They can tie it up for years. All it would take is for Granger to tell his people to back off and we could give it all back to the shareholders."

Peterson had fought with Liechtenstein before, but never won—and didn't expect to this time. He knew that their economy depended on keeping exactly the kind of financial secrets the U.S. Justice Department had an interest in exposing.

"How do you know that Granger is behind Blau Anstalt?" Peterson asked.

Zink shrugged. "That's what Matson says."

Peterson thought for a moment. "Granger just may be one of those guys we need to indict first, unless you've got something new to spook him with."

"Nothing more than what Matson's given us. I've leaned on him every which way I can, but all he's come up with is that Granger was the connection to the guys pushing the stock at Northstead. I feel like I've been digging well after well, but coming up dry."

"Sticking it to brokers isn't going to get us anywhere. We need Granger to roll up, not down."

Peterson saw in Zink's expression that he'd had enough of this particular little snitch. Peterson made a college-try fist, then said, "Let's give it one more shot. But this time, go heavy on him. Push him hard. Maybe Granger bragged about some deal or somebody he knows. We just need a little leverage."

Zink nodded.

Peterson's eyes narrowed. "Granger is what? Late sixties?"

"About."

Peterson looked at his wall calendar. "We just need to get him doing the numbers. Say he goes to trial in sixteen months. Ninety days until he's convicted, and gets sentenced ninety days after that. Say he gets twenty years. They let him out when he's what? Almost ninety?"

"Yeah, if he lives that long."

Peterson nodded slowly. "With a little push, he'll run the numbers and come in. He'll have no choice."

◇◇◇

"You know how Fitzhugh and Granger hooked up, don't you?" Matson asked Zink, as he balled up a potato chip bag and dropped it into a wastebasket next to Zink's desk.

They were meeting in a temporary office Zink had set up a few blocks from the Federal Building.

"Why don't you tell me?"

"Through Burch." Matson pointed at Zink's uneaten sandwich. "You want that?"

Zink shook his head, then got up and walked to the easel. He drew an arrow from the box containing the name Burch to one containing the name Fitzhugh.

"I thought it was obvious," Matson said, tearing off the plastic wrapper. "Granger and I didn't know anybody in London who could run the holding company or handle the money we were running through China and Vietnam. I thought you understood that."

This guy's a dunce, Matson said to himself. *How did he get into the FBI?*

"That's what led to the Irish software deal. Burch hooked us up. I figured you didn't ask me about that because you already had it covered."

"There are a lot of pieces to this puzzle. I hadn't gotten to that one yet." He turned back toward Matson. "You have any proof?"

Matson nodded. "Sure. I've got paperwork in a box of junk in London. Let me have my passport back and I'll go get it. And there are guys over there who worked with Granger before. I can see if they'll let something slip."

◇◇◇

Zink's step was lighter as he walked back to the Federal Building to get Peterson's approval. He'd gotten what the prosecutor wanted: an angle on Granger. He smiled when he realized that the source of Matson's enthusiasm wasn't the possibility of success, but something else: The weasel probably hasn't gotten laid since that last time he saw his Ukrainian love bunny.

It didn't make any difference to Zink what else Matson did over there as long as he brought back the leverage Peterson needed.

Anyway, Zink thought, *there's nothing—absolutely nothing—he can do that I won't find out about in the end.*

Chapter Twenty-five

Viz was just finishing a large pepperoni and anchovy pizza when Gage climbed into the passenger seat of his blue-green Yukon half a block away from SatTek.

"How can you eat that stuff?" Gage asked. "You'll be burping anchovies for the rest of the day."

"I have a high tolerance for discomfort."

"What about my discomfort?"

"You should've called ahead. I'd have picked up tofu and saltines."

"I'll do that next time."

Viz pointed at a monitor propped on the truck console. It showed a magnified entrance to SatTek, an image captured by a video camera concealed in a gym bag resting on the dashboard. SatTek was housed in a half-block-sized, nearly windowless white concrete block with bold red letters spelling the company name along the front. To the right was the entrance. To the left, a long dock and four metal roll-up doors.

Gage surveyed the wide strips of manicured grass surrounding each building in the industrial complex. A coed group was playing volleyball farther down the block, and across the street from them three young men tossed a Frisbee.

Viz pointed toward SatTek. "See that guy with the brown sports jacket? He's the controller."

Gage focused on the man fifty yards away.

"His name is Robert 'Don't-Call-Me-Bob' Milsberg. Accounting degree from SF State in the early nineties."

Gage watched Milsberg climb into a ten-year-old Nissan station wagon. "What's he been up to?"

"Arrives at 9 A.M. Goes out to lunch at 11:50. Comes back at 12:50. Leaves at 5 P.M. Except yesterday. Yesterday broke the pattern."

Viz noticed movement in the dock area and reached forward to reposition the camera. He then reached again, turning it a quarter inch.

Gage smiled. "Don't leave me hanging."

"It's called dramatic tension," Viz said, smiling back. "I'm thinking about taking a film class."

"You could teach a film class. So what about yesterday?"

"I had one of the guys take over for me here so I could follow him. He went to a mortgage company in Cupertino. Came out looking real grim. I asked Alex Z to run him. Turns out his house is in foreclosure. He's lived there since the eighties. Lots of equity. Refinanced last year. Took out a huge chunk of change. And guess what he did with the money?"

"SatTek stock."

"Bingo. Alex Z looked it up. Milsberg used the whole four hundred thousand dollars plus another eight hundred and fifty thousand, probably from his retirement account."

"And he didn't get out in time?"

"Nope."

"That means Matson didn't clue him in that SatTek was collapsing."

"I guess not. And now he's got almost nothing, literally nothing if he loses his house."

"It must've jangled in his number-crunching brain that something was wrong when the FBI started poking around," Gage said.

"I don't think so. Look over there."

Viz pointed at another white block building housing AccuSoft, an accounting software company whose insider trading scandal rode the front pages for months.

"Gotcha," Gage said, nodding his head. "Don't-Call-Me-Bob must have thought SatTek was targeted for the same reason as they were."

"That's my guess."

Gage's eyes fell on the last slice of Viz's pizza and his mind looped back through their conversation. "Where's he eat lunch?"

"A Chinese place over on Tully."

"Maybe I should join him for a little kung pao chicken tomorrow."

"Great idea, then you can bring me back some pot stickers. And a mandarin beef." Viz held up his forefinger. "No, make it a mu shu pork. Or one of those—"

Gage made a show of studying his watch. "How about you try to decide between today and tomorrow?"

"Sure, boss, deciding on lunch is one of the few diversions for a surveillance guy."

Gage left Viz searching his mental menu, then slipped back into his car. He called Faith on her cell as he was driving back to his office.

"I'm here now." The words came out as a sigh, her tone answering what would've been his next question. There'd been no improvement.

Gage heard shuffling as she walked from Burch's room. "The doctors come by?"

"Kishore was in an hour ago, but only to give Courtney a hug and try to boost her spirits. The new critical care doctor strode into the room a few minutes ago as if he could do something, but after flipping through the chart and shining a light in Jack's eyes, he just stood there, kind of slump-shouldered, then shuffled away. It was heartbreaking and—"

Gage winced as Faith's voice caught. He imagined her and Courtney sitting for hours, their eyes darting toward the monitors, flinching at each beep, then looking to the doctors for reassurance that was never forthcoming.

"Then one of the nurses took Courtney aside and asked whether Jack had an advance directive, and then she just fell apart."

"I'll be there in forty minutes."

Chapter Twenty-six

Don't panic," Gage said when he dropped his business card on the table-for-two in the almost vacant Jade Garden Chinese Restaurant in San Jose twenty-four hours later.

"Private investigator?" the diner asked, looking up. "What did I do?"

"I think it may be something that got done to you." Gage glanced at the empty chair. "May I?"

"Sure. Why not? Things can't get any worse."

Gage sat down and rested his folded hands on the edge of the table, careful to make sure his suit jacket didn't touch. The plastic tablecloth was sticky, the soy sauce bottle was grimy, and the napkin holder was empty.

"How's the food?" Gage asked.

"Cheap and better than bringing my lunch."

Robert Milsberg picked up the card. "Graham Gage, Private Investigator. San Francisco." He then looked at Gage. "I knew somebody would come knocking, I just figured it would be the FBI."

"You mean you haven't been interviewed?"

Milsberg should've been the first on the list at SatTek after Matson.

"Not yet." Milsberg offered a weak smile. "I assumed they were still gathering documents and then they'd call us in one by one."

"About what?"

"The whole freaking thing. Even Matson..." He peered across the table at Gage. "I guess you know about Matson if you're talking to me. Even Matson says they haven't questioned him yet."

"What's the whole freaking thing?"

"You know or you wouldn't be sitting here."

"It looks like a pump and dump with an offshore angle."

Milsberg jabbed the air with his chopsticks. "Bingo. Matson and me both got slammed by Granger and that lawyer in San Francisco, Burch. That son of a bitch. Matson lost almost a million and me one-point-two."

A listless waitress wandered up to the table, order pad in hand.

"What's good?" Gage asked Milsberg.

"Chow fun. Beef chow fun."

"That's fine," Gage told her, and she shuffled off toward the kitchen.

Milsberg cleaned his glasses with a handkerchief. Pale skin surrounded reddened eyes and a comb-over that was graying and far less than adequate. He reminded Gage of those awkward kids in high school whose body parts seemed to grow at different rates.

"Who you working for?" Milsberg asked.

"Some of the shareholders." Gage had planned the lie in advance. Better that Milsberg believed that Gage's clients were fellow victims, rather than one of those he thought were the masterminds. "Most are devastated. Others are just pissed."

"Not half as much as me. Once this all hits the papers, I won't even get hired to count eggs at a chicken farm." He didn't laugh at his own attempted joke. "What's your theory?"

Gage took a chance, saying a little more than he could yet prove. "Fake receivables paid for by selling stock."

Milsberg nodded. "That'll be the headline all right."

"Why are you still hanging around?"

"We still have some orders to fill and somebody's got to do the books. There's enough money coming in to cover our reduced salaries. It's not much, but I've got a kid in college, so a little is better than none."

The waitress set a pot of tea, a cup, and a napkin in front of Gage.

"When did you figure it out?" Gage asked.

"One day too late. There was something weird since just before we went public. We'd get these big orders from Asia, but I never knew how. We never had a sales staff out there. I'd ask Matson. He'd tell me that it was through Granger's connections. That's why the board approved his fees. A couple of hundred grand in two years. I could understand the orders from Europe. Matson was traveling there all the time, working the market. That's what he was always good at, sales. He could sell a pork sandwich to a vegan—twice."

Milsberg poked around in his chow fun with his chopsticks.

"It was only after the collapse that Matson told me that Granger and Burch set up a bunch of burn companies...You know what burn companies are, right?"

Gage nodded.

"When Matson went back after the collapse, the customers were gone. Poof. Up in smoke."

Milsberg set down his chopsticks.

"If it weren't for our pastor, my wife would've divorced me. She's kind of a religious nut. She used to teach this marriage class at the church. You know, 'It's not a contract, it's a covenant with God.' That kind of stuff. Naïve. She says I'm naïve. She never liked Matson. She thought he was slick. And Madge. My wife saw through her the first time they met. But you can't blame Matson. He looks at his wife, he still sees what she was like when they first got together. We're all that way."

Gage had come to the restaurant ready for psychological combat with an accountant constantly calculating his position, but what he saw before him was a fragile, flailing man.

"It's called being human."

"I guess so. But you didn't come here to listen to me ramble on."

"It's okay. You've had a tough couple of months."

"I wasn't sure whether to blow my brains out or Granger's or Burch's."

Gage's eyes went dark.

Milsberg pulled back and held up his hands. "I didn't shoot Burch. It wasn't me." He shook his head. "I haven't the stomach for any kind of violence." He hunched forward again and stared down at this chow fun. "I can only eat this stuff because I don't think about how cow becomes beef."

Gage glanced toward the door. "How about we go for a walk?" he said. "Get some fresh air. Talk a little more."

"Sure. I got nothing much to do at the office. What about your lunch?"

"She can pack it up. I know somebody who'll eat it."

Gage drove Milsberg to Coyote Creek Park. They entered the Japanese Friendship Garden, bought fish food pellets, and walked to the crest of the bridge over the koi pond.

"You don't know me," Gage said, as he tossed a few pellets to the koi schooling below, "and I don't know you."

"That's not quite true."

"How do you figure?"

"I'll bet you've met a lot of Robert Milsbergs in your career and you take them to comforting places like this for a little heart-to-heart."

"You're an insightful guy."

"Sometimes too much. You know what I wanted to be when I was in college? A poet. I wanted to be a poet. And I could write, too." Milsberg tore open his bag of pellets. "There was something heroic about being a poet. Now look at me. I'm as broke as if I was one. But I ain't no hero. I'm a middle-aged guy who screwed up his life."

Milsberg leaned over the wooden railing and stared down toward the water, his eyes losing focus, then he blinked hard and tossed a few pellets to the koi.

"You know haiku?" Milsberg asked, watching the fish vacuum them up.

"Of course."

"Try this one: *The somber wind stills, the dark river of pain speaks, of what might have been.*"

"That could be anyone."

"But it's me. I write haiku to keep from jumping off the Golden Gate Bridge." Milsberg sighed, still staring at the koi. "What do you need?"

"Look at me," Gage said, as if a father to his son.

Milsberg turned to face him.

"You tried to ride this scam, didn't you?"

Milsberg glanced away, then returned his eyes to Gage's.

"I shouldn't have. But I did. Everybody said we had great products, ones the country really needed. And I thought everything would work out in the end."

"But it didn't. And a lot of people suffered, not just you."

"Maybe I'm lucky. I'm still young enough to earn it again."

"But not the old folks who lost all of their retirement money."

Milsberg hesitated, off balance, as if for the first time seeing the victims in his mind's eye. "No. Not them."

"And you knew Matson was in on it?"

"Yes."

"And you did what he told you?"

"Yes. And my name is all over the paperwork. Even the SEC filings."

Gage pulled a photograph out of his suit pocket, holding it by the bottom center between his thumb and forefinger.

"You know what building this is?"

"Sure." Milsberg shrugged. "It's the Federal Building in San Francisco. I went there a few times to pick up tax forms, back when the IRS had an office on the first floor."

"And what's in the Federal Building now?"

"Courts, U.S. Attorney, FBI."

Gage moved his thumb.

Milsberg's head jerked forward. Eyes riveted on the small figure walking toward the entrance. "That son of a bitch!"

Chapter Twenty-seven

Mr. Gage, this is Robert Milsberg."

Gage glanced at his watch. 9:01 A.M. He was surprised by the call so soon after their talk the previous day.

"What's up?"

"I've been thinking about our conversation. And I talked to my wife. She reads situations pretty well. For her everything is basically black and white. Maybe that's what religion does for her. She doesn't think the U.S. Attorney will believe me if I tell him that I was just doing what Matson told me to do. And she figures since they made the deal with him first, he's their guy. She says they're invested, no pun intended. They're invested in him."

"She's right. That's exactly how it works."

"And I'm thinking, they don't need me anyway, except to make their indictment longer and pump up their stats."

"I think so, too."

"You know, there's a rule in writing. It's called show, don't tell. And if they won't believe what I say, then I'll just show them who Matson really is."

Gage held his breath. He was a heartbeat away from getting inside SatTek, but he couldn't risk Milsberg later finding out the truth and bailing out when Gage needed him most. "Robert, there's something you need to know before you tell me anything else."

"About Jack Burch?"

"Yes."

"I was wondering if there was a connection. I saw the look on your face when I talked about wanting to shoot him. His wife hire you?"

"No. I volunteered." Gage knew that he had to give Milsberg a picture of Burch that would give him confidence that he was doing the right thing. "This isn't about money. I've known him half my life. The worst he can be accused of is negligence, not realizing what Matson was really up to—but there's mitigation. Matson showed up right after Burch's wife was diagnosed with breast cancer. We didn't know if she'd survive. He just stopped thinking, his mind followed his heart and his heart was with her."

"Until just now all I knew about Burch was what that asshole Matson told me." Milsberg paused, then said, "I won't help you try to get him off, but I'll do what I can to make sure he gets his day in court. He at least deserves a chance to clear himself."

Gage clenched his fist. "That's enough for me."

Milsberg exhaled. "Now it's time for show, don't tell…Get this. Matson's flying to London tomorrow."

"Did he say why?"

"He didn't say anything. I got a peek at the receptionist's message pad."

"What's the flight?"

"United 930. First-class. Can you believe it? The company is in the tank and he's traveling first-class, 12:50 P.M. out of SFO."

"Good work. Maybe you should've been a private eye."

"No. I should've been a poet. Then I wouldn't have ended up in this mess."

◇◇◇

Gage hung up, checked his contact list, then dialed a London number.

"Mickey, it's Graham."

"You old gaffer. How's work?"

"Complicated. How's retirement?"

"Bloody boring. I couldn't wait to get out of police work, now I miss it like my best chum."

"What's your schedule like for the next few days?"

"The same as always—except when you call with a little job. Cheap tea and the *Times* crossword."

"You ready for another one?"

"Willing and still able. What's the topic?"

"You on the Internet?"

"Only through my grandson."

"Have him do a search on a company called SatTek. It's a stock scam. My friend, a lawyer in San Francisco, is being set up to take the fall."

"What do you need me to do?"

"Help me tail the company president. Two hundred pounds a shift for each guy you need to bring in. I'll be coming in on his flight into Heathrow."

Chapter Twenty-eight

Twenty-four hours later, Gage was standing in the economy line at the international terminal at SFO waiting for Matson. When first-class was called, Gage watched Matson stroll to the front and nonchalantly present his ticket to the ground crew.

Gage pulled out his cell phone, then cupped his hand over his mouth. Mickey picked up the call on the first ring.

"He's about five foot nine, mid-forties, brown hair, a little pudgy," Gage said quietly. "Unless he changes clothes on the plane, he'll be wearing tan slacks, a yellow button-down shirt, and a dark brown sweater. He's carrying an attaché case, a camel overcoat, and a suit bag."

"Will you be able to stay with him?" Mickey asked.

"He'll be getting off before me, so I'll probably lose him at passport control, but I'll catch up at baggage claim."

◇◇◇

Gage called Mickey as he followed Matson through customs, and stayed on the phone as Matson met a woman in the arrivals hall. Gage scanned the crowd until he spotted Mickey by an exit. Late sixties, gray-haired, alert eyes that darted, never resting too long on Matson and not reacting when he spotted Gage.

"Did you see the dumplings on that one?" Mickey asked Gage "She's a tidy package."

"Mickey, you're supposed to be watching *him*."

"May they stay as close together as a banger in a bun for as long as he's in London. Amen."

"I have a feeling they will. What do you think? French? German?"

"With her Eurasian features and those tight pants? I'll bet Russian or Ukrainian."

"In any case," Gage said, "they're all yours. I'm heading for the hotel. Keep me up on what they do."

"With delight," Mickey said. "And by the way, thanks for getting me out of the house."

Gage took the Heathrow Express train to Paddington Underground Station, then caught a cab to his hotel. By the time he checked in and unpacked, Mickey called.

"She took him to a flat in Knightsbridge. Right off Brompton Road. It must've cost a bomb. Top floor. And she was driving a Jaguar XK, red."

"Convertible?" Gage asked.

"Right. How'd you know?"

"You've seen the guy. What else would it be? Did you see the way he draped his sweater over his shoulders like some… what's the word?"

"Would that be a five-letter word down or a seven-letter word across?"

"Take your pick."

"Dandy or coxcomb." Mickey chuckled. "I'm sure either one will do."

"You think you can find out who owns the flat and the car?"

"My dear, dear Gage." Mickey's voice oozed with mock disappointment at Gage's seeming lack of respect for his talents and his remaining connections in the Metropolitan Police.

"Sorry. *Will* you find out who owns the flat and the car?"

"It'll be my pleasure."

"I'm going to take a nap and try to head off some of the jet lag. Come by at 11 A.M. I'm in 1704 at the Carleton Tower."

◇◇◇

Gage knew exactly what time it was when he heard the knock at his door.

"I like the beard," Gage told retired Superintendent of Police Mickey Ransford. "It makes you look like a fuzzy old bear."

"The wife says it tickles. Apparently, after forty-three years of marriage I've become cute again."

Gage smiled to himself as Mickey stepped through the doorway. Just a few years earlier, Mickey's subordinates had variously compared him to a bloodhound, a bulldog, and a pit bull. Somehow, in retirement, he'd devolved into a pug.

Gage directed Mickey to a couch, then poured tea from a service resting on a side table and sat in a matching armchair.

"Any chance Matson spotted you?" Gage asked.

"No. Old men like me are like lost house keys. You don't pay them any mind until they're gone, and then you can't find them."

Mickey stirred sugar into his tea. "There's an old Ukrainian saying." He looked up, winking. "It's something like, 'Old age is not a blessing.'"

"So you were right."

"As always. Alla Petrovna Tarasova. A long-legged Ukrainian with a beautiful name. Tourist visa. Extended."

"And who owns the flat?"

"TAMS Limited, registered in Wales."

"T…A…M…S…Let me guess." Gage smiled. "Tarasova-Alla-Matson-Stuart."

"That's how the smart money is betting."

"Did you happen to find out—"

"Morely Alden Fitzhugh IV, chartered account. Director. A memorable name."

Gage felt SatTek's offshore financial universe begin to rotate around a fixed point. "That's the same guy who's head of a holding company connected to SatTek."

Mickey squinted toward the ceiling and raised a forefinger. "How do your American girls say it?" He grinned, then looked at Gage. "I…don't…*think*…so."

"What? You mean there are two guys with that name?"

"There isn't even one with that name. There was, of course, until last week when his various components were found drifting about in the Thames. As I said, a memorable name. One must pass through the news sections of the *Times* to reach the crossword puzzle."

A wave of jet lag shuddered through Gage's body. The fixed point turned out to be a black hole.

"And no. No one was arrested. The home secretary was quoted as claiming that the Russian *maffiya* was responsible. But it's budget time in Parliament so one can't take these sorts of announcements seriously. Blaming Russian gangsters for everything is quite popular among the political classes. For all we know, there was a domestic quarrel and he simply went to pieces under his wife's wrath."

Mickey's cell phone rang.

"A taxi just picked up Matson," Mickey said. "Shall we join the chase?"

Gage slipped on a jacket and dropped a digital camera into his breast pocket. Mickey guided him from the hotel to a black London cab parked on a bordering street.

"We're lucky," Gage said, after getting into the back with Mickey.

"Luck has nothing to do with it." Mickey aimed a finger at the driver, a stocky man leaning toward the steering wheel, gripping it with both hands. "Meet Hixon One. Sergeant, Metropolitan Police, retired."

"Is there a Hixon Two?"

"Certainly," Mickey answered. "Following Matson."

"Nice to meet you Mr. Gage," Hixon One said, pulling into traffic.

While Mickey relayed the directions from the car following Matson, Hixon One fought the midday traffic from Sloane Street, to Kensington Road, and finally to Kensington High Street, where he pulled over.

"Hixon Two says Matson went into that pub over there." Mickey pointed across the street at a heavy wooden door, the center of which was occupied by a stained glass image of an ax. "Shall I go in?"

"No. Send Hixon Two. But tell him the guy Matson's meeting may not be as naïve as he is."

"You mean her."

"How do you know Matson's meeting a woman?"

"No. Hixon Two is a she."

"My daughter," Hixon One said, smiling and reaching for his cell phone. "Reconnaissance and Surveillance Regiment, SAS, on leave, helping her old man out. Eighteen months from now we'll be Hixon & Hixon, Enquiry Agents, Limited."

Gage scanned the sidewalks, cars, storefronts, and apartment windows above for countersurveillance or for others also tailing Matson.

A young woman wearing black pants and a fur-necked jacket slowed near the entrance to the Ax Man Pub. She stopped to read the specials written in chalk on a green board attached to the wall, then pushed the door open and walked in.

Hixon One glanced over his shoulder at Gage, and smiled with a father's pride. "Lovely, isn't she?"

Gage nodded. "And no one would ever guess what she does for a living." He grabbed the door handle. "I need to get a closer look at some of the guys on the street." He glanced at Hixon One. "Why don't you stay here?" Then at Mickey. "How about a little fresh air?"

Mickey climbed out after him and they walked along the sidewalk to the corner, stopping first at a flower stand, then inside West London Newsagents for cover while surveying the street.

"You see them?" Gage whispered to Mickey, peering out through the window.

"I see one, the rather stout fellow on the opposite corner."

"Look at the third car down from the pub, the dark blue Rover."

"Ah yes," Mickey said, "a disturbingly unattractive little creature. His face looks like a bleached prune." He chuckled. "His mother must be quite embarrassed."

Gage nodded toward a silver Mercedes directly in front of the pub. "I think that one may be part of this, too." He then glanced back and forth between the automobiles. The license plates of both were blocked by the cars bracketing them. "We need the numbers. I'll slip by the Rover."

Gage scanned the news rack and grabbed a London map. Mickey paid for it while Gage headed toward the door and adopted the puzzled but earnest expression of a tourist. He walked toward the next intersection, while Mickey strolled back the way they came.

They met at the cab five minutes later.

"Cheap suit," Mickey said, pointing at the Mercedes and settling into the backseat next to Gage. "Foreign."

"The suit?" Gage asked.

"No, the biceps. Quite expansive. The fellow is an absolute giant. Like one of these Greco-Roman wrestlers in the Olympics. Probably Eastern or Central European."

Hixon One wrote down the plate numbers, then dialed his cell phone and passed them on. After listening for a moment, he disconnected and looked back at Gage. "They're both registered to something called UES Holdings Limited on West Cromwell Road."

Gage called Alex Z. "Sorry to wake you up, but I need you to run something."

"No problem. I was lying awake and thinking about how I'd feel if my father had been shot down like Mr. Burch. If you don't mind, I think I'll meet my dad for breakfast."

"That's a good idea. You're lucky to have him."

"I've been realizing that more and more every day," Alex Z said. "What do you need?"

"Find out everything you can about UES Holdings Limited in London."

Twenty minutes later Alex Z called back.

"I ran a registration search on the UK Companies House Web site. UES has the same address as Fitzhugh. Looks like there are a hundred offices in the building, mostly lawyers and accountants."

"E-mail me everything you downloaded, then run a newspaper search on Fitzhugh. He was murdered last week."

"Jeez. Be careful, boss."

Just then Matson stomped out of the Ax Man. He started to hail a cab, but dropped his arm and marched up Kensington High Street, hands jammed into his coat pockets.

"Mickey," Gage said, "follow him on foot. I'll stay here and take photos. Have Hixon Two pick you up if he grabs a cab. We'll meet at my room when you think he's in for the night."

Chapter Twenty-nine

Hixon One, parked down the block from Matson's flat, gave himself a discreet scratch, then settled in for the evening. Alla emerged a half hour later dressed in a blue Marks & Spencer running suit. She stretched for a few minutes against the black wrought-iron fence surrounding the property, then ran off, her long legs beating a practiced rhythm.

Gage had just disconnected from Hixon One's update when Mickey and Hixon Two arrived at his room. He directed them to the couch and again sat in the wing chair.

"Is Two what people really call you?" Gage asked.

"Family and friends," she said. "My mother died when I was four. Since then it's been Pop and me, One and Two."

She looked even younger up close, but her eyes had a mature depth of experience.

"How long have you been in the service?"

"Almost five years. Three in regular army and two in Reconnaissance and Surveillance. I joined after college. It was Uncle Mickey's idea."

"Where'd they send you?"

Hixon Two grinned. "Around."

"Good answer." Gage leaned forward. "So, tell me what happened inside the Ax Man."

She straightened up, as if preparing to report to a superior.

"Matson met Russians. Or at least Central Europeans who spoke Russian to each other. Mostly friendly. At one point it got tense, then it lightened up. But I'm not sure the meeting ended well."

"That was our impression, too." Gage reached over and opened his laptop to display the digital photos he snapped outside the Ax Man after Matson stormed out. He'd numbered them one through thirty-seven. He turned the computer toward her.

Hixon Two studied the first fifteen spread across the screen. "Number three, six, and eleven were the ones who met with Matson."

She pressed the page-down button, then worked her finger across along the images.

"Sixteen is the bodyguard. A giant. He came in just for a minute, otherwise he was in a Mercedes outside. Number three did almost all the talking." She looked up at Gage. "I don't recognize anyone else."

"Could you hear what they were saying?"

"I played girly-girl at the bar in order not to be too obvious, so I didn't catch much of the conversation. I went to the WC twice so I could walk by the table. All I caught was 'leave him out of it' and 'when the time comes.' At one point Matson raised his voice a little and said 'arranger' or 'ranger' or some word like that a couple of times."

"Could it be Granger?"

"Yes, I think that could be it. At one point number three took off his jacket and rolled up his sleeves. I saw a tattoo on his arm." She reached into her pants pocket and pulled out a bar napkin that bore a detailed drawing. "It was like this." She handed it to Gage. "But I don't know what it means. It's not the kind Russian soldiers get."

"It means number three is a thief-in-the-law," Gage said, "a *vory-v-zakone*. Each point represents a year in prison. There are only a few hundred *vorys* in the world. If they were Italian mafia, we'd call them made men. But these are Russians and Ukrainians and it's a lot tougher to get made. Even a guy like John Gotti wouldn't have made it past gofer."

"Shouldn't they be called thieves outside the law?" Hixon Two asked.

"It's law in the sense of a thief's code."

"Like a no snitching rule?"

"Exactly." Gage closed his laptop. The click echoed in the now silent room. He looked back and forth between her and Mickey. "How about I take you two out for dinner and we can make plans for tomorrow?"

Heads nodded.

"How about Indian?" Mickey said, smiling. "A little chicken tikka, a little tandoori, a few chapattis. Food in London is wonderful. It's the only surviving benefit of imperialism. Anytime we want, we get to eat food from all the colonies we've been thrown out of."

◇◇◇

Gage sent them home after dinner, then returned to his hotel room to check his e-mails. One from Faith was waiting. She'd sent it just after meeting Courtney at the hospital: Burch's doctors had reported that his condition remained unchanged.

After logging off, Gage rose and looked out of his seventeenth floor window at the city lights, the traffic sounds muffled by glass and elevation. He imagined Burch lying in his bed, insulated from life by his coma. For a moment, he wished that Burch could remain there, suspended in time and space, at least long enough for Gage to construct a seawall around him; for if Burch regained consciousness now, it would be only to see a wave cresting above him.

A whelping ambulance siren passing on the street below shook Gage's mind free of the fantasy. Whatever the doctors' intent may have been in saying it, the notion that Burch's condition could be unchanged was at best an evasion to comfort Courtney, and at worst a delusion. The truth was that each day he would get weaker and his body would become less able to fight toward daylight.

Chapter Thirty

Plump little Totie Fitzhugh had spent the week after her husband's murder sorting through his papers—at least the ones the police and Agent Zink hadn't taken, and the ones hidden in the pantry. As she was the only employee, she was not unfamiliar with the companies her husband managed, and where he secreted what he called his Special Project files.

Agent Zink had seemed pleased when he left and said he'd covered all the bases, an American idiom she didn't at all understand. He also invited her to San Francisco to testify at a grand jury two weeks later. Expenses paid. She'd never visited San Francisco, so she gladly accepted. One never knew, perhaps she might find a stash of her husband's money there.

◇◇◇

As Alla drove them toward the Fitzhughs' detached cottage west of London, Matson didn't know how Totie would greet him. Calling her Isabella, the name of Fitzhugh's Lugano girlfriend, the first time they met hadn't been a good beginning. Matson wondered whether this was the reason she hadn't returned his increasingly urgent calls since he'd arrived in London.

Mickey, trying to stay with Alla through the morning commute traffic, nearly croqueted a Mini into the rear of her Jaguar when she sped up unexpectedly, then abruptly slowed. For the first mile, Gage thought she was engaged in rather daring countersurveillance, but then concluded that it was rather daring for her to be driving at all.

Jet lag hadn't ceased making occasional visits to Gage, so over Mickey's small objection, he opened the passenger window of the boxy white Volvo sedan. The chilly mid-November air buffeted the interior and cleared his head as they drove into the countryside. The image of Fitzhugh as a black hole returned, but with the sense that, at least for the moment, he remained the gravitational center of the SatTek's offshore money flow.

Alla turned from a narrow lane into a hedge-lined driveway. The stucco and timber Tudor cottage sat toward the back of the large, wooded lot. She parked near the front door.

Mickey pointed at the house number, "It's Fitzhugh's." He then pulled to a stop across the lane in a spot offering just a glimpse of Matson and Alla as they stood knocking, Alla in a waist-length fur jacket and gray slacks, Matson in a black wool overcoat.

"Bli-mey," Mickey said. "Look at those legs."

Gage watched Matson knock, first lightly, then vigorously. Alla pinched her nose and brushed away a bug buzzing around Matson's face, then swiped at one near her ear and scurried back into the Jaguar. Matson knocked a few more times, then also returned to the car. The two of them sat looking at the unanswered door as if deciding whether to wait or come back later when the occupant returned. After a few minutes they drove off.

"I think we better go in," Gage said, "before the police do. It may be the only chance we'll ever have."

"I was thinking the same thing. I'll ring up Hixon One and ask him to catch on to Matson when they return to the flat."

Five minutes after the Jaguar pulled away, Mickey drove to the front of the cottage. Neither he nor Gage bothered to knock on the front door. Gage walked down the left side of the house peering into the windows. Mickey took the right. They met at the rear.

"She's in the dining room," Gage said.

Since he was the younger by nearly twenty years, it fell to Gage to kick in the back door. Impatient houseflies pursuing decaying flesh raced in with them.

◇◇◇

An hour and a half later Chief Inspector Devlin and Homicide Inspector Rees arrived to assume control over the crime scene from the local branch of the Metropolitan Police.

"Superintendent Ransford," Devlin said, reaching out his hand. "I never expected to find you in a place like this again."

"Well, Eamonn, if it weren't for my friend Mr. Gage here, I wouldn't be." Mickey pointed first to his left, then to his right. "Mr. Gage, Chief Inspector Devlin. By the way Eamonn, I'm now officially Mickey."

"So…Mickey. What do we have here and how did you end up in the middle of it?"

"I'll let Mr. Gage fill you in."

◇◇◇

"Apparently, you failed to mention to Devlin that we followed Matson out to the Fitzhugh cottage," Mickey said, as he and Gage sat in a borrowed blue Fiat parked just west of Matson's flat late in the afternoon.

"There were so many details to remember, it could've slipped my mind. How about I'll drop him a line when I get back to the States?"

"Excellent." Mickey's eyes lit up. "And equally excellent is the timely emergence of the lovely Alla, as if a butterfly from a cocoon. Unfortunately, the water beetle is with her."

Mickey fell in behind Alla's Jaguar as she led them haltingly from Knightsbridge, through Kensington toward Notting Hill Gate, then pulled into a space near Holland Park. Mickey found a spot near the squash courts and crawled out of the Fiat to follow Matson and Alla on foot. He returned fifteen minutes later, mixed in among the aging pigeon feeders while he checked for countersurveillance, then drifted away and called Gage.

"They both went into the Ukrainian consulate. She presented a packet of papers to a clerk. I couldn't tell what it was. But I saw Matson reach for something in his coat pocket and pull out airline tickets to get to it. The ticket jackets were for Aurigny

Airlines. Bright red and yellow. Aurigny flies to Jersey, Guernsey, and Alderney in the Channel Islands."

Gage thought for a moment. "There's a company in Guernsey that's connected to SatTek, Cobalt Partners. Find out what Hixon Two is doing for the next few days."

"You don't want to do it?"

"No. I've got something else to take care of."

Matson and Alla returned to their car and drove directly back to the flat. After Gage was certain that they were in for the night, he returned to the hotel to start his something else.

Chapter Thirty-one

A *llo*," the heavy voice spoke into the phone.

"*Dobredin*, Slava, this is Graham Gage."

"What can I say? Little misunderstanding. We friends again. Right?" Slava didn't wait for a response. "Your little interpreter from America. What's his name?"

"Pavel."

"*Da*, Pavel." Slava laughed. "Saved your fucking life and he can't tell nobody how."

Pavel did it by losing bladder control when he thought the leader of Russia's largest organized crime group was about to blow Gage's brains down a Moscow street just weeks earlier. Gage smiled to himself as he remembered Slava's shadowed face transforming from fury to puzzlement as he watched a puddle form on the sidewalk around Pavel's shoes.

Slava laughed until he erupted in choking, wheezing coughs.

"Those cigars will kill you," Gage said, after Slava's coughing died down.

"No, other *vory-v-zakone* kill me, I just be smoking at time."

"I read about that car bomb in Tbilisi in the *Herald Tribune*. Helluva close call. I didn't even know you worked in Georgia."

"I went hunting."

"For whom?"

"For *what*. Wild boars."

"Somehow I can't imagine you hiking through the woods trying to sneak up on pigs."

"*Nyet*. Like farm. You sit in wood hut with bottle vodka, little fish *satsivi*, and rifle. After time, they come walking, and boom."

"Speaking of boom…"

"I all sorry I…" Slava paused as if he knew he hadn't gotten the phrasing quite right. "That how you say it?"

"Close enough."

"That guy, you know who I mean, I can't say name on phone, tricked me to think you set me up for hit. I not realize you just want to talk about natural gas deal. It broke my heart, you know, I thinking I have to kill you."

"You didn't *look* sorry."

"I cry on inside, really."

Gage didn't believe it. He found it hard to imagine that Slava ever cried, even as a baby. He let it go.

"You're almost forgiven."

"*Spaseeba*."

"And you're almost welcome."

Gage heard Slava draw on his cigar, then clear his throat. "I know you not call to talk old times," Slava said. "What you need?"

"To see you. Just an hour or so."

"Sure. I owe you."

"How about tomorrow in the city by the big lake?"

"Why not?" Slava once again erupted into hacking, followed by an explosive spit. "I want to visit my money anyway."

◇◇◇

By eleven o'clock on the following morning, Hixons One and Two had followed Matson and Alla to Victoria Station, then to Gatwick Airport, where Two followed them onto an Aurigny Airlines flight to Guernsey.

By 2:15 Gage was walking down the long neoclassical hallway from the reception area to the restaurant in the Metropole Hotel across a wide boulevard from Lake Geneva. As he crossed the threshold, he felt the enormous presence of Viacheslav Gregorovich Akimov, aka Slava. Gage's eyes were drawn to his right as if by gravitation. He spotted Slava sitting at a corner table with a bodyguard who carried Slava's same weight but on a frame that was a foot taller. Slava struggled to his feet as Gage approached. He was wearing his usual black wool suit and matching turtleneck, both in enormous sizes. He stuck out a hand and Gage shook as much of it as he could, then sat down. Slava introduced his bodyguard as Ivan Ivanovich, the Russian version of John Smith.

"You want little something?" Slava asked, signaling to the black-tied waiter, who approached with a menu.

Gage glanced at the first page, then handed it back. "Just smoked salmon and artichoke soup. What are you having?"

"Page two," Slava said, then stuffed most of a dinner roll into his mouth.

"Just one bodyguard?" Gage asked when the waiter was out of earshot.

"Here. Neutral. Meeting back in '92. Miami. Agreement. No hits in Switzerland." Slava laughed. "Bad to bleed on money."

Slava sniffed a half-filled glass of fifteen-year-old Bordeaux and smacked his lips. "Ah! Only good thing about France."

Gage watched Slava take a sip, then close his eyes and slosh the wine around in his mouth; his ruthless criminality redeemed for a few seconds—but only for a few—in his willingness to suspend himself in the pleasure of the moment.

Slava opened his eyes, then nodded. "Sveta would like this."

"How is she?"

"Good. Good. At spa in Montreux. Keep her relaxed. Thank God." Slava looked heavenward, then sighed. He picked up a piece of dried *Grisons* beef and shoved it into his mouth just ahead of a much more aggressive draw on the Bordeaux.

"Hey, I got something for your wife." Slava wiped his hands on the white tablecloth, then reached into his coat pocket and retrieved a satin pouch. He poured a ruby onto the white tablecloth.

"Is this hot?" Gage asked, picking it up and examining it.

"Stolen?" Slava stretched out his hands, palms up. "I not give you nothing stolen. I paid. Myself. Out my own pocket."

"And the money?"

"Money is money."

"Thanks." Gage set down the stone. "But I'll pass."

"Gage, you always too straight for your own good. But that's why I trust you...except that once. So what you want to talk about?"

"I need to see if you can identify some guys I saw in London."

Slava narrowed his eyes at Gage. "How come?"

"A friend of mine is in a little trouble."

"Good friend?"

"Best. Jack Burch."

"Burch?" Slava glanced toward his bodyguard, then toward the entrance. He leaned forward, clenching his fists on the table, his face turning crimson.

Gage realized too late that he introduced the subject in the wrong way. While natural gas was off his radar, it was still blinking in the center of Slava's.

Slava's voice was as insistent as a diesel rock crusher. "I not have anything to do with that. If that's why you—"

Gage flattened his palms against the bottom of the table, ready to flip it over on them if Ivan or Slava made a move. "That's not—"

"Nobody in gas deal touch Burch. Nobody. Not Russia. Not Ukraine. My people look. Turn everything upside down."

Gage shook his head. "It was something else. A stock fraud. A company called SatTek."

Slava hesitated, then relaxed his fists and leaned back. A self-conscious smile appeared on his face and he shook his head and exhaled. "I think I need vacation. Get too tense, too fast. Maybe I go to Montreux after Sveta leave."

Gage lowered his hands to his lap. "The place not big enough for the two of you?"

"Few places big enough for one of me." Slava grinned, then took a gulp of wine and set the glass down. "Okay. Business. What kind trouble your friend?"

"He set up some companies that were used in a fraud."

"In States?" Slava shrugged. "I know nothing about States."

"The stock was issued in the U.S., but the companies that bought it were in all the usual offshore tax havens."

Gage pulled out prints of the photos he took outside the Ax Man Pub.

Slava pushed his plate away and laid them out. He picked up each in turn, inspected it, then laid it down. He took a sip of wine, then gazed out of the side window toward the landmark Jet d'Eau fountain. He then focused on photo number three, showing a blockish, square-headed, flat-faced, forty-year-old man with thin lips surrounded by ruddy skin. To Gage it gave the impression of a face that led its body up the hard way and was fated to live on for another generation in photo lineups and grainy covert videos.

"Gravilov," Slava said. "*Vory-v-zakone* from Moscow. He protect Ukraine president son. Like umbrella. You know, *krysha*, roof. Son in dirty stuff. Needs one of us to protect interests. Big man needs a big *krysha*. Gravilov is biggest in Eastern Ukraine since I left for Moscow."

"As in the Russian Gravilov Group?"

"*Da*. Does lots of paper scams. Got people in States."

Slava examined the others. "Number six, I not know. Eleven is Velichko, Boris Vasilievich. Russian, too. Independent. *Biznessman*." He turned sixteen toward Ivan Ivanovich, who grunted his professional opinion.

"Molotok," Slava said. "Hammer. Work for Gravilov. Can't tie own shoes."

"Why does Gravilov keep him around?"

Slava smirked. "To stop bullet. What else?"

"And the little guy in the Rover?"

"Chechen. His name is Britva. I see him in Kiev once. Ugly." Slava pointed toward Quai Général Guisan, the tree-lined boulevard bordering Lake Geneva. "I think one time of putting contract on him to celebrate day where everybody clean streets."

"International Earth Day."

"*Da*. International Earth Day."

"What's Britva mean?"

"Razor. He like cutting people. Maybe revenge for disgusting appearance. Face all twisted."

Gage pointed at the photos. "What would bring Gravilov and Velichko together?"

"Big money. Maybe even your stock fraud. Velichko is launderer. Offshore. Otherwise I not know. I ask my people. More Russians or Ukrainians in this?"

"A stockbroker named Kovalenko in California. He handled the domestic sale of SatTek stock."

Slava squinted into the distance for a moment. "I knew a Kovalenko once. In Belarus. Old, old man. No sons."

The waiter approached with Gage's meal. Slava covered the photos.

"How this scam work?" Slava asked. "Maybe I learn something."

While they ate Gage described the SatTek false invoices, the offshore companies, the bank accounts, and the pump and dump. He also described the shooting of Burch and the murders of the Fitzhughs.

"I think Matson is trying to cut a deal with the U.S. Attorney to lay the whole thing off on Burch," Gage concluded. "And somebody is trying to contain the case by killing off the potential defendants."

"Strange," Slava said, expressionless as a shark. "Usually we just kill witness."

"I didn't need to hear that."

"You heard worse."

"Yeah. I've heard worse." Gage thought for a moment. "There's one more. A woman Matson is involved with in London. Alla Tarasova."

Slava drew back. "Tarasova?"

"Yeah."

"What's her patronymic?"

"Petrovna. Alla Petrovna Tarasova."

Slava looked at Ivan Ivanovich, then clucked.

"Petrov Tarasov. Got to be father. Budapest. Business there. Sell Ukraine steel. But real money in protection racket and money laundering." Slava raised his eyebrows. "Maybe even SatTek money. You know *skhodka*?"

"Sure, the *vory-v-zakone* internal court."

"One in Budapest last year. Tarasov was head. I sat. Maybe he use daughter to stay close to guy in scam." Slava propped his forearms on the table and cupped his hands together. "Maybe Tarasov even make syndicate to do deal. How much money?"

"At least fifty million shares were sold, maybe more. It started at two dollars but topped out at over six."

"So maybe two-fifty, three hundred million dollars?"

"At least."

Slava shook his head. "Matson better watch back. When Alla Petrovna tell Poppa time for Matson to go, he go. And that happen right after Gravilov and Tarasov grab Matson money." He grinned. "Matson think they launder for him, but they take him to cleaners."

◇◇◇

After leaving Slava to finish the menu, Gage walked along Lake Geneva. He needed to get himself oriented in a new SatTek world, one that now contained two gangsters nearly at Slava's level and linked to Matson, either of whom could've reached across the Atlantic and ordered the hit on Jack Burch.

He called Faith. She was driving to UC Berkeley to teach an early morning anthro class.

"Jack opened his eyes," Faith told him, her voice giddy. "He's out of the coma. I just got the call." Gage's legs wobbled as if a weight was lifted from his shoulders and he wasn't ready. He stopped, then leaned against a tree. "Graham?"

"I'm still here. I just…"

"I know. He still needs the breathing tube. But he's responding, so they hope there's no brain damage. Where are you?"

"Geneva."

"I can't wait until you get home."

"Me too. Tell Jack…"

"I will."

Gage started walking toward Rue du Leman to find a taxi, wishing he was flying back to San Francisco, then called Spike Pacheco at SFPD Homicide.

"Sorry, man," Spike said. "I'm no closer to finding the shooter."

"I don't think it was road rage. It has to be SatTek and it somehow involves Russians and Ukrainians. I don't know how it all fits together but they're everywhere I turn."

"I'll throw it in the mix and see if it fizzes," Spike said. "Anything else new?"

"Yeah. Jack's back."

Chapter Thirty-two

They only had eyes for each other," Mickey told Gage when he slid into the Volvo outside Heathrow Airport after his Swiss Air flight from Geneva. "Two could've followed them right into their Guernsey hotel room and they wouldn't have seen her."

"How'd they spend the day?"

"They got themselves a room at the Old Government House Hotel in St. Peter Port," Mickey said, "then met with a lawyer at LaFleur & Sedgwick. They finished the day with a late dinner on the waterfront. Two said the owner greeted Matson like a regular and kissed the lovely Alla like she was his own daughter."

"Trust me. He doesn't want a daughter like her."

"Oh no." Mickey's head swung toward Gage. "Don't ruin an old man's fantasy."

"Her pop is a crime boss working out of Budapest. She may have fingered my friend and the Fitzhughs."

Mickey sighed. "So the beauty is a beast."

"That's all the more reason Two has to stick with them."

"She's gotten the best training the British Army can provide. She's like a chameleon. If she can't, no one can."

◇◇◇

Gage spent the next morning in his hotel room reading and responding to e-mail updates from investigators in his office, all the while grateful that he'd been able to recruit men and women with the judgment both to manage their own investigations and to understand how much Gage needed to know in order to manage the firm.

When Mickey arrived for lunch, he reported that Two had followed Matson and Alla from Guernsey to Lugano.

"And get this," Mickey said, as he held up his forkful of Mediterranean chicken in the Park Lane Brasserie. "Alla was using a Panamanian passport. Two saw it, but couldn't see the name."

"Which means she could evaporate any time."

Mickey nodded, then washed the chicken down with a sip of beer. "What do you want to do this afternoon?"

"Research two UK companies. Why don't you finish up here and I'll get the information my office sent."

Mickey grinned. "And the papers you stole from Fitzhugh's house?"

Gage looked over and winked. "Those, too."

◇◇◇

By 4:40 P.M. the Companies House clerk was alternately glancing at the clock and at Gage. A few more minutes and she wouldn't have to accept any more file requests, and could gather up her coat and purse in preparation for her escape from the fortresslike repository of the histories of the two million companies registered in the UK.

Preoccupied with the clock, she didn't see Mickey sliding in just under the wire. "Thanks, darling," he said, after she accepted the file request. He could see in her smile that she found him too cute to get annoyed at.

Mickey's cell phone rang. He answered it, then walked over to where Gage sat before a monitor examining scanned corporate filings and financial statements. "Two has an update."

Gage took the phone and stepped outside the building.

"I think I better break it off," Two said. "I've been around them too long."

"Where'd they go today?"

"They spent about a half hour at Banca Rober and about an hour at Barclays. Now it looks like they're on the way to the airport. I'll probably get burned if I follow them in. They had 'good job, well done' looks on their faces when they left the last meeting so they may be on their way back to London."

At 8:30 P.M., Gage received a call from Hixon One at Gatwick. "The lovebirds have landed."

Chapter Thirty-three

Faith was waiting curbside when Gage walked out of the international terminal at San Francisco Airport the next afternoon, a few hours after Matson's flight had landed. Gage gave her a kiss, then climbed in.

"How's Jack?" Gage asked as they drove away.

Faith's quick smile gave him most of the answer.

"The tube is out of his throat," she said. "He's alert but has a hard time talking. They moved him from SF Medical to UCSF this morning. He really wants to see you. Courtney was hoping you wouldn't be too jet-lagged."

"It's not too bad. Knowing Jack came out of the coma made it easier to sleep on the plane." Gage glanced at the dashboard clock. "Let's stop by the office on the way."

"That reminds me. Alex Z asked me to pass on a message. He said you'd be annoyed when you got it. A U.S. Attorney named Peterson called about Jack."

Gage felt his fists clench. Burch was barely out of a coma and Peterson was already pouncing.

"Alex Z was right."

"Who's Peterson?"

"The guy who wants to put Jack in jail."

"Jack 'n Jail." She glanced over at Gage. "Is that a new game in the U.S. Attorney's office?"

"Apparently."

Faith handed over the number and Gage punched it into his cell phone as she eased her way around the cars stacked up along the curbs in front of the domestic airlines.

"This is Gage."

"Graham." Peterson's tone was jocular. "I heard you've been in London."

Gage didn't rise to it. "Nothing new in that."

"How about a little sit-down?"

"Depends on how you found out."

"From Devlin in the Serious Fraud Office."

"If you agree not to tell Matson, then we can meet."

"No problem. How about my office at 10 A.M. tomorrow?"

"How about mine? I don't want anyone over there putting the same two-and-two together like I did."

Gage disconnected.

"How come you didn't ask him what he wanted to talk about?" Faith asked.

"Because I already know—and because he might've told me, and canceled the meeting. I want to see his face when he tries to scare me off. I need to figure out whether he has Matson in his pocket, or it's the other way around."

Faith merged into the freeway traffic heading north toward San Francisco.

"Sounds like you and Peterson know each other."

"We do. He's okay, just too ambitious for his own good. Always thinking about how cases will play in the media. And this one would be big. Jack goes from road-rage victim to international crook. I can already hear the six o'clock lead: *In a stunning turn of events…*"

"You think you can get Jack out of this?"

"I don't know. I'm still at the edges. The only thing that's clear at the moment is that all the cops and crooks in the case have an interest in making Jack look guilty."

◇◇◇

"Can I see some ID?" the officer on duty asked Gage an hour later as he and Faith approached Burch's room in the critical care unit at the University of California Hospital.

Gage extended his folding ID case.

"Graham Gage?" The officer smiled. "Spike's friend?"

Gage nodded.

"He came by a little while ago. Talked to Burch." His smile faded. "Sorry there hasn't been much progress in the case."

"You're keeping him alive, that's good enough. Thanks."

Courtney hugged Faith and Gage, then used the push button control to raise Burch's bed a few degrees. A myriad of plastic tributaries spread out from Burch's bruised arms. He held a pillow against his chest to allow him to cough without exploding his still-healing sternum. An oxygen mask covered his nose. His lips were chapped.

Despite the devastation, Gage felt his heart lift as he leaned over the bed. "How are you doing, champ?"

Burch pulled the oxygen mask away from his nose. "Been… better."

Courtney put it back, then pointed to the oxygen level on the monitor. "When it gets to ninety-five percent, they'll take it off."

"Too dry," he said, squeaking out a smile. "Like dead… dingo's…donger."

"Now, Jack," Courtney said, reddening.

Gage took his hand. "It's okay, I'm not sure we qualify as polite company."

Burch pointed at his breastbone. "Maybe…someday…we can…compare…bullet…wounds."

"I was twenty-five years younger. It bounced off."

Burch smiled, then coughed, gripping the pillow against his chest.

Gage patted Burch's shoulder. "I think we better let you take it easy."

"Wait." Burch looked at Courtney. "The photos."

"The lieutenant came by with photographs of possible suspects," Courtney said, "but Jack didn't see the man who shot him. Their heads were all too round or blockish. Jack thought the men in the photos all looked Russian."

Burch nodded, then his eyelids lowered and he drifted off to sleep.

Courtney held her forefinger to her lips, then pointed toward the door. They followed her into the hallway.

"I'm not sure Jack got a good enough look at the man," Courtney said. Her resigned tone told Gage that she had no hope Jack would ever be able to pick the shooter out of a lineup. "He just got a glimpse of a thin face and a gun in the man's left hand. That's all." She peered up into Gage's eyes. "The man who shot him will always be out there, won't he?"

Gage reached his arm around her shoulders. "It's all right if Jack can't identify him. I'm going at it from another direction."

Chapter Thirty-four

Peterson and Zink arrived ten minutes early for their meeting with Gage. He met them in his first floor conference room, bringing with him photos of Gravilov and the other gangsters who had met with Matson, the files he'd taken from Fitzhugh's cottage, and records he'd collected at the Companies House in London—ready for a little show-and-tell.

"I don't think you can get your friend Burch out of this one," Peterson began. "He went too far."

"Based on what?" Gage kept his voice flat. He wanted to provoke Peterson into laying out his case, not into an argument.

Peterson grinned, then settled back in his chair. "You show me yours and maybe I'll show you mine."

Gage crossed his forearms on the desk and fixed his eyes on Peterson. "All Burch did was act on a referral from a big name in venture capital. I looked at records in London. Granger and Fitzhugh dummied up an appraisal for a failing company in Dublin, then flipped it to SatTek for three million shares. That was Granger's big payoff."

Peterson glanced at Zink, who clenched his teeth. "I'm still working on it."

Gage hit his punch line hard. "Fitzhugh was Granger's guy, not Burch's."

Peterson sat forward "You got it wrong." He nodded at Zink. "Show him."

Zink lifted a briefcase from the floor. He pulled out a file and slid it toward Peterson.

"These are Burch's phone records from two months *before* Matson went to see him for the first time," Peterson said. "There are six calls from Burch to Fitzhugh. Every wheel has a hub and Burch was it. Fitzhugh was Burch's guy."

Peterson was on a roll. He couldn't wait to show the rest of his.

"Burch put Fitzhugh in the middle of the fake product sales to Asia, then put him in the middle of the offshore stock sales—and there's more on the domestic side."

Gage threw up his hands. "You're not claiming he brought in Kovalenko?"

Peterson slapped the desk. "Bingo." He then flicked his head toward Zink, who slid over another file while smirking at Gage. Peterson withdrew the top page.

"These are the State of Nevada records for Kovalenko's companies. Chuck Verona is the registered agent. Kovalenko even has his name on a couple."

Peterson withdrew another sheet.

"These are all the companies Verona is the agent for. A bunch of them were set up by Burch. Like the one that owns Kovalenko's car." Peterson grinned. "For that one, Kovalenko is the president, secretary, and water boy. If that's not enough, look at Burch's phone records for September, last year. Right in the middle of the pump and dump. There's a call from Burch's inside line to Kovalenko's inside line at Northstead Securities."

Peterson reached in again.

"This is Burch's brokerage account statement. He bought a hundred thousand shares of SatTek at two bucks, then dumped it like all the other insiders at five. He cleared a cool, crooked three hundred grand—on top of his enormous legal fee."

"Then how do you explain the hits on Burch and Fitzhugh?"

"Burch wasn't a hit. It was road rage. While you were wasting your time in London, another jogger was shot in the Mission District. Same MO. As for Fitzhugh and his wife? The London police say they did a little work for Russian organized crime. Zink looked through Fitzhugh's files. There was nothing to connect SatTek to any of Fitzhugh's Russian clients."

Gage started to reach for his folder to show Peterson the photos he took of the Russians Matson met with in London, then hesitated. He hadn't heard the punch line yet.

"And Matson can tie the whole thing together. Trust me. He's given us everything he's got and he's been going out and gathering up more every day."

Gage thought back on Matson's route. London. Guernsey. Lugano. *Maybe he was putting the financial pieces together for Peterson. Maybe he was still trying to snare Granger. In the end it didn't make any difference. Matson was Peterson's boy, and Peterson believed Matson's every word.*

"One thing you don't have is motive—"

Peterson flashed a palm at Gage. "We don't need motive. The facts speak for themselves."

"You may not," Gage said, "but juries want to hear it—and Burch didn't need the money."

"Needing and wanting are two different things."

"He gives away three times your salary to charity every year. He handles the money for a dozen international relief organizations—never a hint that he skimmed a dime."

"Big fucking deal. What he does for charity is a sentencing issue. Maybe it'll buy him a downward departure. Get him down to twenty-eight years instead of thirty." Peterson jabbed a forefinger at Gage. "We both know why these do-gooders want to use him. It's because he knows how to move money so corrupt governments can't get ahold of it. We call it money laundering for a good cause. That's why we look the other way." Peterson smirked. "You think we don't suspect what you two did in Afghanistan? Is there a federal crime you guys didn't commit setting that up?"

A nightmare came to life in Gage's mind: Burch being arrested in the critical care unit and Spike's uniformed cop being replaced by a U.S. Marshal. Peterson had everything he needed: a paper trail, a money trail, and Matson to tell the story—and Gage hadn't seen it coming. He didn't look over, but he felt

Zink grinning like a teenage punk who didn't have a clue what was friendship, or grief, or tragedy. He clenched his jaws and kept his face expressionless. He wasn't going to give Peterson the satisfaction.

"When will you indict him?"

"As soon as we can roll him into court. From what I hear he's making good progress." Peterson paused. Gage saw in his eyes that, at least for a moment, he grasped what this meant to Gage. But the moment passed. "Sorry, man, you can't win 'em all."

◇◇◇

Gage returned to his office after escorting Peterson and Zink to the lobby, each step accompanied by the anguish that Faith had been right: Burch's rage against Courtney's cancer had indeed expressed itself as greed.

But then two poem fragments spoke to him as he settled into his chair and gazed out toward the bay: *I was much too far out all my life…not waving but drowning.* And he wondered whether that had been Jack Burch from the beginning. Maybe that was why the memory of their first meeting came to him in the emergency room hallway the morning Burch was shot.

Maybe it wasn't greed after all, but simply self-destructive recklessness.

Gage took in a breath, feeling the same unease that had troubled him along the Smith River twenty-five years earlier. He remembered watching a young fisherman walk past him into a cliffside café overlooking the river, his gait and earnest face announcing that his mind was too much on the water, his arms and back already feeling the tension of the fly line tight in the guides of a bowed rod.

"Watch out for the Oregon Hole," Gage had warned him and pointed at three off-kilter crosses jammed into lava rocks atop the canyon wall. "Those rapids will beat you to death."

Burch had glanced back over his shoulder, grinned, and answered without breaking stride, "Thanks, mate. I'll take care."

At midday, another moment of unease. Gage looking down from the cliff, catching sight of a slight shifting of Burch's shoulders and hips as he dug his wading boots into the sandy river bottom. Then again, at sunset, with long shadows falling across the river. Gage slowing as he drove across the suspension bridge and glanced down into the gorge, wondering where was the fisherman whose mind had been too much on the river—and catching sight of flailing arms and a fly rod whipping the air.

Maybe that was it all along, Gage thought, turning away from the window and sitting up in his chair. Maybe that had always been Burch: not waving, but drowning.

Gage folded his hands on his desk, his duty—to Jack, to Courtney, and to himself—now framed both by memory and by the fear that instead of asking what and who and how, he should've been asking why.

Chapter Thirty-five

The middle-aged foreperson seated at a semicircular raised judge's bench looked over her reading glasses at a phalanx of occupied student-style Formica desks filling the grand jury room. A clerk sat to her left and the court reporter sat one level below her. The witness box to her right was empty. The foreperson first directed the secretary to take the roll, then invited Assistant United States Attorney William Peterson to address the grand jurors.

Peterson rose from his seat at the prosecutor's table front and center in the grand jury room, picked up his SatTek notes, and then stepped to the podium.

"Today, the government will begin presenting testimonial evidence that it expects to show conspiracy to commit wire fraud, conspiracy to commit securities fraud, and money laundering by SatTek Incorporated of San Jose and by its officers, agents, lawyers, and consultants."

Peterson looked down the far left row of jurors and counted to six. From others in the office he knew that Grand Juror Number Six, a wild-haired, middle-aged former middle manager, was a runaway. Number Six thought he had a mind of his own. Even worse, he thought the grand jury was supposed to possess a collective mind of its own. He was big trouble.

Number Six didn't take an interest in every case, just a few, and he telegraphed his move by taking notes right from day one.

No one in the office knew how he chose a case to go rabid on. He just did and wasted an enormous amount of time asking questions ad nauseam in a nasally whine that made everyone in the room cringe and their palms sweat. One prosecutor had told Peterson that after one of these episodes, the foreperson had whispered to him in the hallway that because of Number Six, the eighteen-month grand jury term felt like a life sentence.

Everyone in the U.S. Attorney's Office figured that someday they'd spot Number Six on a park bench or in the public library with the other loonies scribbling stream-of-consciousness notes in a weathered spiral notebook. But the scuttlebutt was that you could beat him down if you worked at it and he'd vote with the rest of the sheep when the time came—it was just that nobody in the office liked playing sheepdog.

"You'll recall that a month ago the grand jury approved the issuance of subpoenas for stock and bank records relating to SatTek. At that time I outlined our suspicions and also described the roles of the SatTek officers, advisers such as Edward Granger, attorneys such as Jack Burch, and offshore agents such as Morely Alden Fitzhugh. Beginning today you will see the fruits of the subpoenas and learn the details of our investigative labors."

Peterson checked off the first item on his outline.

"I should point out at this juncture that Mr. Fitzhugh, who I mentioned to you a few weeks ago, is no longer a target, as he's deceased." Peterson quickly pushed on, not wanting to answer questions about the circumstances of Fitzhugh's murder. "My summary witness will be FBI Special Agent Lyle Zink. Beginning tomorrow he'll outline the structure of the conspiracy, the coconspirators, the bank accounts, and the offshore companies."

Peterson checked off two more items.

"Stuart Matson has become a cooperating defendant and we expect there will be others. He signed a plea agreement that requires him to disgorge his profits but makes no promises regarding sentencing. Assuming that Mr. Matson is entirely truthful, pursuant to 5K of the Federal Sentencing Guidelines, the U.S. Attorney's Office will move the district court to grant a downward departure from the mandatory minimum in this matter which is approximately twenty years. He could receive a sentence as low as probation, depending on his performance.

"There will be additional witnesses, including employees of SatTek, bank officers, representatives of the SEC, and others. I expect that presenting all of this testimony will require that we meet about twice a week for the next few weeks."

Peterson set aside his outline, rested his hands on the top edges of the podium, then paused. He let his eyes scan the grand jurors just a moment longer than any of them found comfortable.

"In accordance with rule six of the Federal Rules of Criminal Procedure, I must remind each and every one of the grand jurors that the proceedings of the grand jury are secret. Secrecy protects you from intimidation, it prevents the escape of grand jury targets, and it prevents the tampering with or the intimidation of witnesses. Please bear this in mind."

Peterson reached for a binder labeled "SatTek Syllabus" lying on a table next to him.

"Now, let me outline the elements of the crimes of conspiracy, wire fraud, securities fraud, and money laundering."

Peterson looked up at Grand Juror Number Six. He was already taking notes. *Damn.*

Chapter Thirty-six

Edward Granger arrived at the driving range of his country club at sunrise. He purchased two baskets of balls, then selected the driving station farthest from the other golfers. The grass never smelled sweeter, the fall air never felt more crisp and expansive. He paused to watch the caged cart sweeping up spent balls, wondering whether prisons had grass anymore, or whether anything at all grew in them except men growing older. He also wondered how many rounds he would have time to play before he joined the other inmates wasting their days, replacing golf with chess or checkers or bridge or just unrelenting boredom.

Granger teed up a ball, addressed it with his titanium driver, then swung. The ball cracked off the club like a gunshot. He caught sight of it just as it reached its apex. He watched it until it hit the netting three hundred yards away, dropped to the grass, and came to rest. He looked over at the few other golfers at the range. Some hit the ball, then reached into their baskets for another before it stopped rolling, sometimes while it was still in flight. Not Granger. He thought of nothing while the ball was in motion, just the beauty of it. In Granger's mind, that was the point, the whole point.

Granger paused, thinking back on his conversation with Graham Gage in the clubhouse the previous day. Gage had walked in, handed him a business card, looked him in the eye, and said, "We need to talk about Jack Burch."

No raised voice. No explanation. Just the invisible force of a riptide. It told Granger even before they'd made the short walk from the bar to the booth, that his day planner would have a bunch of new entries by the time he stood up.

Gage's leadoff question did it. It convinced him that the first thing he'd need to do was fire his attorney, Sid Lavender. He liked Sid. He respected Sid. But Sid wouldn't represent a snitch. Sid said it was a matter of principle—and Granger was about to become one.

Snitch. An ugly word. *Switch. Bitch. Snitch.* But Granger knew he'd eventually get used to it.

"What do you know about Fitzhugh and the engineering software company in Ireland?" Gage had asked.

The question vibrated through Granger. Gage had figured it out. And so would the government. Or Gage would explain it to them.

"I don't know anything about it." His tone was flat, unconvincing. They both knew it.

"That's the wrong answer," Gage said.

"I know. But there's nothing you can offer me that'll give you the right one."

Granger leaned back, smiling. It was neither aggressive nor defensive. Granger didn't play those games. It was simply melancholy.

"At least tell me this," Gage said. "Was Burch in on it? I don't need you to say whether you were. You and I already know that answer."

Granger thought back to the beginning. He smiled to himself. *Some people think in clichés, I think in analogies.*

"Let me put it this way," Granger finally said. "Do you tell the lumberyard what you plan to use the plywood for?"

Granger didn't expect Gage to answer. There was no need to. He could see by Gage's face that he'd given Gage what he wanted to hear: Peterson couldn't prove intent.

"What about Matson? How did he use the plywood?"

"That's the last one you get," Granger said, knowing that it was already one more than he'd prepared himself to answer. "You're a smart guy. Listen carefully...Sometimes children grow up to do things you never expected in your wildest imagination. And trust me, I've got a wild imagination."

"So I've heard. Will you tell Peterson?"

"When the time comes."

◇◇◇

Granger fired Sid an hour later, then let his fingers do their walking through his Rolodex to Bobby Harrington, a member of the country club and a white-collar lawyer he hoped had enough pull to cut him a deal.

"Bobby, this is Ed Granger."

"How's the old putter?"

"Stiff and straight. How's yours?"

"Don't believe what you read. It's not the smallest club in the bag. What can I do for you?"

"You still have any connections left in the U.S. Attorney's office?"

"Sure, I ran the place under two presidents. My picture is still on the wall somewhere, darts and all. What's up?"

"I've got a little situation."

"How little?"

Granger hesitated, knowing that once he spoke the words that had echoed in his mind as he lay in bed the night before, there'd be no turning back, and nothing would ever be the same.

"I won't kid you or myself," Granger finally said. "I'll be doing time. No way around it. But I'm willing to trade what I know for what they want. I just need a release date soon enough to get in a few rounds before I check out."

"Sounds bad."

"It's SatTek."

"Ouch."

"Yeah. A lot worse than I expected. How much do you want to come into the case to cut a deal?"

"Fifty."

"Might as well charge whatever you want, the government is going to forfeit what's left."

"Fifty thousand is fine. Who's the Assistant U.S. Attorney?"

"Peterson."

"True believer. But we can deal with him. I'm the one that hired him, right out of law school. Who's the agent?"

"Zink."

"An idiot. He's been pretty much neutered because of a DUI a few years ago. I wouldn't worry about him."

"There's another guy involved. He's the reason I've got to make a deal."

"Who's that?"

"Graham Gage. He's ready to hand my head to Peterson to keep his pal Jack Burch from being indicted. No stopping him."

"You sized him up right," Harrington said. "He's the guy I'd hire if I was on the hunt. And I'd be fucking terrified if he was doing it on his own dime. You better jump on board before the train runs you over."

"That's what I was afraid of."

"You know they'll want to put you in front of the grand jury?"

"I figured. I've got the feeling that they're already meeting. A guy in the scam named Matson has been acting real squirrelly."

"Then we'll have to move fast. I'll call Peterson this afternoon and tell him you want to come in. And you start putting money together for bail."

Granger then called his banker and the next morning was among the first on the driving range.

Granger swung like a pro. Smooth. Flowing. Decisive. Each time, the ball cracked off the tee like a gunshot.

Chapter Thirty-seven

A voice mail from Peterson was waiting for Gage when he arrived at his office. He thought of Granger's promise to come clean with Peterson *when the time comes*. As he reached for his phone, Gage hoped for Burch's sake that the moment had already arrived.

"Let me put you on conference," Peterson said.

Gage heard nothing for a moment, then the static of the speakerphone.

"Zink is here with me."

"What's up?" Gage asked.

"Just like your pal Burch, you're a hub around a very bad wheel."

Gage heard Zink snort in the background.

"What do you mean?"

"You meet with Granger?"

"Maybe."

"He got murdered this morning. At the driving range. Shot once in the head."

Gage's whole body tensed. The linchpin that held together his strategy to rotate the case away from Burch had broken off.

"Damn." Gage said the word more to himself than to Peterson.

"Why damn?" Peterson asked. "He was about to finger Burch."

"No he wasn't." Gage sat forward in his chair. His voice intensified. "You *wanted* him to finger Burch. That was the one thing he told me he *wouldn't* do. And he had something on Matson. Something big."

"So you say." Peterson's snide tone made him sound like a schoolgirl gossiping at the lunch table.

Gage blew past it. "Look, I needed him more than you did."

"Being needed by you is a very dangerous occupation. First Burch, then Fitzhugh, and now Granger. My indictment is getting shorter every day. It looks like we'll need to cast the net a little bit wider."

"Is that a threat?"

"Against you? No. Unless you know something I don't. But we'll be looking real hard at anything that connects to Burch."

Gage hung up, then rose from his desk and stepped to a window. He watched a tugboat, its nose to the bow of a container ship, nudging it toward the Oakland Port. He realized that this was what he'd been trying to do with Peterson's indictment, steer it from the outside. But it wasn't going to work. Peterson had too much momentum, and with Granger dead, Gage had nothing left to push with.

◇◇◇

Gage called Courtney, trying to sound upbeat, wanting to protect her and Burch from the world closing in around his ICU room.

"How's he doing?" Gage asked.

"Not good." Her tone was weary. "He's got an infection, maybe pneumonia. They're working on him now."

Gage heard conversation in the background.

"What's that?"

She didn't answer immediately. "The doctor is talking to one of the nurses…Oh, dear. They're going to put the breathing tube back in."

"I'll call back."

"Wait. They want me to step outside."

Gage heard her footsteps on the linoleum floor, then the room sounds faded.

"I hear something in your voice," Courtney said. "Is something wrong?"

"No. Other people are trying to blame Jack for things they did. But it's nothing to worry about. I'll take care of it."

Gage hung up, then examined the flowcharts covering the walls of his office. Too many arrows pointed at Burch and the companies he'd set up for Matson.

He wished he'd hung up two sentences sooner.

Chapter Thirty-eight

You're right," Gage said, "the beef chow fun isn't bad."

Gage and Milsberg were sitting on a wooden bench near the Japanese Friendship Garden, eating out of Styrofoam containers. A group of schoolchildren bunched up along the shore a few yards away were staring down at orange and yellow and blue koi looking up, waiting to be fed.

Milsberg laughed. "You didn't believe me. I really am a man of taste and culture. In fact, I composed a new haiku: *chow fun, mu shu pork, heartburn at midnight.*" He raised his eyebrows. "Am I ready for prime time?"

"Not quite," Gage said.

"Yeah. There aren't enough syllables. It's supposed to be five, seven, five. A shame, I used to be good with numbers."

"But accounting wasn't your first choice."

"Maybe that's been the problem all along." Milsberg set down his chopsticks. "I read about Granger in the paper." He held his hands out toward Gage. "No need to check for gunshot residue. I didn't do that one, either."

"It didn't cross my mind."

While Milsberg took a sip of Coke, Gage took out a notepad from his jacket pocket.

"Did you bring everything?" Gage asked.

"Just about. I have a dozen boxes of old financial files for you, but the really important things are these backup tapes."

Milsberg removed three cassettes from a paper bag and laid them on the bench. "Tape one holds all of the accounting records and everything on the workstations. Two is a backup of the intellectual property division. It's got device drawings, specs, anything related to hardware design and software development. The third one covers the production line. It has the metrology database and the manufacturing execution system. You'll find the specs and history of every product that's ever been sent out of SatTek."

"How did you get them?" Gage smiled. "Maybe you should've been a private eye after all."

Milsberg shook his head. "Dumb luck. The IT guy resigned yesterday and I was the only one around he could surrender his keys to."

"What about phone records?"

"Tape one. I'll give you the numbers that Matson calls out on. I've got a file of his cell records. I think he has another cell phone in London but I don't have any of those records."

"E-mails?"

"Tape one."

"Shipping and receiving?"

"Tape two."

"Stock sales?"

"Ditto."

"Almost perfect," Gage said. "Now for the home run. What about enterprise resource planning software?"

"Sure." Milsberg grinned. "ERP on tape three."

"Very poetic."

Milsberg looked skyward. "Finally."

◇◇◇

Alex Z's eyes lit up like stage lights when Gage set the SatTek backup tapes on the conference room table, but went dark after he picked up one and read the label.

"Jeez, boss, even if these are only half full, there's got to be at least ten terabytes of data here."

"How long do you think it'll take to make them searchable?"

Alex Z's head rocked back and forth as he thought. "Eight or ten hours, but I won't know for sure until I see how much is really there."

"Get to work. We need to figure out what Granger was planning to trade. While you work on the tapes, I'll be down in the storeroom going through a bunch of boxes of financial documents Milsberg gave me."

Gage's cell phone rang two hours after Alex Z left.

"It's going to take longer than I thought," Alex Z said. "Even if I can get them copied by midnight, it'll probably take until morning for our computers to index the data."

"My end isn't going any better. The hard copy records I've found so far are too old to be useful, but I'll keep pushing through them. Let's meet in my office for breakfast. See if you can be ready to abstract some information from their accounting system."

Gage thought for a moment.

"For guys like Matson, greed can be both their strength and their weakness. We just need to find a way to turn it from one to the other."

Chapter Thirty-nine

When Gage walked into his office the next morning carrying two cups of coffee, he found Alex Z asleep, slumped in a chair across from his desk. A ramen noodle fragment was stuck to his gray T-shirt and his right sleeve was smudged with chocolate, as though he'd wiped his mouth while staring at his monitor.

Alex Z shook himself awake, then rubbed his red, dark-ringed eyes with his palms.

"Were you up all night?" Gage asked, handing him a cup.

Alex Z stretched, then looked at his watch. "I guess not quite all of it. I came in to drop off something about fifteen minutes ago, but I guess I'm the one that dropped off."

"You awake enough to show me how to get into the financial data?"

Alex Z reached down and picked up a folder from the floor and handed it to Gage. "I wrote it out." He pushed his scraggly hair away from his face, then took a sip of coffee. "I ran a few searches just to test them out, and the results kept me awake. They didn't match my understanding of how the scam worked. I got sort of panicky and wanted to figure it out before you came in."

Gage sat down behind his desk. "What didn't make sense?"

"I thought all of the SatTek sales outside the U.S. were bogus and only the domestic ones were real. But then I looked at the product descriptions and discovered that SatTek sold millions of dollars of DVLAs, ERDLVAs and LNAs that weren't controlled under the ECCNs."

Gage smiled. "Could you translate that into English?"

Alex Z's face reddened. "Sorry, boss. I had to learn a new language to figure this stuff out. That just means they sold sound and video detection devices overseas that didn't need government approval. Low-power ones. Under 10.5 gigahertz. Like the kind used in electronic testing equipment."

"Why do you think they're real sales?"

"Because the accounting system shows a lot of small orders, mostly between thirty and eight hundred thousand dollars, some a little higher. It also shows partial payments. Odd numbers. The fake payments were big round ones. One million even, two million even. Like those from the dummy Asian companies. The ones that look authentic were in amounts like $246,231 and $513,952."

Alex Z struggled to stay focused, like a marathoner approaching the finish line.

"And I found another thing. They assigned internal purchase order numbers and used them to track the manufacturing, from ordering parts to the final shipping cost. So they knew exactly how much each device cost to build. But the fake sales didn't track all the way through."

Gage nodded slowly, trying to visualize the product flow through SatTek.

Alex Z faded for a moment, then blinked. "And this is interesting. It looks like the fake orders were all for the same kind of device. All digital video amplifiers with the same model number."

"Is that what SatTek dumped in the storage rooms in China and Vietnam?"

"You got it, boss. Every single one. I can't find any real buyers in Asia, only in the U.S. and the European Union. England, France, and Germany."

Alex Z's mind drifted away as he finished the sentence. He stared blankly at Gage.

"I think you need to get a nap," Gage said.

"What? What did you want?" Alex Z blinked again and shook his head. "No problem. What country?"

"I said nap, you should get a nap."

"Oh. I thought you said map."

Gage came around the desk as Alex Z heaved himself to his feet. "How about I'll take a look at what you downloaded, while you take a n-a-p."

While Alex Z slogged off to sleep, Gage worked his way through the SatTek files, troubled by the offshore sales. He located a copy of the hard drive of the workstation used in the sales office, then found the correspondence directory, organized by country.

One stood out. A company in Ukraine, not a member of the European Union, had tried to buy twenty 18-gigahertz, military-grade video amplifiers. The application to export the devices to TeleTron Ukraina had been handled by a SatTek employee named Katie Palan.

The denial notice was blunt:

> This application is rejected pursuant to the Arms Export Control Act of 2000. The Bureau of Industry and Security, in consultation with the Department of Defense, has concluded that this export would be detrimental to the national security interests of the United States.

Gage wasn't surprised. There was no way the U.S. would allow the export of military-grade devices to Ukraine; their next stop would've been Iran or Syria. Since Ukraine no longer had any enemies, its defense industry now existed solely to generate hard currency for a struggling economy.

He ran an Internet search on TeleTron Ukraina and found the congressional testimony of the director of the Bureau of Industry and Security:

Chairperson: Do you find that dual-use devices are redirected from civilian to military uses?

Director: Repeatedly. And it's for that reason that we investigate who the real end users of technology are likely to be. For example, we recently discovered that a company named TeleTron Ukraina was merely a front for the Yuzhmash Defense Production Plant in Dnepropetrovsk, Ukraine. This plant conducted most of the research for various Ukrainian radar and missile targeting systems. Additionally, I would point out that the president of Ukraine, the former head of the Yuzhmash Plant, personally approved the sale of a hundred-million-dollar Kolchuga radar system to Iraq in violation of the arms embargo.

Chairperson: Do you know what front company they're using now?

Director: I'm sorry to say I don't.

Gage called Robert Milsberg.

"You know how I can contact Katie Palan?"

"You can't. She died in a car accident eighteen or nineteen months ago on her way to the company picnic." Milsberg sighed. "She was really a sweet kid. The Highway Patrol figured a deer ran across the road—the area is lousy with them—and she swerved and tumbled down a ravine. It really devastated her parents. They blamed themselves."

"Why'd they think it was their fault?"

"They fled Ukraine because they despised the corruption and violence, but figured if they'd stayed there, she'd still be alive."

"The name Katie Palan doesn't sound Ukrainian."

"Ekaterina. Palan was her ex-husband's name. In addition to her native language, she spoke Russian, German, and a little French, so she was involved in most of the European sales."

After hanging up, Gage sent an e-mail to Alex Z for him to retrieve when he awoke:

"Z: Get me the names of every Ukrainian company that shows up in SatTek records. Market research. Purchase orders. Sales. E-mails. Everything."

Alex Z answered immediately:

"I'll get right on it."

"What happened to the nap?"

"Couldn't sleep—it must have been the sound of your mind working that kept me awake."

Chapter Forty

When Gage and his interpreter, Pavel, were invited into the one-bedroom San Jose apartment of Katie Palan's parents, Gage felt as if he'd been warped back a generation earlier and thousands of miles to rural Ukraine. The living room contained a heavily embroidered couch and matching chairs, a two-door pinewood cabinet painted in vibrant green and red, three flat-weave rugs, and half a dozen egg-shaped Russian Orthodox icons.

Katie's father, Tolenko Palchinsky, a balding, stocky man still wearing his BIG Security Company uniform, answered the door. His wife, Olena, scurried up behind him, drying her hands on a flowery but threadbare full-length apron. Air wafting from the apartment was still thick with the aroma of beef and potatoes, herring and sour cream, and horseradish. It bore a scent of family and of coziness that couldn't soften the strained faces of isolation that greeted Gage.

Tears of a sailor daydreaming of home came to Tolenko's eyes when Pavel introduced Gage and said in Ukrainian, "Ekaterina, we're here about Ekaterina."

And after a long, uncertain moment, Tolenko glanced back at Olena and then invited them inside.

"You know," Tolenko said, after they'd sat down and Olena had brought out tea, "I was a mining engineer in Ukraine—"

"No one wants to hear about Ukraine," Olena interrupted. "Ukraine is dead."

Pavel, caught in the crossfire, cast Gage a weak look as he translated.

"Ukraine is not yet dead," Tolenko said, sullenly repeating the title of the national anthem. "As long as there's corruption and gangster capitalism, it will live. When there's nothing left to steal, then it will die."

"It's dead for us," Olena said.

Gage knew it was a conversation they had before. Unlike Tolenko, Olena had apparently resolved that if you're never going home, don't look back.

"Where are you from in Ukraine?" Gage asked.

"Lugansk," Tolenko answered, then glanced at Olena. "We agree about Lugansk. It's dead. Rotting. Flooded coal mines, slag heaps, sickness."

"Is that where you worked?"

"As if they listened to me." Tolenko jammed his fist into his chest, then pointed at a phantom. "They just dug tunnels. Tunnels and tunnels and tunnels. The government didn't care if miners died as long as they got the coal out before the tunnels collapsed." Tolenko spoke quickly, almost too quickly for Pavel to keep up. "They only hired engineers so there would be someone to blame."

Tolenko gritted his teeth and shook his head, a sign of the fury that boiled within, that drove him to flee with bitterness as the lasting taste of home.

"Tell me about Ekaterina."

"Ekaterina…she…" The grief in Tolenko's heart choked off his voice.

"She was everything to us," Olena said. "So kind. So smart. She studied economics and English at Kiev University and enrolled in business administration courses as soon as she got here." The pride in her voice shone even through Pavel's even-voiced translation. "She was taking classes in asset analysis. She wanted to work at one of the big investment firms, specializing in Central Europe."

"Did she sponsor you to the U.S.?"

Olena nodded. "She married an American she worked with in the trade section of the U.S. embassy in Kiev. We came after they divorced. He was a good boy but he wanted adventure and travel, Ekaterina wanted predictability. She'd lived her whole life in uncertainty. We all did."

"Where's her husband?"

"He's been posted to St. Petersburg for the last two years. He came to San Jose for Ekaterina's funeral."

"Was he here when Ekaterina was killed?"

Tolenko's eyes locked on Gage. "What are you saying?"

"I'm wondering if Ekaterina's death wasn't an accident."

"I know it wasn't her husband," Olena said quickly, her voice edgy. "I called him in Russia an hour after the police came."

"But you've thought about this, haven't you?" Gage asked Olena.

She turned toward her husband and answered, "Yes." She then looked down at her tightly gripped hands. "Every day."

"Have you tried to find out?"

"How?" She looked up, face red, voice rising. "From whom? We're two foreigners who speak little English. When you don't speak good English, you're treated like a child. And when you're a parent and you say your child was murdered and the police won't listen, people think you're crazy. At the bakery where I work, they think I'm paranoid—at best. So I don't talk about it anymore."

Gage leaned forward, resting his forearms on his thighs, trying to look smaller, less threatening. "What do you think happened?"

Tolenko cut in again. "You haven't explained why you want to know."

Olena squirmed, on the verge of not caring who Gage was and why he was asking, just wanting to blurt out the story to anyone who would listen.

Gage turned his head toward Tolenko. "I think SatTek was involved in illegal activities and your daughter may have figured it out."

Olena nodded vigorously, then opened her mouth to speak. Tolenko held up his palm toward her.

"What illegal activities?" Tolenko asked.

"Something involving a company called TeleTron Ukraina."

Tolenko's palm failed to hold back Olena's defense of her daughter. "But she didn't know until afterwards. Please believe us, she didn't know."

"That's what I thought. But did she have proof?"

Olena looked at her husband as if to say that Gage was the only person who would ever listen to them. It was Tolenko's turn to nod.

She hurried from the living room, returning less than a minute later gripping a soiled SatTek envelope, an English-Ukrainian dictionary, and a laptop computer. She sat down, pulled out the papers, then began to search through the dictionary. She looked up at Pavel. An embarrassed smile came over her face. She didn't need the book now. Pavel was a walking dictionary. She handed the papers to Gage, who slowly thumbed through them.

"I tried to translate the sheets," Olena said. "But they didn't make sense. A word here and word there. Too technical." She wrung her hands, eyes searching Gage's face, then Pavel's. "Please tell me what they say. Please."

Gage finally reached out and took her hands in his. "They say that Olena Palchinsky isn't paranoid."

◇◇◇

Gage called Alex Z as he was driving away.

"I checked everywhere," Alex Z said. "There were no sales of exactly twenty Model STV–18 video amplifiers after August last year. There were sales of twenty Model STV–04s to a company called Kiev Industries. The 04 means that it was 4 gigahertz. It didn't need U.S. government approval since 04s are low power and don't have military applications—"

"But you couldn't find any resource planning records showing that twenty STV–04s were ever manufactured for Kiev Industries."

"Jeez, boss, how'd you know?"

Gage glanced down at Katie's file and her laptop resting on the seat next to him. A graceful hand had made checkmarks next to the STV–04 serial numbers.

"Katie Palan figured out that serial numbers on the 18s and 4s were the same," Gage said. "SatTek must've sent the same 18-gigahertz devices back to Ukraine, pretending that they were the 4s."

"No shit!" Alex Z voice rose, hitting a pitch somewhere between incredulity and outrage. "Isn't that like treason or something? You know what those are used for? Hellfire air-to-ground missiles, like on Cobra helicopters and Predator drones. And Ukraine will sell them to anybody. Man, wasn't Matson making enough money off the stock scam?"

Chapter Forty-one

Let me get this straight," Peterson said, his sarcasm reverberating through the phone line the following morning. "You knew you were going to lose on the facts of what Burch did, so you decided to take a shot at impeaching Matson instead? I thought you had more self-respect than that."

"You don't know what the facts are, only what Matson is telling you."

Peterson laughed. "If that's what Granger—may he rest in hell—planned to trade for a ticket out of jail, he was sadly mistaken. SatTek self-disclosed."

Gage caught his breath. He felt as if he'd been sneaking through a forest toward an enemy, only to get caught in an ambush. He looked down at Katie Palan's notes, bewildered by why she'd bothered to track it—unless...Unless she was the first to discover it.

"When did they turn themselves in?"

"Right after it happened. Somebody in the shipping department ran to Matson after he realized that the orders had been mixed up and they'd sent 18s to Ukraine instead of 4s. Matson scurried over to Hackett, who shot off a fax to the Bureau of Industry and Security. It was referred to the FBI and Zink got assigned. He speaks Russian and a little Ukrainian from when he worked in the Eurasian Organized Crime Group. Since he'd looked into the SatTek shipment, he stayed with it after the stock fraud tip came in.

"We know that we can't stop other countries from building missiles, but we sure as hell need to stop them from getting the technology that would allow them to make the kinds of surgical strikes we can. You remember the Varese case? Hackett sure did. Varese got fourteen years in the pen for just one of those devices. Twenty would've gotten Matson life plus a hundred. Hackett sent him over to Ukraine to retrieve them. Matson was a nervous little puppy. He knew the whole U.S. government would've landed on his back if one of his video amplifiers was found in an Iranian missile."

Gage heard the creak of Peterson's chair as he slowly rocked back and forth. He imagined Peterson's expression of self-satisfaction, as if he were standing over a prone quarterback in the end zone.

"Nice try with the arms-trafficking angle, Gage. But it's not going to get you anywhere. Look, I know Burch is your friend. And there's something to be said for loyalty. But there's also such a thing as being loyal to a fault—and I think that's just where you've gone."

Peterson stopped rocking.

"I know about you risking your life pulling him out of the Smith River. It was a helluva thing. But look—man to man—he's in too deep this time. Way too deep. And there's no way you're going to pull him out."

◇◇◇

"What's wrong, boss?" Alex Z asked, walking into Gage's office.

Gage looked at his watch. He hadn't realized that he'd spent the five minutes since he hung up staring out at the bay. He swiveled his chair toward Alex Z.

"Peterson was a step ahead of us on the Ukraine angle," Gage said. "He knew all about it."

Alex Z dropped into a chair and slid three folders across the desk.

"What are these?" Gage asked.

"Good news and bad news. From the look on your face, I better start with the good news."

"Shoot."

"I spent the day looking through the records that Mr. Burch's law firm sent over. They show that Mr. Burch billed from 1:35 P.M. until exactly 2 P.M. for a meeting with Matson. The call from his line to that stockbroker Kovalenko was from 2:04 until 2:09. But Mr. Burch started billing his next meeting at 2:05. Unless Mr. Burch was cheating, he couldn't have made the call."

"I'll find out whether Jack's line is accessible at his secretary's desk or the conference room next to his office. Maybe Matson hung around after the meeting and made the call."

"There are also the Nevada companies. Peterson claimed that Mr. Burch set up a company for Kovalenko with Verona as the registered agent."

"That's what he was suggesting."

"I looked at the secretary of state's records. Kovalenko wasn't one of the original officers. He bought it from someone else. And Verona runs a company that does nothing but act as registered agents. If you're incorporated in Nevada, you need a registered agent there. If you don't, you can't operate."

"And if you don't operate there, you can't get the Nevada tax breaks."

"It looks like half the corporate lawyers in San Francisco use Verona, not just Mr. Burch."

"What about the Fitzhugh connection?" Gage asked. "Peterson claims that Fitzhugh was Jack's boy."

"I found the calls from Mr. Burch to Fitzhugh. And the international call records you took out of Fitzhugh's house in London show a bunch of calls to Mr. Burch that Peterson doesn't know about." Alex Z pointed at the folders. "The bottom one has copies of Fitzhugh's cell phone bills matched up with Mr. Burch's."

Gage flipped it open and scanned a half-dozen lines Alex Z had highlighted in yellow.

"This doesn't look good."

"Sorry boss, but I figured you should know."

"Faith and I will visit Jack tonight," Gage said, closing the file. "I'll ask him about it."

Alex Z rose to his feet and headed toward the door.

"Alex?"

Alex Z turned back.

"Thanks," Gage said.

Chapter Forty-two

Burch was sitting in a reclining chair when Gage and Faith entered his hospital room. The IV lines running to his still-bruised arms were undiminished, but the breathing tube had been removed. If the good color in Burch's face was a reliable indicator, it was gone for good.

The oxygen mask hung below his chin while he performed breathing exercises with a spirometer measuring lung capacity.

"Come on, Jack," Courtney said, a cheerleader's smile on her face, "a little harder. Up to one thousand. You can do it."

Burch was pink and sweaty from effort and used the excuse of their arrival to stop.

"How are you doing, champ?" Gage gripped his shoulder and gave it a squeeze.

"O…okay."

"What are the doctors saying?"

"Another six…" Burch broke into a fit of coughing. Gage reached for a tissue and handed it to him.

Courtney took over. "As soon as he gets over this lung infection, they'll let him go home. Probably no more than six days. Hopefully by Thanksgiving. It's partly up to Jack." She frowned at Burch as if he was her child, not her husband. "He won't eat. He needs to. He's lost fifteen pounds. They want him to gain five back before he leaves."

"The food…terrible…leather and…cardboard." Burch placed the oxygen mask over his face.

"Has Spike come by?" Gage asked, turning toward Courtney.

"This morning," Courtney said. "He told us about the other jogger who got shot. He's thinking maybe he doesn't need to keep the officer guarding the room."

Gage had also spoken to Spike. The truth was that Spike was under pressure from his department. The chief knew that the U.S. Attorney would soon indict Jack and figured it would look bad in the press if SFPD was protecting a grand jury target.

Gage looked down at Burch. "What do you say we bring in our own people? I'd sleep better at night knowing you had somebody with you all the time, especially since you'll be moving around a little more."

"Just tell us who you want us to hire," Courtney said.

Gage nodded, then looked over at Faith and made a slight motion with his head.

"Courtney," Faith said, "let's go down to the cafeteria. You need a break and I'd like some tea."

"Will you be all right, Jack?" Courtney asked, then looked at Gage. "Of course you will. Boy talk."

"Just a little," Gage said.

Gage waited until the door closed, then sat down next to Burch and leaned in close. "I need to know about Fitzhugh."

Burch drew in a breath, then removed the oxygen mask.

"A disappointment. A great…disappointment. Should've told before. But I didn't understand…how he fit in."

"How does he?"

Gage winced as Burch erupted into coughing.

"Let me tell you about…" He coughed again, then wiped his mouth. "About how I met him."

"Just try short sentences, Jack."

Burch nodded. "Conference. In London." Burch drew on the oxygen. "Recommended by colleague…Nothing dodgy about him…My London people…too busy. Matson seemed low risk. So I gave him Fitzhugh to…to manage the holding company."

"What happened?"

"Him and Matson. And Granger. Must've done things. On their own. Used my name, my connections. Changed the companies. Got new ones."

Burch drew on the oxygen. Short, hard gasps on the edge of gagging. Body weakened, wracked by coughs. Breath raspy, wheezy.

Gage reached again for his shoulder. "Why don't we do this later?"

Burch shook his head. "Got to finish…All in my head …too long.…Fitzhugh and Matson…Matson came to my office…asked me to set up a company…to buy real estate and make investments. TAMS Limited."

"Why didn't Fitzhugh do it himself?"

"Said Matson was my client…Didn't want to steal him." Burch took in a breath, then looked up. "I didn't understand where Matson was getting his money…He said stock options. But it was too soon…for him to exercise them…Then said inheritance."

"So you backed off?"

"No choice."

Gage didn't show the relief he felt. At least Peterson couldn't link Burch to SatTek's money laundering.

Burch's eyes teared. "Maybe if Fitzhugh hadn't set up TAMS…"

"So you know?"

"Murdered. Horrible…My secretary found out. His wife, too." Burch looked up at Gage. Childlike. Tears spilling from his eyes. No longer seeming the international lawyer or daredevil skier, no longer living on the edge by choice.

"Graham, I'm afraid."

Gage reached his arm around Burch's shoulders.

"I know. Don't worry, champ. They had their chance at you, and they're not getting another."

◇◇◇

Gage remained at Burch's bedside until his friend fell asleep, then went in search of Faith and Courtney. He found them in the hallway walking back from the cafeteria.

"Courtney," Faith said, reaching around her shoulders, "you need to tell Graham."

Courtney looked up at Gage. "Promise you won't say anything to Jack yet, please."

Gage nodded. Burch's tears had told him that the less Burch knew about what was going on outside his hospital room, the better.

"A man came to serve Jack with a subpoena for his files. A class action suit." She glanced at her husband's room. "I had to block the door to keep him outside."

Gage knew this skirmish in the battle would be coming; he just didn't know when and what angle they'd take. "Did they name Jack?"

"No. They just want his records. Jack will be devastated if he gets named. It'll be bad enough just to testify."

"Who's the law firm?"

"Simpson & Braunegg."

"I'll see what I can do."

Gage tried to herd Courtney toward Burch's room, but she remained planted.

"Graham," Courtney peered up into Gage's eyes, "tell me the truth. Did Jack do something wrong?"

He looked toward Faith as if to say he wasn't ready for this conversation, then back at Courtney. "I don't think so, at least not intentionally."

She shook her head. "You're not telling me everything. I need to know. It's my life, too."

Gage tried to fend her off, not with a lie, but with the truth. "I don't know the whole story yet."

"Tell me what you do know."

"I need to look into a few more things."

Courtney's eyes were still fixed on him. "Please."

He felt his resistance break under the recognition that if he was in her place, he would've demanded the truth, too. Without it there'd be no firm ground on which to stand in the face of the gathering storm.

"Let's sit down."

He led them to a corner of the waiting room, where they huddled in chairs under an indoor palm. Gage outlined what he'd learned, and how the case was closing in around Burch. By the end Courtney was no longer looking at him, her head hung, eyes focused on her interwoven fingers resting on her lap. Faith reached her arm around Courtney's shoulders.

"I think Peterson is aiming at a conspiracy case based on the substantive offenses of wire fraud, securities fraud, and money laundering. That way he can go after Jack for crimes committed by the others, even if he didn't know exactly what they did. Peterson just needs to show what the others did was foreseeable."

Courtney looked up. "But if he wasn't part of it, how can anything they did be foreseeable?"

"That's the burden of proof in conspiracy cases."

"But what's that based on?" Courtney's face bore the bewilderment of a person lost in a maze of underground tunnels. "I mean, how do they prove—"

"Words. Conspiracies are words. And proof in conspiracy cases is how the words are repeated."

"But that's hearsay. I thought—"

"Conspiracies are the exception to the hearsay rule."

Courtney's shoulders slumped. "So it's whatever Matson says."

Gage nodded. "And to be of value to the government, Matson needs to say that Jack was a coconspirator. That's what the government wants to hear. In fact, that's all they'll accept. Peterson has spent a lot of time and a lot of the government's money on this case and it all hinges on Matson."

Courtney turned fully toward Gage. "But you still haven't answered my question."

Gage searched his mind for a way to begin that wouldn't end by crushing her determination to fight. He decided to start at a distance.

"Part of what Jack does is tax law. In fact, that has a lot to do with how Jack structured SatTek's offshore companies. He set them up so that the profits from sales made outside of the U.S. wouldn't be taxed here."

"But he didn't know they were all fake."

Gage nodded and took her hand. "Of course he didn't."

"But—"

Gage held up his palm. "Let me finish."

She nodded.

"Everybody knows what a burglary is. It's just a matter of overlaying the law onto the facts. But tax law is different, it's made by people testing limits. And that's because there is no way the U.S. Congress or the Russian Duma or the Hong Kong Executive Council can anticipate all the inventive ways people do business.

"The problem is that Jack sometimes works the way he skis. Naïvely. Overconfidently. Always on the edge. And his clients are always trying to push him over, sometimes just by not telling him exactly what they're up to. Then, if the client gets in trouble, he says, 'My lawyer told me it was all right.' It's cowardly, but that's what they do."

"But this is a lot more serious than a tax case."

"Yes."

"How serious?"

Gage shrugged. "I don't know for sure."

"Graham." Her eyes searched his face.

"I haven't figured it out. The sentencing guidelines are about a thousand pages long. Then you need to do a lot of calculating. Points are added for some things, deducted from other things. And you have to figure in the amount of the loss. So it's very complicated."

"Graham, I need to know."

"Courtney—"

"Please."

Gage looked up at Faith. She nodded. Courtney needed an answer.

"If Peterson got the indictment he wants and Jack got convicted of everything, it would be kind of long…"

"How long is long?"

"Maybe about..." Gage hesitated, hating to say the words that would stab at Courtney's heart. "Twenty years."

Faith drew her close as Courtney's eyes filled with tears.

"But I know he didn't do it," Courtney said, voice rising. "Jack doesn't work for money. It's all just play for him. You know that, Graham, don't you?"

"I know that. So does everybody who knows Jack. But our first chance to prove it to everyone else may not be until the trial."

Courtney lowered her head, then wiped her eyes with a tissue. Gage and Faith sat silently, not diminishing her by backtracking, and pretending the truth was otherwise.

After a minute, Courtney looked up. She took Gage and Faith's hands. "Thank you."

◇◇◇

"This case has turned into a steamroller," Gage said to Faith as they drove away an hour later. "Between Washington wanting a whipping boy for corporate crime and the class action lawyers looking to make a killing, I don't think there's a way to stop it."

"What do you know about Simpson & Braunegg?" Faith asked.

"That they're disgusting. It's one of those firms that deceives itself into thinking it's on the side of truth and justice, when it's really just after the money—sometimes ruthlessly. It almost makes you respect gangsters like Matson's pal Gravilov. At least they don't pretend to be serving the public good." Gage exhaled and shook his head as he stared at the car taillights in front of them. "Simpson & Braunegg will sue Jack whether they believe he was in the wrong or not. He has deep pockets and his firm has deep pockets."

"Why didn't they just name him now?"

"Because they don't want a big fight over his files. They want him to believe that he's just going to be a witness. They're hoping he'll give them everything if he thinks it'll keep them from naming him."

"Jack may be weak at the moment, but he's not stupid."

"And you know what else?" Gage wasn't looking for an answer. "I think Peterson fed them the case."

Faith's head swung toward him. "But isn't that unethical? U.S. Attorneys aren't supposed to do that, are they?"

"No, they're not. But we won't be able to prove it and, even if we did, nobody'll care. Not with Simpson & Braunegg on the courthouse steps showing off a bunch of retirees who lost everything."

"Can you do anything?"

"I don't know." Gage felt the pressure of two clocks ticking. The criminal case and the civil suit, each counting down toward explosions that would rip Jack and Courtney's lives apart. "There's one thing I do know. I need to buy some time."

Chapter Forty-three

Derrell Williams, an ex–FBI special agent who'd worked with Gage for almost a decade, intercepted him as he walked from his car toward the front steps of his building.

"Hey, Chief. I had a meeting over at the U.S. Attorney's Office on your antitrust case. The good news is that they were so thrilled to have the thing handed to them in a package that they did a little more tongue wagging than they should've."

"And the bad news?" Gage asked, eyes fixed on Williams.

"You better watch your back. The word is that Peterson is pretending to be playing the SatTek case like it's a game of Sunday touch football, but inside his four walls he's been screaming that you're screwing up his indictment and that he's going to hammer you."

Gage nodded. "Thanks for the heads-up."

Williams smiled. "That's what you always say, and then you do whatever you were going to do anyway." His smile faded. "But I'm not sure that's a safe way to go this time. My old partner was at the meeting. On the way out, he whispered that Peterson asked him whether there's a connection between you and a Hong Kong company called TD Limited. He thought it was chickenshit. But it sounds to me like Peterson is following your tracks, trying to get you into his crosshairs."

Gage knew Williams was right. Peterson was looking for a way to make him duck and run. Toxic Disposal Limited was a front company he and Burch created to smuggle medical supplies through Pakistan by mislabeling them as contaminated equipment sent for recycling. It was the only way to keep it from being stolen and sold on the black market. The problem was that the scheme required first presenting fraudulent export documents to U.S. Customs, a felony that could cost Gage both his license and a year in federal prison.

"Sounds that way to me, too," Gage said, "but I'm working on getting Peterson into mine. We'll see who locks on first."

◇◇◇

Alex Z hustled to catch up with Gage as he walked down the hallway toward his office.

"You guessed it, boss," Alex Z said, following him inside. "There's a connection. The partner at Simpson & Braunegg who's handling the SatTek suit was a frat brother of Peterson at Cal. Franklin Braunegg. And they're golfing buddies now. They even belong to the same country club."

Gage pointed at a chair in front of his desk. "How'd you find out?"

"Alumni bulletins. That kind of thing." Alex Z sat, then flipped open a folder and turned it toward Gage. "I even found a photo of them holding up a trophy from a tournament. They play in what's called the Winter Circuit."

"Can you find out whether Peterson was ever—"

"Already did." He slid over a spreadsheet. "I found three securities cases where Peterson was the prosecutor and Braunegg was the class action lawyer. A total of about fifty-five million dollars."

Gage gazed out of the window while doing his own calculation. "If Braunegg's firm got thirty to forty percent, that would be fifteen or twenty million. Even if they had a few million in expenses, they made out like bandits in slam-dunk cases."

"Slam-dunk? I thought these cases are more complicated than that."

Gage looked back at Alex Z. "If Peterson can prove a criminal case to a jury beyond a reasonable doubt, then even a second- or third-rate attorney can reach a preponderance of the evidence in a civil trial. It's not that hard to tip the scales, especially when the defendants all have fraud convictions."

Alex Z's eyes widened. "You mean a guy driving on a suspended license facing a four-hundred-dollar fine can't be convicted unless the jury finds him one hundred percent guilty beyond a reasonable doubt, but Mr. Burch could be wiped out based on fifty-one percent to forty-nine percent?"

"Pretty close."

Alex Z threw up his hands. "That's absurd." He looked down, shaking his head, then up at Gage. "I see what Braunegg gets out of it, but what about Peterson?"

"Peterson can use Braunegg to take advantage of civil discovery rules that force defendants into depositions. The smart thing is for Jack to take the Fifth. He could do it secretly in front of the grand jury. But he knows if he did it in a deposition, Braunegg would leak it to the media."

Gage cringed as he imagined the press stationed on the sidewalk in front of Burch's house, and the humiliation inflicted by cameras riveted on his car window as he drove from his underground garage.

But there was something worse: "In a criminal case, a jury can't hold it against you if you take the take the Fifth; in a civil trial they can. Braunegg would crush Jack with it."

"But I thought they delayed—"

Gage shook his head. "There's no way a judge would delay the civil case until the criminal trial is over. A lot of the shareholders are elderly. The court will want them to get their money back, not die waiting."

"Well, then Mr. Burch should just let himself be deposed. Maybe once everyone hears the truth that will be the end of it."

"It'll only make things worse. Not only will Peterson assume Jack is lying, but it'll give Matson a chance to adapt his story to Jack's defense. In fact..." Gage imagined Braunegg and Peterson forehanding Burch back and forth like a tennis ball on an imaginary red clay court at a very real old boys' club. "Braunegg can tailor his questions to what Peterson is forcing out of witnesses at the grand jury."

Alex Z drew back. "That's not right. Grand juries are supposed to be secret."

"Only in theory."

"But I thought Peterson was a straight shooter. NFL and all that."

"Sports build muscles, not character. How many times do you think Peterson held a blocker, tripped a halfback, forearmed a quarterback, took a penalty rather than let the other side score? You think any coach ever complained? The only thing a coach ever said to him was, 'Don't get caught next time.'"

"And Braunegg?"

"A calculating little scavenger."

Chapter Forty-four

Franklin Braunegg was just biting into a BLT when Gage pulled up a third chair to his table for two at the Hidden Valley Country Club. Over the years, Gage had watched Braunegg try to transform himself from a personal injury street fighter into a white-collar sophisticate, but he only ended up looking slick. Eyes too predatory. Hair dyed too dark. Too many rings on his clawlike hands.

"Where's your pal, Peterson?" Gage asked, glancing at the half-eaten Cobb salad across the table from Braunegg.

Gage knew the answer. He'd spotted an FBI agent driving Peterson away a few minutes earlier.

"Hadda go inta the offish," Braunegg said, trying to chew and answer at the same time. Braunegg swallowed hard, then took a sip of ice tea. "How ya doing, Graham?"

"I'm a little concerned about a friend of mine."

"So I heard."

Gage tilted his head toward the parking lot. "From Peterson?"

"A little bird."

"I think Peterson would find that description insulting."

Braunegg laughed, spitting out a piece of bacon that landed in Peterson's abandoned salad.

"So what do you want?" Braunegg asked.

"I want you to lay off Burch. Withdraw your subpoena and don't name him as a defendant for a few months."

"Not possible." Braunegg sucked on his teeth. "I've got a thousand plaintiffs who want his head. And, of course, his money, which he has a lot of. I need to keep the clients happy. Happy clients are grateful clients. Grateful clients refer friends and family."

"But that's not how you got SatTek."

Braunegg shrugged. "I don't know how we got it. The case just came in. Maybe the shareholders saw me on FOX News and liked my spiel."

"I don't think so," Gage said, finally repaying the wink.

"What are you suggesting?" Braunegg's face flared. "I don't need to sit here—"

"Then get up."

Braunegg threw his napkin onto his plate, but didn't rise.

"Peterson fed you SatTek just like he fed you your last three securities fraud cases."

"I'd like to see you prove it."

"No you wouldn't. That's the last thing you want me to do."

Braunegg glanced around the restaurant. Gage imagined that he was worried that members seated near them had noticed his loss of control in throwing down his napkin.

"You want to take a little walk?" Gage asked.

Braunegg signaled a waiter and signed his tab, then Gage led him out to the parking lot.

"So what if Peterson sent over the plaintiffs," Braunegg said, as they stood next to Gage's car. "It's not a crime."

"That depends."

"Depends on what?"

"What else got put on your tab besides an overpriced salad and whether he also sent over grand jury material."

"You'd have a hard time proving either one."

"Not so hard." Gage leaned in close, pointing at Braunegg's chest. "You're too flashy. It's the reason why you never did well in trial. You show your hand too soon, no self-control."

Braunegg drew back. "Look, Gage, I don't have to stand here and take this shit from you."

"First you don't want to sit, now you don't want to stand. Which is it?"

"How about just show me your cards and let's get this over with?"

"I talked to Hackett. Matson isn't cooperating with you. I talked to Granger's lawyer and Granger wasn't cooperating with you, either."

Braunegg remained silent. His face set. Not sure where Gage was headed.

"Read over your complaint. You have allegations in there that could've only come from Matson and Granger. And only Matson was talking—and not to you."

"Like what?"

"The alleged connection between Burch and Fitzhugh. That went from Matson to Peterson to you."

Braunegg blanched like he just got caught stuffing jumbo shrimp into his wife's purse at a cocktail party.

"And that's all you want? We hold off of Burch? Why not just go to the press? Take a shot at making us pull out of the case? You might even get Peterson fired."

"Because somebody else would take it over and I'd just have to come up with a way to lean on them—and I don't have time. And it doesn't help me to end Peterson's career. Another U.S. Attorney would just come into the case and we're back where we started."

Braunegg looked toward the parking lot exit, as if there was a street sign in the distance to tell him which way to turn, then decided to call for help. "I'll talk to my partner."

Gage pulled out his business card, wrote a telephone number on the back, then handed it to Braunegg. "This is the telephone number of Kenny Leals at the *New York Times*. You can either call me in one hour agreeing or call him in two hours explaining. Do yourself and Peterson a favor. Call me in one."

Gage had driven less than a mile away from the Hidden Valley Country Club when his cell phone rang.

"You've got a deal. Two months. But someday the shoe's going to be on the other foot," Braunegg said. "What goes around comes around."

There was only one type of person Gage hated more than liars: people who thought in clichés. They couldn't help but lie to themselves.

"No it won't and no it doesn't."

"You better watch your back."

Not another one. Better answer in a way he understands.

"You couldn't sneak up on the dead."

Chapter Forty-five

I think we've got a leak from the grand jury in the SatTek case," Peterson told United States Attorney Willie Rose at the weekly meeting of the senior staff in the windowless conference room on the eleventh floor of the Federal Building.

Spread around the table along with Peterson, as head of Securities Fraud, were the chiefs of Major Crimes, White Collar, Organized Crime, Anti-Terrorism, and the Drug Enforcement Task Force. All of them looked at Rose with uncertainty. The first black federal district judge in the Eastern District of California, Rose had resigned a year earlier to assume leadership of what the press called the "troubled" U.S. Attorney's Office for the Northern District of California. And while each knew they had been promoted as part of Rose's solution to the troubles, they all feared becoming vehicles for his political ambition.

"If we had somebody in Congress with balls enough to sponsor a constitutional amendment," Rose said, "we'd get rid of the stupid thing. We don't need a damn grand jury to tell us we have a case. We tell *them*. It's a waste of our time and taxpayers' money." Rose tossed his pen onto his yellow legal pad, then looked over at Peterson. "Why do you think you've got a leak?"

Everyone at the table, and their assistants sitting behind them, alerted like golden retrievers. Peterson wasn't a guy who said whatever happened to flit through his mind. If he raised an issue, he'd thought about it.

"We've had two grand jury targets murdered and one who barely survived." Peterson glanced around at the others. "Some of you know him, Jack Burch. The dead ones are a chartered accountant in London named Fitzhugh, and Edward Granger, a venture capital guy who we had just told the grand jury would be coming in to testify as a cooperating defendant."

"I thought Burch was road rage," Rose said.

"That's the party line, but I'm not sure. The later shooting that I thought was road rage wasn't. It was domestic. The wife thought hubby was having an affair with a woman he jogged with in the mornings. But even if we set that aside, we have Fitzhugh and Granger. It's like somebody is trying to contain the case and somebody in the grand jury is tipping them off."

The tension in the room ratcheted up.

Rose shifted into cross-examination mode. "What's your evidence?"

"It's less evidence than a pattern. Shortly after I introduce the case to the grand jury, Burch and Fitzhugh get hit. Then we tell them that Granger is about to cooperate and he gets taken out."

"What about Matson?"

"Nobody's bothered him and he says he's not afraid."

Rose peered over at Peterson as if the solution was obvious. "Doesn't that tell you that he's somehow in on it?"

Peterson shook his head. "I've spent a lot of time with him. He doesn't have the balls."

"Then what?"

"My guess is that there's something we don't know that connects Burch, Fitzhugh, and Granger that's separate from Matson, and somebody doesn't want it to come out."

"Who were the stockbrokers?" asked Lily Willison, the leader of the Organized Crime Division, known as Mainframe because of her computerlike memory.

"Northstead Securities in San Diego. Kovalenko. Yuri."

Willison looked toward the ceiling, searching her mental database, then back at Peterson. "He's as ganged-up as they come. Just like his dead brother. Maybe he's the one trying to contain this thing."

"I considered that," Peterson said. "But as far as we can tell, Kovalenko's only connection to SatTek was pump and dump. And he isn't afraid of doing a couple of years. He won't get involved in murder just to save himself a short vacation in minimum security. And even if it is him, the information about who to target had to come from somewhere."

"Why not just ask the court to impanel another grand jury…" Willison hesitated, her face flushing. She swallowed, then finished the question, voice rising to a squeak. "And start over?"

The question hung in the air like a raised sledgehammer. Everyone knew, Willison most of all, that she was about to get thumped.

"Let's back up," Rose said, setting up the blow. "How many indictments has that grand jury issued?"

"Fifty, sixty, something like that," Peterson said.

Willison's interlaced fingers began to dig into the backs of her hands.

"How many defendants altogether?"

"Two hundred or so. Maybe more. They did two racketeering indictments with about thirty defendants each."

Rose looked at Willison, then swung down. "Are you ready to disclose grand jury misconduct to two hundred defense lawyers? Ready to answer two hundred motions to dismiss? Maybe a hundred speedy trial motions? Maybe even a bunch of grand jury abuse motions? When we don't even know for sure what happened?"

Willison shook her head, but held his gaze.

Rose reached for his pen, then began drumming it on the conference table, looking from face to face, lowered eyes ducking guilt by association.

"I see there aren't any volunteers for a little motion exercise."

Rose exhaled. It was moments like these that reminded him how much easier life was on the bench. He took the U.S. Attorney appointment only to get his name in the media to set up a run for governor, and planned to kick it off with Burch's indictment and a no-one-is-above-the-law-time-to-get-the-big-time-lawyers press conference. But grand jury problems were messy. The public wouldn't understand and the mess would slop back onto him.

Rose glanced at Peterson. "You and I need to visit the chief judge. Anybody have anything else?" Rose paused, then looked around the table. "No? Then we're done."

◇◇◇

The chief judge cleared his calendar for the meeting, and later that day Peterson called Zink into his office.

"The chief judge authorized an investigation. I told Rose you've done great work on the case and you're in the best position to connect the dots. He agrees."

Zink settled into a chair across from Peterson. "Thanks for the vote of confidence, but this could spin out of control. You think any of the grand jurors will go to the press if they get wind of what we're doing?"

"Only one I can think of."

"Number Six?"

"Yeah, Number Six," Peterson said. "And just wait until we have one grand jury investigating another. They'll be giving me funny looks, wondering if we're going after them, too."

"Where do you want to start?"

"The attendance records and notebooks. They're required to store their notes at the clerk's office when they're not in session. Let's see who was present at each hearing and what they wrote. But let's be careful we don't focus too much on Number Six. Being a runaway doesn't mean he's the one. It's a huge jump from being a little hyperactive to fingering people for hits."

Zink glanced up in the direction of the grand jury room. "How will I get the notebooks?"

"The chief judge is sending an order to the clerk. He authorized you to make copies each evening after they've been collected. But you have to give the copies back to the clerk when your investigation is done. Same with the attendance records."

Peterson paused, leaned back, and looked up toward the ceiling.

"I wonder if it's just SatTek or if this guy, if it is a guy, is also doing this in other cases." He glanced at Zink. "How about you get me the other indictments? I'll find out if anything hinky happened in those cases. Maybe not murders, but witnesses knowing they're about to be subpoenaed or targets getting advance warning of their indictments and making a last-second run. Maybe this guy shops his wares around to everybody."

"Will Rose back you if this blows up?"

"Not if he wants to get elected governor. He'd never get past the primary."

◇◇◇

By the time Peterson arrived at Zink's office the following morning, Zink had profiled each of the twenty-three grand jurors and posted leads from the jurors' notebooks on a cork board tacked to the wall.

"I've got it reduced down to the three most likely," Zink began after Peterson sat down next to his desk. "Number Six, Number Thirteen, and Number Twenty-two."

Zink stepped to his chart, using a Bic pen as a pointer. "Number Six. Not only does he summarize everything, but he makes margin notes of his opinions. His favorite word is 'asshole'..." Zink paused for a moment. "And he most often applies it to you."

Peterson shrugged.

"He never liked you as a football player and is thrilled you never made it into the hall of fame. And he doesn't like Matson, thinks he's a scumbag. He wrote that he wishes this was a capital case and that he'd like to blow the brains out of anybody who was part of the scheme."

"So he's in the postal worker category."

"Exactly. Number Thirteen maybe is just unlucky. He got caught talking about a case in the hallway. They all do it one time or another. The grand jury clerk told me she overheard the chief judge reading him the riot act. The guy was real upset. He begged to stay on. Maybe he became resentful enough to want to sabotage the whole thing."

Peterson shook his head as if to say that this investigation would be going nowhere. "Another weak candidate."

Zink nodded, then tapped Number Twenty-two. "But here's a contender. What got my attention is that he wrote down Kovalenko's patronymic not as 'B-o-r-i-s-o-v-i-c-h,' but as 'B-o-r-*y*-s-o-v-i-c-h,' old style. I figured he's got a Russian background. And bingo. His family name was Toshenko. When his grandparents got to Ellis Island in the early 1920s, the immigration people anglicized it to Thomas."

"That's not unusual. It happened all the time."

Zink raised his eyebrows. "Guess who his cousin is?"

"I couldn't guess." Peterson frowned, not in the mood for game playing.

"Scuzzy Thomas."

Peterson sat up. "No fucking way!"

Peterson slammed his fist on Zink's desk. Pens and notebooks jumped. The computer monitor shook. "Are you telling me that we've got a relative of a mobster who's in the joint for jury tampering sitting on a federal grand jury? Rose is gonna go nuts... Did you look at his juror questionnaire?"

"No, they're under seal. We'll need a court order."

Peterson stood up. "I'll get an order for all of them. This is a fucking can of worms." He looked at the chart, shaking his head. "I'm starting to wish I never opened it."

He started toward the door, then hesitated and looked back at Zink. "Did it cross your mind that whoever wants all these other guys dead also wants to keep Matson alive?" He then turned away and marched down the hallway.

Chapter Forty-six

Why is somebody keeping Matson alive?" Gage wondered aloud when Alex Z walked into the office kitchen where he was making a pot of coffee.

"Keeping or leaving?"

"Leaving means he's harmless, keeping means he's got something somebody wants."

Alex Z reached into the cabinet and pulled out two cups. "If I was him, I'd get a bodyguard."

"He must have a *krysha*, a roof." Gage held his hand above his head, palm down. "Somebody is protecting him." Gage lowered his arm. "Slava thought that Gravilov would squeeze Matson for money and it was Alla Tarasova's job to keep an eye on him."

"Protecting him so they can squeeze him?"

"That's what a protection racket is all about. They protect you from other crooks so you can keep paying."

"Why not just put a gun to his head?" Alex Z formed his hand into the shape of a revolver. "You know, 'Gimme all you got.'"

"What would you do if somebody did that to you?"

"I'd need to run out and sell my guitars and stuff."

"So would Matson. We need to figure out where his money is." Gage flicked his thumb toward Alex Z's office. "Why don't you go over Matson's phone records and the ones I got out of Fitzhugh's house? See if you can tell who they were calling. Maybe we can find a pattern."

Alex Z brought a computer printout with him into Gage's office a few hours later.

"It's pretty clear Matson only used his office phone for SatTek business calls," Alex Z reported. "In fact, all the overseas calls were to companies on the sales leads or customer lists or to suppliers of manufacturing equipment. Germany and France. I checked a bunch of the numbers. Almost all were listed. But his cell phone records show calls to a bunch of unlisted and disconnected numbers in places that haven't even been on the horizon. Like Singapore. Why would he be calling Singapore? Or Taiwan? Switzerland I can understand. Liechtenstein, yeah. UK, sure. But Singapore?"

"Any pattern?"

"Pattern? Yes. Explanation? No—but whatever it was, Fitzhugh was in the middle of it. Calls to him kept crisscrossing all the others. Switzerland, Fitzhugh. Singapore, Fitzhugh. Taiwan, Fitzhugh. He'd get a call from Matson, then right away call a bank or a law office in Lugano, or Guernsey, or London. Bang, bang. Just like that."

Gage turned his head and squinted toward the light coming into his office window, then back at Alex Z with the barest hint of a smile.

"There's something we haven't thought much about," Gage said. "Matson's exit strategy. How does he think this'll end? He knows the government will make him forfeit all the money. Peterson isn't a fool. A jury asked to convict Burch wouldn't be too pleased if he let Matson keep any. But Matson's not a fool, either. He's got to have a stash. He doesn't want to come out of this thing broke. And the best place to hide money is where nobody would think to look."

"You think maybe Alla is part of his exit strategy? Dump the wife and disappear?"

"If Slava is reading this correctly, he'll disappear, all right."

"I don't know, boss, her name is just too pretty for a crook. Alla Tarasova. It's musical, even lyrical. It sort of floats in the air."

Gage remembered someone else who'd talked about her in almost the same way, as a butterfly with a beautiful name.

"That's what Mickey thought, too."

Chapter Forty-seven

Mickey took it. He just lay there and took it. He didn't scream. He didn't yell for help. He knew if they'd intended to kill him, he'd already be dead.

The giant kicked him one last time in the ribs as he lay sprawled in the shadows of Azenby Road in Southeast London, then lumbered into a waiting Mercedes and sped away.

Mickey didn't remember passing out. He just remembered the message and the pain when a constable passing by just after sunrise mistook him for a vagrant and shook him back into consciousness.

◇◇◇

The Metropolitan Police officer who followed the ambulance down Peckham Road and up Denmark Hill to the King's College Hospital recognized Mickey as soon as the blood was washed off his face. Superintendent Michael Ransford was a legend whose retirement picture hung in the station to which the officer was assigned.

The officer winced as he inspected the superintendent's shattered face, for a moment imagining it was his own infirm grandfather lying there. But then he caught himself. Ransford was a pro. The best. He'd remember the details that civilian victims forget. He felt lucky to be the officer assigned to do the interview.

"Superintendent?"

Mickey opened his eyes.

"What did he look like, Superintendent?"

Mickey squeezed his answer out through his fractured jaw. "Never saw him."

"Would you recognize his voice?"

"No."

The officer hesitated, almost bewildered. Of course he should recognize a voice...unless he was senile.

"What did he say to you?"

"Don't remember."

"What about his accent?"

"Cockney."

Finally. At least the superintendent remembered something they could build on later. He pushed ahead.

"What were you doing on Azenby Road, sir?"

"Walking. Just walking."

The officer watched Mickey's eyes close, then shook his head while gazing down at the battered man, wondering why one of the top detectives in Metropolitan Police history had deteriorated so quickly in retirement. He thought again of his grandfather, and an answer appeared: Alzheimer's. Perhaps he should call the superintendent's wife, offer to help keep an eye on him; maybe even gather up some other officers and take turns. Clearly the old man shouldn't be permitted to wander the streets alone.

◇◇◇

The Russian was smart, Mickey thought as he listened to the officer's footsteps fade toward the door. *If they'd killed me, Peckham would've been swarming with police. No one gets away with murdering a retired superintendent. An assault case with no leads? Well, that's an altogether different thing.*

◇◇◇

"Uncle Mickey's hurt."

The grim voice of Hixon Two followed a ringing that startled Gage and Faith as they sat on the couch near midnight watching the last embers in the fireplace turn dark.

"What is it?" Faith asked. "Jack? Did they take Jack back to the ICU?"

Gage shook his head, then placed a hand on her arm.

"Will he be okay?" Gage asked Hixon Two.

Hixon Two took in a short breath, trying to maintain her soldier's composure. "He'll live. But they beat the bloody hell out of him."

Gage covered the mouthpiece and turned to Faith. "Mickey's been hurt."

"Gravilov's thugs," Hixon Two continued. "Hammer and Britva. Ribs, right arm, right eye socket, jaw, a gash on his forehead."

Gage winced at the image. "How did it—"

"He enjoyed the taste of work again, so he went out on his own."

"I never should've—"

"Don't blame yourself. He said you'd do that."

"What was he thinking? These are dangerous people."

"He was thinking that maybe he'd learn something that would help you. He started following Gravilov, but they led him into a trap. Azenby Road is a tiny street that dead ends at Warwick Gardens. He was trapped."

"Can I talk to him?"

"He's still under. They went in to find the source of internal bleeding and they'll wire his jaw. I could tell he learned something, but they raced him into surgery before he could finish."

Gage disconnected the call and remained sitting on the edge of the couch.

"Mickey thought he was invisible," he told Faith, "like lost keys." He felt himself well up. "I never should've gotten him into this."

"It's not your fault. The little jobs you gave him made him feel important, still useful in the world."

Gage turned toward her. "But I always made sure somebody younger and stronger was with him."

"He never realized it, did he?"

Gage shook his head. "I didn't want to hurt his feelings… For something like this, he should've called me to come do it, not tried it himself."

"Maybe he didn't want to look stupid if he was wrong."

"Sometimes it's not worth being right."

Chapter Forty-eight

Hixon Two called back early the next morning, catching Gage on the drive down the hill toward the flatlands and the Bay Bridge.

"He's got a sparkle in his eye and is quite proud of himself." The worry was gone from her voice.

"Wait till the painkillers wear off."

"I don't think it'll make a difference."

"Can he talk?"

"Yes, but he sounds like he has a lisping Chinese accent from a 1940s film. He kept saying he 'crowsht a shirkle.'"

"Closed a circle? What'd he mean?"

"Get this." She paused as she'd been instructed by Mickey to set Gage up for the surprise. "He spotted Gravilov coming out of Alla's building three days ago."

"Now *that's* what I would call closing a circle." The black hole left by Fitzhugh had been filled with Alla Tarasova. He paused, trying to visualize the possible orbits, then thought out loud. "Either she's now Matson's proxy or she's got a separate deal with Gravilov. Maybe Slava is right, she and her father are working with Gravilov."

But that was all step two. Step one was still Mickey.

"Do you think Gravilov had any idea why Mickey was following them? SatTek can't be the only scam he's got running."

"No way to tell. They just beat him up and warned him not to talk. That's it."

After Hixon Two rang off, Gage found himself lost in circles. There were too many threads doubling back on each other, and he couldn't get his head clear. He decided it was time to go beat on something. He cut off the freeway at the last exit before the bridge and headed east.

Twenty minutes later, Stymie Jackson came limping out of his East Oakland gym office. Gage had just slipped on his bag gloves. The sixty-eight-year-old former middleweight contender waved to Gage, then pulled up a stool next to the heavy bag.

"Where ya been?" he asked Gage. "You missed a few weeks."

"A friend of mine is in a little trouble."

Over thirty years since Stymie had first trained Gage for the police Olympics, he had learned never to ask Gage for details. He reached for the stopwatch hanging on a lanyard around his neck, and nodded.

Gage threw two left jabs and then a right uppercut that made the hundred-and-thirty-pound bag jump three inches.

"That's it. Stick it. Jab, jab, power jab. Come on. Jab, jab, power jab. Step into it. Jab, jab, power jab."

The word "trouble" echoed back. Gage then realized that there was something that had drawn him there. "My trouble" was the phrase Stymie always used to describe the day in the late fifties when he refused to take a fall in a fight. Chicago gangsters mangled his right leg as punishment, both for the money they'd lost and for not keeping his mouth shut. Stymie used to tell Gage: *They was telling me that everybody'd be betting against me like crazy on the next fight expecting me to lose—and they'd let me win. The bad guys said it was for the good of the game. But their game really wasn't boxing, it was something else.*

Gage stopped punching. He wiped his brow with the backs of his bag gloves, then glanced around the empty gym. Speed bags still. Ring empty. Jump ropes hung on hooks. A thought was lurking in his mind, but it was still too deep to dredge.

"Did I say it's time to stop?" Stymie looked down at his stopwatch. "You got forty-five seconds left. Come on, stick it."

Gage got back into the rhythm, then switched to a series of straight rights. The phrase "for the good of the game" repeated itself with each punch. For the *thump* of the game, for the *thump* of the game, for the *thump* of the game.

"Stop."

Gage slipped a towel off a worn wooden bench, gripped it between his gloves, and wiped the sweat from his face. He wondered whether the mobsters would've let Stymie keep fighting if he'd kept silent; just a broken leg, not a mangled one that destroyed his career.

Maybe that's it, Gage thought as he stared at the still swinging bag. Then the answer arrived in Stymie's voice: *So what if Matson's talkin'? He ain't talkin' about things the bad guys don't want him talkin' about.*

But Gage didn't have a clue what that was.

Chapter Forty-nine

Gage called Alex Z into his office after driving in from Stymie's.

"What's up, boss?" Alex Z said as he dropped into a chair.

Gage got up from behind his desk and walked to an easel, marker in hand.

"I need your help thinking this through."

He started a fresh charting of the players, drawing arrows showing the known relationships.

"We know how everybody connects together except for Matson, Alla, and Gravilov," Gage said, then stepped back from the chart.

"Three people can all meet each other in six different sequences," Alex Z said, shaking his head. "And when you factor in all of the rest, you spin off into infinity."

"That's exactly the problem," Gage said. "Too many moving parts."

Alex Z made a show of looking around the office. At the bookcases lined with files, the fireproof safes anchored to the floor, and a network server containing millions of scanned documents. "I thought those were the only kinds of cases you did."

"But this one we need to simplify before it gets away from us."

Gage crossed his arms across his chest. "Let's start at the beginning. Who introduced whom?" He glanced at Alex Z's SatTek chronology hanging from the wall, then back at the chart. "Matson travels to London just before the IPO, he hooks up with Alla...or she hooks up with him...Why? Was she looking to snag him? Or maybe they meet by chance...In any case, he brags. He says 'I've got an IPO coming up,' and she calls Budapest to tell her gangster daddy." Gage pointed at the lines connecting Matson, Alla, and Gravilov. "What did Granger say?...*Sometimes children grow up and do things you never expected in your wildest imagination*...Gage looked at Alex Z. "What does Granger do when he figures it out—whatever it was? Nothing. Absolutely nothing. He's unhappy, maybe about not getting a cut, but he has to keep his mouth shut. He can't snitch off Matson without snitching off himself."

"You think Matson has told the government about Gravilov?" Alex Z asked.

Gage repeated the question aloud, then shook his head and smiled. "That's it. That's exactly what Granger had to trade. And what shocked the hell out of him was that Matson had the balls to deal directly with a gangster at Gravilov's level." He looked again at the Granger circle, now transfixed. "Wait a second... Wait a second."

Alex Z's eyes followed Gage as if he was a high-wire artist balancing over a canyon.

Gage flipped the marker back and forth between his hands a few times, then stopped and looked at Alex Z. "If Granger had lived long enough to tell Peterson that Matson and Gravilov were working together, then Matson would've been no good to the government. It would've busted Matson's plea deal because he got caught lying. Peterson couldn't use him. A jury would never believe a word he said."

"Then Peterson gives Granger a chance to work off some time."

"Exactly. Granger could give up everybody Matson could. And he's untainted. He steps in and pushes Matson out of the way. Matson does the hard time and Granger gets no more than a couple of years."

"So Matson kills Granger?"

Gage shook his head. "I don't see a runt like him killing anybody. He's got somebody protecting him, maybe somebody sent by Gravilov…And whoever is behind the murder of Granger is also behind the murders of the Fitzhughs and the attempt on Jack and the burglary at his office."

"But why Mr. Burch?"

"He knows something. Fitzhugh and Matson asked him to set up TAMS Limited, the company that owns the London flat. Maybe Matson used Tarasova-Alla-Matson-Stuart Limited for whatever deal he had with Gravilov. Him and Alla working together…"

Gage paused as a shudder passed through his body, an image of Burch, weak and vulnerable, appeared in his mind. "It could be a lot worse. Jack may know something he doesn't realize he knows."

Gage tossed the marking pen onto his desk and surveyed the chart and the chronology hanging next to it.

"I have a feeling that regardless of whether this all started with Alla meeting Matson by chance or with her targeting him," Gage finally said, "it'll end up at the same place."

"Where's that?"

"I don't know yet. But we've got to get there before they do."

Chapter Fifty

Mr. Gage, you've got to stop him."

Milsberg's panicked voice wrenched Gage away from trying to project the future from the fragments of a partially known past.

Gage leaned forward in his chair and pressed his phone to his ear. "Stop who from doing what?"

"Matson. If he shuts this place down, I'm out of a job and I've got no place to go. Nobody's going to hire me."

"What makes you think he wants to shut it down?"

"It dawned on the rat that he can sell the manufacturing equipment and the SatTek proprietary technology to pay back a little money to the shareholders and make himself look better at sentencing time and in the civil suit." Milsberg's voice turned sarcastic. "He gets the benefit and all we get is unemployment."

"Whether there is any benefit depends on what everything is worth."

"Most of the value is in the intellectual property, but you'd need to ask somebody in the field." Milsberg paused. "That'll be tough because of the trade secrets problem. You'll need to show the material to someone in a position to evaluate it and those would be competitors."

"Let's worry about that later," Gage said. "How far along are you?"

"I've inventoried all of the hard assets and a software engineer has just finished working on intellectual property, like the code we developed for the low noise and video amplifiers. He's put together four or five DVDs."

"Can you make copies and smuggle out a 20-gigahertz video device? I need them this afternoon."

Milsberg didn't answer right away.

"Don't let me down, Robert."

Milsberg sighed, then answered. "But you'll have to watch my back. I don't think there'd be a big market for *The Prison Poetry of Robert Milsberg, CPA*."

Gage heard Milsberg shuffle papers.

"And there's more bad news. I got a grand jury subpoena yesterday. An FBI agent named Zink dropped it off."

Gage knew it would be coming. The meeting at his office and the call about Katie Palan showed that Peterson had mastered enough of the case to get it through a grand jury.

"When do they want you?"

"The date on the subpoena is for next Wednesday." Milsberg sighed. "But that's not the bad part. There was a target letter attached. I knew there would be, but it's a punch in the face when you actually see one with your name on it."

"Did you hire a lawyer?"

"I'm broke. Completely busted. But I was hoping I could just say, 'I refuse to answer on the grounds of self-incrimination' and they'd let me go."

"That's only about things that really could incriminate you. If they ask you where you stored invoices, you may be required to answer."

"Damn. I was afraid it wouldn't be that easy. Maybe that's why I keep having Jonah dreams."

"Sounds like you need a harpoon." Gage thought for a moment. "I've got somebody in mind."

◇◇◇

"Hey, Clara. You want to have some fun?"

He heard a laugh at the other end of the line, then: "I take it that means a freebie?"

"What about personal satisfaction? Isn't that why you left corporate law? Or is that just a line you feed the press?"

Clara Nance was on everybody's list of the top ten women lawyers in the country. Her real and only satisfaction in life was crushing opponents, and sometimes clients who didn't follow her orders. Gage had seen prosecutors cringe when she drew her six-foot frame to its full height and announced to the court that she was coming into a case.

"Don't make fun, Graham. Oprah about wept when I told her my epiphany story."

"Now you have a name for it?"

"And it's mostly true. Well, about as true as any of my closing arguments. But enough chitchat. What am I doing?"

"A grand jury target in a securities fraud case. He's a small fry but he's helping out in something that's real important to me."

"Does it have to do with your pal Jack Burch?"

"How'd you guess?"

"A fresh rumor in the Federal Building."

"How specific was it?"

"Just that Peterson went to the grand jury with the SatTek case and Burch had something to do with it. Also, somebody spoke to Hackett in the attorneys' lounge. He was all puffed up like he gets in a big-fee case. He talked about spending a lot of time outside the grand jury room, which means that his guy is cooperating—of course, his clients always cooperate. So what's new. Who's he got?"

"The president of the company, Stuart Matson."

"Who's mine?"

"Robert Milsberg, the controller. I think you'll like him."

"I'll like him if he does what I tell him, if he doesn't, I ream him a new—"

"Hey, don't talk like that about your client. He's a sensitive guy, writes haiku. Maybe if he gets through this, someday he'll write you a check."

"More likely a haiku about how he can't pay. Who's the agent?"

"Zink."

"Ick!"

"What do you mean 'ick'? Clara Nance doesn't say 'ick.'"

"That perverted crotch gawker once spent half a day trying to look up my skirt—from the witness stand, no less."

"But you wear slacks."

"Now I do."

◇◇◇

Gage checked his watch after he hung up. Faith was just finishing up a seminar. He left her a message to call him, and his phone rang a couple of minutes later.

"Did they get the test results yet?" Gage asked.

"The infections are gone. Courtney said Jack can go home tomorrow. He's ready to go. Believe me. The nurses caught him chewing on a leg from that Thanksgiving turkey you sent in. Everyone smelled the stuffing and sweet potatoes from the moment the delivery kid stepped off the elevator. Dr. Kishore thought it was a riot. It was good to see a smile on his face, the way he's been batted around by doctors."

"The problem is that he may be making himself just healthy enough to get batted around by the lawyers. Things are heating up on the civil side. Matson thinks it's to his advantage to shut down SatTek and sell off the pieces."

"Should Jack's firm intervene to try to stop him?"

"I won't know until I figure out whether SatTek is worth more than the sum of its parts, and that means first finding out what the intellectual property is worth. Do you know anyone in the electrical engineering department at Cal who can help me out? Even better, someone who's retired?"

"And who has a sense of adventure and can keep his mouth shut?"

"Exactly."

"I know just the guy."

Chapter Fifty-one

The ranch-style house on Grizzly Peak Road, high in the Berkeley Hills, was surrounded by a garden so geometrically perfect as to be unnerving. The heavy, gray-haired man who met Gage at the door wasn't. Seventy-three-year-old retired professor Ben Blanchard, dressed in blue baggy-kneed sweatpants, a coffee-stained white top, and running shoes that had never run, led Gage through a museumlike living room, out a sliding glass door, and through a covered patio to his workshop. A desk and two chairs were jammed into the far corner, heated and partially illuminated by a lone radiant heater.

"My wife calls this The Fort," Blanchard said, smiling. "She's not far wrong. The most attractive aspect of academic life is one they don't list on the employment announcement, an everlasting childhood."

Blanchard laughed, as he undoubtedly had the four or five thousand previous times he'd used the line. His timing, as he well recognized, was perfect, and Gage laughed on cue.

Gage glanced around The Fort as Blanchard led him to his desk. Apparently unfinished projects seemed to immeasurably outnumber the apparently finished. One on the workbench seemed to be close to completion.

"What are you working on?" Gage asked.

Blanchard cast Gage a teasing look. "I don't know you well enough."

"For what?"

"It's top secret."

"From whom?"

"My wife."

Blanchard's conspiratorial pause invited the obvious question.

"And it is...?"

"A real cool garage door opener. Very sophisticated. It practically knows my name."

"Unless it also opens a missile silo, I'm not sure it qualifies as top secret."

"It does too." Blanchard grinned. "My wife thinks I'm fixing the microwave."

Blanchard knocked papers off a metal folding chair. "Have a seat. You want a beer?"

"Sure."

Blanchard reached into a half-height refrigerator and pulled out two Budweisers. "I know this is Berkeley so I'm supposed to drink a microbrew, but it's my fort and I'll drink what I want." He handed one bottle to Gage, then twisted the cap off his own. "Faith says you have something top secret, too."

Gage opened his briefcase and displayed the DVDs and a black plastic box Milsberg had delivered. "I don't want to put you in a difficult position, but these contain the trade secrets of a defense contractor in Silicon Valley. SatTek."

"SatTek? Very interesting." Blanchard pointed at the box. "What's in there?"

"A video detector for a Hellfire missile."

A look of delight followed Blanchard's raised eyebrows. "Even more interesting, but I'm not worried. The Fort is like international waters, and its citizens, of which you are now one, are immune from prosecution."

Gage laid the items on Blanchard's desk, then outlined the case that was being framed around Burch and Matson's efforts to appraise the assets of SatTek.

"I need to understand what their intellectual property is worth, but it may be a little complicated to figure out. Not only do they produce offensive devices like video detectors, but they also manufacture defensive ones, like bi-static radar and acoustic amplifiers."

"I know exactly what you're talking about." Blanchard tapped his forefinger on his desk. "If we'd had those devices along the border between Afghanistan and Pakistan, Osama bin Laden never would have escaped. You can pick up the sound of a sandal stepping into sand." He shrugged. "Of course, there was no way the U.S. would've let Pakistan have anything this sophisticated. They'd use them against us someday."

Blanchard stood up and began to pace.

"I can tell you this right off. The technology for these products is hugely expensive to develop. First, because it uses embedded software, burned into the hardware, that allows a device to respond on its own to stimuli in the environment. Very, very sophisticated. And second, because it has to interface with large, complicated systems, and device failures can reverberate throughout with catastrophic results. So there's no room for error."

Blanchard realized that he'd begun lecturing and sat down, substituting gesticulating for pacing.

"The applications range far beyond what SatTek was doing. From cell phones to nuclear power plants—"

"And Dr. Blanchard's garage opening system?"

"Exactly. It may take a couple of days but I can help you out. I suspect that some of the design work was at least partially done by former students of mine. It's not rocket science." Blanchard smiled. "Well, actually, it is. In any case, it'll be fun, and an excellent excuse to avoid the microwave."

Blanchard led Gage back through the house and down the garden walkway to his car.

"Scary, isn't it," Blanchard said.

"What? SatTek?"

"No, the garden. Versailles is the Australian Outback compared to this place. Trust me, I've seen both. My wife trims the hedges with a nail clipper." Blanchard fingered a precisely angled leaf of a Fuji hedge. "At least it keeps her off my back, dear person that she is."

Gage pointed back at The Fort. "You want to meet up back here after you've had a chance to look at everything?"

"No. At my old lab at Cal. The disadvantage of having emeritus after your name is that colleagues treat you like their senile grandfather. The advantage is that they still give you free rein of the place—as long as you don't run with sharp objects."

"How soon can you get to it?"

"I'll start tonight after everyone has gone home."

Chapter Fifty-two

I'm sorry I sounded so panicky on the phone," Milsberg said, sitting across from Gage at the small table in the Jade Garden Restaurant. "Thanks for coming down. I know you're under a lot of pressure, but Franklin Braunegg coming by my house last night scared the hell out of me."

"He's threatening humiliation so you'll give up whatever money you have without a fight."

"It's not money he wants from me. It's testimony. In order to really stick it to Burch, he needs someone to corroborate a story that Matson told. Braunegg tried to get me to say that I saw him and Burch huddled together at SatTek a few months into the scam. But I never did. Never saw Burch over there. And that's what I told him, and that's when the son of a bitch threatened to bring my kid into it." Milsberg's face flushed. "We named our son after me because we thought he'd be proud to carry my name, and now he's going to have to change it."

"Don't get ahead of yourself, Robert. I don't want you freezing up on me. There are things I need to understand about SatTek and you're the only one who can explain them."

Milsberg took in a long breath and exhaled. "Like what?"

"Warrants. That's the reason I called you. In searching through the backup tapes we found a list of people and companies that received warrants to buy stock."

"That was another of Matson's slick little maneuvers. He used to hand out stock options and warrants like candy, but the warrants were the real prize. They gave a select few the right to buy shares at the issue price anytime they wanted, regardless of how high the stock went. That's how insiders were still able to get it at two bucks a share from SatTek long after it hit five on the public market."

"Did you get any?"

"Unfortunately."

"How many?"

"Ten thousand."

"Did you ever exercise them?"

"Yes. And that's what I'm most worried about now. Sure as hell makes me look guilty."

"You *are* guilty."

"Yeah, I guess there's that, too."

The waitress delivered a plate of pot stickers. Gage slid a couple onto Milsberg's plate and onto his own.

"Thanks," Milsberg said. "And thanks for hooking me up with that lawyer. She's tough."

Milsberg reached over to a neighboring table and grabbed a small bottle of hot chili oil. He poured a tablespoon on each pot sticker, followed by an equal amount of rice vinegar.

"Cheap thrill?" Gage asked.

"You got that right."

Gage poured a lesser amount of each on his.

"You told me that Matson claimed he lost a million dollars when the stock collapsed," Gage said. "But the shareholder list on the backup tape doesn't show him owning that much stock."

"I never checked. He must've owned and sold a lot over time. He was living way beyond his salary. I assumed it was from selling stock. And his wife was worse than him. She could put anybody into the poorhouse."

Milsberg popped a pot sticker into his mouth. His eyes teared as he chewed. "Poor guy."

"You crying for Matson?" Gage asked, smiling.

"No way," Milsberg gasped, then sipped his tea and wiped his eyes. "Whew! That was a killer."

Milsberg paused, then took another sip.

"Interesting thing," Milsberg said, setting down his cup. "I was in Matson's office one day and I noticed a deed of trust on his house from a foreign lender. Cobalt Partners. But it was never recorded. A million dollars on what I've heard is a two-million-dollar house."

"It's a money laundering gimmick. He used Cobalt to sell stock offshore and needed to get the profits back into the U.S. He just loaned money to himself."

Milsberg shook his head. "Man, I sure underestimated that guy."

"I think everybody did."

Gage got through a pot sticker without tearing up.

"Can you think of any domestic lenders Matson had dealings with?" Gage asked.

"Just one. He was looking for somebody to buy the SatTek facility and lease it back. It was a short-term gimmick to pump a lot of money into the company. In the end, Goldstake Bank in San Francisco bought it." Milsberg laughed and set down his chopsticks. "It was crazy. Goldstake Bank had a partner company, Goldstake Securities, that traded a lot of SatTek stock. A whole lot. The difference between the two was a fiction. No...it was a joke. The address was the same, the officers were the same. One day we'd get a call from a guy saying he was with Goldstake Bank and the next day from the same guy calling from Goldstake Securities."

"But selling the building would require board of directors' approval. How did Matson get them to go along?"

"Easy." Milsberg smiled as if he was about to take a bow. "Warrants. He'd been feeding them warrants. They did anything Matson and Granger told them to do because they were making hundreds of thousands of dollars for doing nothing but calling their brokers and saying, 'Sell.'"

◇◇◇

Gage called Courtney as he was driving away.

"How's Jack doing?"

"Wonderful. Being home made all the difference. His color is good and his cough is almost gone."

"Would you ask him if he knows anything about Goldstake Bank?"

"Sure. Hold on."

Gage heard a thunk as Courtney set the phone down, then her receding steps. She picked up the phone a minute later.

"Jack thinks it would be better if you came by."

◇◇◇

Burch was napping in a recliner in the slate-floored sunroom of his house when Gage walked in. He opened his eyes at the sound of Gage introducing himself to the bodyguard sitting by the stone fireplace in the living room, then raised his hand in a low wave.

Gage walked over, pulled an armchair to face him, then sat down. "How's it feel to be home?"

Burch spread his hands as if to encompass the house. "It's either a prison…" He cleared his throat while pressing his hands against his chest. "Or a fortress. I'm not sure yet."

On the drive over, Gage had considered asking a few questions, then leaving and thereby postponing Burch's confrontation with the case Peterson and Braunegg were building around him. But Burch took the decision out of his hands.

"I heard Courtney arguing with someone outside of my door at the hospital," Burch said. "I finally convinced her to tell me why." He reached over and picked up a glass of water from a low table, then took a sip. "How'd you get them to withdraw the subpoena?"

Gage shrugged. "Let's say I appealed to their good consciences."

Burch offered a weak smile. "Assumes facts not in evidence." He coughed lightly, then continued. "But it's time I learned what the facts are."

Burch's earnest expression told Gage he was ready to do more than simply answer questions. He wanted to know where he stood.

Gage watched Burch's mood rise and fall, his eyes widen and narrow, as he listened to Gage describe what he'd done and what he'd learned since the shooting. He told Burch everything except what happened to Mickey. That was something for him to feel responsible for, not Burch.

Burch didn't interrupt. Thirty years of listening to clients try to explain complex issues had taught him discipline and patience, but he appeared so drawn and drained at the end that Gage feared he'd gone too far and exposed Burch to too much all at once.

But Burch wasn't thinking about himself. "I had no idea…I didn't want you to devote your whole life to…"

Gage reached over and patted his forearm. "It's okay, champ. You'd do the same for me. We both know it."

"Still…"

Gage stopped him with a wagging forefinger, then changed the subject. "I need to know about Goldstake."

Burch thought for a moment, as if unwilling to leave something unsaid. Gage pointed at him and smiled. "Goldstake."

"Okay." He smiled back, then spoke. "It's owned by the Moscow Bank of Commerce." Burch licked his dry lips and swallowed. "Contacted me about five years ago. A referral from the Bank of America, wanting a bank license in the States. It was funded with foreign capital." Burch glanced toward his bodyguard in the next room, then leaned toward Gage and lowered his voice. "But there was a problem. When I was dealing with the Moscow bank, it was owned by a client who made his money in the natural gas market." Burch cleared his throat and took another sip of water. "But things changed. When the oligarchs…and that's what the client was…went to war, the Russian government couldn't protect the bank so he turned to the *maffiya*. And I resigned."

"Who became your client's roof?"

Burch leaned farther toward Gage. "There were two. One was the Podolskaya Group…and since the client had investments in Ukraine—"

Gage held up his hand. "Don't tell me. It's Gravilov."

Burch sat up, then flinched in pain and pressed his palms against his chest. "Does Peterson know?" Burch's voice rose. "Is he talking about two indictments? Like I'm some kind of mob lawyer?"

Gage shook his head. "I don't think so. I'm not sure he even knows all the ways Goldstake Bank is connected to SatTek—"

"It's what?" The color drained from Burch's face. "That can't be—"

Gage nodded. "Goldstake Bank now owns the SatTek facility."

Burch slumped. "And that means Peterson can connect me at both ends, make me look like the one who put this whole thing together. Bigger even than Granger. Just like he's been trying to do all along."

"Not yet, but it's just a matter of time." Gage looked down and thought for a moment. "Maybe…" Then back up at Burch. "We need to loop back, before SatTek. You know anybody at Granger's old firm in New York?"

Chapter Fifty-three

Westbrae Ventures Executive VP Herb Smothers was wiping his mouth with a cloth napkin as he answered the front door of his Westchester County colonial outside New York City the following night. He was still dressed in his suit slacks, starched blue shirt, and red tie. His sandy hair was short and graying at the temples. His face was open and friendly, as if expecting a neighbor—until Gage identified himself and said, "Jack Burch suggested I talk to you."

Smothers' Ivy League face slammed shut. He clenched his teeth and locked his eyes on Gage. "And I told Jack I had nothing to say."

Gage heard the clunk of rubber cleats on the walkway behind him, then a male voice saying, "We sure fucked up those assholes." Then another male voice laughing and hands slapping. He glanced over his shoulder as two men in their early twenties, wearing mud-splattered blue and yellow striped rugby shirts, emerged from the darkness and into the light cast by the porch fixture. They alerted like Rottweilers to the tension on their father's face and came to a stop behind Gage.

The larger of the two pointed at Gage's back. "This guy giving you a problem, Pop?" The two stepped forward, bracketing Gage, their shoulders touching his and their stale beer breath wafting toward him.

Smothers looked back and forth between his sons. Uncertainty clouded his face as he grasped the absurdity of having his drunk sons come to his rescue.

Smothers fixed his eyes on Gage, but spoke to his sons, "I'll take care of it."

Gage turned sideways to allow them to pass, then back toward Smothers as they thunked across the marble foyer and toward the kitchen.

"Smart move," Gage said. "Now tell me about Granger."

Smothers shook his head. "You wasted the trip." Smothers' voice was now firm, as if a businesslike tone could convince Gage to leave with his questions unanswered. "I couldn't even if I wanted to." He then tried a limp my-hands-are-tied shrug. "Corporate counsel locked the whole thing down the moment Granger walked away from Westbrae. It was mutual. He doesn't talk about us. We don't talk about him."

"Granger's dead. It's not like he can sue anybody. And somebody in Westbrae has got to start showing some courage—and it might as well be you."

"It's just..." Smothers' voice weakened. He leaned forward and peered into the darkness. Fear showed in his eyes. "You don't understand who Granger was...and the people who he..."

But Gage did understand. "You're afraid of something worse than getting fired."

Smothers nodded, then swallowed hard. "I can always get another job—"

"But not another life."

Smothers flinched at the words, then spread his hands in acknowledgment and defeat. "After what happened to Jack and to Granger, I can't..."

Gage's mind flashed on a bouquet that had stood by Burch's bedside in the hospital.

"I know you want to help Jack. That was the message you were really sending with the flowers." He looked back over his shoulder and made a show of inspecting the cars parked in the shadows along the street. Then once again at Smothers. "What do you say we step inside? I'll make my pitch and you decide whether you can help."

Smothers thought for a moment, studying Gage as if the answer lay with Gage, not within himself.

"The grand jury is already meeting, moving like a locomotive," Gage said. "And I'm running out of time to derail it." Gage shrugged. "If Jack gets indicted, it's all going to be out of my hands. His lawyers are going to hit Westbrae with subpoenas for every piece of paper and e-mail that has anything to do with Granger, and probe into every crooked thing he did and what Westbrae knew about it. They'll lay Westbrae open like a filleted catfish."

Gage slowly shook his head, as if in commiseration. "I won't be able to stop it." He then tossed Smothers a lifeline. "But I don't need everything, I only want to know about one thing... Just one thing." Gage locked his eyes on Smothers. "And just between you and me."

Smothers swallowed. "What's that?"

Gage pointed into the house. "I think we better talk inside."

◇◇◇

Driving back to the airport an hour later, Gage had what he needed, but was furious that with the grand jury clock ticking down, he'd consumed eighteen hours getting it.

But it finally made sense why Granger suddenly showed up in California. He had used Kovalenko and Goldstake Securities in a pump and dump with a Midwestern restaurant chain, and Westbrae had buried the crime in money before the SEC could find out about the scam.

The links in the SatTek chain snapped tight as Gage approached the rental car return at JFK. Gravilov had been running the SatTek scam from the beginning: first through Granger, then through Kovalenko, and, finally, through Alla Tarasova—and had been protecting it one dead body at a time.

Gage flashed back on the burglar's shoulder crushing into him outside Burch's office, then shuddered at the irony. The burglary had probably saved Burch's life. If there was anything in the SatTek file suggesting that Burch had connected SatTek to Goldstake, Gravilov would've had to finish Burch off.

Gage pulled to the stop in the Hertz return line and reached toward the glove compartment for the rental agreement, but his hand froze as his heart sank. Gravilov's people had been watching Granger the whole time. And by forcing him to run to the government to make a deal, Gage had flushed him out so they could pick him off.

He looked into his rearview mirror, now chilled by the thought that he might have led Smothers into the same trap—but then caught himself. It was a trap the coward deserved to be in. If Westbrae hadn't concealed Granger's crime, there never would've been a SatTek scam—and no need for a cover-up that left Burch bullet-ridden and Granger and the Fitzhughs dead.

But at least tonight, for whatever reason, Smothers had done the right thing.

Gage reached for his cell phone. "You have any vacation time?" he asked, but he didn't wait for Smothers to answer. "Take it, now. And as far away as you can get."

Chapter Fifty-four

Can you come to the lab?"

"When?" Gage asked, swinging his legs over the edge of his bed. He smiled to himself. The excitement in Blanchard's voice dissipated the gloom that had enveloped Gage during the sleepless night.

"Now's a good time."

"Who is it?" Faith asked, propping herself up on a pillow.

Gage covered his cell phone's mouthpiece. "It's Blanchard."

"Unless he's invented a perpetual motion machine, I'm not sure what excuse is good enough for waking me up at...at..."

"Five-fifteen."

"So, can you make it?" Blanchard asked.

"Sure. Forty-five minutes."

Instead of heading north to Berkeley, Gage took the tunnel toward the Central Valley, then looped back over the hills. Only after he was sure he'd shaken any surveillance he might have picked up after his meeting with Smothers did he drive toward the campus.

The professor was waiting at the entrance to the concrete and glass Cory Hall at UC Berkeley when Gage arrived.

"Matson is an idiot, a greedy idiot," Blanchard said. "The detector video amplifier is brilliant. Absolutely brilliant." He peeked out toward the dark campus, and then headed down the hall toward the lab. "If any of these nerds get here early, just say you're my nephew from...where do you want to be from?"

"Tulsa. I'd like to be from Tulsa."

"Okay, you're my nephew from Tulsa. What's your name?"

"Elmore."

"What about your last name?"

"Blanchard. I'm from your side of the family. Did you forget or are you just embarrassed?"

"Embarrassed? Never. Even as a small child I was proud of you...Little League and all that."

Gage gave him a thumbs-up. "I think we got the story down."

Blanchard led Gage to a computer monitor, then spread his hands as if introducing Gage to a dear friend. "Look at this."

Gage stared at meaningless oscillations with equally obscure labels, "Pulse Response," "Rise Time," and "Fall Time," all measured in nanoseconds.

"I'd like to meet the team that designed this device. It's pure genius," Blanchard said. "Say you installed one like this in a submarine periscope. You could see a sardine do a backflip ten miles away."

Blanchard punched a couple of keys, and a moving bar graph appeared on the screen.

"And footprint, talk about footprint. This draws so little power, you could run it off of a hearing aid battery." Blanchard grinned. "Well, maybe not. I exaggerate when I get excited."

"How much is it worth?"

"I could sell the design to Vidyne Industries for ten million by lunchtime. They'd just need to market a couple hundred of the devices and they'd have made their money back, including production costs."

Gage found himself nodding slowly. "That's it. That's Matson's exit strategy. The government seizes all his stock fraud profits, and he slips away with SatTek's intellectual property while no one is watching."

"And there's also the low-noise amplifier. I imagine that's worth a helluva lot, too."

Blanchard glanced down at the monitor. "The funny thing is that Matson could've legitimately made a bundle on this if he was just patient and knew how to market it."

Gage shook his head. "No. SatTek would have made a bundle. All he would've gotten was a salary and maybe a Christmas bonus, and only got those until the board members realized that they could find someone better." He paused, trying to figure out how to set a trap for Matson and drive him into it. "I think it may be time to apply the stick."

"Or perhaps the carrot?"

Gage looked over and smiled. "Professor Blanchard, you have an evil mind."

Chapter Fifty-five

Alex Z designed business cards for Gage and Blanchard and purchased pay-as-you-go cell phones. Gage was Mr. Green of Technology Brokers. Blanchard was Mr. Black of Detector Consultants.

"Good morning, Mr. Black," Gage said twenty-four hours later, as Blanchard sat down in the passenger seat of the rental car outside the Embarcadero BART Station in San Francisco. "I like your suit. But isn't black a little cliché for a conspiracy?"

"It's my funeral suit. You don't know what a relief it is to be dressed up and not to be going to one, or the opera. And it still fits me as long as I don't button it." He sighed. "I thought I'd shrink as I aged but discovered Ben & Jerry's just about when that was supposed to happen." He patted his stomach. "Cherry Garcia."

"Did you practice your part?"

"I didn't need to." Blanchard flashed a grin. "You're used to fake people who play fake parts. I'm a real person playing a fake part." He peered over at Gage. "But there's one thing that bothers me."

"Shoot."

"Isn't this entrapment?"

"It's only entrapment when the police do it. When we do it we're just coconspirators."

"My wife won't be too pleased to hear me referred to as a coconspirator." He laughed, then slapped Gage on the knee. "On the other hand, it could spice up the bedroom a bit. Maybe you can teach me gangster talk."

"Maybe I'll introduce you to a real gangster."

"Maybe not. I think I'll stick with the fantasy."

"Here's a little reality." Gage pointed at the dashboard. "In the glove box you'll find a cell phone, business cards, and a pen in a blue case."

Blanchard removed the items and put the cell phone and cards into his coat pocket. He smiled as he inspected the pen. "It's a transmitter, just like in the movies. What's the range?"

"Fifty yards."

"Maybe I can tweak it a bit for you later."

Gage cast Blanchard a mock disapproving glance. "Are you done with the microwave?"

Blanchard drew back. "Whose side are you on?"

"Neither. I don't get involved in domestic cases. It's safer."

The professor scanned the road ahead as Gage took the Highway 101 on-ramp. "Where's our friend Mr. Matson meeting us?"

"A hole-in-the-wall diner in South San Francisco."

"What's that mean?"

"It means he watches too much television."

Gage and Blanchard rode in silence until they reached the Grand Avenue exit, halfway between the 49ers' stadium and the airport.

"Give me the pen," Gage said.

Blanchard removed it from his pocket and handed it over.

"I want a clean tape. So don't say anything after I turn it on until we meet him. And then don't say anything after the meeting ends, until we get back to the car."

"Okay." Blanchard licked his lips, and swallowed. "I'll follow your lead."

Gage looked over and smiled. "Don't worry, you'll do fine."

"Just a few butterflies."

"Play yourself. You're the good guy in this—and don't react to what I do. I'll probably need to scare him. Remember, it's just acting."

Blanchard nodded.

"I'll do an introduction as we get close. Date, time, and what we expect to happen. It's for our protection and to use as evidence."

Gage parked down the block from the café, then did the tape introduction.

As they entered the café, Gage spotted Matson sitting alone in a booth at the back. A few of the tables were occupied by what appeared to be regulars. Matson was dressed in a pink Izod golf shirt overlaid with a tan sweater vest. Gage caught Matson's eye as they entered.

"I'm Mr. Green and this is Mr. Black," Gage said after they sat down. Matson slid his unopened *Wall Street Journal* toward the wall. Gage and Blanchard then reached across the table and handed Matson their business cards.

Gage looked hard at Matson. "You make sure nobody followed you here?"

Matson nodded. "I've been driving around for hours. I went all through the Presidio and Golden Gate Park and Chinatown, and stayed off the freeway coming back down."

Gage signaled the waitress and they turned their coffee cups right side up.

"Who goes first?" Matson asked.

"Me." Gage glanced around the half-empty café, then leaned forward and crossed his forearms on the table. "As I told you on the phone, one of your competitors is interested in obtaining certain technology you possess."

"Which one?"

"If I told you that, you'd cut me out. Right?"

Matson smiled. "It crossed my mind."

"That wouldn't be a good move. You'd lose your insulation." Gage jabbed his own breastbone hard enough to make a thump. "And I'm your insulation."

Matson's smile faded.

"Suppose somebody figures out where my client got it?" Gage pointed at Matson. "You want a trail back to you?"

Matson shook his head.

Gage leaned back and spread his hands for a moment. "So what if it gets traced to me? I'll already be Mr. White or Mr. Blue or Mr. Orange the second this deal is done." Gage locked his eyes on Matson. "You understand?"

Matson swallowed, then nodded.

"So we're not going to play any games," Gage said.

"No. No games."

They fell silent as the waitress arrived to fill their cups.

Gage tilted his head toward Blanchard after she walked away. "Mr. Black here will tell me what the technology is worth."

Matson looked at Blanchard, whose face remained impassive, then back at Gage. "What if he's wrong?"

"He'll be right. When he's done looking at the devices he'll give me a number. It'll be my only offer."

"What if I don't like it?"

"Then we never met. But you need to think about something." Gage paused until he saw a glimmer of bewilderment in Matson's eyes. "How many Mr. Greens have come knocking on your door?"

"Well..." Matson looked back and forth between them, then chewed on his thumbnail before finally focusing his eyes on Gage. "How do I get paid if we do the deal?"

"That's up to you."

Matson was quick to answer. "I want cash."

Gage tapped his forefinger on the table. "Cash will cost me ten percent. I'll need to deduct it from your end."

"That's a little steep."

"It's also a little risky. Money laundering will get me a lot more time than a little trade secrets beef."

Matson's eyes darted around the café, as if he was expecting FBI agents to spring from behind opened newspapers.

"If we can agree on a price," Matson finally said, "I'll take it in cash."

"No problem. Why don't you tell me what you think it's worth?" Gage slipped his arm under the table and gripped the top of Blanchard's thigh to keep him from reacting to Matson's answer.

Matson took a sip of his coffee. The cup rattled slightly when he set it down. He leaned forward.

Gage tightened his hold on Blanchard's thigh.

"Three million."

Gage paused. "I think Mr. Black may find that a little high."

"I'll need to examine the devices," Blanchard said.

Gage removed his hand.

"See," Gage said with a slight grin. "That's why I trust him. He doesn't just tell me what I want to hear. When can he get a look at them?"

"There are a few more things I want to know," Matson said.

"Shoot."

"How do I know you won't try to steal the technology?"

Gage smiled. "First, because I'm not in a labor-intensive business. I don't work for a living. I merely put people who have something together with people who want something. Second, you know as well as I do that you can't reverse-engineer these things. You need the code. And third, all Mr. Black needs is access to your facility to run a few tests. He won't remove anything. Right, Mr. Black?"

"Right." Blanchard sounded relaxed, friendly, now into the part. "That's all I need. I don't need to take anything and I don't need to look at your code."

Matson nodded. "Okay. I'll go that far."

"There's one other thing," Gage said. "Companies auction off their assets when they fold. I don't want you including the intellectual property."

Matson blanched.

Gage smiled to himself as he watched Matson's plan to sell the IP twice evaporate, and then said, "I'll arrange a leak to the financial press that the run-of-the-mill SatTek products are the same as everybody else's and the higher-end technology is quickly becoming dated. Everybody will think the IP is more trouble than it's worth. And I'll throw in that SatTek conceded that one of your competitors makes the best devices in the field."

"So then I just auction off the hardware?"

"Right. And if somebody wants to look at the IP, Mr. Black will screw around with the software until it travels in circles. Right, Mr. Black?"

Blanchard hesitated as if thinking through how he could rewrite the code, then nodded. "No problem."

"When can he get in?" Gage asked.

Matson looked at his watch. "I want to get this over with. Let's make it this afternoon."

"We'll be there at two o'clock."

Gage and Blanchard slipped from the booth, then headed for the door, leaving Matson to deduct the three coffees from his end.

Once in the car, Gage retrieved the pen from Blanchard's shirt pocket, repeated the date and the new time, then clicked it off.

"Matson has no idea what it's worth," Blanchard said as they drove away. "It's a good thing you grabbed my leg, I would've laughed out loud."

"As soon as he asked, 'Who goes first?' I knew he hadn't thought everything through. He's forgotten SatTek had a real product. For him it's now just numbers. How much he needs, not what it's worth. I'll bet he was thinking he'd ask for five, but the words "money laundering" punched him in the gut."

"It punched *me* in the gut. Why did Matson go for it so easily?"

"He hasn't yet, but he will. There are only two things he needs to worry about. One, that we don't rip him off. And two, that we're not cops. And he knows we're not cops." Gage looked over and smiled. "When is the last time anybody your age worked undercover?"

Blanchard drew back. "In Berkeley we call that ageism. But what's the real reason?"

"It's because the one lesson he's learned since he started cooperating with the U.S. Attorney is that the cops are on his side. He knows they need him. He's told them lots of lies, held back things he didn't want them to know. He's figured out that they'll believe anything he tells them because they *want* to believe him."

"But wouldn't they test him once in a while? Just to see if he lies."

"It would be the end of their case."

"Then why don't you just take the recording of our meeting to the prosecutor?"

"Because Matson will say he was setting us up, trying to deliver something new in order to work more time off of his sentence—and they'll believe him."

Blanchard shook his head. "Suddenly electromagnetics and plasma physics seem somewhat less confusing than law."

"This isn't law, it's called the gray area."

Gage reached for his phone and called Milsberg.

"I need you to make yourself scarce this afternoon, and don't ask why."

He disconnected and made a quick call to Viz, then took the on-ramp to 101 South toward San Jose.

◇◇◇

Matson met them in the SatTek lobby.

"How long will this take?" Matson asked Gage, eyes darting toward the entrance, then back and forth between the hallway toward the lab and the one toward the accounting and marketing departments.

"A couple hours. If anybody asks questions, just tell them we're interested in bidding on the inventory."

Matson stayed in the lab long enough to watch Blanchard hooking lines up to the RF input and the video output of the same model video amplifier he'd already tested.

"So what do you want to do for two hours?" Gage asked, after the door closed behind Matson.

"I'll give you a lesson in how these things work."

Matson looked in every fifteen or twenty minutes, each time observing Blanchard pointing at a device or at a computer monitor and making notes.

They left SatTek at four o'clock with an understanding they'd meet Matson at seven for dinner.

Gage called Viz as they drove toward the freeway. "Where'd you find Milsberg?"

"The AccuSoft parking lot, spying on SatTek."

"Let me talk to him."

"I'm sorry, Mr. Gage," Milsberg pleaded before Gage had a chance to speak. "Viz scared the daylights out of me. It was like this huge shadow fell across my windshield, like an eclipse. I'll never do it again. I promise."

Gage adopted the stern tone he'd used as Mr. Green. "Look, Robert. I can't take a chance of you screwing up, and that sometimes means you can't know some of the things I'm doing. You understand?"

"I'm sorry. I messed up—"

"If you need our help, we'll help you. But we don't have time to waste."

Chapter Fifty-six

We've done everything we can," Peterson said when he stopped by U.S. Attorney Willie Rose's office at the end of the day. "We can't find the grand jury leak."

Rose wasn't pleased. He could read the headlines before they'd been written: "Grand Jury Scandal Rocks Federal Court. U.S. Attorney's Office Forced to Dismiss Two Hundred Indictments."

Peterson sat down in a chair and passed a folder across Rose's desk.

"These are Zink's reports. The chief judge knew that Number Twenty-two's cousin was Scuzzy Thomas. He put it in his jury questionnaire. In any case, we've followed him day and night. Work. Church. Soccer with the kids. We even checked his phone records going back five years. No contact at all with Scuzzy's part of the family. But Zink will stay on him, just in case."

"What about Number Six?"

"Nothing. The guy annoys people everywhere, not just U.S. Attorneys in the grand jury. He's always calling the police on his neighbor, whose only crime is having a dog that does what everybody wants their dog to do: bark at strangers. The dispatchers cringe when they see his name and address pop up on the 911 screen."

"What about the one the chief judge read the riot act to?"

"That's Number Thirteen. Zink found out that he's showed up at the arraignments of everybody this grand jury indicted. He really enjoys seeing people humiliated in public. Killing them would take the fun out of it."

"So we're at a dead end?"

"That's the way it looks."

"Have you come up with any ideas that won't force us to reindict two hundred defendants?"

Peterson came prepared to answer that question, but knew he had to give it in exactly the right manner. He propped his forearms on the armrests of his chair and steepled his hands.

"Let me put it this way. We have no proof there's a leak from this grand jury. We have no proof there have been prior leaks from this grand jury. Everybody indicted by this grand jury deserved it. They're all righteous cases. This grand jury worked long and hard. Very, very long and hard."

Rose arched his eyebrows. "How long is very long?"

"Their term expires in ten days."

"Tsk, tsk." Rose smiled his understanding of what Peterson was trying to say, then pushed the unopened folder of Zink's reports back across the desk. "What a shame to have labored so diligently on SatTek, then to run out of time."

"That's just what I thought."

Rose leaned back in his chair, then gazed out toward the fog oozing into downtown San Francisco from the Pacific. There were other headlines he was worried about, ones generated by crime victims' groups demanding to know when something would finally be done to punish the crooks behind SatTek.

He looked back at Peterson. "Suppose you got a new grand jury impaneled the moment the old one expires, then jammed them real hard, ten hours a day. How long would it take to get an indictment?"

Peterson was ready with that answer, too. "A week."

Chapter Fifty-seven

Matson arrived for his dinner meeting with Mr. Green and Mr. Black, driving a metallic blue Mercedes 600 Roadster and wearing a navy sports jacket and a yellow button-down shirt. After handing his keys to the valet, he waited by the entrance to Buccio's Italian Cuisine for Gage and Blanchard, who were pulling into a parking space.

Gage had been amused by Matson's choice. The chateau-style restaurant, standing at the far end of a commercial district that trailed off into a neighborhood of Tudors and California bungalows, had for two generations served as the meeting place and watering hole for the criminal and financial elite on the Peninsula.

Blanchard looked over at Gage and smiled. "Isn't this the place where—"

Gage nodded. A year earlier, an FBI bug hidden in the men's restroom as part of a racketeering investigation revealed that the mayor of San Jose not only was on the take from a local contractor, but had severe prostate problems.

"Matson's an idiot," Gage said, as he turned off the ignition. "This is out of a mafia movie. If he says ba-da-bing I'll strangle him. It's a damn good thing we're not for real." He glanced at Blanchard. "Turn on the transmitter. Do the date and time and put it in your coat pocket."

"Is this the lab part of the course?"

"It counts for fifty percent of your grade."

They crossed the parking lot, then nodded to Matson and followed him inside, where the maître d' greeted him by name.

Matson left for the restroom shortly after they were seated. Gage followed him. By the time he arrived, Matson was in a stall. He came out a minute later and stepped up to wash his hands. Gage dried his own, then reached over and grabbed Matson by his back collar, spun him around, and jammed him back inside.

Matson pawed the walls as Gage forced him to look down toward the clean, clear water in the bowl.

"You fucking amateur."

Matson hadn't used the toilet, so he hadn't flushed.

Gage yanked Matson out of the stall, patted him down, then spun him back around. He reached into Matson's right breast pocket, pulled out a small digital tape recorder. The screen showed that it had been running for only thirty seconds. Gage dropped it on the floor and crushed it with his heel.

"Are you some fucking snitch?" For a moment Gage really felt like Mr. Green, and showed it. "Are you setting me up, you fucking asshole?"

"No, no. I just...protection. I needed protection...in case you rip me off. That's all. Really, that's all."

Sweat beaded on Matson's face as he tried to lick his lips with a dry tongue. His eyes were wide, as if imagining himself strangled, propped up on the toilet until his body was discovered at closing time, or maybe not until the following day. Gage released his grip moments before Matson's bladder would've given way.

"You try this shit again and I'll blow your fucking brains out." Gage stared down into Matson's reddening eyes. "You got it?"

"Yes. I got it."

"Let's go back."

Matson grimaced. "I need to pee."

"I'll wait."

Gage walked behind Matson as they left the restroom. Matson snagged a napkin from a supply cart near the kitchen, wiped his face and then dropped it into a dirty dish tub. Gage gave Blanchard a thumbs-up as they approached the table.

A waitress distributed menus as soon as they were reseated, and then laid the wine list in front of Mr. Matson, the regular.

Matson lowered his menu, mouth looking sour. "I'm not very hungry."

"Come on, man," Gage said. "Everything's gonna be okay."

Matson rubbed his forehead, still hot and moist, then let out a sigh while looking around the restaurant at the normalcy around him. The well-heeled diners sipping their wines and savoring their pastas. The waiters poised to serve.

"It's a dog-eat-dog world," Gage continued. "Anybody with a brain will grab a little money for themselves. It's called business."

"Yeah...I guess."

"I've heard you're a smart guy. A smooth operator. Somebody who knows how to seize an opportunity."

Matson brightened. "Yeah, I've done that a few times."

"Us, too. And this one will make us a lot of money." Gage smiled. "Let's celebrate. On me. You pick the wine."

Matson reached under his menu and pulled out the wine list. He turned the pages back and forth, working his finger up and down the lists, until he finally settled on a Cavallotto Barolo Boschis '98. Gage signaled the wine steward, who remained expressionless as Matson mispronounced his selection. He slipped away, returning a minute later, bottle in hand. He and Matson did the label-cork-taste dance, which ended with filled glasses.

Gage picked his up first. "To business."

Then Blanchard, "To business."

Finally and unenthusiastically, Matson said, "To business."

It wasn't until their salads arrived that Matson was ready to pop the money question.

"I think we can go as high as two-point-five," Gage said. "Three is just way too much."

"Does that include the ten percent?"

"No, that'll drop it to two-point-two-five."

"How about we split the difference?"

Gage shook his head. "No can do. I trust Mr. Black. He told me what we can sell it for and I believe him."

"What if I didn't take it in cash?"

"Then you keep the ten percent. But you'll need to tell me how you want it."

"I don't know yet." Matson glanced down at his glass and swirled the wine. "Well, I guess I really want it in cash. The FBI can trace wire transfers anywhere."

"They sure can."

"But I'll need some help."

Gage leaned forward, resting his forearms on the cloth-covered table. "What do you want to happen with it? You want to pay taxes on it and make it legit?"

Matson nodded.

"I'll give you an example of something you could do yourself," Gage said. "Thousand-dollar slots."

Matson jerked back. "No way I'm doing that. I could lose everything."

Gage shook his head. "Hear me out. You ever play slot machines in Las Vegas?"

"Sure. I put in a little money now and then, but I never really win anything."

"But you've seen the billboards, right? They promise you'll win ninety-four percent of the time. And they have to be telling the truth because they've got the Nevada Gaming Commission watching everything they do."

Matson nodded. "I guess so."

"That means that if you put in a million, you get back nine hundred and forty thousand dollars. You just got to have somebody set things up for you."

"But that would take weeks."

"Nope. You'd get it done in a day. A slot machine cycle is five seconds. Two thousand times. Ten thousand seconds. Two-point-eight hours, max. You feed in cash, they pay you in checks. Spread it out over a couple of days, even a couple of weeks. Give the IRS its cut and the money's clean."

"That's fucking amazing."

"Let me know if you want to do it. I've got a guy in Vegas who has a special machine in one of the small casinos. No big wins and no big losses. It just eats six percent of your money and gives you back the rest."

"Man, I wish I'd met you last year."

"Why's that?"

"Nothing." Matson's voice fell. "Just another business thing. I've got money stashed somewhere."

"If you've got to move it, let me know. I can take care of it. Move it anywhere."

Matson's eyes widened. "Where's anywhere?"

"All the way around."

"All the way around where?"

Gage leaned back in his chair. "The way I figure it, halfway around is about Abu Dhabi. So all the way around is right where we're sitting."

◇◇◇

"What the devil happened in the bathroom?" Blanchard asked, after turning off the transmitter as they drove from the parking lot onto a long commercial boulevard toward the highway north.

Gage smiled. "It turns out that Mr. Green has a real mean streak."

"What about Mr. Gage?"

"He's a sweetheart who's very convincing in the role of Mr. Green."

"And Matson?"

"A lonely guy. A greedy, lonely guy."

Gage looked into his mirror to check for surveillance and then reached for his cell phone. "Anybody follow us?" he asked Viz.

"You're clean." Viz laughed. "The guy I've got behind Matson says it looks like the idiot is driving side streets all the way from the restaurant to his house. It'll take him two hours to get home."

"Go ahead and break off from us, but stay on Matson, just in case."

Gage disconnected and looked over at Blanchard. "You ever go to Cal basketball games?"

"Season tickets."

"Ever see a kid play above his head?"

"Sure. The stars in the heavens are aligned and he scores a career-high twenty points, fifteen above his average. For the first time in his life he can keep up with the big boys."

"What does he think right after the game is over?"

"That he can do it anytime. The coach just needs to give him enough minutes on the floor."

"And what does he realize the next time he steps on the court?"

"That he was playing above his head."

"Exactly. And that's what Matson's been doing. And now he's all alone. Granger and Fitzhugh, the guys he relied on, are dead. Gravilov scares him. And the season's not over."

"I think *you* scared him."

"Sure, I scared him. He's the ideal hostage. He's the kind of guy who'd volunteer to make tea for his kidnappers."

"And he's double-crossing the government."

"Right. So who can he trust now? Nobody."

"You said he had a girlfriend in London, Alla something."

"That's a rowboat he's paddling through rough waters. He's cheating on his wife, just like he's cheating on the government. His relationship with Alla is filled with uncertainty. He'll always be on the edge with her. Suppose she starts to see through him? What if his wife finds out? What if Alla bails on him? Even worse, blackmails him?"

"Maybe that's why he's worried about the money he's got stashed."

"I think it's more than that. My guess is that he's told the government where some of his overseas money is, but the rest is hidden. Stuck somewhere. Fitzhugh was Matson's offshore link to banks and money managers. Now those folks are terrified. They don't want anything to do with Fitzhugh's old clients. Cutting a deal is a whole lot different than cutting up the dealmaker. They want to wash their hands of Matson and his money as soon as possible."

Blanchard pointed at an HSBC branch as they passed by. "Then he should transfer the money to some other bank."

"Without the insulation that Fitzhugh provided, he'd have to put his own name on the account opening form. The bank would perform its standard due diligence, the class action suit would pop up, and they'd show him the door. And he's probably got a more pressing problem. He's adjusted his lifestyle to his income and the inflow of money is drying up. Notice that matching Mercedes and sports jacket? All that takes cash."

Gage pulled to a curb just before the on-ramp to the bridge heading to the East Bay so he could confirm that Viz was correct about the absence of surveillance.

"What's next?" Blanchard asked.

"Now that I've scared him..." Gage watched cars pass them by, then smiled. "I need to make him love me."

"How do you go about doing that?"

"Pretty soon he'll start wondering if he's being set up. After all, it was a whirlwind day. So he'll call me, but I won't pick up. Then he'll try you on the cell I gave you. Wait a day, then call and tell him I'm in Switzerland and everything is on schedule."

"But shouldn't you stay around to close the deal?"

Gage flashed a grin at Blanchard. "I'm not going to Switzerland. Mr. Green is."

"Oh, I see. Why is Mr. Green going?"

"Because for Matson, Switzerland means only one thing—and it ain't clocks and chocolate. And equally important, distance makes the heart grow fonder."

"Where should Mr. Black go?"

"To help Professor Blanchard fix the microwave." Gage glanced over his shoulder, then accelerated toward the bridge. "I hear his wife is a little ticked off."

Chapter Fifty-eight

Gage rolled out of bed at 6 A.M. and called Milsberg.

"I'm really sorry about not doing what you told me," Milsberg said, right after he recognized Gage's voice. "My curiosity got the better of me."

"You only have one job, Robert, and that's helping me keep you out of federal prison." Gage wasn't interested in hearing another apology, so he pushed on to the subject of his call. "Did you actually check to see whether all of the components you listed on the inventory were actually there?"

"They have to be," Milsberg insisted. "It's right out of our resource management computer system. It shows what we ordered, what we received, what we used, and what's left."

"That wasn't my question—and don't apologize. Just go look."

◇◇◇

Gage's cell phone rang as he pulled into a parking place behind his building an hour later.

"I'm in the secure storage area," Milsberg whispered. "Empty boxes. Lots of tiny empty boxes. We must be missing a thousand MMIC chips. A quarter-million dollars' worth."

"What's MMIC stand for?"

"Monolithic microwave integrated circuits. Cutting edge. We keep them in secure storage because they're dual use. On the military side, they amplify signals in radar systems. Any of our competitors would grab them up in a heartbeat."

"Any left?"

"Six hundred. Grouped into batches, like someone is getting ready to ship them out."

Gage thought for a moment, then said, "Remember Viz, the guy that appeared out of nowhere?"

"I'll never forget."

"He'll call you on your cell in a few minutes. Do what he says."

"Will it get me into trouble?"

"Robert, you already are."

◇◇◇

Viz materialized next to Gage's desk twenty-four hours later.

"I wish you wouldn't do that," Gage said.

"Do what?"

"You should knock or shuffle your feet or clear your throat next time. Faith will be really annoyed if you give me a heart attack."

"I'm sure I'll find it very upsetting, too," Viz said, grinning. "You need an aspirin or something?"

"Not at the moment, but keep one handy." Gage pointed at the DVD in Viz's hand. "What have you got?"

Viz handed it to Gage, then dropped into a chair across from his desk. Gage slipped it into his computer and the viewing software activated, beginning with an image of the secure storage room at SatTek.

"Good color."

"I got a couple of new microvideo cameras. Well, you did. I'm not sure I mentioned it before."

"How much did I spend?"

"Less than you imagine." Viz pointed at the monitor. "Guess who?"

Matson was loading the batches of plastic-encased MMIC chips into a file storage box.

"He came in around 2 A.M.," Viz said. "It looks like he took about five hundred."

After Matson disappeared from view, Gage reached to eject the DVD.

Viz held up his palm toward Gage. "Wait, boss."

The video cut to an empty office with a large hardwood desk and matching credenza. There was a flat-screen monitor on the desk and a tiny basketball hoop above the corner wastebasket.

"Since I was there," Viz said. "I thought I'd…"

"Good thinking."

Matson came into view. He set down the storage box on the desk and left the office. He returned a minute later carrying three rectangular FedEx parcel boxes and air bills. He distributed the chips among the boxes, then filled out and attached the air bills.

"You want me to enhance the image to try to read the air bill numbers?"

"No, I can get them."

Gage reached for his phone.

"How's our project?" he asked Milsberg.

"Almost done. I'll e-mail you a final list of missing components by the end of the day."

"Good work. Matson sent off three FedEx boxes yesterday. Check the SatTek account and find out where they went."

Gage turned back to Viz after he hung up.

"You want me to retrieve the video equipment?" Viz asked.

"No. Leave it there until we get the rest of the inventory. Matson may dip in again."

◊◊◊

At noon, Gage took a walk along the Embarcadero to the Ferry Building at the end of Market Street, where he bought Faith chocolate-covered ginger before sitting on a bench facing the bay to eat his lunch. The blustery wind chopped at the water. Small sailboats broncoed their way back toward the South Beach Marina while Leviathan-sized container ships ground toward the Port of Oakland. Gage watched their radars spinning, sweeping the bay, as if the radar would spot something the crewmembers' home-yearning eyes missed.

The ring of his cell phone was nearly drowned out by the wind beating against his face and ears.

"Mr. Green, this is Mr. Black."

"Good afternoon. What's new in the Berkeley hills?"

"Our friend Mr. Scooby called, just like you said he would. Quite desperate when you didn't return his calls, and grateful when I did. Now he wants to speak to you."

"Of course he does. What did you tell him?"

"That you would call when you returned from Switzerland and got to a secure phone." Blanchard chuckled. "He just loved that phrase."

"Sounds like he's getting into the cloak-and-dagger."

"Not just him. Is there anything else Mr. Black can help you with?"

"No. I'm afraid it's time for Mr. Black to retire."

"Shoot. I was beginning to like the guy."

"But Professor Blanchard could be useful in the next couple of days. I'll e-mail a list of components that Matson stole from SatTek. Maybe it'll tell you something."

"Glad to do it." Blanchard chuckled again. "By the way, I have some very good news."

"What's that?"

"I fixed the microwave."

Chapter Fifty-nine

Mr. Green returned Matson's calls when he arrived back from Switzerland.

"I'd like to talk to you about something," Matson said. "In person. It's kinda urgent."

"I'm tied up in LA for the next couple of days. Meet me this afternoon at the Beverly Wilshire."

Gage hung up, then booked himself a flight from SFO to Burbank.

◇◇◇

Gage was sitting on a couch in the lobby lounge of the Beverly Wilshire Hotel when Matson entered at 4 P.M. He scanned the room until he spotted Gage and walked over. Gage directed him to sit to his right.

"I appreciate you making time for me," Matson said. "Especially on short notice. Mr. Black told me you were..." Matson glanced around, then lowered his voice. "In Switzerland. So I'm sure you're really busy."

Gage adopted the tone of Mr. Green. "So let's get to it. What do you need?"

Matson glanced around again, his eyes pausing momentarily on a swarthy man sitting fifteen feet away whose black double-breasted suit stretched tight against a mammoth chest and massive biceps. Matson leaned over toward Gage and whispered, "I need a bank account."

"Where?"

"Offshore."

"Everything outside of the U.S. is offshore."

"I don't know where."

"Why do you need it?"

"I need to move some money." Matson swallowed hard. "A lot of money."

The glint in Matson's eyes told Gage that he was thinking about more than just a couple of hundred thousand dollars of microchip money.

"So open an account," Gage said. "What's stopping you?"

"I'm a little hot at the moment." Matson's eyes darted around the lobby as if fearing he'd be recognized. "The class action suit against SatTek is getting a lot of press." He then bumped the side of Gage's knee with his knuckle and tilted his head toward where the man was sitting. "I think that man is watching us."

"Don't worry about it," Gage said, reaching for his coffee cup on the low table. "So what you're looking for is a bank account on an island somewhere."

"What do you mean don't worry about it?"

"He's mine." Gage took a sip and set down his cup.

"Oh, okay." Matson took a moment to digest Gage's idea. "Yes, that's what I want, on an island someplace."

"How about Nauru?"

"What's Nauru?"

"An island out in the Pacific."

Matson's eyes widened, as if imagining stacks of cash in a faraway vault. "How far out?"

"You know where Samoa is?"

Matson shook his head.

"How about the Marshall Islands?"

"No."

"New Guinea?"

Matson shrugged.

"Didn't you study geography in school?" Gage looked at him like a disappointed teacher. "How about Australia?"

"Sure. I know where that is."

"Nauru is a couple of thousand miles northeast of Australia."

Matson squinted into the distance as if studying a map on a classroom wall. "You mean near Hawaii?"

Gage shook his head. "I can see geography is just not your thing." He then looked up at a passing waiter. He didn't ask Matson if he wanted coffee, but merely pointed at his own cup and held up two fingers. When he looked back, Matson was again staring at the imaginary map.

"You mean I'll have to travel way out into the middle of the fucking ocean to put my money into the account?"

Gage drew back a little, adopting an incredulous expression. "You don't get how this works, do you?"

Matson shrugged. "Somebody else used to take care of all this for me, but he, uh, retired."

"It's like this." Gage settled back. "People put money in these offshore banks by..." He cast Matson a questioning look. "You know how correspondent accounts work?"

Matson shook his head.

"Say I've got money in Deutsche Bank in Munich and I want to put it into Credit Suisse in Geneva. Do I hand carry the money? Of course not. Each of those banks owns an account at an intermediary bank. If it's for dollars, it'll be in, say, the Bank of New York. Deutsche Bank and Credit Suisse have correspondent accounts there. So the money goes from Germany to Switzerland by way of these correspondent accounts."

Matson brightened. "I get it. The Nauru bank has a correspondent account somewhere. I just need to put the money into that account."

Gage nodded, smiling like a proud teacher. "You just earned yourself an A."

"And once it's in Nauru's jurisdiction—"

"Nobody can touch it except you."

The waiter appeared with Matson's coffee and refilled Gage's. Gage stirred in sugar, waiting for Matson to work himself to the next step.

"Where'll the Nauru bank have its correspondent accounts?" Matson finally asked.

"In the ones I just named, and lots of others. They set them up wherever they expect to receive money."

"How much will it cost?"

"I don't think cost is an issue."

Matson smiled weakly. "I guess you're right. It's just habit."

"But I'll do you a favor." Gage took a sip from his cup, then set it back down. "Usually I charge a hundred for this kind of thing. But since we've got the other deal, I'll make it fifty thousand." He turned toward Matson. "On one condition."

Matson swallowed, his distressed expression saying that he'd seen a thousand deals fall apart because of what was presented as a final detail.

"We pay you for the other thing in this account so I won't have to handle cash."

Matson let the suggestion sit for a moment, biting his lower lip, then nodded. "But I'll still have to figure out how to get the money back into the States."

Gage smiled. "Piece of cake. There are dozens of ways. Carry cash back. Buy something in Europe and sell it over here." Gage furrowed his brows, as if searching his mind for ideas. "Say you buy a dozen classic Rolexes in Switzerland; thirty, forty thousand each. They're worth the same here as there. Who's to know? Maybe you take a little loss, so what? Buy rice or steel or whatever anybody needs. Find out what people want and go get it."

Matson nodded.

Gage pointed a forefinger at Matson's chest.

"And one more thing. The main way they catch money laundering is that funds come into an account and then go out right away." Gage wagged the finger back and forth. "It doesn't make any difference how much you put in your Nauru account, just don't take out more than about one percent at any one time during the first year. And send the bank a fake contract, like for steel, so it looks like you're really buying something. But make it odd numbers. Round numbers get attention. Nobody buys exactly a million dollars' worth of steel. Got it?"

"Yeah." Matson sighed. "I wish I'd understood how all this worked before."

Gage rose from the couch. Matson hesitated, then did the same.

"I'm real busy for the next couple of days," Gage said, "then I need to travel out of the country. I'll give you a phone number. When you've got the fifty grand, call it. My friend over there will meet you somewhere in LA. It'll take two days to set things up after we get the money. You understand?"

"I understand. What's his name?"

"Just call him Eddie."

Gage wrote out a phone number on a blank scrap of paper and handed it to Matson.

"You go out first. He'll follow. If he spots a tail on you, you'll never see me again." Gage looked hard into Matson's eyes. "If he spots a tail on me, you're in big fucking trouble."

Chapter Sixty

Are you ready for a little work?" Gage began his call to Burch. Matson's fifty thousand dollars was piled on Gage's desk.

"How I've waited to hear those words, but the doctors won't let me leave the bloody house. I'm not even sure I can make it down the stairs."

"You can do it from home. Matson needs a company and an account to put money he's got stashed, but he doesn't have Granger and Fitzhugh to do it anymore."

"It wasn't just them." The weight of the pending indictment crushed the enthusiasm out of Burch's voice. "It was Granger, Fitzhugh, and me."

"Hang in there, champ. They knew what was going on, you didn't."

Gage heard Burch take in a breath and exhale, as if recharging his resolve. "Where?"

"I sold him on Nauru."

"What?" Burch laughed. "Let me guess. You convinced him that he'll have actual cash piled up out in the Pacific?"

Gage felt his fear that Burch's mind had lost its quickness and strategic sense dissolve.

"And we'll need to use a correspondent account in Switzerland."

The humor disappeared from Burch's voice. "But what if something goes wrong? It'll look exactly like what Peterson is accusing me of, helping Matson launder money."

"Jack, you're forgetting the Afghanistan rule. If they ever get us—"

"It'll only be for something we didn't do. But this time I'm doing it, and they're probably going to find out."

"Don't worry. I know a prosecutor in Geneva. I'll tell him in advance what we're up to and give him the name of the bank and the account number."

Gage thought for a moment. He had planned to handle the second part of the setup himself, but decided that rebuilding Burch's confidence required bringing him along. "What do you know about Chuck Verona?"

"Just a paper shuffler. His job is just to make sure corporate fees get paid and do whatever I need to maintain companies in Nevada. And not just me, everybody in the business in San Francisco uses him. Russian immigrant. Grateful to be in the States."

"Any Russian organized crime connections?"

"None that I ever heard of. There's always a risk that he was unwittingly used—I know how that is."

"Does he trust you?"

"Of course. I'm the one who passed his name around."

"Matson sent three FedEx boxes to a company called Checker Trading in Las Vegas that Verona runs. They contain microchips he's stealing to fund his lifestyle until he can tap his offshore money again. Find out from Verona what he did with them—"

"I see where you're going. Then we backtrack the money from the Swiss correspondent account—"

"And dress the little punk in prison stripes and drop him on Peterson's doorstep."

◇◇◇

Gage's cell phone rang the moment he hung up from Burch. It was Milsberg.

"He's traveling again. To London. First-class. And we're running out of money for office supplies. I searched his office when he went out to lunch and found the ticket in his briefcase. Same flight as last time, and—this is the good part—a book about Kiev. Brand-new."

"Is there a ticket for Ukraine?"

"No. But he must be traveling there. Matson isn't a reader."

◇◇◇

Gage got up from his desk, looked over the charts and chronologies hanging on his wall, wondering both what Peterson expected to learn as a result of allowing Matson to travel out of the country again and why Matson hadn't booked his flight all the way through to Kiev.

Does Peterson even know he's traveling? Gage asked himself. *And is Kiev part of Matson's exit strategy? Slip out of London and break the chain connecting his neck to Peterson's hand? Maybe even make the sale to Mr. Green in the comfortable surroundings of a Ukrainian dacha?*

Gage snagged an international treaty book from the shelf, checked the index, and turned to the U.S./Ukraine section.

There wasn't an extradition agreement.

The U.S. couldn't touch him any more than it could touch Gravilov or the other gangsters involved in the scam. Matson and Alla would live happily ever after, just out of reach.

But treaties only bound governments.

Gage flipped the volume closed and reached for his cell phone to call a man who didn't accept the legitimacy of either.

Chapter Sixty-one

Gage's flight landed at Borispol Airport fifty kilometers west of Kiev four hours after Matson, who'd stayed in London only long enough to pick up Alla. Gage had waited in Zurich until he got word from Slava that Matson had arrived. He'd been fortunate to get a seat since journalists from around the world were rushing to Kiev to chronicle the Bread and Freedom Revolution, an uprising triggered by the revelation that the president had diverted a fifty-million-dollar IMF agricultural loan into his election war chest.

One of Slava's impassive bodyguards met Gage in the unheated arrivals hall and led him to an armored Mercedes sedan in the parking lot. Gage got into the backseat with Slava while the bodyguard entered a trailing silver Land Cruiser. Slava appeared so relaxed that Gage wondered whether he'd taken his own advice in Geneva and spent a week soaking in the aromatic steam baths of Montreux.

"What's happening in Kiev?" Gage asked him.

"Opposition took over Independence Square. Hundred thousand. Demand new election."

"Will there be one?"

"Wrong question."

"What's the right one?"

"What difference it make."

Gage glanced over. "I didn't think you took such an interest in politics."

"I take interest in business." Slava flashed a predator's smile. "Politics is business in Ukraine."

The driver sped out from the tree-lined airport road onto the highway toward the city.

"Where's Matson staying?" Gage asked, as they passed a sprinkling of two-story stucco dachas owned by the Ukrainian nouveau riche.

"Where else? Lesya Palace Hotel."

"Apparently he's not afraid of being seen."

"Or heard. Bugs everywhere. For Soviets, state secrets. For capitalists, business secrets." Slava snapped his hand shut. "Like mousetrap."

"Do you have any way to find out what goes on inside?"

"Only little. Waiters and doormen. Guys in president's entourage took it over right after independence. Gravilov maybe own a piece."

Gage smiled. "Am I in a mousetrap, too?"

"Your place clean. My people check it."

Gage gave him an I-wasn't-born-yesterday look.

"What? You think I plant something? I thought we trust each other again. Like partners."

"I brought a little device of my own," Gage said. "But there are a few things I need."

Slava spread his hands. "You want. I get."

"A fur *ushanka* and a black overcoat. I need to blend in. A hat and coat should be enough."

"You get in hour."

"Thanks. What's Matson doing?"

"So far, nothing. Reservation for dinner at hotel restaurant."

After passing concrete Soviet-era apartment blocks, concentrated together as if to squeeze out everything soft or green or human, Slava's driver sped across Paton's Bridge over the Dnepr River. He slipped between the botanical garden and the Monument to the Great Patriotic War, then aimed for the heart of Kiev. As a light rain fell, the driver skirted around

Independence Square, its chanting crowd of a hundred thousand spilling into the side streets, their tone celebratory.

The driver pulled up to the arched driveway of a white six-story apartment building built in the anonymously ornate style dictated by Moscow in the 1950s. He honked once. Moments later the iron-framed wooden gate swung open and he drove through the courtyard into a two-car garage on the opposite side. Once the garage door was closed, Slava heaved himself out of the car. Gage stepped out behind him.

"You should think about losing a few pounds," Gage said.

"Few not do it."

Gage followed Slava into an elevator that took them to the top floor.

"Okay?" Slava said after his bodyguard opened the apartment door.

Gage walked into an Italianate living room, gilded to the barest limits of good taste.

"Sveta do," Slava said.

"I didn't realize your wife was an interior decorator."

"She not. She like to spend money. When she get enough things we hire somebody to do something with them. Some of it match."

Slava ran a finger along the back of one of two aqua and gold Louis IX armchairs. His eyes blurred for a moment.

"When I was boy, ten families live ten years on what this cost."

◇◇◇

As soon as Slava left, Gage removed a debugger from his briefcase and checked the apartment. He disabled four bugs, but left them in place. He then set up a local Internet connection and checked his e-mails.

Boss:

Mr. Burch called. Chuck Verona said he forwarded Matson's FedExed boxes from Checker Trading to New York. He couldn't remember the name of the company, but will find out.

Everything is in order as far as Matson's new account is concerned. Mr. Burch is still wondering why you chose the name KTMG Limited. He thinks "TMG" is The Matson Group, but he can't understand what the "K" means. I think I do. Cute.

Blanchard called. He reviewed the list of what was missing and said the most valuable were the monolithic microwave circuits. He suspects that a competitor is using gray market SatTek components to make their own devices. He'll put together a list of possible companies and I'll research them.

Alex Z

Gage looked at his watch. It was 5 A.M. in California. He didn't want to wake up Faith by calling her on their home phone, so he decided to leave a message on her cell.

Faith answered on the first ring. "Did you make it there okay?"

"I just got in. Why are you awake so early?"

"I was watching the news last night and saw how tense things have become in Kiev. The chaos reminded me of when you and Jack were in Karachi."

"That's why I called. I thought you might be worried."

Gage walked to an east-facing living room window with a view of Independence Square. Through the now freezing rain, he saw thousands of yellow flags bearing images of wheat stalks, the symbol of the Bread and Freedom Revolution, and the tent city in which the demonstrators spent the subzero nights.

"I can see it out of my window. Listen to this."

Gage cracked open the window and faced his phone toward the crowd cheering the opposition leaders as they condemned the president and his corrupt administration.

When he put the phone back to his ear, he heard an echo of the demonstration.

"I just turned on CNN," Faith said. "They're panning the streets leading to the square. Can you see the troops?"

On a side street leading to the square, Gage spotted police clad in blue and soldiers in green waiting for orders, running their numbing hands over the barrels and trigger guards of their AK-47s to keep them from icing up.

"The cheers sounded heroic, almost triumphant as we were driving in," Gage said. "Now they just sound naïve. These people think they're marching toward the promised land, but they're really just backing toward the edge of the abyss."

Gage didn't wait for Faith's next question before answering it. "I'll try to get out of here before that happens."

Chapter Sixty-two

When Gage walked into Kiev's Pechersk Restaurant, he found that it possessed no dining room and no windows. It was nothing more than six private rooms spread along a narrow Siberian birch–paneled hallway. There was no cashier, not even a cash register. The china was gilded, the utensils were silver, and the glasses were crystal.

The dozen armored Mercedes in the parking lot, along with the gauntlet of bodyguards he passed, told Gage that a properly aimed and timed missile would reduce the Ukrainian crime rate by half—and Slava acted like he owned the place.

"Gage," Slava said, as Gage walked into the last room, "this is Ninchenko."

Ninchenko rose stiffly, shook Gage's hand across the table, and introduced himself by his first name and patronymic: Mykola Ivanovich. Gage sat opposite Slava. Ninchenko to Slava's left. Six feet, one-eighty, mid-forties, slightly receding black hair, high cheekbones supporting skin reddened by the icy December wind.

The spaces between the three place settings were filled with plates of smoked sturgeon and salmon, red and black caviar, and fresh and pickled vegetables. Two vodka bottles stood in the center of the table.

"Major Ninchenko retired from SBU last month," Slava said, popping a pickle into his mouth. "Twenty years."

"I served for two years," Ninchenko said, "then left to attend law school and returned for another eighteen."

Ninchenko spoke with only a faint accent, which Gage recognized was a rarity for someone who grew up when Ukraine was still a Russian satellite.

"Where'd you learn English?" Gage asked. "You speak it better than most Americans."

Ninchenko smiled at the compliment. "Kiev State University, and my parents. They worked in the Foreign Ministry in Soviet times."

"And since then?"

Ninchenko shrugged. "Business, like everyone else."

"What about you?" Gage raised an eyebrow toward Slava, who laughed through his smoked sturgeon–filled mouth.

Ninchenko glanced at Slava. "My division formed a private company to provide security during our off hours. *Zherebec.* It means stallion. Stallion Security Services. Marx was wrong, except about one thing, the withering away of the state. The state in Ukraine is nothing, just a way for the rich to make money. Business needs protection and predictability. Stallion provides it. The state can't."

"What is government anyway," Slava interjected, "except protection racket? Protect some rich people from other rich people and all rich people from poor people. State always *krysha* for rich and when state not roof, we roof."

"What about the Bread and Freedom Revolution?" Gage asked.

"At this point it's only a protest," Ninchenko said. "We'll see if it becomes a revolution. And remember, revolutions in this part of the world tend not to overturn as much as fully revolve."

"So Ukraine will end up where it started."

"That's what happened in Russia. They started with Brezhnev, toyed with Gorbachev and Yeltsin, and then ended up with Putin, the velvet glove on the iron fist. There won't be truly free elections there for another generation."

Gage looked over at Slava and watched him shove a buttered slice of baguette piled high with black caviar into his mouth. In his nonchalance, Gage recognized that Slava believed that despite how violently Ukraine was wrenched about, he'd stay on his feet.

"Tell me about Gravilov," Gage said. "I'm wondering whether Matson is counting on him to provide the nest for him to land in."

"The timing would be right," Ninchenko said, his tone changing from a theorizing political scientist to a reporting intelligence officer. "Gravilov flew into Kiev yesterday, the domestic airport. He was in Ukraine already. He's the roof for the Dnepropetrovsk clan, the president's people."

"If he's imbedded here," Gage asked, "why would he get so personally involved in a United States stock fraud and risk putting himself in the FBI's crosshairs?"

"Hard currency. Euros, dollars, francs." Ninchenko pointed west, as if toward its sources. "Our money is worth nothing outside of Ukraine and barely anything here. And times have changed. It used to be you could pay off a plant director and get steel at half the international price, then sell it on the world market. But the World Bank threatened to cut us off if we didn't clean up the steel trade. So Gravilov had to find other sources of hard currency."

Gage stabbed a piece of smoked salmon, cut it in two on his plate, and took a bite. He nodded at Slava in approval, then looked back at Ninchenko. "For what?"

Ninchenko raised a forefinger. "One example. Suppose the government is preparing to privatize a state-owned factory. How does Gravilov make sure that his bid is accepted? Say the plant is worth a hundred million Ukrainian hryvnia. He pays the government ten million in hryvnia for the plant domestically and a two-million-dollar bribe offshore."

"How can he get away with paying a tenth of what it's worth?"

"What's 'worth'?" Ninchenko spread his hands and shrugged. "Even in Soviet times the government calculated depreciation. Five percent a year for twenty years. So, on paper, a plant can be worth exactly zero, even if it is the largest in the world."

Gage did the calculation. "If Gravilov cleared ten million dollars from SatTek," Gage said, "he can convert that into a hundred million dollars in Ukrainian assets."

Ninchenko nodded.

"So who's he paying off?"

"Makarov, Hadeon Alexandervich. The president's son."

"Hadeon. Is that Russian or Ukrainian?"

"Ukrainian. It means 'destroyer.'"

"Destroyer? What kind of man names a baby Destroyer?"

"Man who plan to make dynasty by crushing everybody," Slava answered. "But son has bad genes. Hadeon Alexandervich is reckless. No limits."

"Do you think he got a cut of SatTek?"

"At least indirectly," Ninchenko answered. "It's a complicated relationship. Basically, Gravilov provides physical protection and intelligence. Hadeon Alexandervich has lots of enemies, and Gravilov keeps track of what they're doing, especially the political opposition. He also leans on people if Hadeon Alexandervich takes an interest in a factory or a business. Like his father, Hadeon Alexandervich is insatiable. He has to be fed all the time."

"The Thais have an expression for corruption," Gage said. "They call it eating the state."

"If not for me," Slava said, "he eat everything. I elbow him once in a while to keep my seat at table—but there is difference." Slava thumped the table with his forefinger. "I never take from poor. No one freeze in winter because of me."

Slava opened a vodka bottle, poured three shots, then pushed himself to his feet, rattling the glasses and dishes on the table. Gage and Ninchenko also stood.

"To Hadeon Alexandervich, may he go to hell. Headfirst." Slava paused to let the image complete itself in his mind. "On heels of fucking father."

Slava clinked his glass against Gage's and Ninchenko's, then tossed the vodka to the back of his throat and swallowed. He then noticed that Gage hadn't emptied his glass.

"I not say I send, just he go."

Gage downed the vodka, and then the three of them sat down.

A waiter in a tuxedo shirt and black pants knocked, then entered and removed the appetizers and their plates. He returned a minute later with bowls of red beet borscht, a dollop of sour cream centered in each one.

As Gage stirred his soup, his mind looped back through the conversation.

"Matson needs a place to hide his assets where the U.S. can't reach them," Gage said. "And Gravilov needs hard currency. It's a perfect marriage."

"But first they need to find something for him to invest in," Ninchenko said. "In a way that allows Gravilov to take a cut."

"That must be on tomorrow's agenda."

"Why not just go to the prosecutor now?" Ninchenko asked. "And tell him what you think Matson is doing over here."

"I can't take the chance. For all I know the U.S. Attorney sent him to meet up with Gravilov. He let him travel to London once before."

"They allow informants to do that?"

"They've let them travel to Afghanistan to put heroin deals together and to Colombia to fly cocaine back to the U.S., so sending a financial crook like Matson to Europe isn't considered much of a risk."

"Except to him," Slava said. "Matson may think he buy, but he not keep. Alla poppa and Gravilov take everything."

Slava went silent as Gage tasted the soup.

"What you think?" Slava asked.

"I think Matson may end up dead."

"Of course." Slava pointed at Gage's bowl. "But I mean about soup."

"Perfect."

"It proves the rule about borscht," Ninchenko said. "There's no in-between. It's either good or bad."

Slava smiled. "Not like Ukraine. Everything here is in-between."

Gage smiled back. "Maybe you should've been a philosopher or a food critic, instead of a…"

"Gangster?" Slava finished the sentence.

"I was trying to think of a euphemism."

Slava looked uncertainly at Ninchenko.

"It's a word that means the same thing," Ninchenko explained, "but doesn't sound quite so derogatory."

Slava's puzzlement didn't fade.

"Bad. Derogatory sort of means bad."

Slava grinned. "Just like gangster."

The waiter returned, removed their soup bowls and replaced them with plates bearing wild partridge in juniper sauce, potatoes, and sauerkraut salad with carrots and apples.

Ninchenko's cell phone rang. He answered it, but didn't speak until the waiter left the room.

"Matson and his lady have retired for the evening," Ninchenko said, after hanging up. "They ordered room service breakfast for eight o'clock."

Gage looked at Slava, then back at Ninchenko. "I wonder if he'll live long enough to digest it."

Chapter Sixty-three

At 9 A.M. Gage and Ninchenko entered a battered Volkswagen van in the courtyard of his apartment building. Two boxy Russian-made Lada chase cars, one white and one light blue, were already stationed along Shevchenko Boulevard outside the Lesya Palace Hotel, ready to follow Matson whichever direction he traveled.

Ninchenko's cell phone rang like a starter pistol.

"Matson just got in the car," Ninchenko reported five seconds later. "Alla isn't with him. Black Mercedes 430. Four-digit plate, 0087. Government. The police aren't allowed to stop it. Whoever is inside has immunity."

"A get-out-of-jail-free card," Gage said.

"I've never heard of such a thing." Ninchenko glanced over at Gage. "Do you have those in the States?"

"No, it's a card in a game called Monopoly."

"A monopoly I've heard of." Ninchenko grinned. "That's what we were told the great Soviet struggle was against."

"Now you have your own," Gage said.

Ninchenko made a call to check the plate while his driver sped from the courtyard onto Pushkinskaya, and then right onto Shevchenko, following 0087 from a block behind. The low clouds that had released a steady flow of mist overnight turned Kiev's streets into black ice. The van's defroster struggled against the condensation on the windshield while the wipers swept away light raindrops. The other windows were scummed with dirty water that the driver had splashed on to provide cover for Ninchenko and Gage in the rear seat.

"We'll find out who it is in an hour," Ninchenko said, after disconnecting. "My guess is that it is a representative of the State Property Fund. They handle privatizations of government-owned assets."

"You'd think somebody like him would be more discreet. Wouldn't anyone who saw him with a foreigner like Matson assume that he'll be getting an offshore kickback for setting up a deal?"

"Discretion isn't much of an issue because there are no secrets in Ukraine. Everything gets found out in the end. The president knows everyone's schemes."

"And he doesn't stop them?"

Ninchenko signaled their driver to drop back and allow the blue Lada to take over close surveillance. They then followed it onto Oleny Telihy, heading toward the northern part of Kiev.

"You need to ask yourself how the president keeps power," Ninchenko said. "But don't think like a Westerner. He's violent. He's corrupt. He's universally hated. He was elected through fraud."

"He stays in power the way other corrupt leaders do," Gage said. "Through fear."

Ninchenko looked over. "Fear of what?"

"Illegal arrest, imprisonment, execution. The same things people in dictatorial regimes all over the world are afraid of."

"This isn't everywhere else. This is Ukraine. It is a new kind of political order. Ukrainians are afraid of everything all of the time, so they don't suffer particular fears. There's almost nothing they do that isn't in violation of some law. You want to license a car, pay a bribe. You want to get your child into school, bribe the principal. You want a passing grade, bribe the teacher. You need over sixty separate permits to open a business in Kiev. You think there's a single business in Kiev that has them all? No. They couldn't afford all the bribes. Sure, officials occasionally get arrested for corruption. And while those arrests might seem random from the outside looking in, they're strategic from the inside looking out."

Gage shook his head. "That's no different than any other corrupt government in the world."

"It's fundamentally different—and it's invisible unless you've been here awhile. The president of Ukraine rules not by fear, but by blackmail."

Ninchenko let his words sink in as they gazed out at the storefront pharmacies and markets and cafés along the four-lane street. Rising above them were apartments privatized after independence and, in the distance, an office tower under construction. Each an opportunity for graft.

Gage's mind marched along behind Ninchenko's logic, until he reached what seemed to be an impossible conclusion. He looked at Ninchenko. "You mean that the president actually encourages corruption?"

"Exactly. Because it creates leverage. That's the real function of State Security and the Intelligence Directorate. Leverage. It's information gathering for the sake of blackmail."

"And the opposition?"

"Opposition politicians gather their own intelligence to try to control the president and his entourage. I provide it to them. So does Slava."

Gage felt slightly off balance, as on his first day in Bulgaria ten years earlier, where people nodded when saying no, and shook their heads when saying yes.

Ninchenko smiled, watching his words impact Gage, then pushed on. "And Slava gives the opposition more than just intelligence. I suspect he put the equivalent of ten or fifteen million dollars into the opposition presidential campaign."

"Ten or fifteen *million*?"

"Like he said yesterday. Politics is business. It's an investment. He'll get it back twenty-fold."

"But only if the opposition wins."

"Of course."

In the silence that followed, Gage found himself viewing Ninchenko as larger than the role Slava had put him in.

"Pardon my saying so," Gage said, "but you don't seem like the kind of guy who works for a man like Slava."

"And you don't seem like a guy who works *with* a man like Slava."

"Touché. But you know what I mean."

Ninchenko looked over at Gage, appraising him. "You and I aren't that different. We grew up reading Mark Twain and Jack London and Tennessee Williams. You studied philosophy in college. Me, Marxist theory. We both went into law enforcement. You left to attend graduate school and didn't go back. I left to attend law school, and did go back. We both work in the gray area. You, light gray. Me, dark gray."

"I see you've done a little research."

"Just made a call. You've been in Ukraine three times before. Once in a money laundering case, once to locate a Russian fugitive from the States, and once as part of a delegation from the International Association of Fraud Investigators. State Security has a file."

"You know why I'm here this time, but you haven't answered why you're with me."

Ninchenko wiped away condensation from his window.

"You know what that is?" He pointed with his thumb toward the northeast as they turned left onto a broad boulevard crosshatched by trolley lines.

Gage looked over at the desolate expanse of dead grass, leafless trees, and a stark television tower piercing the gray sky.

"That's Babiy Yar," Ninchenko said. "Grandmother's Ravine. We're still in Kiev. Thirty-three thousand Jews were murdered here by the Nazis in two days. A million people heard the shots and the screams of victims being buried alive. There was no secret, but Ukraine denied it to the world for fifty years. Why? Because they wanted them dead. And some still do."

"Like who?"

"The OUN, Organization of Ukrainian Nationalists. It's a terrorist group that wants to drive everyone out of the country who doesn't meet their criteria of Ukrainians. Russians, Poles, Jews."

"You say that like you're Jewish."

"Literally, I'm not. Figuratively, all Ukrainians are Jews, they just don't recognize it. Stalin intentionally starved to death six million Ukrainians during the Great Famine in the thirties. But now forty percent of Ukrainians believe life was better back then. They still don't understand that Ukrainians were the Jews of the Soviet Union. And those forty percent are most of the people who support the president."

Ninchenko's window clouded over as he spoke.

"So why Slava?" Gage asked.

"Why Slava?" Ninchenko paused as if preparing to explain something that he'd thought through. "Because he provides a real service. He doesn't deceive himself about who he is. He's a man of his word. He has a sense of fairness."

Ninchenko glanced at Gage. "Why is he helping you? He's pretty sure you can get Gravilov indicted in the States without him. He probably could simply wait, then make his move. But he did you wrong by not trusting you in the natural gas deal, so he owes you."

Gage had seen Slava's rage and had looked up the barrel of his 9mm. Both had impaired his view of Slava as a dispassionate public servant.

"He's not what anyone would call a saint," Gage said.

"Of course not. Has he killed? Who knows how many times."

Gage didn't ask the question that came to his mind: *What about you?*

"Slava lives in the same kind of a parallel universe you've seen all over the world," Ninchenko continued. "The rules are the same, they're just applied differently. You and I are just visitors there. Would I kill for Slava just so he can grab somebody else's money? No. And he knows it. Would I kill because it must be done? Of course. You have and you will. That's why he brought me in on this job and why he's willing to work with you even though you're an outsider. He says you have heart."

Gage wasn't sure how to take that kind of compliment from a man like Slava—but he didn't have time to consider it.

Ninchenko pointed ahead toward the wrought-iron gate and guardhouse of a fenced pine forest.

"Puscha Voditsa. A military sanatorium. They've already turned in."

Gage's head snapped toward Ninchenko.

"Military?"

His mind raced ahead before Ninchenko could respond: If Matson was willing to betray SatTek shareholders by selling SatTek's intellectual property to Mr. Green, would he be willing to betray his country by—

Gage knew the answer before he had even fully formed the question. He felt his body tense in self-reproach. He should've guessed it weeks ago.

"Matson didn't come to Kiev to hide," Gage said. "The punk is here to sell missile and anti-terror technology to Ukraine."

"That's insane." Ninchenko shook his head in disgust. "Transferring that kind of expertise to Ukraine is the same as releasing it to Iran and Syria."

"Can you get us inside?" Gage said, eyes fixed on the sanatorium entrance.

Ninchenko nodded. "We can use my old SBU identification. They'd be afraid to look too closely at a major's documents."

Ninchenko's cell phone rang after the guard had waved them through the gate. He engaged in a quick conversation, then said, "They're headed toward the medical center."

They drove past an iced-over lake surrounded by tennis, volleyball, and badminton courts. They passed an empty swimming pool and a dining hall, finally arriving at a white stucco building, where the driver parked in a lot filled with black Mercedes and BMWs and a scattering of camouflaged Morozov personnel carriers.

"They give medical-sounding names to things soldiers simply like to do," Ninchenko said. "A steam bath is called climate therapy. A hot tub is called balneotherapy. A sanatorium is really just a place to hide out from the family—"

"And buy the technology to build radar and missile targeting devices."

"No better place." Ninchenko opened his door. "Let me take a look."

Ninchenko blended in with the men entering the medical center. The driver assumed his waiting position: seat back lowered, window a crack open, cap over his eyes. Gage pulled his coat up around his neck, then slid down in his seat as the cold air seeped into the van.

Ninchenko returned ten minutes later and Gage rolled down the window.

"You're right," Ninchenko said, leaning down toward Gage and glancing back toward the entrance, "Matson met with two air force generals in the bar, then they headed off to the sauna. They must be pretty far along in the deal. They wouldn't have taken Matson with them unless they considered him part of the team."

"Who are they?"

"Traitors. They raided their own squadron and sold off a dozen MIG fighters to Iraq, then tried to keep all the money for themselves. They must've kicked back a lot of it to Hadeon Alexandervich after they were caught in order to stay out of jail."

Ninchenko's cell phone rang. He listened for a moment, then said, "The plate 0087 isn't used by the State Property Fund, but by the Ministry of the Military Complex."

He disconnected and reentered the van. "Do you think Matson brought the devices and code with him to Ukraine?"

"Probably. They're easy to carry. The video and audio detectors are each about the size of a VHS cassette, and all of the documentation fits on a DVD. Schematics, software, everything. I suspect that Alla is guarding it all in their hotel room."

Ninchenko's eyes focused on the medical center. "Those generals may be crooks, but they're smart. Their mistake was in their greed, not in their cunning." He looked at Gage. "Is Matson smart enough not to get taken?"

Gage didn't answer immediately. "Smart" wasn't the right word. "It's more a matter of instinct. He knows sales better than anything else and his instinct will make him hold something back until he gets at least part of the money."

"And that would be?"

"The software. The code that gets embedded into the hardware. If I were him, I'd let them examine the devices and look at the schematics. That way they'll know it's real, but he keeps complete control over it because it can't be reverse-engineered."

Ninchenko said something in Russian to the driver, then glanced at Gage. "Let's go. The others will stay with him. We'll set up along the road so we can follow him back to the city."

Gage took a last look at the medical center and then said, "Maybe we should tell Slava what's going on."

◇◇◇

Slava was waiting for them in his Land Rover a half mile down a forest road on the outskirts of Kiev.

Gage climbed into the backseat with Slava, and Ninchenko got in front.

Slava reached into his coat pocket and retrieved a copy of the arrival card Matson submitted to Ukrainian immigration.

"Interesting thing," Slava said, handing it to Gage. "My people get this at airport."

Gage read it over. "Matson is traveling under a Panamanian passport and he's using Alla's last name. He can disappear anytime he wants."

"You underestimate this man?"

"Maybe." Gage passed it back. "But not who he's involved with."

Ninchenko related to Slava what they had discovered at the sanatorium.

"Does the meeting with the generals mean that the deal is done?" Gage asked.

Slava shook his head. "Maybe yes, maybe no. Not simple to do."

Ninchenko nodded. "Since it would be a national security matter for the U.S., it becomes a diplomatic issue for Ukraine. Take Israel. If SatTek targeting devices were discovered in missiles landing on Haifa, it would lean on the U.S. and the U.S. would not only cut off foreign aid, but would pressure the World Bank and the IMF to cut off loans, and soon the poorest of Ukrainians would be starving."

Slava pointed his thumb over his shoulder. "Many more people in Independence Square if that happen."

"Does that mean Ukraine wouldn't buy it?" Gage asked.

"Not necessarily," Ninchenko said. "Ukraine has only one reason for maintaining a defense industry. Export. The world only wants two things from Ukraine: steel and weapons. And that will be true even if the opposition takes power."

"Ukraine not make radar and missiles because we think somebody attack us or we attack somebody," Slava said. "Ukraine do because other people attack each other."

"So the decision to buy would need to be made high up."

"The highest. All of these decisions, what to buy, what to sell, are made by the president. Gravilov would take the deal to Hadeon Alexandervich, then Hadeon Alexandervich would take it to his father. It is his calculation how much diplomatic pressure the country will be able to withstand when the U.S. finds out."

"And who to kill to hide president part in deal," Slava added.

The words snapped the subject back from the abstractions of diplomacy to an image of Matson lying dead in a Kiev alley. Gage looked first at Slava, then at Ninchenko.

"Meaning what?"

"Remember when the president ordered the sale of the Kolchuga radar system to Iraq?" Ninchenko asked. "It was during the arms embargo against Saddam Hussein."

"Sure. Through Jordan."

"You know what happened to the link between the president and the deal?" Ninchenko asked.

"Malev. His name Malev, Valeri Ivanovich," Slava said. "Head of State Arms Export Agency."

"Murdered. Three days after the U.S. started investigating. It was made to look like an auto accident."

"Murder not solved. Investigation end." Slava spoke in a tone that reported a rule, not an exception. "Matson not understand that they always break chain."

Chapter Sixty-four

Lovers' quarrel," Ninchenko said after he disconnected his cell phone. He and Gage were parked a block away from the Lesya Palace. "Alla just ran out of the hotel restaurant where they were having lunch."

"What did Matson do?"

"Apparently just turned red and sat there eating his borscht."

"Any idea what the argument was about?"

"The only thing Slava's people heard was her crying as she got into the elevator."

"It's out of character. Gangsters don't cry." Gage thought for a moment. "It may have something to do with the meeting at Puscha Voditsa. Maybe a little you-don't-trust-me-with-the-money manipulation." He glanced over at Ninchenko. "I'm not sure we understand all the ways she may fit in." Gage smiled. "And what acting school she went to."

Gage recalled Slava telling him in Geneva that he and Alla's father had sat together on an underworld tribunal.

"Slava and Petrov Tarasov served on a *skhodka* last year. Maybe he can pry some information out of her father without alerting him that we know what she's up to."

After Ninchenko made the call to Slava, Gage asked, "Do you know where Gravilov and Hadeon Alexandervich are this afternoon?"

"Gravilov has been in his apartment since he arrived in Kiev. The radio reported that Hadeon Alexandervich was at Rima Casino until 5 A.M. I expect he's still sleeping it off."

"Sounds as though the Destroyer likes to party."

Ninchenko shook. "Not party. Humiliate women. The strippers at Rima dread him. They never know if he'll stuff thousands of dollars in their thongs or urinate on them. Or both—and his father isn't much better. Once he made all of the cabinet ministers strip to their underwear at a banquet and sing the national anthem."

"Why would they put up with that?"

"You mean why would they pay to do it? It costs anywhere between a million and five million dollars to buy a spot in the Cabinet of Ministers, depending on how much money can be made in the position. Energy and defense are the most lucrative, so they're the most expensive. One energy minister skimmed eighty million dollars in just one year. Whenever the president needs a little money, he just fires an official and sells the job to someone else."

"And when the kid wants money?"

"Until the last few months he didn't want money, he wanted things, big things. Now it's all about cash on hand. If the opposition wins, they'll try to take back all the factories he and the other oligarchs stole. There hasn't been a privatization of a major steel works, truck factory, defense plant, farm, or electric generation facility that he doesn't partly own through nominees or dummy companies. And it's all at risk."

Gage watched the passing traffic as he tried to fix in his mind the relationship between Hadeon Alexandervich and the president. "I was assuming the son was just a nominee for his dad."

"Hadeon Alexandervich got some things on his own and some things he got because people thought they were paying off his father. Not that different than what the European press used to say about the second George Bush and his oil interests."

"Assuming that Hadeon Alexandervich decides to buy what Matson is selling, he has either got to flip it quickly or take it with him when he flees the country."

"My guess is that he'll flip it," Ninchenko said. "He needs assets that are liquid."

Gage pointed down the street. "There's 0087."

They watched the government Mercedes pull to the curb in front of the hotel, followed by a dark green BMW 530i.

Matson and Alla stepped out the hotel entrance and waited at the top of the steps.

"It looks like the lovers' quarrel isn't over," Gage said. "I saw her in London, a scowl is not her normal expression...I hope she's not armed. I want Matson to live long enough to go to jail."

"I better find out who owns the BMW," Ninchenko said. He made a call, then read off the license number and waited.

"No such number is registered," he reported a minute later. "It's probably State Security."

"Matson's having a big day," Gage said. "Sauna with the generals, fight with the girlfriend, protection by SBU."

"And probably a meeting with Hadeon Alexandervich. That's Gravilov's Mercedes SUV pulling up. There are only a couple of G55s in Kiev. Everybody knows which one is his. It's better armored than most banks in Ukraine."

They watched Matson and Alla walk down the steps and enter Gravilov's G55. The procession pulled away, speeding along Shevchenko Boulevard, skirting the main part of Kiev, then into the exclusive Pechersk District of wide boulevards and expensive apartments.

"Looks like the meeting is at Hadeon Alexandervich's apartment," Ninchenko said. "We'll need to break this off when we get close. There's too much security. Many government officials live in that building. Video cameras sweep all sides and the streets."

"So it's a black box?"

"Yes, a black box," Ninchenko looked over at Gage. "How would it play out if they make a deal?"

"My guess is that Matson would give them at least one low-noise amplifier and one video amplifier to test. Then they'd have to negotiate a price. At some point he'd have to give up the software. And then the money would have to be moved."

"So it will take a few days."

"Probably," Gage said. "Any chance of searching his hotel room?"

Ninchenko considered it for a moment, then shook his head. "Too risky."

Gage fell silent as Ninchenko directed the driver to break off the chase. He felt a wave of frustration. He'd been reduced to a spectator, watching Matson travel from place to place, powerless to intervene, not even knowing how far along Matson was in the deal.

Then a moment of self-blame. He should've prevented Matson from leaving the U.S.—but maybe it wasn't too late to backtrack. He reached for his cell phone and called Alex Z.

"Did you find out where FedEx delivered the MMIC chips?"

He heard Alex Z yawn before he answered. It was 4 A.M. in San Francisco.

"They dead-ended at a mail drop in Trenton, New Jersey. The receiving company is registered in Delaware, but is owned by a Florida corporation."

Gage sent Alex Z back to bed, then disconnected. He had his answer about where the chips went: into a maze. And it would take a month of dead ends to get to the other side.

He was still a spectator.

Chapter Sixty-five

Ninchenko bumped Gage with his elbow as they drove toward the center of Kiev, then pointed up at the building housing the Cabinet of Ministers, a stucco monstrosity resting on granite blocks.

"That," Ninchenko said, "along with most of Kiev, was leveled by the Nazis during the Great Patriotic War." He gestured toward the building as they passed by. "The government kept German prisoners for two years after the war was over to rebuild it. As slave laborers. Some of them were just twelve- and thirteen-year-old children forced into the army by the Nazis in the last days of the war." Gage heard regret in Ninchenko's voice, as if it was a crime he had failed to prevent. "And not all of them survived." He shook his head. "I hate even to look at it."

Instead of turning west toward Independence Square and the apartment, the driver continued north, up a long, curving cobblestone street past the National Philharmonic, a yellow brick building looking to Gage more like a place of commerce than culture. They crested the hill and looked down at the blue Dnepr River and the four-story cruise ships moored for the winter at the Podil embankment terminal.

Gage didn't mind the ride. He needed to think, and preferred to do it outside the confinement of the apartment.

Ninchenko's driver wound his way up Castle Hill, then pulled into a space near the Orthodox church at the top. The few trees surrounding the small structure were bare and the parking lot was empty.

"Let's get out here," Ninchenko said. "I want to show you something."

Gage followed Ninchenko to a low wall overlooking the city.

"This is where Kiev was founded," Ninchenko said. "Not by the tribes living in the area, but by Lithuanian invaders. Ukraine, the word, means nothing more than 'borderland.' A gap, a void, an emptiness. One that is usually filled by others."

A sharp gust blew up from the river. Gage turned up his collar and pulled down on his *ushanka* to cover the tops of his ears. Ninchenko shivered, then did the same.

"You don't seem to be particularly proud to be Ukrainian," Gage said.

"Ukraine is the product of hundreds of years of madness. It's the Blanche DuBois of Europe, relying always on the kindness of strangers. Strangers gave Ukraine its capital, its industry, its culture, its religion. Russian was even the national language until a few years ago. And the world subconsciously recognizes it. Most people in the West think Kiev is part of Russia. They even refer to it as 'The Ukraine,' as if it was merely a region and not a nation."

"I don't want to offend you," Gage said, "but there does seem to be a certain hollowness in Ukraine. I feel it every time I come here. Americans expect a certain depth, maybe a certain weightiness, in this part of the world. Cossacks, plagues, famines, suffering. The kinds of things that create great art and literature."

"All of that only taught narrow-minded self-interest," Ninchenko said. "That's why Ukraine will sell arms to anyone. In fact, ethnic cleansing in the Balkans wouldn't have been quite so effective without the weapons supplied by Ukraine. Too many Ukrainians live like there's no tomorrow, and they expect that no one else has the right to."

Ninchenko pointed north. "You know what's just up that way?" Gage's gaze followed Ninchenko's arm toward treed, rolling hills. "Chernobyl. One hundred kilometers. A wind in this direction would've brought radiation to Kiev in two hours. You know how long it took the government to warn the people of Kiev about the nuclear accident? Two weeks. And you know what the government sent to the contaminated people in the zone? Red wine and instructions to wash their floors. Five hundred thousand people were evacuated, but not until they were fully bathed in the fallout and condemned to death."

Ninchenko turned toward Gage. "But we didn't come here to discuss history and literature and culture."

Gage smiled. "I think we did."

Ninchenko shrugged, not at all embarrassed to have been found out. "Apparently I'm not as subtle as I thought."

"I get your point: Matson needs to be stopped before he turns over the technology."

"But you came here to do more than that."

"I think I may be trying to do too many things. Clear my friend. Recover the money. Expose Gravilov. Stop the sale. And snagging Matson would be the linchpin for doing it all." Gage shook his head slowly. "There isn't time to do everything."

"What is there time to do?"

Gage turned toward Ninchenko. He not only wanted to hear Ninchenko's answer, he wanted to see it—for the city tour could end in the infamous State Security dungeon.

"How much of a risk are you willing to take?" Gage asked.

Ninchenko kept his eyes locked on Gage's, but pointed once again toward Chernobyl. "My older brother was a police officer. Among the first on the scene of the fire." His eyes moistened and his voice quivered, but he didn't look away. "He died within hours." Ninchenko tilted his head at the church. "We had his memorial here. You know what my mother asked the government representative? She asked him what was the half-life of grief—and he just turned away, pretending he hadn't heard her."

A gust of wind rattled the frozen leaves at their feet.

Only then did Ninchenko glance away, back toward the Cabinet of Ministers in the distance. "I despise those people as much as they despise us." He then folded his arms across his chest. "What do you need?"

"You have a place I can stash Matson?" Ninchenko didn't flinch at Gage's words. "We need to grab him, Alla, and whatever he brought with him."

"And then what?"

"Get them out of Ukraine."

Ninchenko's gaze swept north and west. "Poland, Russia. Too hard to cross the borders."

"We need to get him to a NATO country," Gage said.

"Romania or Hungary or Slovakia. But those are also difficult borders."

"What about Istanbul? By boat across the Black Sea from Odessa."

"I'll see if Slava is willing to set it up."

Ninchenko made the call as they drove down the hill.

"He agrees," Ninchenko said, after he disconnected. "But says that we better snatch them tonight. He just found out that they made plane reservations to Dnepropetrovsk tomorrow morning. Hadeon Alexandervich owns an electronics factory there. Slava thinks that's where they're going to test the devices. He wants Matson stopped before that happens."

"He wants Matson stopped? I thought politics was just a form of business to him."

"Remember what I said about Ukrainians being the Jews of the Soviet Union? Slava isn't a figurative Jew, he's an actual one. Aboveground, he travels on an Israeli passport, and he doesn't want any more weapons falling into the hands of Israel's enemies."

◇◇◇

Ninchenko dropped Gage off at the apartment. He packed a few things to take on the boat, then made a cup of tea and imagined Faith lying in bed, on his side, where she always slept when he was away. He called their home number and pictured her reaching over to pick up the handset.

She answered on the first ring. "Graham?"

"How do you always know?"

She laughed. "When you're in love, the ring sounds different."

"You okay?"

"Other than worrying about you, I'm fine."

"No need to worry. I'm almost done, but I'll be traveling for a few days through an area without cell service."

"Going where?"

"I better not say."

He thought for a moment, searching for a way to reduce the uncertainty he knew she felt. "You recall what I had delivered to Jack in the hospital?"

"Let me think…in the hospital…" She laughed again.

He smiled to himself as they both said the word silently to themselves: *Turkey*.

Chapter Sixty-six

I think they finally made up," Gage said to Ninchenko, as Matson and Alla walked arm-in-arm from the entrance of the Lesya Palace Hotel to the waiting Mercedes. "It's a good thing. I wasn't looking forward to them squabbling all the way to Istanbul."

Gravilov's enforcer, Razor, trailed Matson in a security car. Ninchenko's driver followed them from two blocks behind and let the other two surveillance cars work the perimeter.

Matson's driver wound his way east, northeast, then northwest to Artema Street, a mixed-use boulevard of offices, apartments, restaurants, and car dealerships.

Gage's cell phone rang as they drove. It was Slava.

"I talk to Alla Petrovna father in Budapest," Slava said. "He say he not have daughter. What you call disown. Look like she follow in father business, but not follow father."

"Maybe it's genetic. She must have a crook chromosome."

Ninchenko chuckled.

"What chrome zome?" Slava asked.

"I'll have Ninchenko explain it later."

"Maybe American humor not translate."

"Afraid not. Is everything ready for the happy couple?"

"*Da*. Nice room. No view."

Ninchenko's driver pulled over as they approached the end of Artema Street, then pointed toward the Madison Restaurant, a casual New York–style steakhouse and bar. Matson and Alla were walking in. Razor had parked his car on a street to the west of the building, and Matson's Mercedes had swung in behind.

Gage directed the driver to position the van on the opposite side of Artema, with a view of the entrance and the long row of restaurant windows. Ninchenko then ordered his two chase cars to bracket Razor's and the Mercedes, ready to freeze them in place while Gage and Ninchenko grabbed Matson and Alla as they left the restaurant.

"Are they too close?" Gage asked Ninchenko, tilting his head toward the chase cars.

"No. Many of the patrons bring security. Razor'll think our men are merely comrades suffering in the cold while the bosses eat in comfort. He's too arrogant for his own good. He shouldn't have let himself get boxed in."

Ninchenko handed binoculars to Gage.

Gage scanned the restaurant interior. Matson and Alla sat in an oversized leather booth in the wood-paneled restaurant. Down lighting from recessed ceiling coffers illuminated their table.

A wine steward approached to take Matson's order, then entered the glassed-in circular wine vault. He made his selection, then returned to Matson's table.

Matson swirled the wine, then tasted it and nodded.

"Matson thinks he's a real charmer, a *debonair* man about town," Gage said. "Look at his little pinky sticking out, like a society matron...He looks ridiculous."

The wine steward filled Alla's glass, then added to Matson's.

Gage watched Alla's face brighten as she reached across the table to clink glasses. She smiled, then slid around the table so that she was next to Matson and her back was to Gage.

The waiter approached to take their dinner orders and moved Alla's place setting. She lowered her menu as if to defer ordering to Matson, then reached her arm through Matson's and snuggled close.

"Suppertime," Ninchenko said, retrieving a bag from the floorboard and handing Gage a sausage sandwich and a Coke.

◇◇◇

After Matson and Alla's dessert dishes were removed, Ninchenko signaled his chase cars. The four occupants exited the Ladas, two taking positions against the building out of the wind and lighting cigarettes, while the others simply stretched, then stamped their feet on the icy grass, their breath rising in swirling clouds that quickly condensed into invisibility. One walked up to Razor's window and offered him a cigarette. Another approached Matson's driver, holding out a flask of vodka.

Alla gave Matson a light kiss on the cheek, then walked toward the far left rear corner of the dining room and disappeared down a hallway leading to the restrooms. Matson left the table and followed the same route. A minute later Alla reappeared. She glanced toward the empty booth as she walked toward the coatroom. She retrieved a black, fur-collared overcoat, then walked toward the entrance.

Gage lost sight of her when she passed on the opposite side of the reception station, then spotted her again as she descended the concrete front steps. She looked toward Razor and the Mercedes, but Ninchenko's men blocked her view. She then walked behind a large fountain near the entrance.

"Tell your men to stand by until Matson comes outside," Gage said. "And get them out of here fast. We don't want Razor thinking there's anything left to fight over."

Ninchenko gave the order as Gage looked toward the restaurant window. Matson had not yet returned from the restroom. A slight motion caught Gage's eyes.

"She's running! She's running!" Gage yelled at their driver and pointed at Alla fleeing across Artema, and then said to Ninchenko, "Razor hasn't noticed yet. Have your men keep him diverted."

Gage fixed his eyes on Alla as their driver pulled away from the curb.

"What should we do about Matson?" Ninchenko asked.

"Nothing yet," Gage said. He pointed at Ninchenko's phone. "Keep your guy on the line and reporting what Matson does."

They followed Alla as she cut south, then slipped into a small residential street running southeast. Gage lost sight of her until their driver looped around the block to cut her off, but she was already beyond them.

Ninchenko held his phone tight to his ear, then said, "Matson is back at the table, waiting for his credit card receipt." He then pointed at Alla. "She's fast."

"One of our surveillance people in London said she was a jogger," Gage said. "But how the devil did she know we were here?"

Gage felt anger rise within as he turned toward Ninchenko. "Did one of your people sell us out?"

"I don't know—but we will know in a couple of minutes."

"I don't want her hurt. Leave it up to me."

Alla slowed as she approached a group of theatergoers strolling toward the Zoloti Vorota Theatre, mixing into the crowd to conceal herself and catch her breath. The driver pulled over until she separated and began scampering farther south.

Ninchenko raised his hand as he listened on the phone. "Matson is walking toward the coatrack." He looked at Gage. "What should we do?"

"Have someone go in pretending to be a friend of Alla's from her hometown. Say she walked down to his apartment to say hello to his wife. She'll be back in ten minutes. Have him buy Matson a drink in the bar."

Ninchenko passed on the order as Alla cut onto a side street angling northeast.

"She's heading back toward Artema," Ninchenko said. "Lots of places to escape into. Apartments, stores, even embassies."

"We better get her now."

The driver sped up until he was ten yards beyond her, then cut into a blind alley to block her way. Gage and Ninchenko leaped out and grabbed her just as her feet slipped from under her when she tried to stop on the icy sidewalk.

Alla struggled against them, squirming, kicking, trying to shake free by wiggling out of her coat. She then went limp.

Ninchenko smiled at Gage, but instead of loosening his grip, held her even more firmly, turning her coat into a straitjacket.

"Let me go!" she yelled in Ukrainian. "Let me go."

Ninchenko covered her mouth. Gage pointed down the shadowed alley, and Ninchenko dragged her to the end. The driver backed in and then walked around to the rear of the van to tie her hands. They lowered the tailgate and sat her down.

"We're not going to hurt you," Ninchenko said. "If we were, you'd be gagged and hooded. We just want you to answer some questions about Stuart Matson."

Alla's eyes flashed, then she nodded and he removed his hand.

"Who are you running from?"

"Everyone."

"Who's everyone?" Gage asked.

"Shit," Alla spat out, her face red not only from exertion, but now from anger. "Another fucking American."

"That's not an answer. You were just kissing an American ten minutes ago."

"That's nothing. I would've gone down on a toad to get that bastard."

Gage glanced toward Ninchenko. "I think I made a mistake about her."

Alla kicked at Gage, who skipped back a step. "You bet you did. Wait until my father gets ahold of you."

"From what I hear Petrov Tarasov doesn't have a daughter anymore."

"Who *are* you?"

"Graham Gage. I'm a private investigator from San Francisco."

"Whose side are you on?"

"Not Matson's," Gage said. "He's trying to frame a friend of mine and I'm here to stop him. Where were you heading?"

"The U.S. embassy."

"A little late in the day."

"So what. They'll open the door for me."

Gage shook his head. "Not over a lovers' quarrel."

"It's worse than that," she said.

"How much worse?"

Alla shrugged. "How do I know you won't send me back?"

"You can trust me on that. I'm not letting you go at all. Tomorrow you'll be on a slow boat to Istanbul."

Gage tensed, expecting her to kick at him again, or push off against the tailgate in a final attempt to flee. Instead she asked, "What about Stuart?"

"He's next. I've already got him, he just doesn't know it. He has something other people want and I need to stop him from turning it over."

Alla laughed with frustration and disgust. "You're about six months too late."

"What do you mean?"

"What do I get?"

"What do you want?"

"The whole truth and to see that son of a bitch hung by his heels in Shevchenko Park."

Gage glanced over at Ninchenko to see whether his picture of Alla had also turned inside out.

Ninchenko raised an eyebrow in response, then asked Alla in English, "What was your fight about the other day?"

Alla's eyes widened. "It was…" She hesitated and looked back and forth between Gage and Ninchenko. "Why should I trust you two?"

Gage pointed back toward the street. "You notice anybody out there that wants to stop him besides us?"

"How do I know you don't want to steal it?"

"Because I could've done that in California."

"The fight?" Ninchenko asked again.

"It was…" Alla looked back and forth between them. "It was about what he's really doing here. Before we came, he said he wanted to make an investment. But that's not the truth, or at least not the whole truth. The investment had already been made."

"Is that what the meetings in London with Gravilov were about?"

She drew back, then smiled as if Gage had walked in on her in the shower. "Have you been living in my flat and I somehow missed it?"

"No, just close by."

"I wish I knew you were there." Her smile faded. "This would all be over by now."

"Unfortunately, your background suggested that you were carrying on the family business, or at least working for Gravilov."

"He tried to recruit me to spy on Stuart. One Ukrainian to another. I didn't want his money...that fucking gangster."

"Does Gravilov know who your father is?"

"I don't think so. I didn't want to get caught in a crossfire between him and my father's people so I used my ex-husband's last name when he came by." Alla looked down and sighed. "How did I get into this mess? All this time I thought Stuart was different, but he turned into the same kind of predator I was trying to escape from."

"People fall in love with the same person over and over again," Gage said. "It's just the names that change."

Alla looked up at Gage. "You must know my ex-husband."

Gage shrugged. "Just a guess." He circled back to the fight. "What investment?"

"Stuart, Gravilov, and Hadeon Alexandervich built a plant in Dnepropetrovsk, to manufacture missile guidance systems."

Gage caught his breath. He felt as if life had been fast-forwarded and he'd blinked at all the wrong times. Rage mushroomed inside him, at Matson for his treason and at himself for failing to recognizing what Matson had been up to.

"Stuart got caught sending over military-grade video amplifiers, so Gravilov suggested that he manufacture them over here." She emitted a bitter laugh. "Stuart liked to brag that SatTek can drop a missile into a coffee cup, but he never seemed to grasp that it's people, not coffee cups, who get blown up."

"How far have they gotten?" Gage said, keeping his voice steady, concealing his anger.

"They've already built fifteen hundred." She glanced over at Ninchenko. "Stuart ordered the parts, mostly through intermediaries in Taiwan and Singapore, and shipped them over. Gravilov and Stuart fronted the money." She glanced over her shoulder. "A FedEx box from Germany arrived at the hotel."

Gage tensed as he said the words, "MMIC controller chips."

Alla nodded. "The last five hundred. They were repackaged in Munich to disguise them as computer components. Gravilov's bodyguard snatched them right out of Stuart's hands and headed for the plant. All that's left is to embed the software."

"How do you know—"

"I studied engineering in college. I understand the process better than Stuart does." She shook her head. "Putting weapons in the hands of these people is lunacy…sheer lunacy."

Alla glanced in the direction of the restaurant. "Now what?"

Gage looked at his watch and asked Ninchenko, "What's Matson doing?"

Ninchenko passed on the question, listened for a moment, then answered. "He's still at the bar."

"How'd you get Matson to tell you all of this?" Gage asked her.

"I told you what I'd do to a toad," she said, unsmiling, "so use your imagination. And it didn't hurt that Stuart has painted himself into a corner. Gravilov gave him a down payment of five million dollars for the software and Stuart's afraid that if he hands it over, he'll never get the rest of the money and they might even force him to give the five million back. He knows he's already lost his investment in the plant."

"Where's the software?" Gage asked.

"Stuart told them it's with his lawyer in London, but it's really on his laptop. The idea is that he stays in Ukraine until the payment is wired into his account. Then he gives them the software and they're supposed to let him leave."

"Supposed to?"

"That's what's got him worried most of all."

Gage looked at Ninchenko, who shrugged his shoulders as if to say, *Use your best judgment*. Then back at Alla. "Would you go back to him if I asked you to?"

She shook her head. "If they don't let Stuart leave, there's no way they'll let me. Why not just kidnap him and the laptop?" She jutted her chin toward the restaurant. "I'll make sure he cooperates."

"Things have gone too far. We need to disable the devices so no one can ever use them."

Ninchenko held up a finger and again listened to his phone. "Matson has looked at his watch a couple of times."

Alla peered up at Gage. "You seemed to be good at following people. How good are you at rescuing them?"

Gage glanced at Ninchenko and smiled. "Even better. There'll always be people just minutes away."

"And if I say I want out?"

"We'll get you out."

She turned sideways and rolled her shoulder. "You'll need to untie me."

"You going to run?"

"No." She flashed a smile. "I think I'd like a ride back."

Gage nodded, then Ninchenko released her. Gage then pointed at the front passenger door and said to Alla, "You ride in front."

She slipped down from the tailgate, rubbing her wrists, then walked around and climbed in. Gage and Ninchenko got into the back.

Alla turned toward them as the driver pulled out into the street. She locked her eyes on Ninchenko, and then tilted her head toward Gage. "I know how he fits in. What about you?"

"I work for an enemy of Gravilov—"

"I should have guessed." She glared at Ninchenko. "The enemy of my enemy. It's the Ukrainian way."

"Except," Ninchenko continued, "this enemy agrees with you and Mr. Gage. The devices have to be disabled. They mustn't fall into the wrong hands."

"They better be disabled, and fast." Alla looked back at Gage. "You know what Stuart's leverage for more money is?"

Gage shook his head.

"The video amplifiers are supposed to be installed in Ukrainian air-to-ground missiles next week. Like your Hellfires. Orders were placed. Part of the money has already changed hands. And they're in a hurry to get it done. Hadeon Alexandervich is afraid the opposition will win the new election. Within weeks there'll be a new prime minister and a new chief prosecutor. Hadeon Alexandervich knows he's target number one. He wants the rest of his money. Now."

"How much?"

"For the missiles? His profit is going to be about two hundred and seventy million. And Stuart is supposed to get twenty million. Same as Gravilov."

"Who's buying them?"

"Stuart doesn't know exactly. He heard Gravilov refer to his Middle Eastern friends, but that may just mean the intermediary, like the Jordanian in the sale of the Kolchuga radar to Iraq. But I know this: Whoever the buyer is will be at a demonstration at the Black Sea the day after the installation is completed. If he's satisfied, they'll be shipped out right afterwards. A boat is already waiting."

"Isn't Matson afraid of these people?"

"Yes, but he doesn't quite get it. Violence to him is an abstract concept."

"And I take it he doesn't understand what protection means over here, either."

Alla shook her head. "He doesn't have the slightest idea."

The driver pulled into the shadowed alley behind the restaurant.

"Where do I tell Stuart I was?" Alla asked.

Ninchenko told her the story his man had used.

"You have a cell phone?" Gage asked.

"From London."

Gage pulled out his own. "Keep this on you. You never know when you'll have a chance to sneak a call." He deleted the numbers in the memory except for Ninchenko's, then looked at the battery meter. "It has about four days of power left. There's just one number programmed in, Mr. Ninchenko's." He thought for a moment. "If anybody finds the phone, tell them it's a local one you use for convenience."

"Whose number do I say is in memory?" Alla asked.

"Your cousin, Ivan Ivanovich. Say you've been planning a surprise party for Matson when you get back from Dnepropetrovsk."

"There'll be a fucking surprise all right."

Chapter Sixty-seven

Ninchenko and Gage drove back toward the apartment, leaving Ninchenko's men to watch Alla and Matson's return to the Lesya Palace Hotel.

"I sure didn't see that coming," Gage said as they wound their way back toward central Kiev.

He stared for a moment at the dimly lit street, then shook his head slowly. "Makes me wonder what else I missed."

◇◇◇

"Why not blow up the plant?" Ninchenko asked when he, Gage, and Slava met for a drink at the apartment. They sat at the dining table, bottled water in front of Gage and Ninchenko, vodka in front of Slava.

"I want it," Slava said. "If Gravilov fall or opposition win, I get it. And blow up not solve problem anyway."

"No, it won't," Gage said. "Rubble in Eastern Ukraine isn't evidence."

"Bullet in head solve everybody problem," Slava said.

Gage gave Slava a sour look. "Don't get any ideas."

"Just little joke." Slava poured a shot of vodka into his glass and tossed it down. "Not easy to bury body in forest when ground frozen."

"With Alla on the inside"—Gage glanced at Slava—"and Matson still alive..."

Ninchenko nodded. "Maybe she can gather enough evidence so she can testify about what Matson was really doing over here."

Gage shook his head. "And then spend the rest of her life on the run? Gravilov, Hadeon Alexandervich, and all of Ukrainian security will be tracking her like wolves on the hunt."

"What about your Witness Protection Program?" Ninchenko asked.

"That's only if she's willing and if the U.S. Attorney buys her story—which he has no incentive to do. How will it sound? Daughter of gangster Petrov Tarasov, traveling under Panamanian passport, fights with her boyfriend, then gets even by running to the government with a made-up story?"

Gage stared at the water bottle on the table before him, overcome by a sense of foreboding, worried that he was leading Alla, like Granger before her, into a Gravilov trap—and feeling straitjacketed by conflicting, if not contradictory, goals: making sure the devices never got installed in missile guidance systems while obtaining hard enough evidence to crush the conspiracy of words upon which Peterson was resting his indictment of Burch.

Then a thought.

He looked at Ninchenko. "How many people would it take to break in and destroy the devices? I'll just need to preserve a few for evidence."

"That depends on the security at the plant," Ninchenko said.

"How soon can we get out there?"

"You take my plane at Zhulyany Airport," Slava said, after tossing down another shot of vodka. "Ready in thirty minutes. Two-hour flight to Dnepropetrovsk. Car waiting when you arrive."

"Good. Now let's hope that Alla doesn't snitch us off."

Chapter Sixty-eight

Midnight shadows dominated the wide boulevard sweeping through the heart of Dnepropetrovsk. Sepia-toned sidewalks emerged from a grassy blackness under the light cast by halfhearted yellow bulbs. The only souls Gage observed on the street were heavily coated swing-shift workers and a few vodka-inebriated wanderers, seemingly impervious to the chilly wind off the Dnepr River flowing down from Kiev.

"This is called Karl Marx Avenue," Ninchenko said. "We haven't entirely shaken off the past."

Gage found no opposition protestors camped out in the main square, no opposition banners strung from building to building across the boulevards as in Kiev. Gage pointed at a dozen headstones draped in yellow as they passed a Russian Orthodox cemetery.

"They'll be gone by morning," Ninchenko said. "The president owns Eastern Ukraine. The graveyard is the only place out here where the opposition gathers. He orders the murder of opposition journalists and politicians who show their faces in his hometown."

Gage thought back on the demonstrators in Independence Square encircled by police and soldiers. "Courageous people."

"They don't see that they have a choice but to take the risk if they're going to change the country. The opposition knows it can't win the election without carrying at least thirty percent of the vote out here, so they keep coming."

As they drove past the cemetery, Ninchenko ceased speaking in a moment of respect for those who'd fallen in the cause, then pointed ahead. "We're almost at the hotel."

Gage made out the four-story, redbrick Astoria in the distance. The entrance was dark and the sign in front wasn't illuminated. Clearly, walk-ins weren't welcome.

"Has Slava decided whether to meet us out here?" Gage asked.

"His presence in Dnepropetrovsk could be viewed as a provocation."

"I thought he had investments in the area."

Ninchenko shrugged. "They don't threaten anyone. They're not viewed as a toehold, just a place to put money. A personal visit is another thing altogether. Especially with the country on the verge of chaos."

Ninchenko swung around behind the hotel, stopping at a guarded gate that slowly opened, allowing him to drive into a parking area formed by the L-shape of the building. A beefy man in a *ushanka* and a knee-length leather jacket opened Gage's door and handed him a room key anchored to a brass plate. He passed another one to Ninchenko, then removed their luggage from the trunk and followed them through the back door and into an elevator to their rooms.

He set Gage's on a rack in the bedroom and left without waiting for a tip. Moments later Ninchenko appeared at Gage's door.

"I didn't need all of this," Gage said, gesturing toward the heavy leather couch and chairs and satellite television in the living area. "Just a place to lay my head."

"Slava said you should be comfortable."

"Can we take a look at the plant tonight?"

"One of my local people is bringing over a surveillance van. Let's get something to eat while we wait."

Gage turned the face of his watch toward Ninchenko: 2 A.M.

"Hotel staff in Ukraine work twenty-four-hour shifts." Ninchenko grinned. "They say it gives the guests more continuity but it's really just a holdover from Soviet days. People slept on the job anyway, so the leaders found a better way to schedule their naps."

Ninchenko and Gage walked down to the second floor restaurant, passed through it, then entered a private dining room. One of the four tables was already covered with plates of smoked fish, cheese, pickles, olives, tomatoes, and bread. Ninchenko walked over to the bar and switched on a radio to cover their conversation.

Gage reached his fork toward the smoked sturgeon, then drew it back. "Is this from the Dnepr River?"

"Only the poor eat fish from the Dnepr. It'll be a million years before the Chernobyl radioactivity washes out. This is Siberian."

Gage stabbed a piece and shook it onto his plate.

A bleary-eyed waiter in a wrinkled white shirt appeared with bottles of mineral water, filling both of their glasses, then slinked away.

"When will your helpers from Kiev arrive?" Gage asked.

Ninchenko glanced at his watch. "A few more hours. They'll be staying on the other side of town. No reason for all of us to be seen together."

Gage and Ninchenko ate in silence. The waiter reappeared with a customary bottle of vodka and two shot glasses. They waved him off simultaneously. He walked away bearing a mixed expression of disappointment and violated expectation.

"For the Ukrainian male, a meal without vodka is like Chinese food without rice," Ninchenko said.

"A cultural impossibility?"

"Very close."

Ninchenko's phone rang. He looked at Gage after answering, forming the word "Alla" with his mouth. He listened for thirty seconds, spoke quickly and quietly, then hung up.

"Matson and Alla are confirmed on a commercial flight tomorrow morning."

"She sound okay?"

"Nervous," Ninchenko said, smiling. "She's lost the fire she displayed when she was kicking at you."

"Did she say where they're staying?"

"The Grand Domus Hotel. I know it. Hadeon Alexandervich pried it out of the hands of the former owner through tax inspections. The Ukrainian Tax Authority is like your IRS except it's a political and economic tool of the president. The government seized the hotel and auctioned it to the single qualified bidder."

"And that would be?"

"Hadeon Alexandervich's ninety-year-old great-aunt."

"I take it she's a spry old lady who possesses special skills in hotel management."

"She possesses special skills at keeping her mouth shut and in staying alive. She's already outlived the average Ukrainian by thirty years."

"What's the layout? We'll need a plan to get Alla out of there. I don't want her paying for Matson's crime with her life."

"It won't be easy. The perimeter is composed of high brick walls and wrought-iron fences. She's in good shape, but I doubt that she could climb over either, especially with them iced over."

The waiter reappeared and whispered in Ninchenko's ear.

"The van has arrived," Ninchenko said, pushing his plate away.

Ninchenko led Gage down a staircase and out to the parking lot where a gray, long-haul delivery van was waiting. It bore red lettering and drawings of fruit and vegetables.

Ninchenko introduced Gage to their driver, Kolya, a slight, middle-aged man with deep-set eyes and the earnest expression typical of uncomplaining men devoted to executing the orders of others.

Ninchenko and Kolya engaged in a short conversation in Russian.

Kolya handed Gage a cell phone and charger and gave a thumbs-up. He then walked around to the back of the van and opened the swinging doors, inviting Gage and Ninchenko to climb in. Once inside Gage found a metal table and two chairs bolted to the floor, along with a small refrigerator, a metal cabinet containing a monitor and recorder, and a case of mineral water.

Ninchenko turned on the video and picked up a joystick. The image on the screen scanned a full 360 degrees.

"Impressive," Gage said.

"If we're going to battle State Security, we need to match their tools."

"What conceals the camera?"

"An air vent on the roof."

Ninchenko knocked on the blackened divider and the van began to move. Gage sat down while Ninchenko pointed the camera toward the front of the van, giving them a wide-angled view of the road ahead, illuminated by the van's headlights.

Gage watched the monitor as the van drove down Karl Marx toward the river, following it north past Lenin Street, across a bridge over the Dnepr, then southeast. Bordering the river on each side were aging factories that made the city the heart of the Ukrainian defense industry, starting in Soviet times.

The van slowed after traveling ten blocks. Ninchenko directed the camera toward a concrete two-story building half the size of a football field, then activated the zoom, first focusing on the plant sign, "Electro-Dnepr Joint Stock Company." Razor wire glinted in the perimeter lights. Towers stood at the corners and a guardhouse protected the main gate.

Ninchenko zoomed in, then swept the walls of the building until slowing to track two uniformed guards and their German shepherd. He then focused on each tower and the guardhouse at the main gate, hesitating at each until he confirmed that it was occupied.

"There's no way we're getting in there," Ninchenko said.

Gage thought for a moment, then punched a string of numbers into his new cell phone.

"Professor Blanchard, this is—"

"Mr. Green, I presume?"

"I'm back to Mr. Gage."

"What going on?"

"The video amplifiers are about to be installed in Hellfire-type missiles."

Blanchard's breath caught. "No…"

"I need you to be close to your phone for the next forty-eight hours."

"For what?"

"I'm not sure. Maybe just advice. There are too many parts in motion and I'm not yet sure where to aim."

Chapter Sixty-nine

Low clouds hanging over Dnepropetrovsk muted the daylight that met Gage and Ninchenko as they walked from the hotel to the van where Kolya was waiting. Smoke from industrial stacks towering above the auto, steel, and missile plants in the distance rose until it encountered the denser atmosphere above, then curled downward, filling the air with a leadish haze and a sour and acidic odor.

Ten minutes later, Kolya pulled to a curb southeast of the city along the route from the airport. Matson and Alla would have to pass them whether they drove first to their hotel or to the Electro-Dnepr Company. Ninchenko stationed one surveillance team a half mile from the plant and another a half mile from the hotel.

At 10:25 Ninchenko's phone rang. He answered it, listened, then covered the receiver.

"It's Alla. She's calling from the Dnepropetrovsk Airport bathroom."

"Let me talk to her."

Ninchenko handed the phone to Gage.

"Are you okay?"

"A little nervous," Alla whispered, her voice brittle and edgy. "I've had too much time to think—hold on...It's okay. Just someone passing by outside."

"I need to know the car you'll be in."

"Gravilov's driver brought the G55 from Kiev overnight. Gravilov will meet us at the hotel, then we'll go to the plant. What about you?"

"We'll be close by, but it's better if you don't know the vehicle we're in." Gage didn't want her inadvertently drawing attention to them. "Any talk about price?"

"That's close to being settled." Alla's tone firmed, as if strengthened by her accomplishment in finding out. "Stuart is still telling them that he has to fly back to London to get the code—and they're not happy. I'm pretty sure he'll break down and tell them he's got it with him, just to get this over with. But he's afraid they'll try to force him to return the money after they get it. The result is that he's starting to flail around."

"Just tell him you know how Ukrainians think and you'll guide him through it."

"I will?" She laughed softly. "I don't remember a class in arms trafficking at my college."

"It was an elective." Gage gave Ninchenko a thumbs-up, as if to say that Alla had recovered the confidence they'd originally seen. "Don't worry, I'll tell you what to do when the time comes." He glanced at Ninchenko. "What's the area around the hotel like?"

"It's on a large lot, facing a wide street," Ninchenko said. "The back borders a large park. Lots of trees and benches. There are always people out there, lovers and drunks, even in winter."

Gage spoke into the phone. "Ask for a lower floor room facing the park. That'll be the easiest route if we need to get you out of there."

He confirmed that his new number was saved in her phone's memory, then disconnected.

"Matson is getting a little spooked," Gage told Ninchenko.

"So you'll need to tell him how to commit the crime?"

"Looks like it."

Ninchenko raised his eyebrows, a little grin on his face. "You know any Yiddish?"

"A few words."

"You know *shmegegi*?"

"No."

"It's like *putz*."

Gage laughed. "You use that one over here, too?"

"We're a lot closer to the source than Brooklyn."

◇◇◇

Twenty minutes later, Ninchenko and Gage were parked in the van a half block away from the Grand Domus with a view of the driveway and entrance. The white building, set back about fifteen yards from the street on a half-acre lot, looked more like a small townhouse complex than a hotel. Tall brown-brick apartment buildings flanked it.

Kolya joined them in the back. He curled up in the corner and fell asleep.

A few minutes later, a blue four-door Opel sped past, then pulled to the curb between them and the hotel, but neither of the two men inside got out. They slid down in their seats. Gage watched their heads swiveling, attentive to their surroundings. There were no other vehicles near them on the street.

"What do you think?" Gage asked.

"They're not mine," Ninchenko answered.

Gage thought for a moment. "Maybe it's somebody who wants to keep an eye on Gravilov."

"Hadeon Alexandervich?"

"Could be."

"How about Alla? You think they got to her somehow?"

"She asked me what vehicle we were in, but I didn't tell her." Gage glanced at the monitor. "If these guys knew someone was out here, they'd have parked behind us or on the other side of the hotel with a view back this way. That way they could watch everything on the street."

Gage and Ninchenko watched on the monitor as one of the men leaned over and kissed the other on the lips, then got out of the car. The driver sped away.

"Not everything is a conspiracy," Gage said.

"Or at least not our conspiracy," Ninchenko said, raising his teacup. "To love."

"*L'chayim.*"

Ninchenko pointed at the monitor. "She's pulling up."

"Turn on the recorder," Gage said. "I want to put together a little piece on how Scoob Matson spent his winter vacation."

Ninchenko reached over and activated it.

The wrought-iron gate slid open to permit Gravilov's G55 to enter the hotel grounds. Ninchenko tracked it until it stopped at the entrance, then drew back for a wide view of the vehicle, the hotel entrance, and the sidewalk in between. A driver and a bodyguard stepped down and immediately reached to open the two passenger doors. Alla got out of the one closest to the entrance and glanced back toward the street. Her eyes scanned the cars and trucks along the curbs, but didn't come to rest on the van.

The driver reached for Matson's briefcase as he came around the back of the SUV, but Matson pulled it away. The bodyguard retrieved the luggage and followed Matson and Alla up the stairs and inside.

Ten minutes later an enormous silver Mercedes sedan approached the hotel. It hesitated until the gate slid open, then drove onto the grounds. Gravilov got out, then walked around the left side of the building, out of Gage's view.

"Where's he going?"

"The restaurant is downstairs. It has an outside entrance."

"What do you suppose they're having?"

"I know it's not this." Ninchenko reached into the refrigerator and withdrew three ham sandwiches and three Cokes.

"It's okay," Gage said. "We have better ambience."

"And company."

They clinked their Cokes, then woke Kolya.

◇◇◇

"How much time do we have?" Ninchenko asked after they finished eating and Kolya was once again curled up in the corner of the van.

"It depends on when they make the deal and when Matson's bank confirms that the payment arrived."

Gage's phone rang.

"It's me," Alla said.

"Stop—where are you?"

"In the hotel room."

"Turn on the radio. The room is probably bugged."

Gage heard the rustling of Alla walking, then Ukrainian pop-rock music in the background.

"They gave us a suite on the floor above the lobby," Alla said. "It faces the park. There's even a balcony."

"What's the layout?"

"The suite runs the length of this side of the hotel. There's a bedroom, a dining area, and an office. The balcony is off of the office."

"How's Matson?"

"He confessed to me that people were murdered. He thinks Gravilov and Hadeon Alexandervich might kill him whether they get their money back or not. Everybody who was killed was in a position to hurt Gravilov. Stuart said he did something stupid but won't tell me what it was. He just went into the bathroom and threw up his lunch. He's pretending that he caught the flu, but the truth is that he's getting really scared."

Gage knew Matson wasn't the only one, and pretending otherwise would destroy her trust. "And you are, too."

"I think I better get away. There are rumors that the opposition is planning mass corruption trials in January if they win, so Hadeon Alexandervich and Gravilov have nothing to lose. I have cousins further east, near the Russian border. I can hide there."

"They'll hunt you down in no time. You know too much. You've known too much since Gravilov visited you in London. You're safer being close to us."

"But I've got to come up with something to tell Stuart, otherwise—"

"How badly does Gravilov want the low-noise software?"

"Very."

"Tell Matson to give Gravilov the video amplifier software after the money arrives, but hold back the low-noise. Say it's in London. Make sure he erases it from his laptop."

"I don't think he knows the software well enough to tell which is which. He'd be too nervous anyway, afraid he'd delete the wrong thing and end up in worse trouble."

"Is there a high-speed Internet connection in your room?"

"Yes."

"Will he give you time alone on the computer if you tell him you can figure it out?"

"He may be too afraid I'll make a mistake and then Gravilov will—"

"Is he still throwing up?"

Alla paused and Gage heard the faint flush of a toilet. "Yes."

"Then he'll give you all the time you need."

"But I know nothing about this kind of software—he's coming out."

The line went dead.

Gage called Blanchard.

"Is there an easy way to differentiate between the video and low-noise software on Matson's laptop?"

"Sure. But files could be spread over several different directories."

"How long would it take to delete just the low-noise amplifier software from Matson's laptop?"

"How competent is the person doing it?"

"She studied engineering, but knows nothing about this kind of code."

"She probably couldn't."

"What about you?"

"Get me connected and I'll give it a shot."

Gage thought for a moment. He didn't come to Ukraine to help Matson commit a crime, but to stop him. Then an idea. Maybe he was wrong when he told Ninchenko on Castle Hill that he couldn't do everything.

"I want to use Matson as a Trojan horse," Gage said. "Can you do that, too?"

Blanchard didn't respond right way. Gage imagined him sitting in his little workshop, his mind racing toward a solution.

"It'll be difficult…let me think…The changes will have to be very subtle. If they're too gross, they'll be spotted on a first pass… Remember when we talked about embedded software testing? There are three parts. The hardware, which I assume is nearly assembled, given the timeframe you mentioned. The software. And the device with the software embedded…" Blanchard's voice trailed off. Then the sound of his hand slapping his workbench. "I got it. Do you know where SatTek's previous test data can be found? It would be in something called the metrology database."

"On the backup tapes at my office. Alex Z from my office will bring them to you and set up a remote connection to Matson's computer."

Gage heard the beep of an incoming call an instant before he broke off from Blanchard.

"He's back in the bathroom," Alla whispered. "I suggested he hold back the low-noise amplifier software. He likes the idea."

"Were there negotiations during lunch?"

"No. They'll finalize the figure this afternoon."

"We can't let that happen. I don't want them transferring the funds during banking hours in Switzerland today. Matson needs to make the low-noise proposal, then move the meeting to dinner."

"But I don't think I can delay them. Gravilov doesn't take me seriously."

"Then play mother to Matson. If you pretend he's sick, he'll keep believing it and will be convincing when he postpones his visit to the plant. There's really no reason to go, they're just using it to pressure him."

"Then what?"

"Tuck him in bed, then get his laptop connected to a service called Connector1+1. Enter SatTek as the username and eight 2s for the password. As soon as you're hooked up, someone at my office will take over. You just sit there and pretend. Leave the laptop on when you're done."

Gage rang off, woke up Alex Z, and sent him to Blanchard's.

◇◇◇

Alla called three hours later.

"We've got a problem." Her voice was panicky. "Gravilov came to the room and saw that the computer was hooked up and unplugged it. He said the line wasn't secure. I couldn't connect again because he left Hammer with me while they met in the bedroom."

"How long was the connection active?"

"An hour and a half. I'm sorry. I messed up. I should've blocked his view."

"You can't think of everything. We'll have to try again."

"We won't have a chance. Stuart told me that Gravilov is insisting that everything be settled tonight. Stuart is angry at himself because he didn't resolve this when they argued about it in London. He's also angry that he let himself get trapped here. Gravilov told him that the president has readied contingency plans to ground all commercial aircraft if he decides to move against the opposition. Stuart asked me if I knew of anyone who could get him out of Ukraine."

"Does he know who your father is?"

"I won't ask my father for help," Alla snapped.

"That wasn't my question."

"Sorry. I'm a little on edge...No, I haven't told him."

"How is Matson's mental state otherwise? Can he pull this off?"

"He's now sounding more angry than scared. I think we've given him a plan that makes him feel like he's in control."

Gage disconnected and called Blanchard. "How'd you do?"

"I don't know. The line went dead just as I was checking to see whether he hid backups somewhere else on the drive. He would've been an idiot not to."

"Stand by. We can't give up on this. There's too much at stake."

◇◇◇

Gage and Ninchenko watched Gravilov drive from the hotel grounds, heading north toward the Dnepr River.

"What's next?" Ninchenko asked.

"We wait for Gravilov to come back and make a deal."

"But is Matson predictable? Will he follow your plan?"

"Amateurs are never predictable if left to their own devices. But they can be guided." Gage reached for his cell phone. "Let me find out how well I'm doing."

"How are you feeling?" Gage asked Burch when he answered his home phone in San Francisco.

"Stronger every day. Where are you?"

"In a little Ukrainian icebox." Gage looked up at Ninchenko and smiled. "But I'm in good company."

"Did the KTMG Limited account I set up for Matson work out okay?" Burch asked.

"That's why I'm calling. Can you find out if any money arrived?"

"Sure. I set it up through a friend. He receives all of the wire transfer documentation by e-mail from the bank."

"Call him on your cell."

Gage heard Burch set down his home phone.

"Maurice, this is Jack Burch...Fine, getting along better every day...I'm calling to verify that KTMG received some funds...I think I'd rather stand by. The client is anxious about this."

Gage heard Burch pick up the home phone again.

"He's retrieving the e-mails...By the way, my firm called about a partners' meeting next week. They're pretty nervous. Franklin Braunegg's class action suit is getting a lot of press coverage—hold on."

Gage heard Burch speak into his other phone, then come back on the line.

"There were four incoming wire transfers," he told Gage. "About fifteen million dollars altogether."

Gage smiled to himself. "Perfect."

"Ten from Guernsey," Burch continued. "Five from the Cayman Islands."

"The ten is probably stock profit and the five is Gravilov's down payment."

"And Matson has moved two hundred thousand in three transfers to Barclays in London."

"Probably feathering his nest."

"Will you have the rest of the money seized?"

"Not yet. I told him to move only a little at a time. At worst we'll lose a few hundred thousand more, but we can track that later."

Burch laughed. "Clients are always trying to trick me into laundering their money, now I seem to be doing it all on my own. If this ever gets into the papers—"

"That's what you said when we were in Afghanistan. We got away with it and you got a nice little plaque. I saw them give it to you."

"I don't think I'll get a plaque for this one."

Chapter Seventy

At 7:15 P.M. Gravilov's car reappeared at the hotel. Gravilov, his driver, and Razor marched together toward the restaurant, like soldiers into battle.

Gage pointed at the monitor. "Looks like Gravilov has decided he's done talking."

"I don't understand the delay," Ninchenko said. "Why didn't Matson just...what's that word they use in your cowboy movies? Skeedle?"

"Skedaddle."

"That's it, skedaddle. Why didn't he skedaddle?"

"One, he's not sure he can get away. Two, it dawned on him too late that he'd have to settle for less than half of what he was expecting for the software. And three, he had a hard time accepting that he'd lose his investment in the plant."

"And your idea of selling just the video amplifier software is his ticket out."

"I hope that's all it takes."

Gage and Ninchenko watched the monitor for the next hour as a thick mist settled in, dampening the air and haloing the hotel lights.

There was no movement. They'd succumbed to surveillance daze, until startled by Gage's ringing phone.

"They made a deal," Alla said. "Five million more. Gravilov is supposed to transfer the money first thing tomorrow morning.

Matson expects the bank will fax the confirmation to the hotel by 11 A.M."

"Can you reconnect the computer?"

"I tried, but the line's dead."

"Where are they now?"

"They're downstairs drinking like they're best friends."

"Maybe it's just afterglow."

"What's afterglow?"

"You know, the birds and the bees."

"Oh, I get it." She laughed. "Except it's Stuart that got buggered. He just doesn't know it. And I haven't figured out how Gravilov did it."

"Does Gravilov know the video amplifier software is here?"

"Stuart told him his lawyer in London will e-mail it to him tomorrow after he gets the wire transfer confirmation. He claimed that the other software is in the States and only he has access."

"Did Gravilov believe him?"

"I couldn't tell. Right now all he cares about is getting what he needs for the missile firing on the Black Sea."

"Then what?"

"Stuart wants to get out of Ukraine as fast as possible. I made reservations for us on a flight from here to London. At 3 P.M.—and Gravilov is okay with it. He promised Stuart that the flight would get off the ground."

"Why'd Gravilov agree so easily?"

"I have no idea. Maybe he thinks the video software can be checked quickly enough. And get this, Gravilov has already turned the deal for the low-noise software to his advantage. He wants it delivered to Moscow behind Hadeon Alexandervich's back, just in case the opposition wins—they're coming back. I'll call later."

Gage watched Gravilov's driver move the car from the parking area to a position in front of the hotel entrance. The driver got out, but left the motor running, the car backlit by the hotel entrance lights. He walked to the rear passenger door and stood by to open it. Steam rose from the tailpipe and swirled past him.

Gravilov walked down the steps, opened the front passenger door, and got in.

"Why's Gravilov getting into the front seat?" Gage asked, looking from the monitor to Ninchenko, who shrugged his shoulders. Gage looked back—and got his answer. A struggling Alla, gripped between Hammer and Razor, appeared at the entrance.

"Gravilov has taken her hostage," Ninchenko said.

Gage watched as they half carried Alla down the stairs. From the jerky movement of her head Gage guessed she was searching the street for the protection he promised.

"Get your people over here," Gage said, glancing at Ninchenko. "There's no way we can follow them in this van without being spotted."

Ninchenko yelled in Ukrainian into his cell phone.

Razor slid into the car first. Hammer pushed Alla inside and followed her in. The driver then sped off into the half-lit streets of Dnepropetrovsk.

"One car will be here in thirty seconds," Ninchenko told Gage. "What do you want them to do?"

Gage let the pieces reorganize themselves in his mind. "Not start a war, not in Gravilov's town. We'll lose. Just stay with them."

Ninchenko gave the order, then said, "Do you think she told them about us?"

"If she had," Gage said, shaking his head, "they would've snuck out a back door."

Ninchenko turned off the video camera.

Gage thought back on his conversation with Alla. Matson and Gravilov as drinking buddies. He looked back at Ninchenko.

"Gravilov didn't take her hostage," Gage said. "The little runt gave her to Gravilov as security for the low-noise software."

"Will he deliver?"

"I'm sure he's telling himself that he will, but I don't know."

Gage paused, trying to anticipate Matson's next move, thinking that under this kind of pressure, Matson's actions would depend more on character and instinct than tactical ability.

"He didn't give a second thought to the people who got killed until his own life was in danger," Gage said. "He's the kind of guy with the rare capacity not to think." He pointed at Ninchenko. "I want to hear from your people every time they make a turn until they arrive at their destination."

Ninchenko issued the order, then hung up.

"What do you mean, the rare capacity not to think?"

"He's not like a sociopath who enjoys hurting people or like a murderer gets off on reliving the crime. Matson's a guy who just doesn't think about what he's really doing."

Ninchenko's phone rang, he listened for a moment, then reported to Gage. "They're heading south, paralleling the river toward farm country. Gravilov has a dacha out there. Near Taromskoe."

Gage handed Ninchenko a water bottle and opened one for himself.

"You think she'll tell Gravilov who her father is?" Ninchenko asked.

"Only as a last resort. She knows that her father would turn the thing to his advantage, try to get a cut of the deal. He's a respected guy. Nobody'll take Gravilov's side once they find out he took Petrov Tarasov's daughter hostage, and Gravilov would have to make up for disrespecting him by giving him a piece."

"I may quote Yiddish," Ninchenko said, "but you think like *maffiya*."

"I'll take that as a compliment."

Gage stared at the dark monitor and took a sip of water. "Is there somebody who can keep an eye on Matson? He'll stay put until Gravilov comes back for him."

"Sure, I'll take care of it."

◇◇◇

Moments after a blue Lada containing two of Ninchenko's men pulled to the curb twenty-five yards away, Kolya turned the ignition and headed back to the Astoria Hotel.

"I wonder if Gravilov will let her go," Ninchenko said as they neared the yellow-lit columns and blue-lit towers of the train station.

"It depends on whether they think they have leverage to make her keep her mouth shut after the deal is done. They figure they can use the U.S. government to control Matson—if he talks he'll go to jail. On her, they've got nothing."

"Which means?"

"That they'll treat her well until they get the software, then just get rid of her."

Chapter Seventy-one

The sun broke through the previous day's cloudy remnants as Ninchenko drove them just after dawn through the southwestern outskirts of Dnepropetrovsk on their way to Taromskoe, where Alla had been delivered. The green and gold cupolas of the Byzantine Holy Trinity Cathedral struggled against the remaining haze as the industrial stacks, newly liberated from the low clouds, thrust their smoke toward the blue sky. The sun revealed that the buildings and factories that merely appeared a dismal gray on the preceding day, were, in fact, a dismal gray, brooding and unrepentant.

Gage could see on Ninchenko's face that his night had been as restless as Gage's, even with the reassurance from their surveillance people that Alla had arrived safely at Gravilov's dacha.

Within minutes of leaving the city limits, Gage found himself looking out over vast expanses of collective farms. Ninchenko was soon winding through miles of unfenced land and rolling hills. Gage lowered the passenger window of the four-door white Lada. He smelled the acrid odor of industrial-sized cattle breeding operations mixed into the diesel exhaust exploding from ancient commercial trucks lumbering along on the ill-maintained two-lane highway.

"Is that winter wheat?" Gage asked, pointing out toward thousands of acres of green shafts just emerged from the soil.

"So they hope. Last year the February freeze killed ninety percent of the crop."

"Tough way to make a living."

"That's all they know."

Ninchenko tuned to the excited chatter of the Kiev Vedomosti news station as they rode west. They listened for a moment to the announcer's excited voice.

"What are they saying?" Gage asked.

"The Supreme Court ordered a new election for next week, but without their own army they can't force the president to let it happen."

They drove without speaking until Ninchenko cocked his head at the radio, then burst into bitter laughter. "The Foreign Ministry has admitted that it issued three hundred diplomatic passports in the last week, all to members of the presidential administration. They're probably getting ready to escape to Switzerland to join their stolen money."

◇◇◇

Thirty minutes after leaving the city, Ninchenko turned north, back toward the Dnepr River, and passed through two villages that served as the urban centers of a thirty-square-mile collective farm. Just before they crested a hill, he pulled over and parked next to a thick stand of fir trees.

"His dacha is down the other side, along the river."

Gage climbed out of the car, then followed Ninchenko thirty yards through the evergreens, stopping in the shadows on the far side.

Ninchenko handed binoculars to Gage, then pointed toward a museumlike dacha formed by three-story, white stucco wings extending at forty-degree angles from a domed atrium. The driveway encircled a Romanesque fountain populated with Cossacks at play. No other dachas were in sight.

"What's in there?" Gage asked, pointing at a dozen thirty-foot-square cages nestled at the bottom of a hill to the west of the house.

"That's his menagerie. Wolves, bears, even a Bengal tiger. Most were smuggled in. Many are ones that evolution planned for climates other than Ukraine's. But there are a few locals, too."

"Does he take care of them?"

Ninchenko tilted his jaw toward trails of smoke rising in the distance. "They live better than any of the villagers we passed on the way."

Gage surveyed the countryside, looking for observation points. "Where are your people?"

Ninchenko reached for his cell phone.

"*Dobre utra...Dobre...Kak dyela?*"

Ninchenko glanced at Gage. "Apparently it was a little chilly last night." Then spoke into his phone again, "*Donde esta?*"

Gage's head snapped toward Ninchenko. "That ain't Russian, Pancho."

"*Eso es correcto, mi amigo,*" Ninchenko said, grinning. "My helper was stationed in Spain during the late 1980s. He taught me a few words." He listened again, then told Gage, "They're on the hill above the menagerie. They can see Alla's room. It's on the top floor at the end of the wing closest to where they are. She turned on the lights and opened the curtains last night hoping someone would spot her. It looks like she believed you when you said you'd station people close by . . . and Gravilov's car is still in the garage, so he hasn't left yet."

After bidding his man *adios*, Ninchenko walked back to the van to retrieve a thermos of coffee while Gage sat down, leaning back against a tree with a clear view toward the dacha and the Dnepr River just beyond. Through the binoculars, he watched a rusting six-hundred-ton cargo ship pass by, guided downstream by a small tugboat. Crewmen stood on the deck in surplus Russian Navy overcoats and gray lambskin *ushanka*s with flaps pulled hard against their ears. The horn sounded as it approached a bend in the river, the moan seeming less to fade than simply be absorbed by the heavy brush along the shore, the forest beyond, and the low clouds that hovered above the valley.

His cell phone rang as Ninchenko walked up from behind and handed him a cup of coffee.

"This is my second kidnapping this week," Alla said.

Gage smiled at Ninchenko and gestured with his cup at the dacha.

"Technically speaking, you ran into me, so you sort of kidnapped yourself the first time."

"Have I called you a fucking American yet?"

"At least once."

"I hope you're damn close by."

"Did you look out of your window this morning?"

"Yes."

"You see the cages?"

"Yes."

"What's inside?"

"All I can see are wild pigs, antelopes, bears, and disgusting-looking hyenas."

"When a bear growls or a pig snorts or a hyena does whatever a hyena does, we'll both hear it."

"I'm glad you gave me that little phone. They snatched mine."

"Where'd you hide it?"

"Guess. Stuart always tried to get me to wear a thong. It's a good thing I refused."

"What happened last night?"

"Stuart pretended he didn't know what Gravilov was going to do, but he can't act. They cooked it up together. My guess is that they'll keep me here until Stuart brings the other software from the States, except…"

"Except what?"

"I don't think he's coming back."

"Doesn't make a difference."

"It makes a hell of a lot of difference to me. I didn't come back to Ukraine for Gravilov to turn me into hyena food."

"We'll come get you as soon as Matson arrives in the U.S."

"Unless they ground the planes. I'm not sure he'll even make it as far as London."

"The planes will fly. A lot of newly appointed diplomats are looking to get out."

"What if…I mean…" The nervous edge was back in her voice. She couldn't bring herself to finish the sentence.

"There'll be two men on the hill above the menagerie all the time you're here—and if Gravilov moves you they'll be on your tail. Ninchenko will give you their cell number in a minute. But first, what's security like?"

"I don't know. They covered my eyes when they brought me in, but I don't think there's much. I didn't hear many people talking. A woman brings me food. She looks like one of those unisex Bulgarian weightlifters. I can't tell whether she wants to break me in two or have sex with me—or both."

"Is there a way down from your room on the outside?"

"I'd need wings. They took the sheets off the bed so I couldn't make them into a rope."

"We'll get you out in a way that doesn't require flight."

"You better. You got me into this."

"No, you got yourself into it. I just gave you a rather complicated way out."

◊◊◊

An hour later Ninchenko and Gage were following a quarter mile behind Gravilov's Mercedes as he and Hammer rode toward Dnepropetrovsk.

"It makes me a little nervous that he left Razor behind," Gage said. "Guys like him derive sexual pleasure from their work. He may do something preemptive." He glanced at Ninchenko. "What do you know about him?"

"Hammer recruited him for Gravilov in Chechnya at the end of the first war in '96. He worked for warlords and *maffiya*. The rumor was that if he didn't need to eat, he would've worked for free."

"Why would he give it up?"

"Too many enemies at home and age, probably. He's in his early forties now. But don't underestimate him. Gravilov keeps him close because he believes Razor is still at the top of his game. And Gravilov's life depends on him."

"He sure looks the part, with his face twisted like that, his nose angling off to the side. When I saw him in London I felt like reaching out and straightening it."

"Not a good idea. It would be the last thing you ever did with that hand."

◇◇◇

Gravilov's Mercedes was already parked by the time Ninchenko and Gage arrived at a spot on the street with a view of the Grand Domus Hotel.

"I wish we had the van," Ninchenko said. "We're kind of exposed sitting here."

Gage glanced over. "If anybody pays attention to us, feel free to kiss me. I won't tell your wife."

"I'm not married."

"Good. I think Alla is looking for a new boyfriend."

"It won't be me. She's already complained that she keeps picking the same type over and over, first her ex-husband and now Matson, and I don't think I match the profile." Ninchenko nodded toward the hotel entrance. "It looks like the wire transfer went through."

Gravilov and Matson were walking down the hotel steps, preceded by the driver and followed by Hammer, carrying Matson's luggage.

"We just need to babysit Matson until he gets on the plane," Gage said, "then put our plan into effect to rescue Alla."

"Which plan was that?"

Gage looked over. "I was afraid you'd ask that."

Chapter Seventy-two

In the early evening, Hixon One was reclining in his car listening to a motivational tape about how to succeed in small business and watching the entrance to Matson's London flat. Rain was ticking lightly on the windshield. He cracked the window open as a defense against his damp breath condensing on the windshield and blocking his view. His eyes flinched when an occasional gust sprayed droplets through the gap.

He watched as a red cab drove toward him, then stopped in front of the building. Matson stepped out, dragging his luggage behind him. Hixon One saw him hand the driver a few bills, then wave off the change. As the driver rolled up his window Matson turned away, then spun back, knocking on the side of the cab. The cabbie rolled the window back down, listened for a moment, then handed something to Matson.

Hixon One sealed up his car, jumped out, and hustled across the street. As soon as the cab switched on its roof light, he raised his hand and whistled. The cab pulled over and the rear passenger door popped open. Hixon One got in.

"Bloody dismal out, eh?" the cabbie asked. "I'll bet it'll rain like this all the way through Christmas."

"It's good for the taxi business."

"So they say. Where to?"

"St. James Square."

Hixon One waited until the cabbie turned onto Knightsbridge for the long, straight run to Piccadilly. "Any good fares?"

"Mostly short, except for the last one, that American. But at least this shift will end with a good long ride tomorrow morning."

"He reserved you?"

"And paid extra. For 8 A.M., all the way to Heathrow. I imagine he didn't enjoy soaking outside of Paddington Station waiting for a cab earlier tonight."

Hixon One rode the last few blocks to St. James Square in silence. He hopped out, waited for the cabbie to swing around the square and shoot out the other side, then hailed another taxi back to his car.

◇◇◇

As Matson climbed into the cab in front of his building the next morning, Hixon One took up his position outside terminal one at Heathrow. An hour later, Hixon One trailed Matson from the curb to the British Airways first-class check-in. Hixon One bought a refundable ticket on the same flight and trailed Matson through the security checkpoint, then called Gage.

"He's taking the British Airways 10:40 for San Francisco," Hixon One said.

"Stay with him until he gets on the plane. I don't want to take a chance of him escaping onto a flight somewhere else."

◇◇◇

"Why haven't we heard from her?" Ninchenko asked himself aloud for the fourth time in an hour. Gage thought he heard more in Ninchenko's voice than just concern for an operative.

It was 3 A.M. Gage and Ninchenko were stationed on the hill to the west of the dacha from where they could look down on the top of the menagerie, Alla's window, the fountain, and the entrance to the mansion. Two of Ninchenko's men, Maks and Yasha, had kept watch on Gravilov's apartment until they were sure he and Hammer were in for the night, then took up positions in the bushes along the dacha's fifty-yard-long driveway.

"Slava sounded nervous when I told him we may have to go in after her," Gage whispered.

"He's not looking for a war with Gravilov and he's afraid what we're doing here may start one."

Gage's phone rang. It wasn't Alla.

"Graham? This is Viz. Scooby came through customs a minute ago. He's in line for a cab, all fidgety, like a man on the run. Should I stay with him?"

"Just long enough to see whether he heads down to SatTek to get the low-noise software. A hundred says he goes home instead of paying the ransom."

"No way I'll take that bet. Not on that scumbag."

Gage rang off and turned his attention back to the mansion.

"Alla thinks that all Gravilov left here are Razor and the androgynous one," Gage told Ninchenko.

"No need to waste the extra manpower. It wouldn't cross Gravilov's mind that Matson would send someone to rescue her."

Forty-five minutes later, Viz called to report that Matson's cab had turned off from the freeway away from San Jose and was now heading toward Saratoga. "You were right, the little weasel went home."

Gage spotted movement at the entrance to the mansion as he ended the call. Light from the interior illuminated Razor's profile as he lit a cigar, the lighter flame giving his pale, distorted face an orange glow.

Ninchenko slowly shook his head.

"I was thinking the same thing," Gage said. He then hoisted on his backpack and withdrew a semiautomatic from the waistband of his pants. "We're way, way too old for this."

"Don't worry old man, my young helpers will be right behind us."

"To follow us in or carry us out?"

Ninchenko laughed softly. "Probably both." He then called Maks and Yasha and told them to seal off the entrance to the property.

Gage and Ninchenko snuck down the hill, their path through the forest intermittently lit by a last-quarter moon. Halfway down, Gage glimpsed Razor again, the glowing tip of the cigar in his left hand rising and falling. They paused and watched him pass behind the fountain in front, then work his way toward the pens and around the western wing of the house, passing under Alla's window. He disappeared around the back and reappeared a few minutes later, walking around the eastern wing. He walked up the driveway, then back, and began another circuit.

Hooves thumped as Gage and Ninchenko continued down the hillside until they reached the rear of the pens. They stopped moving, but more of the animals alerted to their presence. Bird wings fluttered. Gage sensed the sniffing of a hyena, nose pressed into the chain-link fence three feet away. A wild pig snorted, then scraped at the ground as wolverines began to pace. A slight breeze off the river brought them the smells of fresh straw, dirt, and the odors of animal waste.

Gage looked up toward Alla's window, hoping her phone was on vibrate, then pressed "send." The phone rang four times, then stopped. A low-wattage light flashed in Alla's room. He called again, let the phone ring once, then disconnected.

They waited until Razor completed another circuit and walked up the driveway, then Gage signaled for Ninchenko to head toward the rear of the mansion. As Ninchenko crept forward, angling past the western wing and around to the back, Gage set about to create enough chaos to keep Razor away from the house long enough for Ninchenko to slip in and rescue Alla without engaging in bloodshed that would provoke the gang war Slava wanted to avoid.

Gage shoved the gun under the waistband at the small of his back, then slid off his backpack, removed bolt cutters, and worked his way along the front of the pens. In the darkness, he nearly stumbled over a rake. He felt for the lock on the antelope pen, then carefully slipped the jaw around the shackle and pressed the cutter arms together. The cheap Ukrainian metal parted in silence. Gage twisted the lock free, opened the gate, then moved on. He passed on the wild pigs, then opened the peacock and deer pens in turn.

Gage waited for the animals to realize they were free, but they didn't catch on, so he worked his way back past the antelope pen and retrieved the rake. He felt the length of it. It was heavy like a medieval pike, with a dozen clawlike steel tines. He slipped inside and sidestepped along the fence until he spotted two moonlit eyes fixed on him. A slight breeze disturbed branches above, then moonlight fell on four more eyes and horns pointing skyward. The eyes followed Gage as he tried to sneak behind them, then disappeared into blackness as they turned away from the moon. Gage glimpsed the silhouette of a set of horns, guessed where the rump was, then gave it a whack. The startled antelope led a charge of the four-member herd away from Gage. Using a double-handed grip, he swung the rake in wide arcs until all of them found the open gate.

But the delay had been costly. As Gage followed the charging animals into the gap between the front door and the fountain, he spotted Razor running down the driveway—and Razor spotted him.

The antelopes scattered, leaving Gage without cover and facing Razor, now crouched six feet away with a semiautomatic in his hand. The expression on Razor's face suggested puzzlement, rather than fear or rage, as if it didn't make sense to him that the Matson he'd observed had it in him to organize a rescue.

Razor pointed his gun at the rake and then at the ground, signaling Gage to drop it. Gage bent forward as though in submission and slowly lowered it. Razor's head snapped to his right at the sound of thudding feet in the woods, mistaking the running of panicked animals for more attackers. Gage yanked the rake upward, catching Razor's wrist with the tines. The gun spun free. Razor neither recoiled nor dived for it. He simply reached under his coat and emerged with a Russian combat knife.

Gage didn't think he could get to his gun before Razor got to him, so he kept him at bay with the rake. He heard the crash of Ninchenko kicking in the back door, then the rat-tat-tat of an automatic weapon, followed by two gun blasts, then a third.

The war Slava had hoped to avoid had begun.

Razor charged inside the arc of the swinging rake. Gage ducked, then threw an uppercut at the man's twisted nose.

Razor's hands involuntarily rose to his face. Gage crouched and threw a right cross into the base of his rib cage. Razor grabbed and hugged Gage like a punch-drunk fighter, then gouged at his back with the knife. Gage's body told him he was being hit, while his mind told him he was being stabbed. He dropped to the ground and wrapped his arms around Razor's knees, then rolled, twisting him from his feet, his arms flailing as he fell. Razor's legs kicked and shook but his torso flopped like a rag doll along the ground. Gage heard him grunt, then felt the spasms of his body's uncontrollable jerking until it finally went limp. Gage yanked Razor's lifeless left arm behind his back, then saw that his head lay propped at an awkward angle. Gage pushed it to the side and saw the knife handle and half of the blade sticking out of the dead man's neck.

A window exploded, followed by Alla's screams.

Maks and Yasha ran up as Gage picked up Razor's gun. He pointed toward the front of the house, and they followed him inside. He signaled for them to secure the first floor, then he snuck down the long foyer toward the back of the house until he reached a closed door. He pressed himself against the wall beside it, pushed it open, then dropped to a crouch and ducked his head forward into what turned out to be the kitchen. He spotted Ninchenko's legs to the left and a stocky body curled in a pool of blood on the opposite side of the room, a nearly bloodless bullet hole centered in the man's forehead.

Gage crawled toward Ninchenko, propped against the stove, eyes closed. Ninchenko struggled to raise his gun hand in response to the sound of Gage's movement.

"It's me, *amigo*," Gage whispered, then pressed Ninchenko's hand back down. He saw two holes in Ninchenko's jacket, one below his left shoulder and one in his lower chest.

Ninchenko opened his eyes a fraction, then tilted his head upward toward Alla's room. Gage nodded, then pushed himself to his feet.

Gage met Maks and Yasha in the foyer. He waved them toward the kitchen, saying Ninchenko's name.

Alla screamed again as he ran up the stairs.

He followed the screams up the next flight and toward an open door at the end of a hallway. Gage peeked around the doorjamb. Alla stood on a chair in the far corner, swinging a lamp at a squat woman in a tracksuit who was grabbing at her.

"*Nakonec!*" Alla yelled, looking across the room at Gage.

An androgynous, slug-shaped woman turned toward the door. Alla swung the lamp high in the air and brought it down on the top of the woman's head and she crumpled to the carpet.

"Finally!" Alla repeated, this time in English, then jumped down from the chair and kicked the woman in the ribs.

Gage ran over and pulled her away.

Alla struggled against his grip. "Let me go."

"We don't have time for you to get even. Ninchenko's hurt."

Gage tied the woman's hands with the lamp cord so she couldn't get to a phone to warn Gravilov when she regained consciousness, then they dashed down the stairs and to the front of the mansion, where they spotted Yasha easing Ninchenko into the backseat of a car. Maks ran from the direction of the menagerie carrying Gage's backpack and bolt cutters, and Razor's knife.

Gage and Alla got in on either side of Ninchenko in the backseat while the others jumped into the front. Gage unbuttoned Ninchenko's jacket, then reached inside, pressing a palm against each wound.

Maks called ahead to the hospital as they sped through the countryside. By the time they neared the city limits, Ninchenko lay slumped in the seat, motionless, his skin ghostlike in the dashboard lights.

Chapter Seventy-three

A white-coated doctor waited in the darkness just off the grounds of the Dnepropetrovsk Clinical Hospital. Maks stopped the car and handed a roll of bills to the doctor, who then followed the car to the emergency entrance.

The doctor snapped orders in Russian, then spoke softly to a nurse as he walked into the hospital. Gage and Alla followed behind as orderlies lifted Ninchenko onto a gurney and raced him down a grimy pale green hallway into pre-op. They watched through an open door as his clothes were cut off and he was rolled into the operating room.

"What did the doctor tell the admitting nurse to put in the record?" Gage asked Alla.

"That Ninchenko was in a car accident. Internal bleeding."

Gage leaned back against the wall as an elderly couple shuffled by, carrying clean sheets and towels and containers of food. Bleary eyes spoke of a long journey on Soviet-era streetcars and of a hospital too poor or too corrupt to meet even the most basic needs of its patients.

"What happened outside of the dacha?" Alla asked.

Gage shrugged, then looked over. "Let's just say Razor gave his life for the greater good."

She smirked. "Self-sacrifice didn't seem to be his game."

"I think he surprised himself."

"You surprised *me*," Alla said. "I had no idea you were coming until the phone vibrated the second time."

Alla fell silent as a nurse passed by, then said, "Stuart wasn't coming back, was he?"

Gage shook his head. "And we needed to move in before Gravilov figured that out." He turned away from the wall to face her. "I didn't tell you before because I was afraid you'd panic and try to take them on yourself."

Alla stepped forward, pulling Gage's shoulder farther away from the wall.

"What's that?" She ran her fingers over red smears on the paint, then showed them to Gage. "This is blood."

Alla pulled Gage around until his back was to her.

"He slashed you. Can't you feel it?"

She reached up with both hands and grasped his collar, pulled his coat down, and dropped it to the floor in one motion. Blood on his shirt circled the wounds.

"It just feels bruised," Gage said, reaching around to probe his back. Alla pulled his hand away.

"Wait here." She strode down the hallway, returning a minute later with a pouting nurse with a large mole on her cheek, who led them to an examining room. Gage removed his shirt, then the nurse cleaned the wounds.

"How bad is it?" Gage asked.

"They're about two inches across and about a quarter-inch deep," Alla said. "It looks like he was stabbing at an angle."

Alla spoke with the nurse in Russian, then said, "She wants to stitch them."

Gage reached into his wallet, withdrew a twenty-dollar bill, and held it up. "Tell her I want a new needle, unopened surgical thread, and a course of antibiotics. German."

Alla translated.

The nurse smiled, accepted the money, and left the room. She returned a few minutes later and laid out the items for Gage's inspection. Both the needle and thread were sealed in plastic. She opened the box of antibiotic tablets to show they hadn't been tampered with.

"O-kay?" she asked in English.

◇◇◇

Two hours later, the doctor emerged from the operating room wearing a bloodstained smock. He and Alla conversed briefly in Russian near the swinging doors. After he walked away, Alla turned toward Gage with a quick smile and a thumbs-up.

"What did he say?" Gage asked as she approached.

"The first thing was that he wanted to know when he'd get the rest of his money."

"And?"

"We'll need to bring in clean sheets and more money for syringes, IVs, and the rest. He'll give us a list of the food that will have to be brought in."

Gage glared at the doctor's office door. "At what point did he mention Ninchenko's condition?"

"Only after he said that he'll take care of paying off the nurses and that he'll be in his office for the next half hour waiting for the cash."

Gage shook his head in disgust. "At least he's got his priorities in order." He looked back at Alla. "How much extra for a private room?"

"It's included."

"Why? Is he having a sale today?"

Alla's tone was even more sarcastic than Gage's. "I think it must be what you Americans call an early-bird special."

Maks arrived, and she passed on the doctor's instructions.

"We can leave," she told Gage, as he walked away. "Kolya's waiting outside. Ninchenko's men will stand guard."

"What about Gravilov? Has he found out yet?"

"I don't know. Maybe not. Maks says that he's still in his apartment."

◇◇◇

As Kolya drove them through the gray-dawn streets toward the Astoria Hotel, Alla wedged herself into the corner of the backseat and rested her head against the window. Gage watched her drift into a confused, chaotic state in which sleep is imperative, but not possible. She shifted her position and her eyes moved under her lids as if watching a replay of the night. He wondered whether she had slept at all during the last few days.

Gage escorted her to the dining room and turned on the radio. He poured her a cup of coffee and inspected her face as she sipped. Her eyes were dark and her cheeks seemed to sag. The adrenaline surge that had carried her through the morning had subsided like an outgoing tide, leaving her vulnerable and exposed.

"I need you to do something," Gage finally said. "Call Matson. Tell him that you've escaped and how grateful you are that he was trying to rescue you."

Alla blinked away the glaze that clouded her eyes. "And I'm supposed to do that without laughing?"

"It has to be done. I don't want him wondering whether you sold him out and cut a deal with Gravilov." Gage thought for a moment. "And tell him that you'll be hiding out with relatives in the mountains for a few weeks."

"Then what?"

"That's up to you. You have money?"

"Stuart set up an account in my name at Barclays in London. There's about a hundred thousand pounds in it. But now that I know where he got it…"

"You earned it, and more. And I'll make sure no one ever gives you trouble about it." He sipped his coffee. "But what will you do after that's gone?"

"I'm eligible for the Skilled Migrant Program in the UK. I'll stay if I can find a job."

"What about Gravilov?"

She paused, then shrugged. "That's a bridge I'm not sure how I'll cross."

"How about coming to the States for a while?"

She shook her head. "I can't get a visa."

"What if I could get you in?"

She forced a smile. "You have some magical powers you've been hiding from me?"

"I can get you what's called an S visa. It's for witnesses who may be willing to testify about a criminal organization."

Her smile died. "I know you want to help your friend, but there's no way I can do that. Gravilov and his people would never forget. Never. They'd hunt me down. Even your Witness Protection Program wouldn't be safe. There's no escape."

Gage reached over and squeezed her hand. "I know. The key word is 'may.' You'll just change your mind once you get to the States."

"Would I get in trouble? I mean, here if you—"

"No. The head of the Criminal Division of the Justice Department will feel pretty bad he didn't help me out a few weeks ago, so he'll let me handle this the way I want to."

Alla looked away and shook her head slowly. Gage knew she was imagining the carnage at the dacha. She finally looked back. "How long would it take?"

◇◇◇

Gage walked Alla to his room, where he let her shower and nap in his bed. He then sent an e-mail to Washington, D.C., constructed to extort a visa, but without disclosing too much of what he knew.

When he leaned back in his desk chair, he felt for the first time the bite of the slashes and stitches in his back. He realized that he had another e-mail to send. He and Faith trusted each other too much for him to conceal from her that he'd been injured. He wrote her what he always did when his middle-aged body got battered around: "I'll need a little chicken soup."

Chapter Seventy-four

Gage and Alla returned to the hospital in early afternoon. Ninchenko was in a third floor, private, two-room suite, the best in the hospital, but looking to Gage like a skid-row hotel room. He was propped up in bed and being fed clear broth as they entered. The nurse wiped Ninchenko's chin, then stepped back. Ninchenko's guard escorted her from the room.

"How do you feel, *amigo*?" Gage asked, leaning close. Alla stood next to him. Both looking down at the pale, hollow-eyed face.

Ninchenko worked up a little smile. "Like an elephant is standing on my chest," he answered in a hoarse whisper, his throat still raw from the anesthetic used during surgery.

"What happened?"

"He came running into the kitchen just as I kicked the door." Ninchenko's voice strengthened. "He got off three shots before I caught my balance. He knew he hit me so he stopped firing."

"Big mistake."

"He picked the wrong line of work. He didn't finish me off."

Gage thought back on the dead man curled up in the kitchen. The man's heart had stopped before Ninchenko fired his last shot.

Ninchenko licked his lips. Alla poured water from a pitcher into a clear plastic glass and brought it to his lips. He took two sips, then shook his head.

"What about you?" Ninchenko asked.

"Let's just say Razor lived by the sword."

Ninchenko offered up another weak smile. "Aristotle was right."

Alla's mouth gaped open at Ninchenko. "What? Aristotle? You're lying in a hospital with two fucking bullet holes and you're talking Greek philosophy?"

"What he means is that things tend toward their natural end," Gage said.

Alla shook her head. "It's still weird." She set down the glass and looked fondly at Ninchenko. "I thought you were just some ex–State Security thug out to make a buck. I'm sorry. I was wrong."

She put a hand on his shoulder. "I'm glad your natural end wasn't to die last night saving me. I'll never forget what you did." She leaned over and kissed him on the forehead.

"We were both wrong," Ninchenko answered. "I hope you'll come back one day."

Alla shrugged her shoulders. "I don't know."

◇◇◇

Three hours into their drive back to Kiev, Gage heard the name Gravilov spoken on the car radio. He poked at Alla, waking her up.

"What are they saying?"

Alla rubbed her eyes. The announcer spoke the name again. She listened for a minute, then smiled.

"It sounds like Ninchenko's people tricked the government into believing that nationalist terrorists attacked Gravilov's mansion. There was a note stuck to the front door that the police think was left by the paramilitary arm of the Organization of Ukrainian Nationalists, demanding that all Russians leave Ukraine, starting with him."

Alla listened for another few moments, then laughed. "They're demanding a ransom for my return. Apparently I'm Gravilov's girlfriend."

She looked hard at the radio, then gasped. "The police found Razor in the hyena pen, chewed into pieces."

Gage now understood what Maks had been doing while Yasha helped Ninchenko to the car.

"What about the woman upstairs?" Gage asked.

"They claim she was raped."

"That couldn't be."

"But it's the kind of thing the government wants people to think OUN terrorists would do." Alla pointed ahead toward Kiev. "That way they'll believe that the president is all that stands between Ukraine and chaos if Bread and Freedom succeeds."

"Will Gravilov really believe that's what happened?"

"Maybe for a few days...nobody believes anything in Ukraine for longer than that."

Chapter Seventy-five

Mr. Green? This is Mr. Black."

Gage swung his legs down from his bed at the Carlton Tower in London as he answered his cell phone, wincing from the pain from the twisting stitches in his back.

"Hey, Professor. What's up?"

"Merry Christmas."

Gage blinked. The words restarted the clock that seemed to have stopped on the day he flew into Kiev. "Likewise."

"Your friend Mr. Matson called. Very upset. Whimpering like a puppy."

"I can only imagine."

"His banker told him the KTMG Limited account has been frozen and he can't find out whether the Swiss did it or the...what do you call people in Nauru? Nauruites? Nauruans? Nauruians?"

"I don't know. It's never come up before."

"Okay, Nauruians...or even why it was frozen."

"A shame."

"He wants to talk to you."

"Tell him I'm out of the country but I'll call him in a couple of days."

"Anything else?"

Gage paused, imagining Matson flailing around as he drifted out to sea.

"I don't want him doing something stupid. Tell him my client wants to close the deal on the technology right away, and in cash, just like we first agreed."

"Okay. But one more thing, just for my edification. How'd his money get frozen?"

"It isn't."

"It isn't?"

"It isn't." Gage looked at his watch, smiling to himself, enjoying the professor's puzzlement. "Got to go. I'll call you when I get back to the States."

Gage knocked on the door to Alla's adjoining room.

"Time to get up and get your hand stamped."

◇◇◇

Gage and Alla arrived just on time for their meeting with the U.S. consul general in London. Gage had learned from his friend in the Justice Department that John Clyde was a careerist near the end of his service who'd topped out just one step short of his goal of becoming an ambassador. The story was that he'd even have taken a posting in Sudan just to wear the title.

An aging Ivy Leaguer with indoor skin and puffy jowls, Clyde met them at the visa section, then escorted them to his office. He sat down behind a large desk framed by U.S. and State Department flags and directed them to sit across from him.

"You must have some kind of pull in Washington," Clyde said, opening a folder and withdrawing Alla's Panamanian passport. "I received a call from the head of the Criminal Division of the Justice Department." He thumbed through the passport until he found the pasted-in visa. "And the ambassador instructed me not to notify the legal attaché or the FBI that I issued this."

Clyde made a show of examining the page. "S visas are quite rare, you know," he said, inviting an explanation from Gage.

"This is a special occasion," Gage said, his voice flat.

"Does it concern London?"

"Does it make a difference?"

Clyde fixed on Gage's impenetrable face for a moment, then shrugged. "I guess it doesn't."

Alla leaned forward in anticipation of receiving the passport, but Clyde remained immobile. She sat back, reddening, as if she had tried to shake his hand and he'd refused.

Clyde flipped to the identification and photo page and grinned. "Somehow the name Alla Petrovna Tarasova doesn't sound Panamanian."

"Look," Gage said. "If you've got a problem, spill it. If not, let us have the passport."

"I don't have a problem, it's just unusual." Clyde closed the passport, tapped its edge against his blotter, then looked over at Alla. "I need to advise you of certain conditions: You must arrive at a U.S. port of entry within ten days. You may stay in the U.S. for no longer than forty-five days. If you fail to leave within that period, you'll be subject to arrest."

He waited until Alla nodded her understanding, then retrieved a sealed envelope from the folder. "You will present this letter to the immigration and customs agent at passport control at your point of entry." Clyde handed Alla the envelope, then retrieved a second one, unsealed. "This is your copy of the same letter."

Clyde slid the second envelope into the passport, then stood and passed it to her. He stepped around his desk and walked toward the office door, as if expecting Gage and Alla to follow like imprinted ducklings. Alla stuck her tongue out at his back, then smiled at Gage as she rose to her feet. She glanced toward Clyde, then snagged a State Department paperweight off his desk and slipped it into her coat pocket.

They followed Clyde back to the visa section, where he opened the door and waved them through to the lobby without another word. As the door swung closed, Alla stopped to place the letters and passport into her purse.

Gage overheard a well-dressed, elderly American woman complain to the clerk behind the bulletproof glass that she'd already waited fifteen minutes past her scheduled appointment time with Clyde. Gage reached into Alla's pocket and pulled out the paperweight, then walked up to the woman.

"The consul general asked me to give this to you to apologize for the wait." Gage handed it to her. "Be sure to mention it to him."

Alla covered her mouth as they left the consulate, stifling her laugh until they reached the sidewalk.

"What was wrong with that man?" Alla said, giggling, her eyes sparkling as she looked up at him.

Gage then noticed the loveliness that other men saw in her, then felt a sadness born of the fear that she'd never grow old with the kind of man she deserved because she'd always be looking past him toward the Matsons of the world.

"Maybe Clyde was offended that we went around him to Washington," Gage said, holding out his hand to hail a cab, "or maybe it's that he knows something."

Gage made flight reservations for the following afternoon as the taxi drove them toward Mickey's house in the suburbs. They stopped in long enough for Gage to assure himself that Mickey was recovering and so that Mickey could gloat about having been right about Alla from the beginning—though for the wrong reasons—and could get a closer look at the woman who'd made his old heart flutter.

From there, it was on to Matson's flat in Kensington.

"Let's make this quick," Gage said as they entered the lobby.

The diminutive doorman greeted Alla by name. "I hope you had a wonderful trip," he said, "this is the longest you've been gone."

"Actually, I cut the trip a little short."

"A shame. Mr. Matson seemed quite worried when he left a few days ago. I hope everything has returned to normal."

"Yes, it has. Thank you." She glanced toward the street. "Has anyone come by for me in the last few days?"

"A Russian gentleman. He said he was a friend who happened to be in London. He didn't leave his name."

"Did he ask for Mr. Matson or just for me?"

"Just you."

"What did he look like?" Gage asked.

The doorman looked at Gage, then back at Alla.

"It's okay," she said.

"A very large man. I do say, a most unfriendly-looking friend."

"Has he come back?"

"No. We've looked in on your flat every day just to make sure he didn't decide to check for himself."

"If he inquires again, tell him I haven't returned to London and you don't know when I'm expected back."

Gage withdrew a couple of ten-pound notes from his wallet and handed them to the doorman, who slipped them into his pants pocket.

The elevator deposited Alla and Gage on the eighth floor, across the hall from the penthouse door. After Alla unlocked it, Gage stepped into the flat, where he found himself time-warped back to an early nineteenth-century London sitting room.

"Was this Matson's idea?"

She nodded. "It's ridiculous, isn't it?"

Alla set her purse on a Regency mahogany writing table, then turned back toward Gage, who was standing just inside the threshold. She followed Gage's eyes, which were focused on a highball glass resting on a pedestal secretaire. He walked over and picked it up, revealing a white water ring on the forty-thousand-dollar piece of furniture.

"He's not coming back," Gage said.

Alla walked across the room and through an open door. She returned moments later. "His clothes are gone."

They searched the apartment, collecting phone records, airline ticket stubs, and notes on scraps of paper. Gage stuffed them into a paper bag while Alla packed.

"Is there anything else you want to take?" Gage asked, as Alla carried a battered brown suitcase toward the door. "I imagine this place will be seized by the UK government. You may never get back in again."

"Nothing here ever really belonged to me. I'm just taking what I came with." She sighed as her eyes swept the apartment. "Sometimes life is completely absurd."

They rode in silence back to the hotel.

"I think I need to be alone for a while," Alla said, as they walked down the carpeted hallway toward their rooms.

"That's fine. Maybe we'll meet for dinner this evening."

Alla slipped her key card into the lock and pushed open the door. She paused, then turned toward Gage and looked up at him with searching eyes.

"Is there something wrong with me?" she asked.

Gage knew the answer, but responded with a question. She needed to say it for herself to make it real. "What do you mean?"

"My husband. Stuart. They were the same greedy, conscienceless men and I didn't see it." She looked down, frowning. "That's not true. I refused to see it. Stuart started to emerge from the clouds of my juvenile imagination and I looked away. I should've gotten out of this when he came back here after SatTek went public."

Tears formed in her eyes as she looked up again. "I'm really no different than him. A self-deceiving little rat. You must think I'm pathetic."

"No, not at all." Gage was tempted to wipe away the tears, but held back, fearing that she'd seek salvation in him, rather than in herself. "You do the right thing when it affects others. You just seem to get lost when you try to create a world you can be happy in."

"But what am I supposed to do?"

"I can't tell you how to live. All anybody can do is try to think about what they're doing, and not lie to themselves. Beyond that, I have no other answer."

Chapter Seventy-six

Special Agent Zink was waiting near the customs scanners when Gage and Alla walked from passport control in the international terminal of the San Francisco Airport late the next afternoon.

"Don't say anything," Gage told her, "except your name. You can show him your passport and the copy of the letter if he asks. Nothing else."

Confusion, verging on panic, flashed in her eyes. "But aren't you required to talk to the police here?"

"No. Name, passport, letter. That's all."

Gage and Alla handed their customs declarations to a uniformed agent, who directed them to the green line and toward the exit. Zink stationed himself in their path as they approached the automatic doors.

Zink pulled his shoulders back. "I need to talk to your friend, Gage."

"Sorry, we're late for an appointment." Gage took Alla's arm and stepped to Zink's left. "Why don't you give me a call next week, I'll see if I can fit you in."

Zink moved over to block them. "You're forcing me to pull rank."

"Pull rank? I'm not in your chain of command, and neither is she."

"She can talk to me now," Zink said, "or I'll subpoena her to the grand jury."

"Do what you gotta do."

"You're verging on obstruction, Gage."

Gage held out his hands as if waiting to be cuffed. "Take your best shot."

Zink reddened. "In time." He looked at Alla, then back at Gage. "Where's she staying?"

"It's on her arrival card, go take a look."

Gage fixed Zink in place with a forearm in front of his chest, then signaled Alla to precede him to the exit.

"You don't like that guy," Alla said as they emerged into the arrivals hall.

"He's a lousy investigator and a snake. He got into the FBI during the height of the cocaine epidemic. Back then they took anybody who knew what crack looked like. Now they're stuck with him. Even worse, he's badged his way out of a DUI and a prostitution arrest."

"What's badged?"

"It means he used his badge, used his position as a federal agent to talk his way out of being arrested."

"And he was a prostitute, too?" Alla asked, drawing back and grinning.

"No, not a prostitute. A john."

"Are you still speaking English?"

"A john is a customer. A DUI is driving under the influence."

"Of what?"

"No one knows. As I said, he badged his way out, both times claiming he was undercover. Ever since he's been trying to prove to the Bureau that he's a real cop. For him, Jack Burch is just a statistic he needs to get back on the promotion trail."

Gage hailed a taxi that took them on the forty-minute ride to the East Bay hills. The sun had set by the time it pulled into the driveway next to the redwood stairs rising up from his house.

As the cab door shut, Gage spotted Faith climbing the steps, now lined with tiny Christmas lights. She threw her arms around Gage, who flinched when her hands pressed against his wounds.

"I'm sorry, dear," Faith said, unwrapping herself. "I got excited."

Faith's motherly look at Alla told Gage that she'd understood his e-mail describing both the courage Alla had shown and her need for a woman in whom to confide. Faith hugged her, then picked up her suitcase. "You must be very tired. All you've been through."

"I'm fine, really. I rested in London."

"Not like you'll rest here." Faith tilted her head toward the stairs. "Come on, I'll show you to your room."

Faith led Alla through the house to a lower-level bedroom. Alla walked directly from the door to the corner windows facing the bay.

"Is that San Francisco?" she asked, wide-eyed at the floor-to-ceiling view that extended from Mount Tamalpias in the north to the airport in the south. The first bit of evening fog was easing its way through the Golden Gate, but had yet to mute the twinkling lights of the city or the sapphire blue of the bay. "It's like a postcard."

"It's real and it's yours as long as you can stay with us. You can freshen up down the hallway, then come back up."

Gage was sitting at the kitchen table when Faith walked in. She took a bottle of Budweiser out of the refrigerator and handed it to him. "From Professor Blanchard. He said you'd understand."

Gage twisted off the top and took a sip. "Sweetheart of a guy."

"He feels indebted to you," Faith said, sitting down.

"It's the other way around."

"That's not how he looks at it. He spent his whole career worrying that his research was being used to make weapons that would end up in the hands of the wrong people. He feels like you gave him a chance to use his knowledge for good."

"Well, he did good. I couldn't have gotten this far without him. I just don't know whether it was enough."

Faith reached over and rested her hand on Gage's forearm. "You look beat."

"A little jet lag, it'll be gone tomorrow."

"You think you can force Peterson to indict Matson for the devices?"

"Based on what? Alla can't get up on the stand. Whoever killed Granger and the Fitzhughs will go after her if she does."

"What about you?"

"Testify about watching Matson from a distance? It was a silent movie without subtitles—and it would be just as dangerous for Alla because I'd have to expose her role." Gage looked across the bay toward the Federal Building, but his eyes fell on the clock tower at the foot of Market Street. "I've got nothing to delay the indictment."

"How soon do you think it will be?"

"A day or two. Milsberg left a message that Zink said he's the second-to-the-last grand jury witness, and they want him in tomorrow. At 10 A.M."

Chapter Seventy-seven

Peterson called seconds after Gage sat down in his office the next morning.

"Hey, hotshot. I heard you've been traveling again."

Gage didn't rise to the aggression rumbling under Peterson's jocular banter.

"A little bit."

"I also heard Matson's girlfriend is in town."

"Ex."

"Ex?"

"Yup."

"How'd you do it?"

"I went over to London a couple of days ago and asked her to come. He shouldn't have left her alone in that big flat."

"What's she gonna say?"

"That Matson told her Burch didn't know what was going on."

Peterson laughed. "That's bullshit. Matson told Zink he didn't let her in on anything. Why would he? He says she was just a plaything and he dangled a green card in front of her nose to keep her around."

"Then you can add lying to a federal agent to his charge sheet."

"Yeah, right. If she was such a hot witness, you'd have run the visa through me."

"Two reasons. One, you'd feed her to the civil lawyers—"

"You've got no proof—"

"And two, I've got an idea about Burch's shooting and the Granger and Fitzhugh murders. My guess is that each one happened right after you focused the grand jury on them."

"What are you saying?"

"You've got a leak."

"That's a dead end. We already checked it out."

"By 'we' you mean that idiot Zink?"

"You underestimate the guy. He turned his career around with this case. He put the whole thing together from the ground up."

"That's a crock. The case was handed to him by an insider at SatTek, Katie Palan. She gave you Matson, then Matson gave you everything else. All Zink did was take notes."

"Who?"

"Katie Palan."

"Oh yeah, the woman who sent the letter."

"That's how it happened. And she's dead, too."

"I heard somebody at SatTek died in a traffic accident. Was that her?"

"That's her. But it wasn't an accident."

"Not again." Peterson adopted an exasperated tone, and seemed to enjoy it. "You sound normal for a while, then you start babbling like a conspiracy lunatic."

"We'll see."

"What do you mean, we'll see?"

"We'll see who's got a better grasp on reality."

"Don't kid yourself, pal. Burch is going down as sure as the sun sets in the west."

"The sun doesn't set. The earth rotates."

"Same difference."

"Nope. It makes all the difference in the world."

Gage hung up and called Burch.

"Any news from Geneva?"

"Matson hasn't tried to move the KTMG Limited money again. He must still think the account's frozen."

"Will your banker friend hang tough?"

"I think so."

"I want you to give him a code phrase. If Matson calls and says 'looking glass,' your friend should do what he says. Get ahold of him as soon as the bank opens."

Gage then called Matson.

"This is Mr. Green."

"Thank God you called. They froze my money and I—"

"Not over the phone."

"But—"

"Not…over…the phone."

"When can we meet?"

"At 3 P.M. The café where we first met."

◇◇◇

When Gage walked into the South San Francisco café, Matson was sitting in the same booth, staring toward the door and pushing his napkin back and forth on the Formica table. Gage walked across Matson's field of vision as he approached.

Matson flinched when Gage sat down. "Where'd you come from?"

Gage jerked his thumb toward the entrance.

"You startled me."

"Tough day?"

"The worst."

"I called my people in Geneva," Gage said, settling back into the role of Mr. Green.

Matson sat up like a puppy waiting for a treat, hands on the edge of the table.

"What did they say?"

"The Swiss have what they call an investigating magistrate," Gage said. "He made Nauru freeze the account."

"Why?"

"Did you try to move too much money at once?"

"I…I don't think so. I did exactly what you said. A little at a time."

"Where'd the money come from?"

Matson sat back, then spread his hands. "I can't tell you."

"You mean you don't know?"

"I mean I know, but I can't say."

"Why not?"

"Because the guy who sent me some of it wouldn't be happy."

Gage adopted a stern expression and aimed a forefinger at Matson. "At the moment you need to worry about keeping me happy. You wanted to see me because you needed me to do something for you. Right?"

Matson swallowed, then nodded.

"And I'm not going to be working in the dark on this, understand?"

Matson glanced toward the door, and his voice rose. "But who's gonna protect me?"

"How much you got in the account? If you got enough money, you can buy all the protection you need."

Matson looked around the restaurant, then leaned in and whispered, "About twenty million."

Gage rolled his eyes. "That's idiotic. Why'd you put that much in one account?"

"It's the only one I had."

"Why didn't you tell me you needed more accounts?"

"I wasn't thinking."

"What else weren't you thinking about?"

Matson shrugged.

Gage leaned back in his seat, then folded his arms across his chest. "What do you expect me to do?"

"I don't know. I just need my money."

"How much are you willing to pay?"

Matson fiddled with his spoon, then said, "Five percent."

Gage laughed. "You want me to stick out my neck for five percent and I don't even know where the money came from? And worse, I don't even know if it really belongs to you."

"Okay." Matson drummed his fingers on the table, biting his lower lip. "How about ten percent?"

Gage shook his head. "You're still not thinking. Thirty percent. First and last offer."

"Six million dollars! To make a call? A helluva Christmas gift."

Gage shook his head again, seemingly disgusted.

"It ain't a gift. Six million buys you my ability to make that call. It also means I'm putting myself in the middle of something I don't have a clue about and I'll need to watch my back forever because you won't tell me what I need to look out for."

"What about me?"

Gage lowered his arms and leaned over the table. "I'll give you a bodyguard for a week. He'll help you set up security for after that."

"Starting when?"

Gage looked at his watch. "Two hours from now."

"And how much will that little service cost?"

"Not a dime."

"But how will you unfreeze the money?"

"I know somebody who can get to the magistrate."

Matson drew back. "What do you mean?"

Gage smiled. "Nobody's gonna hurt the guy. We'll just appeal to his sense of justice."

Matson exhaled. "When can you do all this?"

"At 9 A.M. Geneva time."

"That quick?"

Gage nodded. "At 2 A.M. our time you call your banker and say, 'Mr. Green will call with instructions. He has the looking glass.'"

"Looking glass?…I don't get it."

"You don't need to get it. Just say exactly that—you need to write it down?"

"No. But…but what'll happen to my money?"

"That depends on where you want it to end up."

Matson shrugged. "I don't know."

"How about Costa Rica? Good place. You'll fit in there. Lots of people speak English. But you're gonna need a passport."

Matson smiled, as if he finally had a correct answer. "I have one."

"I'm thinking you don't want the cops to figure out where you are. Right?"

"I thought of that already," Matson said, his voice firm.

"If you use your passport, they can find you."

"I've got a backup. Panama. I've got a Panamanian passport." He smiled again. "And it's real."

"Good thinking. But if it's in your name, they can still find you."

"No. A friend of mine set it up. She has one, too. I used her name."

"What's that?"

"Tarasov."

Gage raised an eyebrow. "Tarasov? You mean like the Russian *maffiya* guy?"

Matson's eyes widened. He swallowed hard, then licked his lips. "What do you mean?" Matson's voice rose to a squeak. "What Russian *maffiya* guy?"

"Well, he's not really Russian. They just call all those guys Russian *maffiya.* He's Ukrainian. Works out of Budapest. Got pushed out of Ukraine by a gangster named Gravilov. I don't know if they ever made up. It's hard to follow these things. You could look him up on the Internet." Gage shrugged. "Of course, I could be wrong, Maybe she's not related to him. There have to be lots of folks in the world named Tarasov."

Gage paused, idly looking about the restaurant, letting Matson founder on the ragged shores of his imagination.

"I can't remember what Tarasov's first name is," Gage finally said, scratching his head as if searching his memory. "No wait… it's P-something. Pavel, Pavlo, Petro…"

Matson glanced toward the door, then mumbled to himself, "Petrovna…"

"Can't be. Petrovna isn't a man's name. It's what they call a woman's patronymic. You know, from the father's name."

"Alla Petrovna Tarasova," Matson whispered.

"What'd you say?"

Matson looked up. "I'm fucked. I'm really fucked."

"What do you mean?"

Matson glanced at the door again. "I need a place to hide—now. Right now."

"What kind of mess are you in?"

"I can't say. I just can't say." Matson ground his hands together on the table. "You'll get your money. Just don't ask me."

◇◇◇

At 2:03 A.M. Gage's cell phone rang as he was lying in bed next to Faith. It was Viz, Matson's new bodyguard.

"Mr. Green. I'm with the guy. He made the call."

At 2:04 Gage called Geneva.

"This is Mr. Green. I have the looking glass."

Faith propped her head on an elbow.

"Yes, Mr. Green," the banker answered.

"In two minutes you'll receive an e-mail containing banking particulars. Transfer the entire KTMG Limited balance to that account except for ten thousand dollars to cover your fees."

"Yes, Mr. Green."

Gage flipped open his laptop on the bed table, sent the pre-written e-mail, then called Viz.

"Tell Matson you'll be taking him north into the mountains for a few days, then to Costa Rica. I'll give him the details when I get up there."

Gage hung up and looked over at Faith, silhouetted against the moonlit sky.

"Mr. Green?" she said, giggling and reaching for him. "Whatever is my husband going to think?"

Chapter Seventy-eight

Alex Z was sitting cross-legged on the landing in front of Gage's office building when Gage walked up the stairs the next morning.

"You listen to the news on your drive in?" Alex Z said, standing up.

"No. Your new tracks. It was the first chance I had since Jack got shot. They're brilliant, even to the ears of an old guy. I'm really proud of you."

"Thanks."

Alex Z swung open the door and held it for Gage.

"Why the special treatment?" Gage asked.

"You'll see."

Alex Z led Gage into the conference room, where he found Professor Blanchard sitting, his bleary eyes fixed on a corner television that displayed CNN coverage of an election-eve opposition demonstration in Kiev.

"Hey, Professor, what're you doing here?"

Blanchard glanced toward Gage, then back at the television. "I was in the neighborhood and thought I'd catch up on Ukrainian politics."

"Since last night." Alex Z smiled and pointed at a cot in the corner. "He snores."

"Your wife finally send you packing for insubordination?"

Blanchard jumped up, pointing at the television. "Here it is!"

"Explosions in Crimea" burst onto the screen, overlaying unfocused, jerky videophone images of a reporter standing against the earth-toned, minareted backdrop of Istanbul.

A shudder of relief passed through Gage as he dropped into a chair.

Then a voiceover: *Turkish authorities reported that NATO satellites over the Black Sea indicate that three explosions occurred at the Ukrainian Crimean missile testing site approximately four hours ago.*

Gage looked over at Blanchard, in awe of the old man with the power to reach into Central Europe and derail an arms-trafficking scheme from his little workshop in the Berkeley hills.

Since the accidental shooting down of a Russian airliner a few years ago, NATO monitors all Ukrainian missile tests. Seventy-eight passengers and crew members died in that incident. As in the case of the airplane disaster, Ukrainian authorities are denying the NATO claim. NATO is expected to release satellite images of the explosions later this evening.

"How'd you do it?" Gage asked.

Blanchard glanced over. "You wanted a Trojan horse, you got one. I made the missiles think they arrived at their targets before they left the ground." He grinned. "And I disguised the flaw by planting a program that invaded their server. When they tested the guidance software, the results screen always displayed SatTek's most successful performance data."

Gage imagined the devastation on the launch pads, concerned not about Gravilov and Hadeon Alexandervich, but about the Ukrainian hourly workers who made their living pushing brooms around the missile site. "You think anybody was hurt?"

"Not unless they were riding it. They're all supposed to be in bunkers."

"Can they fix the other devices?"

"No. Given how close this is to the shipment date, that wasn't a test, but a demonstration. Making these missiles was just a cookie-cutter job. And once the software is embedded in the hardware, that's it. *Finito*. Burned in is burned in."

Gage smiled. "Hadeon Alexandervich must be pissed."

"Who?" Blanchard asked.

"The president's son. This was his deal. His and Gravilov's." Gage paused, thinking about what the Middle Eastern buyers would do next. "I should've said their customer—probably Iran—will be pissed. Hadeon Alexandervich is about to wet his pants. It's a big mistake to annoy the Iranian Ministry of Intelligence." The rest of the future snapped into focus. "My guess is that they'll go after Hadeon Alexandervich, and Hadeon Alexandervich's father will send State Security after Gravilov."

"I thought Gravilov was the president's roof," Alex Z said.

"Looks like the roof just fell in."

"What about Matson, can't he buy his way out?" Alex Z asked.

Gage looked at his watch. The banking day in Geneva was over and the KTMG account was empty. "Nope."

Chapter Seventy-nine

At 3 P.M. Gage turned off the main highway onto a two lane graytop that quickly dwindled to one, then became dirt and gravel for the last six miles toward Hat Creek in Northern California. The four-hour drive took Gage from sea level wetlands, then north along the Sacramento River, and finally east through scrub oak to pines and redwoods at forty-five hundred feet.

As Gage drove into the clearing, he saw Viz rocking in a chair on the front porch of the small, weathered wood cabin, a pump-action shotgun across his lap. His worn black Stetson rested low on his forehead and his eyes stared toward the river flowing almost silently fifty yards away. His head rotated to the right at the sound of Gage's car rolling toward him. He stood up, waiting for Gage to park near an outbuilding, then walked down the steps to meet him.

Viz pointed at the semiautomatic in Gage's shoulder holster. "I didn't even know you owned one that big."

"Spike loaned it to me for the occasion." Gage looked around. "Where's our little pal?"

"By the river." Viz pretended to flinch. "Bark at him and I think he'll start crying. He jumps every time a twig breaks. He thinks he went down there to watch the water, but he really just wants to hide from unexpected noises in the roar of the rapids. The only thing that's keeping him together is the idea of Costa Rica."

"Has he seen the news?"

"No. I told him the satellite dish was broken because I didn't want him in my face all day."

"It's time to fix it."

Gage walked down the pine-treed hill toward the meadow bordering the stream. He saw Matson, wearing a blue parka and slacks, sitting on a fallen tree, mechanically tossing pebbles into the whitewater rapids below him. Gage's footfalls disappeared into the sounds of the river as he approached from behind.

"Matson!" Gage yelled at twice the decibels necessary to pierce through the roar.

Matson cringed, then peeked back over his shoulder. At the sight of Gage, his body slumped and he exhaled through puffed cheeks.

Gage jerked his thumb toward the cabin, then turned away and marched back. Matson, breathless, caught up at the stairs. They climbed the steps together and walked into the house. Gage pointed at a couch that faced the television off to the left and the fireplace directly in front. He then walked past the dining table to the counter that separated the kitchen from the living room.

Matson hung his parka on the coatrack, then sat down on the edge of the couch, arms on his thighs, fingers interlinked. Gage measured out coarse ground coffee from a Folgers tin, filled the coffeemaker with water, and punched the switch. He then returned and took a seat in a matching recliner.

"This place okay?" Gage asked, looking over.

"Yeah. But it's boring. No TV. Nothing."

Matson's eyes were sunken and bloodshot, his breathing still heavy from the hike up from the river.

"That's getting fixed."

"Did you get my money out?"

"No problem. I'll give you the bank info once it gets all the way to Costa Rica."

Matson nodded. "Thanks." The word came out like a sigh.

Viz entered through the back door. "I think I solved the TV problem." He set the shotgun in the gun cabinet along the wall to the left of the fireplace, then walked to the kitchen.

Gage grabbed the remote from the coffee table and turned on the television. He skimmed the channels until he found CNN, and then set it down. The U.S. secretary of state was commenting on the opposition victory in the Ukrainian elections.

"How long do I need to stay here?" Matson asked, peering at Gage.

"Not long. You got anything you need to take care of? You won't be coming back for a while."

"No," Matson said, looking like a dog abandoned at the pound.

"Does your wife know why you gotta go?"

"It doesn't make any difference." Matson stared vacantly at the television. "I'm not taking her."

"You want I should send her a little money?"

"There's a couple of million in equity in the house. She can sell it. I don't care."

Matson let his hands fall between his legs and exhaled.

Viz called over to Matson, "You take sugar in your coffee?"

Matson didn't respond, eyes now riveted on the screen.

Gage saw the words "NATO reports Ukrainian missile explosion" tick along the bottom.

"I guess not," Viz said.

Gage picked up the remote and switched the channel to ESPN.

"Turn it back," Matson said, voice rising. "Turn it back, please."

Gage returned to CNN.

"Cream?" Viz asked, pretending not to notice Matson's bewilderment and terror.

Viz brought the cup into the living room and set it on the coffee table in front of Matson. He picked it up, seemingly more from habit than interest, hands shaking.

A grayscale photo appeared next to the right shoulder of the announcer. *NATO released satellite images of three explosions at a Ukrainian missile testing facility on the Crimean peninsula.*

Gage twisted the knife. "Since you've got a Ukrainian name on your passport, maybe you should pay attention to this one."

The screen was filled by a succession of photos, each showing dark-edged gray blots of slightly different contours against the aerial view of a military installation.

After first denying the explosions, late today the Ukrainian Ministry of Defense acknowledged the mishap and reported that four observers were injured. CNN in Kiev confirmed that one of those injured was the son of the president of Ukraine. His condition is unknown. The president-elect has promised a full investigation.

Matson half rose from the couch, spilling his coffee as he set down the cup. "Shit!" He shook off the hot liquid from his hand. His face reddened as he hyperventilated and dropped back onto the couch, arms rigid on the cushions, as if trying to maintain his balance.

Gage glanced over Viz. "Bring him a paper bag."

Viz brought one, snapped it open, then pushed it up against Matson's face. Matson circled his hands around the top, then sucked air in and out, the bag collapsing, and then expanding with a pop.

Gage waited until Matson's breathing began to slow, then got up and sat next to him on the edge of the couch.

"What's going on?"

Matson pulled the bag away from his mouth. "I…" He gasped a final time. "I can't talk about it."

"You in some kind of trouble you haven't told me about?"

Matson stared at the television, as if waiting for a bulletin that would grant him a reprieve.

Gage leaned back, then signaled with his head for Viz to return to the kitchen.

"If I was to put two and two together," Gage said, "and I think you know what I'm talking about, I'd say those missiles were using SatTek video amplifiers."

"There's no proof that I—"

Gage raised his hand toward Matson. "I'm not saying there is. I'm just saying what you get when you add it up."

Matson leaned back and began to chew on a fingernail.

Gage watched Matson trying to calculate his position. His deal with Peterson, blown. Alla's gangster father maybe coming after him. Gravilov wanting an answer to why the missiles exploded. Hadeon Alexandervich, if he was still alive, wanting revenge against everyone.

"I deal a lot in missile technology," Gage said. "Three explosions. Ukraine tests in three different ranges all at once. I would guess it's probably not a hardware defect. That would be like lightning striking the same tree three times in a row." Gage was making it up as he went along, wondering how easily Blanchard would cut holes in this fictionalized account of why missiles explode. "It would have to be the software. That's my guess."

Gage waited until he felt Matson was done processing the logic of his fiction.

"Maybe somebody sabotaged it." Gage shrugged. "You know, monkeyed with the code."

Matson's eyes widened as a picture seemed to capture his mind. Gage guessed it was of Alla working away on his laptop in Dnepropetrovsk.

"I..." Matson swallowed hard. "I need to use your phone."

Gage walked to the counter, retrieved the handset, and passed it to Matson. Gage watched him punch in the international access code, then the UK country code, London city code, and number. Gage knew what Matson would hear: a script Gage had given Alla to read.

You have reached Alla and Stuart. Sorry we're unable to take your call. If you're trying to reach Stuart, try him on his cell phone in the States. I can be reached at my father's in Budapest. Otherwise, leave a message after the tone.

Matson lowered the phone from his ear, fumbled until he located the end button, and disconnected. He stared at the receiver. Gage reached out to retrieve it. Matson at first didn't notice, then handed it back.

Gage sensed Matson recalculating. Alla: If her job was to sabotage the software, then her gangster father wouldn't be coming after him—but Gravilov would.

"If I was to add two more," Gage said, "I'd say you sold bad devices to Ukraine and somebody is pissed. Maybe even already gunning for you."

"What the fuck do you know?" Matson slapped the armrest. An adrenaline rush pumped him to his feet.

"Take it easy, man," Gage said, looking up. "I'm just doing a little addition. If it doesn't add up, it doesn't add up. Makes no difference to me. I'm only in this for the money and I got enough to keep me happy. But there's something you need to think about."

Matson glared down at Gage. "What the fuck is that?"

"Screwing with national security is a whole lot worse than some diddly-squat stock fraud." Gage stood up, then handed Matson his parka. "Let's take a walk. You got to cool down so you can think things through."

After Matson turned toward the door, Gage signaled Viz to follow with the shotgun.

Matson was waiting at the bottom of the stairs when Gage returned from collecting his jacket from the car. The sun had already fallen behind the six-thousand-foot mountain range to the west of the cabin and the temperature was plummeting toward freezing.

The parka was puffed up around Matson's head. He blinked against the crisp breeze, then wiped his eyes with his sleeve.

Gage heard Matson's feet shuffle and wobble on the gravel as he followed behind through the woods and toward the river. Matson stumbled over a root. Gage looked back in time to see him steady himself against a pine tree, then pull his hand away and try to wipe off grimy sap on his pants.

Gage stopped just before the meadow. The only sounds were the rushing river in the distance and Viz's footfalls coming to a stop five yards behind them.

"You don't need to say anything," Gage said, staring toward the shadowed forest, hands in his coat pockets. "Just let me talk."

Gage's breath condensed into a cloud, then dissipated.

"It seems to me you've got a big problem."

Matson didn't respond.

"Now, you told me you've got a Panamanian passport."

Gage looked over, and Matson nodded.

"I may be wrong here, but I'll bet you used it where you shouldn't have, and if you travel on it people are gonna find you."

Matson nodded again.

"My guess is that you also got lots of different people looking for you. Ukrainians, gangsters, FBI, and pretty soon the CIA. And the world is getting real small."

Gage rolled over a fist-sized piece of granite with his shoe, then reached down and picked it up. Matson's eyes followed the rock as Gage flipped it back and forth in his hands. Gage tossed it into the dark meadow, where it thudded like a head hitting cement.

"My situation is different than yours," Gage continued. "I can disappear anytime. I mean you see me and everything, but I don't really exist."

Matson looked up at Gage, his expression a combination of envy and apprehension.

Gage turned fully toward Matson. "You've got yourself in a pickle and I can see you don't know what to do." Gage shrugged and spread his hands. "I mean, look. We hardly know each other but here I am, taking care of your money, protecting you. I was even gonna get you out of the country until the passport problem came up—and you don't know me from Adam."

Matson's eyes darted toward Viz, then back to Gage. Uncertainty consumed his face. Gage knew what Matson was thinking: He was in the middle of nowhere with two guys he didn't know, one with a shotgun, the other with an enormous handgun dangling a foot away, and all his money stashed somewhere in the ether.

"You shouldn't have ended up in a spot like this," Gage said. "I think you wanted to go big time, but you didn't have the skills—or the heart."

Gage curled his hand and looked down at his fingernails. "You really fucked up."

He watched panic rising in Matson's face. He knew Matson had seen it on television a hundred times: The gangster gazes dismissively at his fingernails, then draws his gun and the victim's guts are spattered against a wall. Matson glanced around the darkening forest, the world closing in.

"Yep. You really fucked up."

Gage waited, letting the panic rage.

Matson flinched when Gage reached out to rest a hand on his shoulder.

"You know what I think?" Gage said.

Matson flinched again as Gage slowly reached under his jacket and toward his gun.

Gage scratched his ribs. "I think you better get some legal advice."

Matson exhaled. "I thought…I thought…Man, you scared the shit out of me."

"I'm sorry." Gage smiled, pretending to be embarrassed at the misunderstanding. "I figured you knew what I was getting at all along."

"Yeah, I guess…I mean…I thought I knew what you had in mind."

Gage dropped his hand from Matson's shoulder.

"I'm thinking you need to consider a different strategy."

Matson nodded.

"I know a lawyer who could help you."

"Is he good?"

"Yeah. The best."

"Could he cut me a deal?"

"Easy."

"You trust him?"

"With my life."

"What's his name?"

"Jack Burch."

Viz racked the shotgun, metal on metal ripping at the still air.

Matson's hands began to shake as if his body understood before his mind. Gage watched him disassociate, lose his bearings.

Gage leaned in toward Matson and grabbed the front of his jacket, just below his chin, and yanked up. "You little runt. Burch took two bullets in the chest because of you."

"You…you are…" Matson's voice failed him.

Unmoved by either anger or sympathy, Gage watched the spectacle. He knew that the actual, the imaginary, and Matson's bewildered attempt to distinguish them had been sucked into a ferocious vortex. He saw Matson's eyes recoil from the images flying at him, the names and faces emerging out of the whirlwind, gouging at his sense of reality.

Matson dropped to his hands and knees, splattering vomit on his parka and pants, and ending with dry heaves that arched his back into spasms. He tried to wipe his mouth with his sleeve as he struggled to his feet, but missed and fell forward, then curled into a fetal ball and began whimpering.

Viz stepped forward and looked down at Matson. "Jeez, boss. I think you broke that son of a bitch."

Chapter Eighty

I've got him stashed," Gage told Peterson across the conference table on the eleventh floor of the Federal Building the following morning. Zink sat at the end of the table near the door, childishly sneering.

"It's called kidnapping and false imprisonment," Peterson said.

"You don't know when to give up." Gage shook his head. "How do you know he doesn't want to be stashed? You've listened to the recording I made last night. Does he sound like a guy who's ready to cozy up to you again?"

Peterson leaned back in his chair. "What do you want?"

"Transactional immunity for Burch. No prosecution ever for anything related to SatTek."

Peterson tossed his pen onto the table, as if Gage's demand was absurd. "I'll only give him use immunity for anything he tells the grand jury."

Gage looked hard at Peterson. "You don't get it. Maybe you don't want to. Maybe you're still addicted to the headlines you'd get bringing down a lawyer like Burch. Maybe his indictment was going to be your ticket to Willie Rose's job after he quits to run for governor." Gage paused for a beat. "I've got news for you: Burch...didn't...do it." Gage stood up. "Maybe your boss will catch on a little faster."

Peterson straightened himself in his chair. He glanced over at Zink. The sneer was gone. "Okay. Sit down."

"What does okay mean?"

"It means transactional."

Gage sat down. "And I want a court order before I leave today."

"Fine. And I assume that's not all you want."

"You got that right. I don't want Burch or his firm named in the civil suit."

"I can't control what Braunegg does," Peterson said. "DOJ policy says I can't interfere."

"It's a little late to start drawing ethical boundaries between you and Braunegg. You're the tit he sucks on. He'll do whatever you tell him."

Peterson smirked. "Anything else on your wish list?"

"Nope. But I've got twenty million dollars that Matson had in a Swiss account. KTMG Limited. I'll wire it to the court's bank when Braunegg confirms that Burch is out of the case."

"Why the court?"

"Because I don't want Braunegg getting a cut of it. If he doesn't recover it on his own, he doesn't get a percentage. His thirty percent will go to the victims."

Peterson picked up the telephone and dialed.

"Franklin Braunegg, please...Frank, this is Bill...Yeah, fine... Look, the complexion of the SatTek case changed...Yeah, just today...I'll fill you in on the details later...You'll need to drop Burch and his firm from the complaint...Yeah, that's what I said...It's gotta be that way...Yeah, how'd you guess? He's sitting right here..." Peterson covered the mouthpiece. "Can they interview Burch?"

Gage shook his head. "They're not coming anywhere near him. I'll tell them what they need to know."

Peterson removed his hand. "He won't go for it...Gage will do it...He's kinda got a gun to our heads on this one...You need to cut your losses...okay...I'll talk to you later."

Peterson hung up. "He agrees."

Gage nodded, then dialed his cell phone. "Bring him in."

Two minutes later the conference room phone rang. Peterson picked it up, listened for a few seconds, then said, "Zink'll come down," and disconnected. Zink pulled himself up from his chair and shuffled out.

Gage watched as Peterson began to write a column of names on a blank yellow pad in front of him. Gage knew what it was without asking: a revised grand jury target list.

"You're pretty light on your feet for a big guy," Gage said.

"It's the only useful lesson from football. Sometimes you have to settle for a field goal."

"Who've you got?"

"Matson, the stockbrokers, Gravilov, the controller at SatTek…what's his name?"

"Milsberg, Robert Milsberg. Leave him off. He's worked his tail off helping me."

"Will he debrief?"

"He'll do what I tell him."

"Okay. He'll be an unindicted coconspirator."

Gage tossed a bone. "Why not the Ukrainian president's son instead? He'd be a prize."

Peterson brightened.

"You'd get headlines around the world. A helluva press conference for your boss."

"Not a bad idea."

"Of course, you'll never get him to trial. No extradition treaty."

"I'm not so sure," Peterson said. "CNN is saying the new president wants to put his predecessor and his cronies on trial. Maybe him and his son will make a run for it and we'll snag him in a country where we do."

Peterson rose and headed toward the door. "You want coffee?"

"Sure. Black." Gage knew Peterson's offer wasn't really about a warm drink. He'd simply made peace with the reality Gage had imposed on him.

Peterson returned just a minute before Viz, Matson, and Zink approached the door. Matson froze at the threshold, glancing first at Gage, then at Peterson, then back at Gage, uncertain where to sit, not sure who now owned him.

Gage pointed at the end of the table, farthest from the door. Viz walked him to a chair and unlocked the handcuffs. Matson rubbed his wrists, then pulled out the chair and sat down. Viz leaned against a bookshelf behind him.

"What about his lawyer?" Peterson asked. "Shouldn't Hackett be here?"

"No." Gage looked at Matson. "Didn't you tell me you wanted to represent yourself?"

"Yeah," Matson said, slumping down in his chair. "I guess so."

"You disappointed me," Peterson said, glaring at Matson. "And you're gonna pay for it."

"I'm willing to do a few years. I told Gage I'd do that."

"A few years won't do it."

"Okay, five, five years." Matson said the words in an expectant tone, as if a negotiation had begun. "I can do five years."

"Not a chance." Peterson's forefinger thumped the table. "There's something called sentencing guidelines and you're now off the fucking chart."

Matson swallowed hard, then sat up rubbing his hands together. "We can work something out. I know we can work something out." He forced a weak half smile, his salesman's instincts taking over. "I got it. Gravilov. He's big. Him and Kovalenko were behind the killings. Absolutely. And they weren't part of my deal. It'll be something new. I can testify about those guys. Then go into Witness Protection."

"No chance," Peterson said. "You were double-dealing behind the back of the United States government. The jury wouldn't believe a word you said."

"What about the missiles? The missiles blew up, right? Can't we say that was the plan all along? I was working undercover. That's what we can say." Matson nodded, glancing back and forth between Peterson and Gage. "Then I can go to Ukraine and testify against the president's son. And I met two generals. I can testify about them, too."

Gage stood up. "You're a hell of a piece of work, Matson."

Viz walked toward the door, and Gage followed behind him.

"Wait," Matson called out. "What does KTMG stand for? I have to know."

Viz laughed.

Gage glanced back at Matson. "Kiss The Money Good-bye."

◇◇◇

Peterson walked with Gage and Viz down the hallway toward the lobby.

"What'll you do with Matson?" Gage asked.

"Zink'll take him over to North County Jail in Oakland. Mix him in with a thousand old gangsters and dope dealers. He might as well start getting used to hard time." Peterson looked over at Gage. "You think he realizes that he'll never get out?"

"I'm not sure it's dawned on him that he'll never even get bail. If I was him I would've bolted for the door when Viz took off the handcuffs. That was his last chance to see daylight."

They walked to the end of the hallway in silence, then Peterson asked, "What now?"

"I'll take Burch up to my cabin for a few days. He's been a prisoner in his house too long."

Peterson paused at the exit before opening the door to the lobby. "Tell Burch I'm sorry about all this. I really thought Matson was being straight. Everything he said seemed to check out."

"Maybe that's because you had Zink doing the checking."

◇◇◇

Courtney was helping her husband down the front stairs as Gage parked his car in their driveway a couple of hours later. She waved at Gage as he opened the passenger door, and then guided Burch to it. Gage helped ease him into the passenger seat.

"Take it slow, champ. No rush."

Burch grimaced as he dropped into the seat, then smiled.

"If I was moving any slower, I'd be standing still."

Gage walked Courtney back up the stairs. She turned at the top and looked back at her husband.

"There may be some things Jack wants to talk to you about once you get settled up at the cabin," she said.

"Did he tell you what they were?"

"He tried, but couldn't find a way to say what he meant. I think he needs to talk it all through with you in order to figure it out."

Chapter Eighty-one

Burch and Gage stared at the flames consuming oak logs in the fireplace of Gage's cabin. Burch's walker stood next to the rocking chair where he sat with a glass of bourbon in his hand and with his legs covered by a plaid wool blanket. Gage reclined on the couch, feet up on the coffee table.

The midnight forest was finally quiet except for an owl hooting in the distance.

"Matson is absolutely certain that Gravilov was behind all the violence," Gage said, after recounting his surrender of Matson to Peterson.

"That explains Fitzhugh. It must've been that fellow Razor. But what about me and Granger?"

"Matson said he had nightmares starting the moment he met that monster Kovalenko at Northstead Securities."

Burch caught his breath. "Kovalenko? It was Kovalenko?"

Gage shook his head. "Not him. He doesn't match the description. He probably brought in some East Coast enforcer from his Goldstake days. But we'll find the guy. It's just a matter of time."

Gage rose, then grabbed the poker and repositioned the logs, buying time to think. In saying those words he grasped that he'd adjusted to Burch's fragility in the two years since Courtney's cancer, accepted it, maybe even contributed to it—and he'd just done it again.

Gage turned to face him. "Sorry, champ, that's not true. We'll never get past Kovalenko to catch the guy who shot you. The

Kovalenkos of the world don't break, and they don't make deals." He paused. "I was just trying—"

"To protect me."

Gage shrugged.

"I know. It took a couple of slugs to help me figure that out." Burch looked past Gage toward the fire. "I've had a lot of time to think." Then back at Gage. "You know what I realized? That I've misunderstood myself all my life. I thought I was like you, but I'm not. I should've learned that lesson in Afghanistan. I spent the two weeks terrified and bewildered. You didn't need me there at all." Burch set down his glass. "In all the things I do. Sailing. Skiing. Even work. I've always oriented myself against a predictable kind of resistance. Ocean breezes, gravity. Then, whenever I felt constrained, I became reckless."

Gage nodded. He hadn't thought about it that way, but Burch was right.

"But when Courtney was diagnosed, the wind just stopped. I felt completely helpless. Adrift. After I got shot, lying there in the hospital, I realized that you had always been protecting me, insulating me. Even when we were in Moscow. I sat in that conference room, forehanding contract provisions back and forth in a contained little space for gentlemen who accepted all the rules. I even saw you going out to meet Slava Akimov and the others as just one more step in an orderly process—risky, but constrained by rational people pursuing their long-term self-interest."

"Does that mean you would've done it differently?" Gage asked, dropping back onto the couch.

Burch shook his head. "I just would've understood it differently. Truthfully." He fell silent and slowly rocked back and forth in his chair. "That's what I've needed all my life."

Gage stared at the fire. There was no reason to say anything more. Burch had arrived where he needed to go.

They sat silent for a few minutes. Then Burch looked over.

"I don't understand how Matson got involved in selling those devices to Ukraine in the first place," Burch said. "Arms trafficking just doesn't seem like something he'd do. When he first came to see me, he seemed like no more than an earnest salesman."

"It didn't happen all at once. Gravilov led him along. First they tried to slip high-power devices into Ukraine labeled as low-power. A woman at SatTek named Katie Palan found out about it. I talked to her parents while you were in the hospital. She'd written an anonymous letter to the FBI, but—"

The word caught in his throat.

Burch squinted toward Gage. "But what?"

Gage pulled his feet off the coffee table and then sat up.

"But SatTek self-disclosed…claimed it was a mistake."

"What's wrong?"

Gage rose and paced in front of the fireplace, trying to order the images and sequences clashing in his head.

"Something doesn't make sense. The timing isn't right."

He stopped pacing, then turned toward Burch. "Katie Palan's car accident was more than a year before the grand jury started hearing the case. Right in the middle of the scam."

"You lost me."

"I thought the leak was from the grand jury. So did Peterson. He sent Zink to investigate it. Somebody was tipping off Gravilov. Your name came up, you got shot. Then Fitzhugh. And when Granger decided to cooperate, he got hit."

Gage walked to the kitchen counter and picked up the telephone. "Maybe I underestimated the guy. Maybe everybody did."

He called information, then dialed an Oakland number.

A woman answered, "North County Jail."

"I'd like to know if you have a federal prisoner there, Stuart Matson."

"You have a DOB?"

"No. But he's mid-forties."

Gage heard keystrokes against the background of light jazz.

"There's no Stuart Matson in custody."

"Maybe he just came in."

"Hold on."

Gage heard the clerk set down the phone, then the sound of footsteps followed by distant voices. "Vernice, is there a Stuart Matson waiting to be booked?... *What's the name?*...Matson... *You got somebody calling?*...Yeah ...*The name's familiar but it's not in my paperwork...*"

Gage heard footsteps approaching the phone.

"No. He's not here...hold on...Matson, yeah...That was him?...You still there?"

"Yes."

"He's a runner. It was on the radio."

"He escaped?"

"Five or six hours ago. From an FBI agent driving him over from San Francisco. Hijacked right at the bottom of the first Oakland off-ramp. A stockbroker or something, right?"

"Sort of. Thanks."

Gage set the phone back into its cradle and turned toward Burch.

"Gravilov had someone snatch Matson."

A squeak of a porch board broke the forest silence, followed by four hard raps on the front door. Gage peeked through the curtain, then opened the door. Zink was standing on the bottom step, his badge extended in his right hand toward the light emerging from the cabin, while the other rested on his gun.

"I tried to call," Zink said, "but there's no cell service out here and the cabin phone is unlisted."

"Come on in."

Zink climbed the last three steps, then crossed the threshold.

"Aren't you supposed to be chasing down Matson?" Gage asked.

"I am. Him and the guys who jacked me." Zink offered a weak smile. "I feel like a fucking idiot."

"Tough break. What can we help you with?"

"I need to talk to you two." Zink remained standing near the door as if hesitant to approach Burch. "See if you have any ideas about where Matson might go, where he might've stashed money. He'll need some cash to live on. And I gotta go through you to speak to Alla, see what she knows."

"Matson turned out to be a lot smarter than any of us figured," Gage said.

"Sure was."

"Well, I'm sure as bloody hell not talking to you," Burch said. "And I have no apologies."

"I know you've got hard feelings, but I was just doing my job."

Burch's face darkened. "Not very well, I'd say."

"Matson was just so believable," Zink said. "He fooled us, me and Peterson."

"Jack'll calm down in a minute," Gage said. Then he felt his heart thump as his mind flashed back on Zink poised on the stairs, but kept his voice steady. "Why don't you take a seat. Maybe we can figure out where he went."

Gage glanced backward, as if looking for a chair, then spun back at the sound of a ripping Velcro holster strap. His right cross hit Zink in the jaw—

"Graham!" Burch yelled. "What're you doing?"

A left jab to the nose brought up Zink's hands, and a right uppercut just below the ribs dropped him to the floor. Gage then knelt down and yanked Zink's gun from his holster, a battered Ruger .357.

"What'd you do, Zink? Buy this on the street? Steal it from the evidence room?"

Zink curled up next to the threshold, covering his head as if expecting the next sound to be the gun butt against his skull.

Gage pulled up Zink's left pant leg, then tore off his ankle holster.

"What's going on? Graham, he's a federal agent."

Gage looked over at Burch, then held up his left hand, trigger finger curled. "The man who shot you now has a face."

Burch's mouth dropped. "But he's…"

Gage glared down at Zink as a nightmarish image sent a tremor through him: Katie Palan's car spinning out of control and tumbling down the hillside.

"It was the letters." Gage glanced at Burch. "First Katie sent an anonymous letter about the illegal sale of video amplifiers to Ukraine, and Zink covered it up. Then she sent a signed one about the stock fraud, so he had to get rid of her."

Instant confirmation appeared in Zink's rodentlike eyes darting around the room. He reached for a table leg and tried to pull himself to his feet.

Gage pointed down, his finger an inch from Zink's bleeding nose. "Don't."

Zink fell back, grimacing as his shoulder hit the floor.

Bending toward Zink, Gage asked, "Why? Why'd you do it?"

A montage of facts, until then shadowed behind the flash of Zink's badge or submerged in the chaos of events, turned stark and sharp-edged in Gage's mind: the sexual harassment complaint that derailed Zink's career, his compulsive cruising for street prostitutes, the arrests he'd slithered out of.

"Blackmail," Gage said, as much to himself as to Zink and Burch. "First it was blackmail...then what?...I'll tell you. They kept you from getting into trouble, even restored you to being a perfect FBI agent, by keeping your sexual addiction satisfied."

Gage rose, then took a step backward and sat on the edge of the coffee table.

"You knew I'd figure out that they'd gotten to you, but you didn't know when." Gage stared at Zink, nodding his head slowly. "And you guessed wrong. Not by much, but you guessed wrong." He stopped nodding. "What did you stop for? Gas? Burger and fries? Coffee? Take a leak on the side of the road?"

Zink's eyes just barely widened.

Gage answered the question himself. "Lack of bladder control." He kept looking at Zink, but spoke to Burch. "He was there when Peterson and me were talking to Matson, him blaming Gravilov and Kovalenko for the killings, for shooting you. He knew we believed Matson and thought we'd wrapped it up. He figured he had all the time in the world."

Gage finally turned toward Burch. "If he'd gotten here thirty seconds earlier, we'd be dead."

He then spun back, grabbed Zink by his shirtfront, and yanked him a foot above the floor. "What did you do with our little friend Scoob?"

Zink stared back without answering.

Gage jammed the Ruger muzzle under Zink's chin, hard against his windpipe. "I said, where's Matson?"

"Car."

"And where's the car?"

"Dirt road."

Gage lowered him and retrieved an extension cord from the kitchen. He hogtied Zink and removed his car keys.

"You have my permission to blow off his head if he moves." Gage handed Burch the revolver, then paused and looked around. "Maybe not his head." He dragged a small table away from Zink's right and pushed a couple of fly rods farther toward the corner. "Shoot him in the stomach. Brain matter is a helluva mess to clean up."

Gage found Zink's car a hundred yards up the road, then slid into the driver's seat. He made no effort to avoid the bumps and potholes on the drive back to the cabin, under the theory that if Matson was dead, he couldn't feel it, and if he was alive, he deserved it. Gage parked in front, then popped the trunk. Matson cowered inside, his bound hands covering his face as if flesh could stop lead.

"You want to ride down the mountain in here?" Gage asked. "Or do you want to climb out?"

Matson peeked upward, eyes widening at the sight of Gage.

Gage untied Matson's feet, then swung them over the lip of the trunk and pulled him out. He reached to untape Matson's mouth, then stopped.

"I really don't want to hear another word out of you."

Chapter Eighty-two

Just after sunrise Gage returned from the FBI's Northern California office in Redding, where he had delivered Matson and Zink. The strands of tulle fog he'd followed from the Central Valley into the mountains interwove the pines and oaks and had thickened into mist, but at least Zink's road to corruption was now clear.

Gage found Burch sitting in a rocker on the porch, Gage's first off-duty weapon, a snub-nosed Colt .38, in his right hand, resting on the blanket covering his lap.

"What's that for?" Gage asked, as he climbed the steps.

"I've had one too many surprises."

"I can understand that." Gage peered at the gun. "Is it cocked?"

"No."

"Keep it that way."

Gage leaned back against the porch railing. "It turns out that while Zink was spying on local gangsters as part of the Organized Crime Task Force, they were spying on him. They figured out his obsession and fed him a sixteen-year-old prostitute, and he wasn't willing to trade his FBI ID for a Bureau of Prisons number. A couple of years ago, they sold him to Gravilov."

"And that cost Katie Palan her life."

Gage nodded.

Burch closed his eyes and rubbed his forehead. "That poor woman. I should've seen what these people were up to." His face reddened in self-reproach. "There must've been something I could have done."

Gage shook his head. "There's no way you could've figured it out. Matson didn't even know where this thing was headed in those days, and he was in the middle of it."

Burch scanned the pines and oaks surrounding the cabin, then looked up at Gage. "But why try to kill me? I didn't have a clue."

"Gravilov was afraid you'd start putting together your pieces of the puzzle and they were still a couple of months away from the missile sale."

"I didn't even know there was any connection between Gravilov and SatTek."

"Gravilov couldn't count on that. Or that Zink was smart enough to contain everything."

"But that doesn't explain Fitzhugh. I thought he was one of them."

"Only at the beginning." Gage exhaled as a wave of fatigue shuddered through him. Two nights without sleep, debriefing first Matson, and then Zink, had pushed his body close to its limit. "Granger had Fitzhugh ingratiate himself with you months before he even met Matson. Granger was looking to run an offshore scam even before he'd heard of SatTek."

"But why kill him?"

"Zink showed up in London two days before he contacted the Metropolitan Police. He met Fitzhugh and decided he'd melt when British cops applied the heat. Razor took care of him while Zink cleaned out his files."

A chill breeze swept through the property and swirled fine raindrops around them. Burch pulled up the blanket to cover his chest.

"And when Granger decided to cooperate with Peterson," Burch added, "I guess he had to go, too."

Gage nodded.

Burch glanced back toward the living room as if Zink was still lying there on the floor. "What did Zink plan to do with Matson?"

"Pretend Matson came up here and killed us, kill him, and then go back to San Francisco and play hero."

"Seems like it would've been smarter to do away with Matson before he got here."

"He needed the fresh blood spatter to make the crime scene look real."

Burch stopped rocking. "He really thought it through like that?"

"He started as a street cop. He knew what homicide detectives would look for."

Burch sat silently for a moment, then said, "I'm still worried about Kovalenko, and now about the gangsters who first got to Zink. Don't they usually clean up the kind of mess that Matson created?"

Before Gage could answer, a low rumble and a crunching of tread on gravel sounded in the distance.

"What now?" Burch threw aside the blanket and struggled to his feet.

Gage raised his hand toward Burch. "What are you doing?"

"What do you think?"

Burch hobbled over to a porch support, then leaned against it, his left palm bracing his gun hand. He glanced at Gage, then jerked his head backward. "Don't just stand there, get behind me."

Gage shook his head. "Let me have the gun."

"Don't you understand? I have to stand up to these guys. I can't spend my life hiding."

Burch lowered himself into a crouch and aimed the barrel dead center on the spot where the road entered the clearing.

As the car approached the last turn and its headlights haloed through the mist-choked trees, Gage slid his hand under Burch's and raised the gun skyward, then pulled it away from him seconds before Faith's car emerged into the clearing.

Burch's whole body sighed. He then slowly pulled himself up using the porch support, and steadied himself against the railing.

While Faith parked the car and Courtney came running toward them, Gage slipped the gun into his back pocket and reached around Burch's shoulders.

"Not today, champ," Gage said. "The bad guys aren't getting you today."

Epilogue

Nine Months Later

Gage pulled his car onto a dirt patch along the winding road where it overlooked the Northern California coast. He gazed through his windshield toward the rolling hills, their crests and valleys covered with oaks and eucalyptus and their sides burned yellow by the summer sun. A lone buzzard circled in the distance, and below it the flattening land disappeared into the hazy nothingness of the Pacific.

He climbed out into the late September heat and walked back along the curving, shimmering blacktop toward a section of aluminum railing far less oxidized than those bracketing it. Its bolts still reflected the morning sun and its posts hadn't yet faded from greenish-brown to the weather-bleached gray of its neighbors.

As he approached the barrier, he scanned the pavement for skid marks, but they were long worn away or paved over during the two years since Katie Palan had been murdered at this place. He nonetheless felt her wrenching terror as her car suddenly fishtailed, and then her panic and bewilderment as it smashed through the thin metal strip and tumbled down the hillside.

He stopped at the top of the ravine and looked down at the sage and fennel and California poppies, long since healed from their thrashing by the plummeting car. He then picked his way down the rocky trail through dusty shards of glass and plastic, and over the chunks of bark and the shattered branches that marked Katie's tormented path to her resting place.

In a small clearing at the bottom he found an oil patch, like an anonymous tombstone marking the spot where she died. He knelt by its edge and rubbed the stained dirt between his fingers, then sat on a granite boulder and watched a gray-brown grasshopper flit away. Only then did he notice the finches and sparrows chirping in the trees and the cu-ca-cow of quail fluttering among the low bushes. When they went mute, he glanced up to see a red-tailed hawk swoop and disappear behind a pine. Moments later, their songs began again.

He tore off a sage leaf and wondered whether Katie had smelled the wild herbs during her last moments; whether she heard the shudder of the wind in the eucalyptus; whether hope swelled at the sound of Zink's footsteps; whether she grasped that he froze in place because he was waiting for her breath to cease; whether, in the last thoughts she spoke to herself, she asked herself why.

Maybe she was lucky, and didn't live long enough for any of that. Zink had refused to say. He'd just shrugged his shoulders when Gage asked.

Gage stared down at the dark soil, thinking of her parents welcoming Faith and Courtney and Jack and him into their little apartment a week earlier. The dining table was centered in the living room, surrounded by chairs borrowed from neighbors. The home was filled with the aromas of Ukraine, and the pall of sadness. A picture of Katie, framed in silver, rested on a bookshelf between two icons. Eyes that would've seemed serious if she was still alive simply looked forlorn.

Jack had taken her mother and father into their bedroom where suitcases and boxes sat half filled in preparation for their return to Ukraine, for there was nothing left to bind them to their adopted country except pain and loss. Jack had closed the door and sat with them, then came out a half hour later, holding Olena's hand and with his arm around Tolenko's shoulders, their eyes moist and red.

◇◇◇

Gage leaned forward to rise from the boulder, but paused when he caught sight of a Russian Orthodox, triple-barred cross standing under a tiny evergreen at the far edge of the clearing. It hadn't been there when he last visited in June. He walked around the oil patch and knelt down to read the laminated note attached to the base, its words written in English, in a man's handwriting Gage had known for a generation: *Dear Katie, rest in peace. I'll make sure your parents will never want for anything.*

◇◇◇

So what if it was blackmail, Gage said to himself as he rose and looked up the ravine. *Maybe even extortion.* He and Jack showing up at Franklin Braunegg's office unannounced a month earlier. Then at Daniel Hackett's. Both lawyers feigning outrage, slamming their fists, claiming they deserved every nickel of the millions they'd profited from the crimes of SatTek.

It wasn't that Gage and Jack had demanded that they surrender all the money; only enough to ensure that poverty wouldn't compound the grief and loneliness of aging parents.

So what if it required a slick bit of money laundering and a Channel Island shell company to funnel the involuntary donations into an offshore account.

So…what.

Gage smiled to himself as he climbed back up to the road.

So what.

He knew the rule. Jack knew the rule.

If they ever get us…it'll only be for something we didn't do.

Note to the Reader and Acknowledgments

Final Target reflects conditions in Ukraine during its first decade and a half of independence. In the course of investigations I conducted there over three years, I met with leading members of both the government and the opposition. Numerous and lengthy conversations with bankers, attorneys, State Security officers, members of Parliament, and two prime ministers, one of whom served in the corrupt and violent Kuchma regime, gave me an inside and troubling view of the practice and psychology of corruption during those years.

The stock fraud described in this book is a composite of various crimes committed in the last ten years and is not intended to stand for any particular one. Further, the characters of Matson, Granger, Gravilov, the stockbrokers, and the offshore bankers and lawyers do not represent actual individuals, but merely the parts that must be played to commit transnational crimes and the sort of people who play them. At the same time, aspects of the physical characteristics, biographies, and personalities of the characters are sometimes composites of individuals I have met in my work, sometimes just in passing. Matson, for example, was inspired by a giddy company president I sat next to on a flight from London to Hong Kong who thought that a Dutch girlfriend, a UK bank account, and "the deal" would fill the vacuum that was his life. Slava, on the other hand, was based on…well, maybe I'll keep that one to myself.

I am better both as an investigator and as a writer due to my good fortune of having worked with interpreters throughout the world who bore the same risks as I under sometimes difficult conditions. They translated my questions into culturally appropriate forms, explained what was meant by what was said, and sometimes simply bought me time to think. Equally important were attorneys who helped me struggle through complex cross-cultural legal and ethical issues. As a representative of them all, I would like to mention the late Senior Advocate Ijaz Hussain Batalvi of Lahore, Pakistan. He will live on in Pakistani history, for ill or for good, as the prosecutor of President Zulfiqar Ali Bhutto and defense attorney for President Nawaz Sharif, but his true pleasures in life were his family and a lamb kebab cooked on the backyard barbecue. Like so many others, he was a joy to work with.

The counterintuitive notion of blackmail as a form of political power was drawn from the work of Keith A. Darden of Yale University, including: "Blackmail as a Tool of State Domination: Ukraine under Kuchma," *East European Constitutional Review*, vol. 10, nos. 2/3 (Spring/Summer 2001), pp. 67–71.

The lines, "I was much too far out all my life, And not waving but drowning," are drawn from Stevie Smith's "Not Waving but Drowning," in *Collected Poems*, p. 303, New Directions Publishing, 1983. "Beauty is the beginning of terror" is a misquotation by Matson of a line from Rainer Maria Rilke's *The Duino Elegies and the Sonnets of Orpheus*, p. 5, Mariner Books, 1977 (A. Poulin, translator).

There is one partially nonfictional piece of dialogue: "If they ever get us, it'll only be for something we didn't do." I first heard a line similar to this as an oblique confession to uncharged crimes by a drug trafficker and later heard a different version that originated with an attorney in the Bay Area.

While one of the thrills in private investigation is finding facts, one of the thrills of writing is that you get to make things up. I have therefore taken liberties with technology, geography, and certain physical locations.

Thanks go to Ray McMullin, Steve Homer, David Agretelis, Marian Sticht, Dennis Barley, Davie Sue Litov, Don Eichler, Randy Schmidt, Carol Keslar, Chris Cannon, and Denise Fleming. To Teresa Wong and Linh Nguyen who helped with translations. To Seth Norman, whose acclaimed angling essays are populated as often by corrupt cops and dead-eyed pit bulls as by artificial flies and actual fish. And to my cousin Bruce Kaplan, a race car driver who has walked away from more crashes on southwestern dirt tracks than Road Runner.

Thanks also to Carl Lennertz of HarperCollins, who took on this book after we met through the Book Passage Bookstore, and to my agent, Helen Zimmermann.

My mother, Martha Gore, and late father, Victor M. Gore, were thrilled to receive an early version of the book, if only hoping to find out what I really do for a living. (Mom, it's fiction. Really.) I haven't given a copy to my mother-in-law, Alice Litov, a minister's widow, as it contains words she doesn't think I even know, much less use.

To receive a free catalog of Poisoned Pen Press titles, please contact us in one of the following ways:

Phone: 1-800-421-3976
Facsimile: 1-480-949-1707
Email: info@poisonedpenpress.com
Website: www.poisonedpenpress.com

Poisoned Pen Press
6962 E. First Ave. Ste. 103
Scottsdale, AZ 85251